Colleen tiptoed into the nursery and approached the crib.

The infant stirred and turned its head toward her. A drop of blood was caught between its lips. She was about to turn and call for help, when the baby's tongue appeared like a tiny snake and wiped away the drop.

Shocked by what she'd seen, Colleen rushed from the room.

BLOODCHILD

Berkley Books by Andrew Neiderman

PLAYMATES
SURROGATE CHILD
PERFECT LITTLE ANGELS
BLOODCHILD

BLOODCHILD

ANDREW NEIDERMAN

BERKLEY BOOKS, NEW YORK

**For Uncle Dave,
who will always be
the judge**

BLOODCHILD

A Berkley Book / published by arrangement with
the author

PRINTING HISTORY
Berkley edition / September 1990

ISBN: 0-425-12044-9

A BERKLEY BOOK® TM 757,375
Berkley Books are published by The Berkley Publishing Group,
200 Madison Avenue, New York, New York 10016.
The name "BERKLEY" and the "B" logo
are trademarks belonging to Berkley Publishing Corporation.

PRINTED IN THE UNITED STATES OF AMERICA

10 9 8 7 6 5 4 3 2 1

"... And the midwife wondered and the women cried, 'Oh, Jesus bless us, he is born with teeth.'"

—*Henry VI, Part III*
William Shakespeare

PROLOGUE

Even before Dr. Friedman looked up, Dana Hamilton knew her baby was dead. She had sensed something happening throughout the delivery. The spiritual bond between mother and child had been broken. She had felt her baby's life break away and drift off like a kite whose string had torn. She was left with the same empty, loose feeling in her hands.

Her husband, Harlan, wearing the milk-white surgical mask, his forehead beaded with sweat, stared at her along with Dr. Friedman and the nurses. They all had the same eyes peering over their masks. Although the faces were covered, everyone's eyes reflected the morbid conclusion.

"I don't understand it," Dr. Friedman said. "It must have been the trauma of the birth."

With his mouth hidden from view, his voice sounded distant to Dana. It was almost as if he were a narrator, physically apart from the tragic scene being acted out before her.

Harlan moved quickly to her side and lowered his surgical mask. His face was now seized with fear, as well as with horror. She looked from him to Dr. Friedman to the nurses and back to Harlan. She saw the corpse of her baby being lifted and handed gently to a nurse, who, because of her years of training, automatically handled it with care despite its silent heart.

When Dr. Friedman lowered his mask like a flag lowered in defeat, she began to scream and scream and scream.

Some time later Dana awoke in her hospital room. For a moment it seemed as if she had been dreaming and all that had happened was only a nightmare. Harlan was standing by the window looking down at the parking lot, his hands clasped behind his back the way they usually were when he lectured to his English students at the community college. But with his shoulders slumped, his chin nearly on his chest, he looked much older than his thirty-seven years and nowhere near his six feet two inches. His demeanor confirmed their tragedy. It had been no nightmare.

Dana moaned, and he turned around quickly to come to her bedside.

"Harlan . . ."

"Don't cry, don't cry. Don't make yourself sicker. Please, I can't lose you too," he said, as if there really were a chance of that. She was weak, but she knew she wasn't in critical condition. He was just being overly dramatic, the way he could be, she thought; but she didn't dislike him for it. It seemed appropriate at that time.

"Why did this happen?"

"They're doing an autopsy now. From what Dr. Friedman told me, the baby's heart stopped beating as the child was emerging."

"But it was going so well," she said, her face crumpling. "He said I was one of the healthiest thirty-five-year-old pregnant women he ever had."

"And you were. It's not your fault. Don't lay there and blame yourself. Please," he pleaded.

"But we wanted a child so badly, Harlan." She closed her eyes and relived the way Dr. Friedman had handed her dead baby to the nurse. "What was it?" she asked in a whisper.

"It was a boy," he said. He smiled as if she had given birth to a healthy, living boy.

"Oh, God." She turned away, pressing her face into the pillow. He stroked her long, light brown hair gently, but she didn't want to be comforted. She realized she was more angry than sad. This was unfair; this was illogical. She had done everything right—the vitamins, the good foods, the avoidance of anything in any way detrimental, the exercise classes, all the preparation—it was unfair. They had been cheated, betrayed, made the object of some terrible celestial joke. God was having fun with them at their expense. Why?

She was going to breast-feed the child; she had read up on the advantages and had come to believe there was truth in the idea that breast feeding developed a stronger bond between mother and child. She had read a lot about child rearing. There were all those books, the videotapes, the magazines, even the classes she'd attended. All for what?

"It's just not fair, Harlan," she said, turning back to him. "It's just not right."

"I know," he said. He took her hand and squeezed it gently, but she could see by the way he was looking at her that he had more to say.

"Was there something I did that was wrong?"

"No, no—God, no. Dr. Friedman told me over and over that you were a great patient. You did everything on the money. He's as disgusted as we are, and as confused."

"Then what is it, Harlan? There's something else, something you want to tell me. What?"

"Well, it's strange, but it's almost as if . . . as if it were fated. Just don't reject it outright," he said quickly, holding both hands up, palms toward her. "I thought I would, but as I stood here watching you and waiting for you to regain consciousness, I couldn't help going over and over it and wondering if it wasn't meant to be."

"What, Harlan? What's meant to be? The death of our child? You want me to accept it as something called fate?"

"No, no. There's a man outside, waiting in the lobby. He's a lawyer, a Mr. Lawrence, Garson Lawrence. He represents a family whose unmarried teenage daughter just gave birth to a baby boy."

"What?" She stared up at him. For some reason all the colors in his face looked more vivid to her. His blue eyes were brighter and his carrot-colored hair seemed more orange. Even the freckles in his forehead looked more abundant to her. "What are you saying?"

"They want to give up the child immediately. Apparently the girl's mother is one of those who believes in breast feeding, too—religiously, in fact—and when Lawrence heard that was what you were going to do . . . well, he came right to me and made the offer."

She didn't say anything. She stared up at him. He shrugged.

"I know it's a horrible thing to think about at this moment, but there are obvious reasons to make a quick decision. I feel that if we did it, we would have more of a sense of the child being ours."

"But it's not ours," she said, grimacing.

"I know," he said softly, closing and then opening his eyes. "It wasn't easy for me to bring this up at this moment, but as

I said, I was standing here thinking . . . could this be fated?"

"Oh, God, Harlan, I don't know. I don't know." She turned away. Why had such a decision been presented to her now? Was Harlan right? Was it part of some divine design?

"We wanted a child very badly, Dana. This one doesn't have a mother yet, and if you bring its lips to your breast now—"

"Who are these people?" she demanded. Her child had been taken from her—literally ripped out of their lives before they even had a chance to accept it, and here were these people, eager to give their child away. The irony . . . the unfairness . . .

"We don't know them. They came here to have the child, to protect their reputation back where they live. They want nothing from us. There's no money involved, nothing but our promise to breast-feed the child."

He looked down quickly, and then up again.

"I saw the baby, Dana. It's a beautiful little boy; he's what our baby should have been. And you won't believe this," he added, smiling widely, "but he has carrot-colored hair. I know it's just a coincidence, but . . ."

"I don't know what to say. It's all so bizarre. Why couldn't things have gone well for us? Why?" she demanded. Harlan looked away. She realized he was in pain, too, and she softened. "Did you call my mother?"

"I haven't told anyone the bad news yet. My sister called from school, but I told her nothing had happened yet."

"You're not suggesting we pretend this other baby is really ours, are you, Harlan?" she asked, pulling herself into more of a sitting position. She understood that to him the idea was viable.

"In a very short time we might very well think of the child as ours. I almost feel as if our baby's soul moved right over into this one."

Unable to speak, she stared at him, her eyes wide.

"If you saw the child," he said, "maybe . . ."

"You don't think I'll be able to have another baby, do you, Harlan? No matter what Dr. Friedman said about my health during this pregnancy?" For a moment he didn't reply.

"I don't know what to think, Dana. Neither do the doctors, if you want to know the truth. They didn't anticipate this, did they?"

She thought for a moment.

"All these people care about is that I breast-feed the child?" The possibility was becoming real to her.

"That's what Mr. Lawrence says. They feel guilty about giving it up, of course, and want to be sure it's got a healthy, happy start in life, is the way he explained it. It's all so horrible, but I agree with him—the quicker a decision is made, the better it will be for the baby and for us," Harlan added with more enthusiasm.

She turned away and thought about her own dead baby. She hadn't really looked that hard at him, and she hadn't seen his face. Could she pretend? Could she cheat fate? Could she right the wrong that had been done to them?

She turned back to Harlan. He looked so confused, so tired, so defeated. These should have been the happiest moments of their five-year marriage. Once again she thought, It isn't fair. Once again she was more angry than sad.

Her decision was impulsive but determined.

"Tell him yes," she said, "and have them bring the baby to me when it's time for its first feeding."

Harlan nodded, and for the first time all day he risked a smile. She lifted her arms toward him and they embraced.

"But I can't help telling you," she said, "that I'm frightened."

"Of what?" he asked. "A baby?"

"I don't know." She pulled back and then smiled up at him. "You're right," she said. "That's silly," she added, and she let the moment pass.

Which was something they would both live to regret.

1

Dana left the maternity ward of **Sullivan County General Hospital** with the infant cradled possessively in her arms. She had no reason to feel threatened; it was just something instinctive, something she couldn't help. The nurses and other hospital personnel past whom she was wheeled on her way to the lobby and exit all smiled warmly. She sensed that hospital employees, who were usually acquainted with the sick and the infirm, were elated by the birth of children. There was a reaffirmation of life, hope, and purpose in each healthy, newborn baby. Sunshine emanated from the maternity ward. The scents and the sounds from it had been heartwarming and had provided some respite from the sounds of heart monitors and the scents of medication and alcohol. Hospitals could be the entranceways to life, as well as the portals to death.

She was happier than ever, and more confident that she and Harlan had made the right decision. As she was wheeled on, she imagined what it would have been like for her to be leaving this hospital without a baby. Pregnancy would have been more like an illness, something from which she had recovered but which had left her weak and diminished. There would have been no smiles, just expressions of pity and sorrow. She would have had to travel through a funereal atmosphere and exit from a tunnel of grief. The pregnancy and her delivery would have been like some nightmare to repress.

Eventually Harlan would have asked **Grant Kaplan** to call her and ask her to return to his accounting office on a full-time basis, thinking that she would have needed to stay occupied. It wasn't that she would have been afraid of going back to work. Her added unhappiness would have come from the fact that she had been preparing for this maternity leave and planning ways in which she could do part-time work. Everyone at the firm would have expected that she wouldn't be there in her old capacity. Every day back there would have been a day reinforcing the tragedy.

But instead of all those terrible possibilities, she was leaving in a state of ecstasy, feeling light and happy, floating through the immaculate corridors and out to the car. When they reached the hospital entrance, Harlan rushed ahead of her to open the door and stand back like a professional chauffeur. People waved; even people she had not met wished her good luck. Harlan put her suitcase in the rear with the baby's things and moved quickly to the driver's seat, his face animated.

"Comfortable?"

She nodded and pulled the soft blue cotton blanket away from the baby's pinkish-white cheeks. Although his cerulean-blue eyes were open, he was quiet, content. She thought her milk was like a magic potion. Ingesting it, the baby not only consumed the nutrition he needed, but also he took on some of the essential parts of her. She felt she was giving him more than her milk; she was giving him personality, knowledge, and emotional contentment, for after each feeding the child stared with uniquely mature eyes, eyes that mesmerized her.

Not having had a child before, nor paying much attention to childbirth until she'd become pregnant, she was not sure what part of her reaction was normal and what, if any, was not. Were all mothers as infatuated with their children? Did all of them lie there eagerly anticipating the infant's arrival for each feeding? Did all of them ever dream about it?

One dream was more like a nightmare, even though there was something sensually pleasing about the images. A nurse had brought the baby to her, but this was a nurse she hadn't seen before. There was a man with her. He wore an intern's white jacket and pants, but he didn't look like a medical student or a doctor. She couldn't make out his face. It was draped in shadow, but there was the occasional flash of teeth and the occasional glow from his eyes. He was at her first.

She started to sit up in the bed, but he put his hands on her shoulders, pressing her back and moving the straps of her nightgown off her shoulders and down her arms as he did so. She wanted to resist, but she found herself so weak that she could barely lift her arm. In moments he exposed her breasts.

Then the nurse brought the baby toward her. The man cupped her right breast and squeezed it gently as the nurse held the baby's lips inches from her nipple. She thought the baby's eyes glowed, and then its lips slipped over her nipple and the suckling began. All throughout the feeding the man held her breast firmly and the nurse held the baby. It was as if they were teaching it how to feed.

When she woke the morning after the dream, her right breast ached. The next time they brought the baby to her, she sensed there was something singularly uncommon about the way he looked at her. Lovingly, she thought. She was identified in his mind as his mother.

Very quickly all the maternity nurses began commenting on his behavior. Few, if any babies, it seemed, slept as long during the day and were so alert and active for such long periods of time during the night.

"He would have slept right through the scheduled feeding," one nurse told her.

"You woke him?" she asked angrily.

"Well . . . it's not usual for an infant to go that long between feedings."

"He feeds well at night. Check your charts," she snapped.

When Harlan arrived, she complained and insisted that they move up her discharge one day, despite Dr. Friedman's concern.

"I didn't have complications," she told Harlan. "My baby did." They had learned that their baby had died from a ruptured aneurysm in the pulmonary artery. That was why the infant had died so quickly. "There is no reason to keep me here longer than women are normally kept," she added curtly.

"Well, he's just being cautious."

"He should have been more cautious before," she replied with uncharacteristic venom. "We've got to take the baby home. They don't know what they're doing here. He's special."

"What?" Harlan started to laugh. "A doting mother already?"

She didn't smile. Harlan was puzzled, but he went to Dr. Friedman and got him to release her a day early.

Actually this wasn't the first thing that made him wonder about Dana since their baby's death and the subsequent adoption of the child. Without any logical explanation she decided to change the name they had agreed upon should the baby be a boy. They were going to call him Frank, after his father, but after the first feeding, when Harlan came to her, she had other ideas.

"I want to name him Nikos," she said.

"Nikos? You're kidding. Nikos?"

"I'm not kidding," she said with vivid indignation. "What's wrong with it?"

"Nothing's wrong with it. It's just . . . well, why Nikos?"

"I don't know. It came to me and I like it so much. Please, Harlan."

Actually it had come to her in a dream, a dream in which she had envisioned Nikos as a handsome young man, only . . . only in the dream he didn't have the carrot-colored hair. He had black hair; dark blue eyes, the whiteness around the pupils almost luminescent; and skin as pale yellow as old bones.

Harlan shrugged. He was disappointed, of course, but he figured she had been the one to go through all the suffering. If Nikos was the name she wanted . . . let it be Nikos.

"Okay." He smiled and shook his head. She kissed him gratefully and he went out to see the baby. Nikos was asleep, just like he was every time he came to the hospital during the day. The only time Harlan saw him awake was in the early evening.

Now, in the car, as if Nikos understood he was being taken from the hospital, he lay in Dana's arms, eyes wide open, quietly expectant.

"Looks like he knows he's going home," Harlan said.

"Of course he does," Dana replied. She kissed the baby's cheek and brought him even closer to her breast. "The nurses told me that during the night he was the most alert infant they'd ever seen. He's going to be very smart, aren't you, Nikos?"

"If he says yes, I'll drive off the road," Harlan kidded, and they started away, heading for their home in Centerville Station. "Oh, I'm going to pick up Jillian at ten-thirty tomorrow. She got the flight into Newark."

Dana didn't even acknowledge what he had said. She continued to stare down at the baby, who stared up at her. It was as if mother and child could not take their eyes off each other, even for an instant.

Jillian, Dana's mother, was flying in from Tampa to help with the baby. That was another thing that struck him as unusual—Dana's reaction to her mother's offer after he had finally decided to call and tell her everything.

"You shouldn't have told her the truth," Dana had said. "You should have let her believe Nikos was actually my baby. Now she thinks I'm an invalid and I can't take care of my own infant."

Harlan was surprised at Dana's comment because he knew that she and her mother had a very good relationship. Although Jillian was in her mid-sixties, she looked more like a woman in her early fifties. He had always known her to have a youthful, vibrant view of life, even after the tragic death of Dana's father in a boating accident off the Florida Keys. Jillian was a strong-willed, independent, and rather beautiful woman. When Dana and she were together, they were more like two sisters.

"You can't be serious, honey," he had replied. "Surely you realize she would have learned the truth shortly after arriving, and then—"

"Then nothing. I can take care of my own infant," she had repeated, and had almost gone into a sulk about it. He imagined it was part of the postdelivery blues, something Dr. Friedman had warned him about only the day before. The trauma, then the drama of burying one child and taking on another the same day had to have some effect on her as well. If he hadn't kept himself so busy these last few days, marking student themes, it would have had as dramatic an effect on him, he thought, and left it at that.

She turned the baby so he could see its face. The child was staring up at him, but he couldn't smile. Of course, he thought, it was only his imagination, but the infant looked angry. It was as if . . . as if it took on Dana's moods instantly, as if all that nonsense about breast feeding developing a strong bond between mother and child were true.

He shook his head and drove on.

Colleen Hamilton paused after she stepped out the south exit of Centerville High and watched as the boys emerged from the gymnasium entrance and ran up to the football field. Already psyched up by the team's impressive winning record, the boys popped out vigorously, shouting after one another. The relatively small junior-senior high school, with a total population of fifteen hundred students, was sitting on top of a volcano of excitement that continually threatened to erupt. That day, the day before the division championship game, was a day filled with anticipation. Twice during the afternoon the high-school students broke out with the school cheer as they passed through the halls from class to class. She thought the excitement had even affected her teachers, putting more enthusiasm into their lectures and questions and more smiles on their faces.

She remained to watch the players come out. With their shoulder pads and black-and-gold uniforms, most looked like clones. Some already wore their gold helmets, and as they appeared, the mid-October Upstate New York sun ignited them, making it look as if they each wore a crown of fire. Characteristically Teddy Becker appeared with his helmet in hand, his ebony hair still neatly styled, and lumbered along slowly, calmly, almost arrogantly, for he was the first-string quarterback. She waved and he stopped, holding his arms up to express his disappointment that she wasn't staying around to watch the practice.

Every day for the past two weeks she had been lingering after school to watch Teddy practice or play; but today she had to hurry home, for her brother and her sister-in-law were bringing home their child. It was still difficult to believe that it was an adopted child and that all that had happened really had happened. She almost wished Harlan had never told her the truth. She probably wouldn't have figured it out, because when she had seen the baby in the hospital, she thought it looked so much like him.

When Harlan had first told her that Dana was pregnant, Colleen felt mixed emotions. She was happy for them because she knew how much they wanted a child, but she couldn't help but wonder how the baby's arrival would change her own life. She had always felt obligated to them for taking her into their home, and she especially felt obligated to Dana, even though Dana rarely, if ever, made her feel uncomfortable or unwanted.

They had a big enough house. It was a two-story, eight-room, light blue Colonial on Highland Avenue, a quiet, dead-end street in Old Centerville Station. The previous year Harlan had replaced the wooden siding with aluminum and had the two tall pillars in front refinished. They painted the white shutters a glossy white, and now, because he had replaced the roof shingles as well, the house looked brand-new.

There were four rooms downstairs: the living room with a picture window facing the street, a dining room, the kitchen, and a den-office in the rear. All four bedrooms were upstairs. Even with the baby taking the large room in the west corner, there was still a guest room. Harlan and Dana had their own bathroom and Colleen had hers. Since she had come to live with her brother after their father's fatal heart attack, she had never felt she was crowding them. In fact, she couldn't think of one uncomfortable moment.

It was painful to leave her old school, where she had made so many friends, but with her mother dead ten years, a victim of cancer, and now with her father deceased, she had no choice. She was just a senior in high school.

Harlan had always seemed more like a father than a brother to her, anyway, because there was such an age difference between them. Her parents had had him when they were very young, and then they had tried to have another child, but her mother had had a miscarriage and the prospects of her having a successful pregnancy diminished. Her parents never gave up, however, and surprisingly, when Colleen's mother was in her early forties, she became pregnant with her. She was a change-of-life baby.

Colleen always liked Dana because Dana never treated her like a child. Even before she had come to live with her and Harlan, Colleen often had had serious and intimate discussions with Dana about boys and romance. Once, when she thanked her for being so frank and mature with her, Dana said, "I know what it was like when I was your age and how I hated being treated like a child when I already had had my period and had the same feelings and thoughts."

Dana was more like a big sister to her and certainly welcomed her into her home openly and warmly. A trust had already been built between them. She could come to her with her problems and Dana would listen; and Dana wouldn't hesitate to tell her about her problems, either, even if they related to Harlan. They had quickly become female allies. Harlan was always jokingly complaining about being outnumbered.

And so, as difficult as it was for her to leave her friends and home, the transition was made quite easily and comfortably because of Dana. Now what troubled her was her anxiety concerning how the baby would change Dana and her relationship with her. She anticipated that they would shortly expect her to be their built-in baby-sitter, but she was resigned to this, thinking she had to have some way to repay them for their kindness and love.

Anyway, it was her last year of high school. Next fall she would be off to college. She was a good student, always on the honor role, and she had dreams of becoming a doctor. Harlan had already told her there was a substantial trust fund for her. Financing her college education was not going to be a problem. In many ways she was better off than a number of her fellow students.

Of course, it was painful to have a family broken and destroyed by illness, but so many of the kids she met and knew came from broken families. Teenagers today were more independent in many ways, whether they wanted to be or not. In any case, she wasn't the type to sit around and mope. Self-pity had never been attractive to her. She was too ambitious, whether it be about schoolwork or romance, to waste time moaning and groaning about life. She was proud of her maturity and her stability, both of which often made her feel superior. She knew her girlfriends envied her for it, and she knew most boys were attracted to her because of that, as well as because of her good looks.

At five feet eight, with an hourglass figure, thick light brown hair, and dark almond eyes, Colleen knew she was a stand-out. Dana, who had a naturally robust and healthy complexion, was always complimenting her on her peaches-and-cream look. Other women who saw them together believed they shared some cosmetic secret and refused to believe there were no special skin creams or makeup involved.

Part of Colleen's self-confidence came from her awareness of just how attractive she was. Although she wasn't arrogant, she was uncomfortable with false modesty. Instead she had found a middle ground that enabled her to accept compliments gracefully without seeming to flaunt herself.

All this contributed to her aura of stability and maturity. Unlike many girls her age, she did not flit from one style or fad to another. And she had democratic tastes when it came to music or movies or television. Some of the things older people liked, she liked; and some of the things girls her age adored, she despised.

In short, Colleen Hamilton was an individual, matured by tragedy and molded by her own sense of self-worth and ambition. During the six weeks she had been attending Centerville High, she had become very popular with both girls and boys, had begun a romance with the football team's handsome quarterback, and had become a favorite of her teachers. Harlan Hamilton had many reasons to be proud of his beautiful teenage sister.

She turned somewhat reluctantly from Teddy Becker and headed for her car. Harlan had bought her a late-model, walnut-brown Mustang, because, as he jokingly said, "I know it's beneath you seniors to ride the school buses."

Centerville High was a semirural school system that drew from five hamlets. The upstate communities, about ninety miles from New York City, had a combined stable population of about ten thousand people. Many were involved in the resort business because this part of the Catskills was a summer vacation area characterized by camping grounds, lakes and rivers, and famous hotels. However, from the fall to the spring, it was a relatively quiet community, with traffic trickling slowly and lazily through its hamlets, most of which had their stores closed until the next summer. To Colleen, when she drove through the village and saw the dark windows and empty streets, it appeared as though the world around her had gone into hibernation. Coming from a lively Westchester community, this took some getting used to; but she had visited here often and knew what to expect.

Now she was nervous because she didn't know what to expect when she got home. These past few days, Harlan had put her on pins and needles because he was continually emphasizing how emotionally volatile the situation was. He had specifically requested that she come home from school as quickly as possible and make as big a deal as she could of the baby's arrival, not that he really had to tell her to do that. She was already very excited.

Harlan's black New Yorker was in the driveway, which meant he had not returned to his college classes. She pulled in beside the New Yorker, gathered her books in her arms, and hurried to the heavy oak front door. As soon as she entered, the first change took place.

Harlan had come to the top of the stairway to tell her to keep the noise down when all she had done was open and close the front door.

"Nikos is asleep," he said.

"Oh," she whispered.

"You can talk. Dana just asked that you don't bang things around or play music loud."

"I don't do that, anyway," she said in a matter-of-fact tone.

"Right," Harlan said, and smiled. "I'm so nervous and excited I don't know what I'm saying or doing. Come on up and say hello to Dana."

Colleen started up the stairs, deliberately tiptoeing even though she knew she wasn't heavy-footed and that the thick, dark brown carpet would smother any sounds. She didn't even touch the dark mahogany balustrade for fear it would creak. She put her books on the light maplewood desk in her room and then quickly followed her brother to his bedroom.

Dana was sitting up in the antique brass bed, her face flushed, her hair pinned back tightly. She wore a bright red cotton nightgown, one that Harlan had just bought for her, at her request, which was something Colleen thought was odd, since she knew Dana wasn't very fond of red, especially bright red.

"Hi," Colleen said, and went quickly to her to give her a kiss.

"Hi, honey," she said. "You just missed him. He had a feeding and went right off."

"Can I peek in?"

"Of course."

"How are you feeling?"

"Wonderful," Dana said. "Fulfilled," she added, her eyes making an emphatic turn upward, almost as though she were going to pass out. Colleen smiled at such dramatic expressiveness. Dana was normally a quite reserved person. In fact, she was often the antithesis of Harlan, who sometimes behaved as though he took Shakespeare literally when Shakespeare wrote, "All the world's a stage."

"It's so exciting, huh?"

"Yes, it is. More exciting than I ever imagined it would be."

Dana squeezed Colleen's hand for emphasis and looked so directly and so hard into her face that Colleen blushed.

Harlan stood there smiling dumbly at both of them, his hands in his tweed pants pockets, his shoulders hunched up. He still had his gray-and-white turtleneck sweater draped over his shoulders, the sleeves tucked together on his chest. He looked more like a college student than a college teacher.

"At least now I have an ally," he said. "In a short while you two won't be terrorizing the males in this house the way you have been. It will be the other way around." He started to laugh, but Dana grimaced.

"What a thing to say, Harlan. Nikos isn't the type to terrorize anyone."

He stared at her a moment, surprised she had taken him so literally, and especially surprised that she referred to the baby as a type . . . as if it already had formed a personality.

"I gotta go see him," Colleen said, and walked out softly. She went to the corner bedroom and pushed on the slightly open door to peer in.

The twelve- by sixteen-foot room had a thick, beige nylon carpet. There were two large windows on the west wall, which permitted sunlight most of the day and gave the room a warm, bright feeling. The walls had been freshly papered with a dark brown box print to match the carpet. To the right was a large walk-in closet. There was a dark maple armoire after that. Across the room were two matching dressers separated by a smaller closet.

The baby was in a dark pecanwood crib. Dana's mother had bought it long-distance by calling an area furniture store and having it delivered nearly a month before Dana's due date. The night after their baby's death and the subsequent adoption, Harlan had told Colleen all of it, and Colleen remembered thinking what it would have been like for Dana to come home without a child and confront that crib.

She tiptoed into the room and approached it. Just as she reached the crib, the infant, its head turned away from her, stirred and turned its head toward her. It opened its eyes, but what attracted her attention was what she thought was a drop of blood caught between its lips. She was about to turn and call for Harlan and Dana when the baby's tongue appeared like a tiny snake and wiped away the drop.

Still shocked by what she thought she had seen, she rushed from the room.

"Isn't he just adorable?" Dana asked as soon as she entered. "Especially when he's sleeping."

"Yes. But he was awake. Dana, I think you should go look in on him."

"Why?" She started to get out of the bed. Colleen looked at Harlan.

"What is it, Colleen?" he asked, moving toward the door.

"I thought I saw blood on his lips."

"What?"

"Blood?" Dana said. Her face whitened and they all moved quickly to the baby's room. Colleen remained back at the door as Harlan and Dana peered into the crib.

"He's asleep," Harlan said. He turned back to Colleen.

Dana reached in and touched the baby's lips, moving them about gently. The infant's eyes fluttered and opened, but he didn't cry. Dana lifted him to her and kissed his cheeks.

"He seems perfectly all right," Harlan said. "Dana?"

"He's fine. Wonderful." She kissed him again and put him back into the crib. Almost immediately the baby closed his eyes. For a moment Harlan and Dana just stood staring down at him. Then they turned to Colleen and headed out of the baby's room. She led them back.

"It just looked like blood to me," she said. "I'm sorry I got everybody excited."

Dana said nothing. She crawled back into bed.

"It's all right," Harlan said. "I suppose it's only natural for us to be nervous about him."

"Of course it's natural," Dana said, and turned to Colleen. "Wait until you're a mother."

"I can wait for that," Colleen said, smiling. Dana did not return the smile.

"Well," Harlan said, "I'll go down and put up the steak. Dana's starving," he explained to Colleen, "so she'll eat before us."

"That's all right. I can cook her supper. No problem," Colleen said.

"Naw, you get to your homework. I've got to do something to keep busy. Still a nervous wreck." He held his hands up in front of his face and shook them. "I've got a son in my house," he added proudly, and left the room. Colleen shook her head.

"I'm sorry if I frightened you."

"It's all right," Dana finally said. Colleen stared at Dana. She couldn't help looking at her because she sensed something different about her. Harlan had explained how emotionally draining the entire experience had been. She could appreciate that. When she had gone to the hospital to see the baby, Dana had been sleeping, so they really hadn't had a chance to talk. Now, with Harlan downstairs cooking Dana's supper, Colleen expected they would have one of their intimate conversations.

"You feel all right, though, don't you?" she asked, moving closer to the bed.

"Of course. I'm just a little tired. Breast feeding can be a little tiring in the beginning, and you've got to eat correctly while you're doing it."

"Uh-huh."

"But I wouldn't have it any other way," she added quickly. "You know, it's a proven fact that children who have been breast-fed have fewer allergies and are healthier later on in life."

"Why don't more women do it, then?" Colleen asked.

"Because they're self-centered. They're worrying about their precious figures. Many women today treat having children the same way they treat buying a new dress or piece of furniture. There's no real commitment," Dana said vehemently.

"I don't know if there are many women like that," Colleen said gently.

"There are. I know," Dana insisted. "Anyway, that's not the way I'm going to be."

Colleen nodded. She looked down at the bed and then up quickly.

"Harlan explained everything to me, all that happened. I felt so bad for you and for what you went through."

For a moment Dana looked confused. She blinked her eyes and then sat forward.

"Went through?"

"You know, with the baby dying and all. It must have been—"

"It was a blessing," Dana said quickly. "A blessing."

"What?" Colleen smiled. Had she heard right? "What do you mean?"

"The baby was imperfect. It would have died sooner or later, and just think, honey. If what happened hadn't happened, I wouldn't have Nikos, would I?"

For a moment Colleen couldn't say anything. She let Dana's answer replay itself.

"But . . . wouldn't you have rather had . . . your own child?"

"Nikos is my own child," Dana snapped. "I don't want to ever, ever hear otherwise while you're in this house. Do you understand me? Do you?" she repeated, her eyes wide, her mouth twisted in an ugly contortion.

Colleen stepped back as though Dana had slapped her across the face.

"I didn't mean anything bad. I—"

"He is my child. He is!" She pounded the bed. "Do you understand?"

Colleen nodded.

"And if you don't feel that way, stay away from him."

"I didn't mean anything bad," Colleen repeated, the tears coming into her eyes. "I just thought—"

"Thought what?" Dana asked, her head tilted.

"Nothing. I gotta do my homework," Colleen said. "I'll see you later."

She hurried from the room, the tears now freely streaming down her cheeks. She went into her own room and closed the door. A short time later Harlan knocked on it.

"Steak all right for you too?" he asked after she told him to come in.

"Okay," she said, turning away quickly.

"Hey, why so sad?" he asked, and she described what had happened.

"Don't think anything of it," he said softly. "I spoke to the doctor again today before I picked her up," he added. "She's experiencing some personality changes because of the tragedy and all. It's common for a woman to experience some depression after delivery. Before the baby comes, all the attention is on the expectant mother, and then afterward, she can feel neglected. The doctor said they call it postpartum blues. Some get so depressed, they need psychological help.

Hopefully this will pass, but it'll take a little time. Until then just go with the flow, okay, Colleen?"

"Uh-huh."

"Great. So, steak à la Harlan Hamilton it is," he said, and slapped his hands together. "Prepare yourself for a gourmet meal."

She laughed. Her brother was one of the good guys. She thought she was lucky to have him.

Half an hour later she came out of her room to go down for dinner and met Dana coming out of the baby's room. For a moment they just stared at each other.

"Everything all right?" Colleen asked.

"Of course," Dana said.

"I'm sorry about before . . . about frightening you."

"Forget it. Tell Harlan to bring me another glass of milk and another piece of steak, okay?" she said in a much friendlier tone of voice.

"Sure."

"You're kidding," Harlan said when she told him. "Lucky we didn't bring home twins. My food bill would go sky-high," he added. Then he stopped what he was doing and thought for a moment. She looked up in anticipation. "It's funny," he said, "but when I think of our baby, I mean our own baby, and then I think of Nikos, it's like they were twins." He paused and stared ahead for a moment and then shook his head. "Just a lucky coincidence." He turned to Colleen as if just remembering she was also there. "Right?"

"Yes," she said, but she couldn't get herself to feel that it was lucky, and she felt terrible about that. She knew all about sibling rivalry and why she had these anxious feelings about the child, but she honestly didn't resent the baby. There was something else.

She was so sure that had been a drop of blood between its lips, and the way he'd lapped it up . . . she shook herself quickly as a chill went through her body.

Best to forget it, she thought.

🔥 2

Colleen woke to the sound of loud whispering just outside her door. For a moment she thought she might have dreamed it. She listened again and heard it again—two distinct voices, their words hard to understand.

She looked over at her Garfield the Cat alarm clock, on her round, white-marble-topped night table, and saw that it was only two A.M. She sat up in bed and continued to listen. The voices drifted away but were still quite audible. Curious now, she got out of bed and went to her door.

The empty hallway was vaguely lit by the small night-light in the wall socket. She listened again and realized that the sounds were coming from within the guest room across the hall. Because of the streetlights on Highland Avenue, illumination spilled through the windows in that room and now cast two distinct shadows on the open door.

Why were Harlan and Dana up so late? she wondered, stepping into the hallway. Almost immediately she was greeted by a putrid odor, the scent of something rancid. The only thing she could think of that resembled it was the odor surrounding the day-old dead cat that had been splattered by an automobile on Turtle Avenue, the next street over.

She cupped her hand over her mouth and swallowed. Then she crossed the hallway quickly and went toward the open door of the guest room. Just before she reached it, she thought she heard the flutter of birds' wings. She looked in. The reeking odor was stronger.

Dana, dressed in her red nightgown but barefoot, stood by the wide-open window. Her hair was loose and brushed down so it lay softly just below her shoulders. She held the baby up, resting him against the inside of her arm, but from Colleen's perspective it looked as though the baby could hold up its head on its own. The baby was wrapped in its soft, blue wool blanket, but the top of its head protruded firmly. She knew enough about babies to know it should be a while before it was supposed to be able to do that.

"My mother's coming tomorrow," Dana told the baby. "She'll be staying in here. She wants to help me with you, but we don't need that kind of help, do we, Nikos? We don't want anyone coming between us. You don't want anyone else to hold you or bathe you, do you, Nikos? Of course not," she said, kissing the top of the baby's head. "I wish she would just make her usual week's visit and leave."

Colleen could have sworn that the baby turned its head to look behind Dana at her as soon as Dana finished speaking. The action caught Dana's attention, and she spun around to confront Colleen in the bedroom doorway.

"What are you doing?" she asked sharply.

"Nothing. I heard you out." She looked around the bedroom. "I thought Harlan was in here too."

"Are you spying on us?" Dana asked.

"What?"

Dana closed the window with her free hand and then walked toward Colleen. She snapped on the overhead light fixture and the room exploded in a hot, overwhelming brightness that made Colleen shade her eyes and squint.

Dana stood before her, and the baby was able to look directly at Colleen. She couldn't believe how alert it seemed for a baby less than a week old. It stared at her with a fixed glare, its eyes catching the illumination from the overhead light in such a way that it was as if it absorbed and fed on the brightness. Its face was flushed, so that even its lips looked pale in comparison to the rest of its complexion.

Colleen stepped back from the doorway and looked to her right, hoping that Harlan would awaken.

"That isn't very nice, Colleen. You don't peek into rooms and listen to other people's conversations."

"That's not what I'm doing, Dana. I heard you and I didn't know what was wrong."

"Nothing's wrong. Nikos is awake, so I am attending to him. You can go to sleep."

"What's that odor? It's terrible," she added, putting her hand over her mouth and nose.

"Probably just a skunk next to the house. I opened the window to air it out. It's dissipating."

"Ugh," Colleen said. "Is there anything I can do?"

"Absolutely not. There's nothing to do. Go back to sleep."

"Okay. 'Night," Colleen said. She paused a moment, then retreated to her bedroom. She closed the door softly, grateful that the horrible aroma hadn't penetrated her room. She returned to her bed, but after she crawled under the covers and lowered her head to the pillow, she vividly relived the way the baby had been glaring at her. It looked like it was really thinking, and she knew there was no way a baby really could be thinking.

She shuddered and tried to think of other things. She heard Dana go downstairs with Nikos, and then all was quiet once more. Sometime before dawn, she woke again to the sound of Dana returning Nikos to his room.

She listened for a few moments, and then she fell asleep and had to be woken by her alarm, something that rarely happened. Usually she woke up just before it went off, but this morning she felt exhausted, not only from being woken a couple of times but also from the nightmares that followed. She was happy she couldn't remember them.

Thankfully the odor was gone from the hallway. Harlan joined her in the kitchen for breakfast. He was up early because he had to go to the airport to pick up Dana's mother, but he was so bright and rested, Colleen had to ask him if he had heard Dana get up to go to the baby late at night.

"You know, I didn't," he said as if just realizing it. "I never even heard the baby cry. Dana slipped out of that bed so softly, I never knew she went to feed him. And I never heard her come back. I guess I didn't realize how tired I was. Dead to the world. But there's nothing unusual about that," he added. "What was it Sir Philip Sidney wrote? 'Come sleep! Oh sleep, the certain knot of peace, the baiting place of wit, the—' "

"She was up all night," Colleen said, interrupting. He stopped his recitation and looked at her. "I heard her in the guest room and spoke with her. There was this terrible odor she said must be a skunk near the house. She was airing out the room. We spoke for a while and then I went back to sleep. She went downstairs. I heard her come back upstairs just before dawn."

"Really? Couldn't get the baby back to sleep, I guess. Well," Harlan said. "That explains why she and the baby are dead to the world. It's exhausting. I'll be glad when Jillian arrives today."

Colleen wondered if she should mention what she had overheard Dana say about Jillian to the baby the night before, but since Dana had accused her of eavesdropping, she thought she would just forget it, even though it was hard to understand why Dana would suddenly resent her. Jillian was never interfering, and Dana was always after her mother to visit and always looked forward to visiting her.

Were these postdelivery blues supposed to have such a dramatic effect on a woman's relationships? When would it end? Colleen could see that it was going to be a great deal harder to get along with Dana while this condition existed. She thought it was probably better for her to find ways to avoid her sister-in-law for a while.

"Jillian will be here by the time you get back from school today," Harlan said.

"I won't be back until after dinner today, Harlan. Today's the big game with Liberty, and afterward, hopefully, I'll be celebrating with Teddy. We're going to the Beast Burger in Middletown. Everyone is."

"Oh, yeah, I forgot. Teddy nervous?"

"Teddy? If he is, he'd never let you know it. That's why they call him Iceman."

"It's a good quality to have when you're in that kind of position. Helps you take the pressure, I'm sure. But," Harlan said, leaning over his coffee and smiling, the patches of freckles under his eyes flashing, "I'm sure you defrost him from time to time."

"Oh, Harlan." She blushed, and then she thought for a moment. "Harlan, I never asked you, but how do you really feel about the baby and all that's happened?"

"What do you mean, Colleen?"

"Well, I know what you told me about Dana and her mental and emotional condition and all, but what about yours? You're part of all this. You've gone through traumatic events too."

He nodded. "Well, I guess I really haven't given myself all that much thought. Dana was so fragile—and still is. Like I said, I think we lucked out with the turn of events, but of course, I can't help thinking about that little tyke who died in the delivery room."

Colleen was fascinated by this. She couldn't help wondering about their own baby herself.

"Did it really look like Nikos?"

"He had carrot-colored hair but he was smaller. I didn't permit myself to look at him all that closely, Colleen. It was too painful, after we realized . . ."

"Yeah, I bet. But how did you come to this other child? You told me about the lawyer. . . ."

"I was out in the hallway. Dr. Friedman was commiserating with me, and to tell you the truth, I was beginning to feel more sorry for him. He really took it badly, since there was no indication that there would be such problems. Anyway, a man approached us and introduced himself as the lawyer for these people. He was a very distinguished-looking man, nearly all gray-haired. The fatherly type," he added, and smiled. "Yes, I remember thinking he was very fatherly—soft-spoken but authoritative, the kind of man you feel you can trust. Apparently he was also a close friend of these people."

"Did you see the people? Were they there too?"

"No."

"What about the teenage girl?" Colleen thought about the tenth-grade girl who was in her eighth month and still attending Centerville High.

"No, I didn't see her," Harlan said. "The lawyer didn't suggest it, and I didn't see the point. I suppose in my own mind I didn't want to make any connections between Nikos and someone else. This way it was as if the baby were just there, just appeared miraculously, you know."

"Uh-huh. But you know the girl's name, right?"

"I know the family name. It was on the papers we all signed. They're Italian, I guess . . . Niccolo was their name."

"Niccolo?"

"Yeah."

"Is that why Dana wanted to call him Nikos? The similarity?"

"No, Dana never really knew their name. She just signed the document where I showed her to sign, and even if she had, she wouldn't have wanted to do anything to remind her of the baby's real family. It brings her such mental and emotional relief to fantasize that Nikos actually is her baby. I might be wrong for permitting her to think that way, but for now I can't see the harm. Later, perhaps, when she is stronger, we'll sit down and talk about it."

"Nikos, though . . . it seems like such a coincidence," Colleen said.

Harlan laughed. "She dreamed it. That's what she told me. Sort of divine inspiration." Colleen nodded. Harlan clapped his hands together and got up. He put his coffee cup in the sink. "Well, I gotta get going, even though the airplanes are rarely, if ever, on time. Can you clean up in here?"

"Of course."

"Thanks, little sister." He kissed Colleen on the cheek. "Have a good day, and wish Teddy luck for me."

"Thanks, Harlan."

She watched him leave, then cleaned up the kitchen, setting the dishes in the dishwasher and wiping down the bright yellow Formica counter and the matching dinette set. She'd always liked this kitchen. Its windows faced east, so the mornings were always bright. Sunlight streaming through the windows would light up the vibrant yellows and greens, making breakfast cheerful. Dana was very good at interior decorating and always seemed to choose colors and patterns that added life and energy to a room.

After Colleen finished in the kitchen she went upstairs to get her books. When she came out of her room, she tiptoed over to Dana's bedroom and listened. The door was closed and all was silent. She started away and then paused, curiosity drawing her back.

She went to the baby's room. The door was slightly open, so she proceeded to enter as quietly as possible. The baby was asleep this time, its eyes closed so tightly that they looked sewn shut. For a few moments she stood there staring down at it.

Colleen really hadn't looked at it all that closely before, or at least studied it enough to recognize its facial features. She knew that a baby's face changed dramatically, especially during the early months. Teddy told her that when his younger brother was born, he and his sister, Steffi, thought that Benny was half baked. Teddy said, "He didn't look like me; he didn't look like Steffi; he didn't look like anybody in the family. Now we argue who he looks like more."

Of course, Colleen knew there was no point in looking for any resemblance to Harlan or Dana in the child. The carrot-colored hair was similarity enough to make any adopted child remarkable, but there was something about the baby's expression in sleep that reminded her of Dana, especially when Dana was in deep thought and unaware of other people in the room. Both she and the baby pulled up the corners of their mouths, and both had that tightness in their chins.

Colleen was fascinated with the baby's hands. Unlike any other young baby she had seen, this baby's fingers and palms had taken full shape. The fingers were exceptionally long, the knuckles sharply defined. There was no puffiness around the baby's wrists, either. Its forearms were lean and graceful.

She shook her head and blinked rapidly. It was as though the baby were developing and maturing right before her eyes. She put her fingers on the crib railing and took a deep breath. Suddenly the baby's eyes opened. Her heart skipped a beat. If it started to cry, Dana would surely bawl her out for coming in here and waking it.

But Nikos didn't cry. He stared up at her silently. She decided to risk touching him and slowly lowered her fingers to the baby's chest. When she made contact, he smiled.

"Hi, Nikos," she whispered. "I never really got a chance to welcome you. Welcome."

The baby seemed to understand. His smile widened. She brought her right forefinger to his cheek, and he smacked his lips together. She laughed to herself and touched the tiny lips. Instantly the baby drew her finger into its mouth. She imagined he thought he was going to breast-feed.

"Uh-oh," she said, pulling her hand back. "Now don't start to cry on me."

The baby grimaced and grunted. She backed away.

"Go back to sleep," she whispered. She heard him whimper. "Shit," she said, and turned quickly to rush out of the room. "I've really done it now."

She paused for a moment outside the baby's room and listened. He didn't start to cry. All was silent. She let out a deep breath and started toward the stairway. Before she reached it, she felt the pinprick of pain on her finger and looked at her hand.

There, at the tip of her right forefinger, the finger that Nikos had so greedily seized into his mouth, was the tiniest bubble of blood, the kind of puncture made when someone was being tested for blood type.

"What the . . ." She brought her finger to her mouth and sucked on it for a moment. Then she looked back at Nikos's room. The baby had no teeth yet. How could it do this? Her body tightened as if it instinctively knew it were under some threat.

She slowly continued toward the staircase. Then she hurried down the steps, eager to leave the house and get on with the excitement that the day promised.

Harlan carried Jillian's bags into the house and paused in the entranceway to listen for Dana. All was deadly quiet. He turned back as Jillian came up behind him, that angelic smile on her face. Dana's mother had soft, small features and almost always wore a kind or gentle expression. Harlan had heard it said that a husband should take a good look at his mother-in-law to see what his wife would be like in twenty years or so. In this case he hoped it was true.

Dana had inherited Jillian's small, graceful nose, her prominent, high cheekbones and delicate lips. They had the same hazel eyes, only Dana's were more often green. Jillian's hair was a darker brown, a color she kept free of gray. She was a small-framed woman who stood just five feet seven but who kept her figure so well that it was difficult for anyone to believe she was indeed sixty-four years old.

Her skin was remarkable. The lines around her eyes and at the corners of her mouth hadn't gotten any deeper or any longer since her late thirties. Her cheeks habitually had a young woman's flush in them, and her neck was as smooth and as graceful as it had been when she was merely twenty. It was as if age itself was in remission when it came to Jillian Stanley.

Her dark green leather suit and white silk blouse looked no worse for travel. That was one of the things Harlan admired about his mother-in-law: She always looked so elegant, so together, no matter what time of the day it was, or what the circumstances were.

Dana had inherited that same meticulousness when it came to her clothing and her appearance. She never left the house, even to go pick up a bottle of milk at the convenience store, unless her hair was neatly brushed and her colors matched.

"You get to appreciate a ranch-style house when you have an infant," Jillian said, looking up the stairs. "We were already in the town house when Dana was born, and carting her up and down or going down for formula made me wish we all slept in the kitchen."

"It's no inconvenience now. You know Dana's breast feeding."

"Oh, that's right. Funny," Jillian said, "how the more things change, the more they stay the same. I didn't breast-feed, but my mother did. Now modern science and medicine renews its faith in the natural way."

"Don't get Dana on the topic; she's an expert. She even makes talks to prospective mothers. The baby-formula companies have taken a contract out on her. If she had her way, they'd be out of business."

Jillian laughed.

"Let's get your bags up to the guest room," he said, and started up the stairs.

"Colleen's not home yet?"

"She won't be home until after dinner. Big football game today, and her boyfriend's the starting quarterback."

"Oh. Wish I had gotten here earlier. I'd have gone to the game with her."

"I bet you would have," Harlan said. He put Jillian's bags in the guest room and the two of them headed for the master bedroom. They paused in the doorway, however. Dana was fast asleep. She was on her back, her head turned to the side, her arms resting comfortably on her thighs.

"Maybe she just finished feeding him," he whispered.

"She does look tired, Harlan," Jillian said. "Drained from the whole experience. Poor thing. To lose a child and then gain one and have to care for it like this . . ."

"Well, he's up a lot at night. Maybe he's a bat," Harlan added, and shrugged.

"Let's look in on him," Jillian said. They went to the baby's room. Nikos was in just as deep a sleep and was also on his back with his head to the side and his arms crossed so that his hands rested on his thighs. "How unusual," Jillian remarked. "Sleeping on his back, but he's adorable," Jillian said. "I can't believe that carrot top."

"Some coincidence, huh?"

Jillian widened her eyes and raised her eyebrows, something Dana often did when she was impressed by something or someone. She studied the baby's face for a moment and then nodded, as though confirming a suspicion.

"Wide forehead. He's going to be brilliant," she said. "He's rather big for a baby less than a month old, isn't he?"

Harlan shrugged.

"You're asking me? I couldn't tell a week-old baby from a month-old baby to save my life. Never really looked at babies," he said, and then indicated the door. She nodded and they walked softly out and back downstairs.

"How about some coffee?" he asked, still not raising his voice much above a whisper.

"Fine. Dana must be exhausted, not even sensing our presence. She was never that deep a sleeper. I remember you couldn't tiptoe past her bedroom without waking her, not that she slept that much. She was so active and full of energy, it practically took a sledgehammer to slow her down and get her into bed."

"She's no different now. If I have a noisy dream, she wakes up."

"I'm surprised she didn't hear us come in and go up the stairs. We weren't exactly quiet."

"Breast feeding is exhausting, I suppose. But don't even suggest she give it up," he added quickly, a note of panic in his voice.

"If that's what she wants to do, fine. I don't mind as long as it's not me."

Harlan laughed, but he sensed her eyes on him as he prepared the coffee. All the way from the airport they had avoided discussing the death of his and Dana's baby and the subsequent adoption. They had circumvented the topic by talking about Nikos as though he were indeed his and Dana's actual child. He had described the baby's hair and had talked about Dana's devotion.

"I'm sure she'll spoil the child," Jillian told him. "It's not uncommon for women to do so when they have children relatively late in life. But Brad and I never spoiled her. Even though she was an only child, she had to work and earn money and be appreciative. Brad was too much old-country for it to be any other way, even though he thought the sun rose and set on Dana's moods."

"Dana's no goof-off. She works far harder than I do. You know she's worked out ways to do part-time work for Grant Kaplan's firm, even while she's on this maternity leave, and she's always borne more than her share of work in the house. I've got to pick up the slack now," Harlan said. "I'm going to start bringing some of my work home. After all, I've got a second career now—fatherhood."

"Well, I'm glad to be of some help to you two. Makes me feel significant," Jillian said. "And not like most of those wealthy, self-centered friends I have in Florida. I swear, some of them actually despise their children and grandchildren. They hate for them to visit, but then again, they hate anything that breaks their comfortable pattern of existence."

They talked about Florida; they talked about Colleen and her future; and Harlan talked a little about his students. The only negative note was sounded when Jillian remarked on her recent phone conversation with Dana, commenting about her aloofness, about a certain coolness in her voice. Harlan nodded, but didn't say anything about it.

Now Jillian was more determined to know. He brought the coffee out to the dining room, and as soon as they sat down, she began.

"I want you to tell me what she's really been like, Harlan," Jillian insisted. "I want to know the details about all this too. Not because I want to be a nosy, interfering mother-in-law; I just want to understand it and see where I can really be of help to you two."

"Sure, Mom, I know." He went on to describe the things the doctor had told him about Dana's emotional condition. He explained how the adoption had occurred and how Dana had taken so quickly to the new baby. "She is a bit obsessive about him right now," he concluded, "but the doctor tells me it's only natural considering what happened to her own child. So," he told her, "don't be shocked if she seems possessive."

"She's not that excited about my being here to help, is that it?" Jillian asked. Harlan knew his mother-in-law was a bright and perceptive woman. There was no point in trying to fool her about things she would eventually realize, anyway, but for some reason—one he did not understand—he was sorry Jillian was so perceptive.

"Well, I don't think she resents you; she wants to do it all herself because, as the doctor said, she's afraid of anything happening to Nikos. Hopefully the paranoia will pass."

Jillian nodded. She put down her coffee cup and sat back in the chair.

"Harlan, where in hell did either of you come up with the name Nikos?"

He looked at her and then laughed.

"It wasn't my idea. Your daughter dreamed it, and considering what she had gone through, I didn't put up any resistance."

"Nikos? Nikos Hamilton?" She laughed. "Oh, well, I suppose before long we'll be calling him Nicky."

"Don't count on it," Harlan said. His tone of voice worried her, and she retreated into her own thoughts before continuing with their conversation. After a while they spoke about other things, Harlan grateful for the opportunity to talk more about his classes and the changes at the college. He told her that the contract negotiations between the faculty and the trustees were on the verge of breaking down. She listened, but he was aware that she rarely had more than half of her attention. He understood why.

They were both surprised at how long it was before Dana woke up. The sun was just about below the horizon and they had had to put on lights. Twice Jillian had gone up to check on Dana, and twice she returned to say that Dana was still in so deep a sleep, she hated to wake her.

The baby woke practically at the same time as its mother. Dana came to the top of the stairway and called down to them.

"Is that you, Mother?"

"Well, well, Sleeping Beauty has arisen," Jillian said, and went to her. They had just embraced when Nikos wailed and Dana broke out of her embrace to go to him.

Jillian followed her to the baby's room and watched as Dana lifted him lovingly out of his crib. As soon as she held him firmly in her arms, his cheek against her breast, the baby stopped crying. Dana kissed his forehead, and Nikos looked at Jillian. She thought he wore a very self-satisfied expression, and it made her laugh.

"Spoiled already?"

"He's not spoiled, Mother," Dana said. "He just . . . just loves me already."

"Really?" Jillian tilted her head the way Dana often did when she was puzzled or even annoyed by something.

"Yes. I can feel it through my whole body when I hold him to me. He radiates it." She lifted the baby and kissed his cheek. Jillian thought it seemed Nikos had smiled. "Time for his feeding," Dana said, and carried him to her bedroom.

Jillian followed and watched as Dana placed herself comfortably in the bed and then slipped the nightgown off her shoulders to expose her breasts. She held the baby up in front of her bosom for a moment, as if giving him his choice. Jillian was surprised to see with what force and control the baby turned its head and brought its lips to her left nipple, ballooning her breast. Dana cupped him in her arms and looked down at him lovingly as he fed. When she looked up at Jillian, she wore an expression of great contentment, her face flushed with excitement. Her eyes were dazzling, the green in them becoming emerald.

Jillian moved toward the bed. The baby's energy and momentum in suckling took her breath away. It looked as though it could consume Dana in one feeding, yet Dana appeared undisturbed by the baby's vehemence. Obviously, if anything, she enjoyed it.

"My God, he's starving," Jillian commented. "Do all babies nurse that vigorously?"

"Of course," Dana replied. "If the mother's milk is good and the baby is healthy."

"He's certainly healthy," Jillian said. She couldn't help shaking her head. Dana smirked.

"Maybe you ought to wait outside, Mother, if this bothers you."

"What?" Jillian felt the heat come into her neck. "I didn't mean it bothers me. If anything, it's a wonder it doesn't bother you."

"Well, it doesn't. Please, Mother. I'd rather be alone when I nurse Nikos. Do you mind?"

For a moment Jillian didn't reply. She just stared. The baby sucked on, its neck muscles straining, its free left arm jerking spasmodically with the fingers of its hand fully extended as it drew the milk from Dana's breast.

"Of course not," Jillian said. "I don't want to make you uncomfortable. I'll go down and help Harlan with dinner," she added. Dana didn't reply. She turned her attention back to the baby, looking down at him adoringly and pressing him even closer to her body.

Jillian looked at her a moment, and then, sensing she had already been dismissed, left the room and went downstairs. Harlan was in the living room making himself a cocktail. She watched him for a moment, sighed, and came forward.

"What's that you're making, Harlan?"

"Bourbon sour," he replied. "I don't do it often, but . . ."

"Never mind how often you do it," Jillian said. "Make me one, too, and make it a double," she added.

He smiled. "What's wrong?"

"Modern motherhood," she said, and dropped herself into the big-cushioned, soft blue chair to the right of the picture window, welcoming the way it swallowed up her diminutive body, practically allowing her to collapse.

While Harlan mixed her drink, she brought her hands to her own breasts, as if they, too, were somehow threatened by the lips of Dana and Harlan's adopted child. Her nipples stiffened as she vicariously experienced the event. She didn't take her hands away from her breast until Harlan turned and she realized from the expression of curiosity on his face just how protectively she was holding her palms over her bosom.

♨ 3

Colleen clutched her hands at her waist as the tension drew her to her feet. The entire Centerville section of the stadium had risen like a wave in the tide of excitement. Teddy and his teammates burst out of their huddle, exploding with determination, and went into their formation. The crowd was screaming at such a high pitch, it sounded like thousands of bees humming. Colleen held her breath. The score was tied; it was the final minute of the fourth quarter. Centerville was on the Liberty fifteen-yard line and it was the third down.

Suddenly an eerie stillness came over the fans as they waited in anticipation. Teddy chanted the numbers, his voice powerful and steady, the voice of the Iceman, she thought, and then the ball was snapped with such force, it looked as though Teddy had drawn it to his hands on a giant rubber band. He turned to his right and faked a run; then he spun to his left, ran laterally for two or three yards, leapt in the air, and threw the football, threading it perfectly between two Liberty players and into the waiting arms of Bobby Reynolds, who was standing in the end zone.

The stadium literally rocked. Colleen felt the structure tremble and had a flash of fear that it would collapse. Her schoolmates were throwing things up in the air, embracing one another, slapping hands, kissing; some of her girlfriends were actually crying. She looked around in stunned amazement and then out to the field. Teddy's teammates were hoisting him onto their shoulders. The referee was blowing his whistle, his cheeks ballooning with the effort, but it looked like a scene from a silent movie because the crowd noise was so great, the sound of the whistle was drowned out.

The game wasn't over; fifteen seconds remained. The umpires and stadium personnel finally got the field cleared, and the ball was put back into play. Danny Singleman kicked the extra point and Centerville was ahead by seven.

The final ten seconds went by quickly because the Liberty team had been depressed by the final events. When the gun was sounded to end the game, it seemed more like a gun fired to start a race. The stadium crowd had been poised to charge forward and instantly broke onto the field to embrace its football heroes. Colleen stood back and caught a glimpse of Teddy being carried off to the locker room.

"Oh, what a game. What a game!" Colleen's girlfriend Audra exclaimed. Even with the animation in her round, ebullient face, her normally wide brown eyes opened to their limits, her soft, thin lips twisted like a string of strawberry licorice, Audra Carson's statement sounded like an understatement. It was the greatest, most exciting game Colleen had ever seen, and not only because she was romantically involved with the quarterback. The lead had seesawed back and forth continually, until the score remained tied for the final minutes of the fourth quarter. Teddy's excellent efforts had been matched by those of the talented Liberty quarterback. It had really been a contest in which both boys had to reach back and call up every bit of skill they had.

Colleen couldn't help but watch the Liberty players retreat from the field. Some looked back enviously at the Centerville crowd and players. She saw that some even wore smiles, probably imagining what it would have been like had the situation been reversed. The Liberty quarterback departed with his head down, his teammates already beseeching him not to feel sorry but to feel proud of the effort he had made.

She turned back just as Teddy was carried into the locker room, and then she followed Audra into the aisle, proceeding to the parking lot, where she would wait for him.

"You're so lucky, so lucky to have him for a boyfriend," Audra said, turning back. Colleen smiled at Audra's unabashed revelation of her feelings. She liked her just for this reason: Audra was refreshingly innocent and open. She was a trusting and warm seventeen-year-old girl who sometimes seemed so oblivious to the way other girls mocked and abused her, it was as if she were from another planet. Colleen often felt the need to protect her. She was indeed Audra's only true friend, but

Audra had been the first to welcome her to the school, and welcome her warmly.

With Audra, Colleen didn't feel the undercurrent of jealousy, jealousy that sometimes took form in vicious ways, that she sensed in other girls at the school. Audra was a pure spirit, vulnerable but full of forgiveness. Colleen couldn't help but like her.

And she liked Audra's mother too. Her father had left them when Audra was just ten, and they had embraced religion, but in a much different, if not strange, manner. They didn't become ardent churchgoers. If anything, Audra's mother, Lucy, seemed to eschew organized religion, as if all churches and all clergy were undercover organizations and agents working for the devil. Their home had become their church, and although they didn't discuss and promote it the way some ardent believers and clergy would, they had a confident belief that God spoke directly to them. There was no need for intermediaries.

They read the Bible together daily, and they had a clear and trusting faith that seemed childish at times. Audra wore her thick silver cross like a shield, sometimes fingering it in private prayer. Others were turned off by this ostentatious religious activity, but Colleen felt comfortable in their home; she felt welcome and sincerely wanted.

She sensed that Lucy Carson was happy and even grateful for Colleen's friendship with Audra, a friendship that was often hard to defend; for her other friends—even Teddy—couldn't understand why she wanted to be friends with such an unsophisticated and, in many ways, strange girl.

"Do you want to come with us to the Beast Burger?" she asked Audra. It wouldn't be the first time she had brought her along with her and Teddy. He had forgiven her for it before, and she was positive he would forgive her for it now, because he would be so elated, nothing she did would make him unhappy.

"Will you be upset if I don't? I promised my mother I would go with her shopping for shoes tonight," Audra said. The five-foot four-inch girl wore an expression of sincere concern.

Colleen shook her head and smiled.

"I'll see you in school tomorrow. Have a good time, and congratulate Teddy for me. I was praying for him to do well."

"I'll tell him. Thanks. See you," Colleen said, and Audra walked off, her dark brown ponytail so long and tied so high, it swung back and forth rigorously.

The moment Audra left Colleen's side, Colleen's other girlfriends approached and gathered around her, everyone talking excitedly. Colleen stood in the center, smiling. She was Teddy's girlfriend. For the moment she was his ambassador. Talking to her and being around her was like talking and being around him. She felt and understood this; it made her feel good. It crowned one of the most exhilarating days of her life, and with all the talk before the game, the game itself, and now in its aftermath, she had little time to think about her strange reaction to her brother's adopted child and the changes in her sister-in-law's personality.

By the time Teddy appeared, Colleen was emotionally exhausted. The girls around her were talking so excitedly, so quickly, their voices so high-pitched, that they sounded as if they had all inhaled helium. First they heard the boys cheering and singing, their voices reverberating in the locker-room corridor, and then Teddy appeared, surrounded by his teammates, all of them in tune with his every move.

His wonderful performance and the team's great victory had inflated him. He looked taller than his six feet one inch and broader and more muscular than his one hundred and eighty pound frame. He had his silky sable hair blow-dried and styled with that wave in the front, and his eyes sparkled like two diamond-shaped pieces of black marble washed by a thousand years of ocean tides. There was a glow about him, and his friends and teammates bathed in the light.

Colleen didn't rush to him. She stood back as the other girls congratulated him, vying for an opportunity to touch him and be touched by him, as though his sports accomplishment had given him divine powers and one could share in the glory simply by a laying-on of hands. She saw the way the girls who touched him and were touched by him turned back to one another, their faces radiant with ecstasy and satisfaction. She wasn't jealous, but she was bothered by it because she saw that it was having a bad effect on Teddy. He didn't need his ego stroked; his head was already too big.

After a few moments he began to search the crowd, and

when he saw her, he moved quickly forward, the others parting to clear his way.

"Hi."

"Hi," she said. She smiled, leaned forward, and kissed him on the cheek. "Nice game."

"That's it? Nice game?"

"For now," she said, looking at the others and then back at him suggestively. His expression of disappointment changed quickly into a knowing smile of anticipation.

"My father let me have the RX-7."

"Great," she said, now happy that Audra had not agreed to come along. The RX-7 sports car had only two seats.

"I'm starving," he announced, and everyone rushed on to their vehicles. He took her hand and they headed into the parking lot. "You know, just before I went into that final huddle, I looked up into the stands and saw you."

"I thought maybe you had."

"You looked so worried."

"I was."

"I just felt it," he said. "I felt I was going to do it. I can't explain it, but it was like a warm glow. It just came over me and I felt so confident."

"I'm glad," she said. They reached the car.

"Then how about really showing it?" He took her by the shoulders and drew her closer to him. They kissed. Some of the other kids howled, but she really didn't hear them. When Teddy pulled back, she sensed another kind of need in him. She felt his hunger for real companionship. Strong feelings, even such good strong feelings, could be overwhelming. They had to be shared in a personal way. For the first time she sensed that he was a lot more sensitive than he made out to be. Harlan was right—she was defrosting the Iceman.

"Want to go somewhere by ourselves?" she whispered. His eyes filled with interest. He took a quick look around at the others, who were getting into cars and pulling out of the lot, screaming at one another, waving at him. He nodded.

"We'll just sneak away," he said. She smiled, happy that he really wanted to be with only her at this moment, that he really didn't need or want the continuous compliments and adoration from the others.

He made a couple of quick turns, downshifted, then sped up

so quickly on the major highway that he lost those who were tailgating. Then, laughing at his deception, he made a turn, working his way back toward the stadium and off to Old Centerville Station. He and Colleen would go to the reservoir and follow the truck road down to the dam where he could park and they could look out over the water, turned silvery by the sinking sun, relinquishing its command of the sky to the full October moon. The reddish-gold orb revealed Nature's plan to continue the Indian summer for at least another day.

After he parked, Teddy got out and went around to the rear of the vehicle. He opened the back and took out a blanket, which he spread over the cleared area just to the right of the car. She watched from inside, pretending not to know what he was doing. For a moment he stood with his hands on his hips. Then she laughed and got out.

"And how did you just happen to bring that along, Teddy Becker?"

"It's always in the car. For emergencies," he explained.

"For what kind of emergencies?"

"Come over here and we'll find out," he said. As soon as she was within reach, he pulled her to him and they kissed again, only this time it was a much longer and much more passionate kiss. She felt herself soften. He pressed his cheek against hers and the two of them lowered themselves to the blanket. There, under the moonlight, with the water just below them, they kissed and stroked each other tenderly, their mutual desire growing more intense with every passing moment. Teddy unbuttoned her light blue sweat-suit jacket and brought his hands to her sides. She felt his fingers slip under her cotton turtlenecked blouse and then move up over her ribs until they touched her breasts.

She sighed and leaned back. He followed her, pressing his mouth against hers, running his lips over her cheeks and chin and down to her neck. He embraced her fully and gracefully unfastened her bra. When the loosened garment lifted under his touch and the tops of his fingers stroked her nipples, she moaned, but suddenly, instead of thinking of him and the moment, she thought about Dana and the new baby.

Teddy stripped off the sweat-suit jacket and peeled up her blouse. In moments he brought his lips to her breasts. He had done this before. Just the week before, they had made love in his room when no one was home, but now, the moment his lips touched her nipple, she imagined Dana's baby bringing its lips to Dana's breast, and the image, for reasons she didn't understand, frightened her. She pulled back, pressing Teddy's head away from her.

"What's the matter?" he asked.

"I . . ." She looked around, unable to explain and yet unwilling to continue. "I feel funny doing this out here. Suppose someone comes along?"

"Out here?" He also looked around, as though that were answer enough, and then went back to her naked bosom. But she tightened again and turned away from him. "Come on, what's wrong? You can't be serious about worrying about anyone. We'd hear or see them coming long before they arrived."

"I don't know. I feel nervous."

"Shit." He sat up. "I can't believe this. And tonight too." He looked away angrily.

"Oh, Teddy." She reached up for him.

He looked down at her. "What?" he asked, his voice filled with confusion.

"Something's wrong. I can't explain it."

"With us?"

"No, not with us. At home," she added softly.

"What do you mean? Someone sick? Problems with the new baby?"

"Yes," she said. "It's the new baby. It's changed things and made me very anxious."

"Well, don't let it get to you. Things will smooth out. Anyway, put it out of your mind for the time being." He started to lean toward her again. She pulled back.

"You're not listening. Dana's different, and the baby is . . ."

"What?" He stopped inches from her lips.

She was going to tell him the truth, that the baby wasn't Harlan's and Dana's, that it was adopted, but all she could say was, "He's weird."

"All babies are weird," he said. Before she could reply, he brought his lips to hers and kissed her so demandingly that he pressed any further conversation back into storage. She allowed herself to be turned into him and let his hands find her breasts again.

"Oh, Teddy."

"God," he said, "when that crowd was cheering and I was out there and I looked up at you, I felt so good. You gave me confidence. I don't know what love's supposed to be," he added, "but it can't be more than this."

His words were enough. She surrendered to his advances and made as many demands of him as he made of her. It all served to help her forget those anxious feelings, and because that was something she wanted to do so much, she was willing to make love more passionately and more completely than before. Those images of Dana and the baby evaporated. The sun slipped completely below the horizon, and darkness, tempered by the moonlight, hung around them like so many thin, black gauze curtains.

Afterward they did not speak. Teddy folded up the blanket and put it back in the car. The two of them moved like shadows of themselves. Their lovemaking had taken them to a higher level of communication. They spoke to each other in gestures and in quick glances. In the car, Colleen lowered her head to his shoulder and they drove out of the darkness, rising out of their own quiet thoughts like two people who had been asleep for a thousand years.

By the time they arrived at the Beast Burger, the crowd had swelled to an unmanageable number. Half the high school had learned where the team had gone to celebrate and was there as well. Throngs of high-school students were gathered outside the doorway of the popular hangout, waiting for an empty seat or even some empty space. Even so, the moment they arrived, a place was made for Teddy and Colleen. They were treated like guests of honor at some community affair.

With all the excitement surrounding her, Colleen didn't think about her family until Teddy drove her up to the house. It looked like all the lights were on.

"Are they having a party?" Teddy asked.

"Oh, Harlan's mother-in-law's here," she said, remembering Jillian's arrival. "But I don't know why every light upstairs is on."

"Want me to come in? I should say hello and see the baby."

"Yes," she said quickly. She wanted him to see the baby,

hoping he might confirm some of her strange, unexplainable feelings.

"Hey, champ," Harlan said, greeting them at the door. "We heard about the game." He shook Teddy's hand. "Congratulations on a terrific game."

"Thanks, Harlan."

"Colleen!" Jillian stepped out of the living room to greet them. "You get more beautiful every time I visit."

"Thank you, Jillian. This is Teddy Becker," she said. "Teddy, Dana's mother, Jillian Stanley."

"Pleased to meet you, Mrs. Stanley." He extended his hand.

"Call me Jillian. So you're the hero?"

"Just one of a group of heroes," Teddy said, smiling.

"Where's Dana and the baby?" Colleen asked. She thought Jillian smirked at the question.

"She went up to feed him. Again," she added.

"It's all right," Dana said, looking down from the top of the stairway. Everyone turned. "The feeding's over." She came down the stairs slowly, carrying Nikos in her arms. She was wearing her white-and-blue velvet robe and matching slippers, and she had her hair pinned up. She appeared fresh and vibrant, that pale, peaked look gone. "Hi, Teddy," she said. "Congratulations on the game."

"Thank you, Dana."

Dana turned the baby and held him up.

"Say hello to the town hero, Nikos. Someday you'll be playing football too."

Nikos opened his eyes and then closed them.

"Typical baby," Dana said. "Unimpressed with football heroes."

Everyone laughed.

"Well, I'd better get my rear end on the road. I'm sure my parents are waiting for me," Teddy said.

"Congratulations again, Ted," Harlan said.

"Thanks. Cute baby," he said, looking at Nikos. The baby burped and everyone laughed. Dana put him over her shoulder and patted his back gently. "'Night," Teddy said. Colleen followed him out to the car. "I don't know what you meant before," he said as they went down the sidewalk.

"What do you mean?"

"About being anxious because of the baby's arrival. Everyone seems happy as hell in there. Dana doesn't seem any different and the baby's cute. What do you mean by saying it was weird?"

"It wasn't that way before," Colleen said. "Dana was different and the baby was . . ."

"What?"

"I don't know." She looked at her finger. Although there was no evidence of any wound, it was still sensitive. How could she explain it to him, anyway? She couldn't explain it to herself.

"Maybe you're imagining some of it," Teddy said. "It's a big change in the house, but you'll get used to it. Believe me." He kissed her and got back into the car.

"Maybe," she said.

"This was one of the greatest days of my life, for many reasons," he said. "But you were the most important reason. See you tomorrow."

She smiled and watched him back out. Then she turned and went back to the house. Just as she walked in, Dana was going back upstairs, carrying the baby so that his head rested on her shoulder. Colleen watched them go up. Suddenly the baby opened its eyes and looked down at her. She saw it lift its head slightly, and then she swore she saw it smile. It was such an unexpected kind of smile, a knowing smile, an arrogant smile. It was as if it were letting her know it had pulled something off.

She couldn't keep her eyes off it until Dana reached the upstairs landing and disappeared around the corner. Then she turned and saw Jillian standing in the living-room doorway staring at her, a worried look on her face.

Teddy was wrong. What she felt wasn't her imagination. But what was it? What did it mean?

"Come," Jillian said, holding out her hand. "Join us for a few minutes and let's catch up."

"Yeah, let's hear the details about the game," Harlan said.

"Forget the game," Jillian said. "I want to hear about her love life."

Colleen smiled. She glanced up the stairway again and then took Jillian's hand and went into the living room with her and Harlan.

* * *

Dana lowered Nikos into his crib. He was wide awake and stared up at her as intently as she stared down at him. She imagined he was just as fascinated with the sight of his mother as she was with the sight of him. Babies were truly miracles, she thought, and the miracle of Nikos was so overwhelming that she had nearly lost the memory of her own infant dying quickly in the delivery room. She could recall only a vague image now—the image of a child being handed up to a nurse who handled it with the greatest of care.

Maybe it wasn't dead; maybe it was Nikos. This memory of her baby dying—it was probably just a nightmare, she thought. As she stared down at Nikos she promoted that idea more and more until she accepted it as fact. There was no other baby but this one. No, there was no other baby. It came to her like a chant. She had to repeat the thought aloud.

"There was no other baby, only you."

Nikos smiled and jerked his arms toward her, as if he understood.

"Yes," she said, smiling, and then she ran her right forefinger down his cheek to his neck. "No other baby."

He smiled and shook his tiny body from side to side, as if struggling to stand up so he could embrace her. His movement and energy took her breath away, and even though she had just placed him in the crib, she couldn't resist taking him into her arms again.

He pressed his face against hers and she stood there feeling his warm lips moving against her skin. Her heart began to throb and she felt her nipples stiffen. She had fed him only a short time ago, yet she felt this great need to bring his mouth to her breast.

The urge to do so was so overwhelming that it made her head spin. She held him away from her and looked into his face. Was it what he wanted? He wasn't crying; he seemed content. Perhaps she would make him sick by feeding him so much. But there was such a heat and a tingle in her bosom now, undulating within her breasts. She closed her eyes. It felt like a man was gently caressing her and then running the tips of his fingers down the outline of the veins that were close to the surface of each breast.

Funny, but when she thought of a man doing this, she didn't

think of Harlan. The man in her imagination was dark-haired and dark-skinned. He was a shadow, the personification of masculinity, rather than any one person from her past or in her memory.

She brought the baby close to her again, and he made a sound in her ear. It wasn't a cry, exactly. It was more like the sound of sucking. It sent a tingle down her spine. Nikos pressed his right hand against her cheek and then wiggled as though to free himself of her embrace and work himself down her body. She was surprised at his strength and determination.

"Okay," she said. "Okay." She started to put him back into the crib, but he screamed and waved his arms at her. He wasn't trying to escape her embrace; he was trying to move himself closer to her bosom. She vaguely wondered if all babies this young had such firm control of their arms and legs.

"What's wrong with you? Don't you want to sleep at all, Nikos?" She lifted him back to her and he stopped crying.

"That's just the way to spoil him," Jillian said, and Dana spun around to confront her mother in the doorway of the baby's room.

"My God, Mother. You frightened me. Why did you sneak in here?" she asked sharply. How long had her mother been standing there, and how much had she seen? she wondered, filled with a guilt she didn't understand.

"I didn't sneak in here, Dana. You probably didn't hear me approaching because you were concentrating on the baby so much," she said. She stepped farther into the room and shook her head. "You can't pick him up every time he cries, Dana. He'll cry all the time, expecting you to. Let him cry himself to sleep, honey."

"He doesn't cry that much, Mother. He won't be spoiled."

"Oh, dear," Jillian said. "You've got to give yourself a break from it, Dana. Put the baby in the crib and come downstairs. You and I have hardly had a chance to talk," Jillian pleaded.

"In a while," Dana said. "I'll come down in a while. I promise."

Jillian shook her head and smiled.

"If your father was alive, he'd be roaring at you like a lion. If there was one thing he couldn't stand to see, it was parents doting on their children."

"I don't dote on him, Mother. I see to his needs. There's a big difference."

"Dana, listen to me—"

"I'll be down in a few minutes, Mother," Dana said more firmly. Jillian saw that she was glaring at her now. Her eyes were glowing with anger, the heat from their embers spreading quickly through her face, tightening her jaw, inflaming her skin. When her lips pulled back, her teeth flashed. Jillian thought she was becoming unrecognizable.

"All right," Jillian said, and left.

Dana waited until she heard her mother going down the stairs. Then she looked at Nikos. His eyes moved with every turn of her head. He was studying her to see what she would do with him; she felt sure of it.

"Poor baby," she said. "I won't leave you yet."

She carried him out of his room to hers and placed him on the bed. He stared up at her silently as she took off her robe. She was wearing a sheer white nightgown. Once again that wave of heat undulated through her bosom. She put her hands under her breasts and felt their fullness. When she opened her eyes, she saw how the baby continued to stare up at her.

She brought the straps of the nightgown over her shoulders and down her arms, permitting the sheer material to slip over her breasts and gather at her waist. Then she stretched out on the bed beside the baby, turning him toward her. He brought his right hand to her left breast and pressed his palm against it. She smiled when he giggled and smacked his lips.

She turned onto her back and lifted the baby so he could rest on her stomach, just below her bosom. She enjoyed the feel of his movement on her body, and for a while she just lay there with her eyes closed.

But it wasn't enough. Her breasts were aching. She cupped them and pressed her palms against them, but nothing stopped the dull but constant agony. She felt like she had been brought to the point of an orgasm and then left to dangle. She couldn't help herself.

She kept telling herself it was bad for the baby to feed so often. Surely he would regurgitate and maybe even get sick, but there was a force working within her that pushed all her motherly concern aside. With her eyes still closed, she reached down and grasped him at the waist. Slowly she brought him up to her breasts until she felt his lips slide over her right nipple.

For a few moments the baby did nothing. When she opened her eyes and looked down, she saw him looking up at her as if he were teasing her. Gently she brought her right hand to the back of his head and pressed him forward, urging him to feed. Then he closed his eyes and she felt the pressure when his lips tightened around her nipple.

In fact, the pressure was so strong that it seemed to her he was drawing out the very marrow from her bones. Even though there was nothing painful about it, she did experience a momentary sensation of fear because it felt as though her whole body were being sucked out through that nipple. The baby was consuming her. In her wild imaginings she saw herself deflate like a balloon and then sucked through his lips until he was left with a swollen, red stomach lying on her nightgown.

The image continued to frighten her so much that she cried out, but the baby went on feeding. She brought her hand to the back of his head and felt his neck muscles working, rippling like the thick body of a python as it ingested and then digested a rat. She couldn't pull her breast from his lips. She could only lay there and wait for him to be satiated once again. She closed her eyes and let it go on.

When she had come into the bedroom, she had left the door open, and now, under the baby's grasp, she forgot about it. In fact, she never heard Harlan come to the door. He started in, coming up to see what she was doing and why she wasn't joining him and Jillian downstairs. As soon as he made the turn into the room, he stopped and stared.

The baby was on its stomach right beside her, his head up, his lips tugging on her right breast. She opened her eyes slightly, the eyelids fluttering, and looked at Harlan. He didn't move; he didn't speak. Then she closed her eyes again. He watched in fascination for a few more moments and then left the room, chased out by the sight of the baby making such dramatic and powerful demands on Dana's body.

He was still flushed when he reached the living room. Jillian looked up from the newspaper expectantly.

"Where is she? What is she doing?"

"She's . . . feeding him."

"Again? Harlan, that's not normal." He shrugged and Jillian got up.

"Don't go up there," he said. "Leave her."

She stared at him. "Why?"

"We'll talk about it later. Please, Jillian. Let's not pressure her just yet."

She thought for a moment, looked up toward the stairway, and then shook her head.

"All right," she said. "But there's something wrong here, and it's more than postdelivery blues. Everything that makes me a mother tells me that," she said. "I'm sure it has something to do with the dramatic events of the past week, but still . . ." She looked up again. "I'm worried about her, Harlan. She's different; she's terribly different."

She turned back to him and he nodded.

"I'll get her to go to the doctor this week," he said. "It'll all be all right, I'm sure."

Jillian stared at him a moment and then sat down again. They waited silently for Dana, but she never came. Colleen, who had been in her room talking on the phone, came down to say good night. Afterward Harlan went up to see about Dana again. This time he returned smiling.

"It's such a cute scene," he said.

"What is?"

"The two of them on the bed. She has the baby lying on her stomach, its head just under her breasts. Dana's fast asleep."

"And the baby?"

"He's lying there so peacefully. When I stuck my head in the door, he looked right at me; he had such an expression of contentment on his face. Face it. Your grandson is something special," he said, but Jillian didn't smile. She just looked up at the ceiling as if she could see through the walls and view the scene he described.

Then she shook her head. "I'll feel better after you've taken her to see the doctor," she said.

He shrugged. "Mothers. They're a breed unto themselves," he said, and turned on the television set. Not long afterward Jillian went upstairs to go to sleep. Before going to her room, she looked in on Dana but found that Dana wasn't there.

She turned and looked at the baby's room. The door was closed. She went to it and turned the knob, but the door was locked.

"Dana?" she called.

After a moment Jillian heard her whisper through the door.
"What is it?"

"What are you doing?"

"Putting the baby to sleep. Go to sleep, Mother. I'll talk to you in the morning."

"But—"

"Go to sleep," Dana repeated.

Jillian turned the knob again to confirm that the door was indeed locked. She stood there for a moment, dumbfounded. Then she turned away and reluctantly went to her room.

Fear and anxiety did not have an easy time settling themselves in the likes of Jillian Stanley, but this night they had their way.

🔥 4

Jillian was already downstairs in the kitchen having coffee when Harlan and Colleen appeared the following morning. She looked up expectantly. She had her hair pinned back neatly and wore a bright blue ankle-length housecoat. Harlan could see that his mother-in-law had not slept well. Rarely, if ever, was the skin under her eyes as puffy, and she usually put on a little lipstick before greeting people, even in the morning. The natural flush in her cheeks that bespoke of her healthy vibrancy was dimmed. She slumped a bit over her coffee cup, inhaling the aroma as though it were medicinal.

"Morning, Mom," Harlan said. He went directly to the pot of coffee.

"Morning, Jillian," Colleen said cheerfully. She opened the refrigerator and took out the orange juice. She had already showered and dressed and tied her hair into a ponytail. She was wearing her black-and-gold school sweatshirt and a pair of stone-washed jeans. She and her girlfriends had burned the telephone wires last night, planning the way the student body should celebrate the team's victory in school. Part of that celebration was the wearing of black and gold, the school colors.

Jillian didn't respond immediately. She looked from Harlan to Colleen and back to Harlan, as though they were both crazy.

"Morning," she said finally. "I imagine Dana is still asleep."

"Like a mummy." He laughed at his own pun and Colleen smiled. "Don't you get it, Mom?"

"I get it, I get it. You guys want eggs? I'll make you some."

"Sure," Harlan said.

"I'm just having some cold cereal today," Colleen said.

Jillian went to the refrigerator and took out the eggs. Harlan noted that she moved abruptly, without her usual grace.

"Scrambled?"

"Right, Mom." Harlan sat down with his coffee. He resisted saying more, even though he sensed that Jillian was very tense. Instead he sipped his coffee quietly and watched Colleen pour her cereal into a bowl. Harlan wasn't one to seek a confrontation or draw out unhappiness from people. He was like his father had been—an avoider—and often, as his mother used to say of his father, one who goes around with his head in the sand: "Mr. Ostrich."

Jillian began beating the eggs vigorously, almost angrily.

"So," he said to Colleen, who seemed either oblivious to Jillian's mood or absorbed in her own thoughts, "school going to have some kind of rally today?"

"There's talk of it. The coach hates them, though, until the season is completely over. We've got the title game to prepare for now. He says rallies before big games put the jinx on."

"Who do we play?"

"Pine Bush. They're undefeated."

"Should be a great game. Maybe I'll be able to—"

"Am I crazy?" Jillian said, spinning on them suddenly, "but you two act as though nothing happened last night."

"Pardon, Mom?"

"What do you mean, Jillian?" Colleen asked. She held her cereal spoon frozen in the air.

Jillian looked incredulously at both of them. "You never heard anything? Neither of you?"

Harlan looked at Colleen and then they both turned back to Jillian.

"Heard what, Mom?"

Jillian stared at them again, as if to confirm that they really meant what they said. Both continued to wear expressions of confusion. Then she turned to the stove and poured the scrambled eggs into the hot pan. She watched the eggs sizzle for a moment before turning back to Harlan and Colleen, both of whom sat back patiently.

"Dana must have been up all night. I had finally fallen asleep when I awoke to the sound of her talking in the hallway, so I got up and looked out. She was walking with the baby. I called to her, but either she didn't hear me or didn't want to. I saw her go downstairs, so I went back to bed, but I couldn't fall asleep."

"I didn't even hear her get up," Harlan said, and looked at Colleen. "But that's nothing. I usually don't."

"I guess I was in a deep sleep, too, this time," she said.

"What do you mean, this time?" Jillian asked with the speed and thrust of a prosecutor.

"I heard her night before last. She did the same thing."

Jillian looked at her thoughtfully. Then she remembered the eggs and put them on a dish for Harlan.

"Thanks, Mom. So Dana was up with the baby—what's so unusual about that?" he asked, reaching for the salt and pepper.

Jillian sat down again across from them and clasped her hands on the table. She looked like someone making a difficult effort to remain calm. Her lips trembled slightly before she began to speak.

"As I said, I didn't fall asleep. I never heard Dana come back upstairs, so I finally got up and went down to see if everything was all right."

"And?" Harlan said, taking his first forkful of eggs.

"The house was totally dark. She hadn't put on a light."

"You're kidding." He looked at Colleen, who shrugged.

"No, I'm not kidding, Harlan. I called to her, but she never responded. At first I thought she might have come back upstairs and I hadn't heard. So I went back up and looked in on the baby's room. The baby wasn't in his crib. Really worried now, I went back downstairs and put on the lights."

"So?" he said after her long pause. He continued to eat, but he looked like someone eating before a television set, engrossed in a suspenseful movie.

"She wasn't anywhere in the house, Harlan."

"What?" He smiled skeptically. "Where was she?"

"I don't know. I thought you would say something about it this morning, but you didn't even hear her get up, and for a moment there, I thought I might have dreamed the whole thing."

"Come on, Mom. You've got to be wrong. Where would she go with an infant in the middle of the night?" His smile widened and he went back to his eggs, as if dismissing the whole thing as Jillian's dream.

Jillian just shook her head. "You'll have to ask her. She wouldn't tell me. I went to the front door, of course, and looked outside, but I didn't see her anywhere. Eventually I put out the lights and went back upstairs, where I lay awake for hours." She leaned forward on the table, her eyes widening. Harlan stopped eating and held his breath. "I said for hours, Harlan. It was nearly morning before I heard her again. The sunlight was just coming over the horizon.

"I got out of bed quickly, but by the time I stepped into the hallway, she was going into the baby's room. Naturally I followed her and watched her put the baby back in his crib. Then I asked her where she had been."

"What did she say?" Harlan asked quickly.

"She said she had been nursing the baby and she told me to go back to sleep. She was very short with me, Harlan. I didn't want to wake you and Colleen, so I just returned to my room. As tired as I was, I couldn't fall asleep, so I got up early and came down to make the coffee."

"Doesn't make any sense, Mom." He shook his head vigorously, as if that was all he had to do to end the mystery.

"You're telling me?"

"Well, when she wakes up, you'll ask her again. I'm sure she'll have some sensible explanation." He started to smile hopefully.

"I don't know how any explanation could be sensible," Jillian said.

Harlan nodded and finished his eggs. "I'm giving an exam to my nine-o'clock class today," he announced, "so I gotta get moving. I feel bad about rushing out like this and leaving you with such worry."

"It's all right. I'll be all right," Jillian said, but it was obvious that she wasn't happy with Harlan's reaction to what she had told him.

"You want me to call you during my lunch hour?" Colleen asked. "Teddy and I could drive over if you need anything."

"No, honey. I should be able to take care of things here. You just enjoy your day. Maybe Harlan's right—maybe there's some sort of sensible explanation."

"Sure. Did you check the bathroom down here? She could have been in there," he said, gulping down the rest of his coffee.

"No, I didn't. But why didn't she put a light on? You'd think she would be afraid to carry an infant in the dark like that."

"Maybe she had it on and then turned it off, not wanting to

wake or disturb the rest of us. Dana's usually very thoughtful."
Jillian nodded, but he saw that she was still not satisfied. "I'm
going to call Dr. Friedman today and make her appointment,"
he added.

"That's good," Jillian said.

"Okay." Harlan stood up. "I'm on my way to sift out the
goof-offs," he announced. He tugged Colleen's hair gently.

"Typical cruel teacher," Colleen said. Harlan laughed and
then started out. She watched him go and then turned back to
Jillian.

"You spoke to her the night before last when she was up
during the night?" Jillian asked, her voice so low that she was
nearly whispering.

"Yes," Colleen said.

"How was she?"

"Like you said . . . short with me." Colleen looked down
and then up quickly. "She accused me of spying on her."

Jillian's eyes grew smaller as she thought intensely for a
moment. Then she sat back in her seat, bringing her right hand
to the bottom of her throat, as if she were about to hear the
most terrible news.

"Then what did she do?"

"Like you said . . . she went downstairs. I went back into
my room and I didn't hear her until much later, but I was afraid
to look out to see what she was doing. I don't know if she had
the lights on or not."

"Something is different about her," Jillian said sadly. She
shook her head. "You sense it?"

"Yes," Colleen said, "but I just figure it has something to do
with all that's happened. Harlan thinks so." Worry seized
Jillian's face and seemed to age it in moments: Her forehead
wrinkled, her eyes dimmed, and the corners of her mouth
dipped. Colleen felt very bad for her. "It's going to take a little
time yet," Colleen said. "Don't worry. She'll be all right after
a while, I'm sure."

"I just hope she's not going through some kind of a nervous
breakdown. I'll feel better when the doctor sees her again, and
I'm going along to talk to him," she added with determination.
Colleen nodded. She started to clean up. "Just leave it, honey.
I need things to do to keep my mind off everything else."

"Sure. Should I call you later?"

Jillian hesitated.

"Yes," she said. "Call. I didn't want to tell you to do so in front of Harlan. He has a lot on his mind without my adding any of my own anxiety. Anyway, you're probably right. It will all pass in time. Can't help worrying, though," she said, and forced a smile. "Wait until you're a mother."

"That's what Dana said."

"Oh?"

"When I asked her if she was nervous about Nikos. Only she got very defensive and said, 'Wait until you're a mother.'"

"What did you say?"

"I said I can wait."

Jillian laughed. It felt good to do so. She took a deep breath and shook her head.

"You're right, sweetheart. Take your time. It all goes so fast as it is. Seems like just yesterday Dana was your age, going to football games, worrying about some boy. No need to speed things up."

She followed Colleen to the front door and then stood there watching her get into her car and drive off. When she turned around to go back to the kitchen, she was struck by how quiet the house was. It was as quiet as a tomb, she thought, and then she thought, Maybe it's only natural for it to be this way. At least until the baby was a bit older and Dana wouldn't get so exhausted feeding and caring for him. It had been so long since she'd been the mother of an infant, and she had had little or no contact with any women who had been since. She had just forgotten what it could be like, she thought. Harlan was probably right—it was ridiculous to be this nervous.

Even so, she couldn't help herself. She had to go upstairs quietly and peek in on Dana. She was so intent on moving silently that she was even aware of the soft squish her footsteps made on the corridor rug. Dana's bedroom door was open slightly. Gently she opened it farther. The room was dismal because the shades were drawn on the windows, so she took a few steps in. She could see her clearly because of the light from the hallway. She was just the way she had been when she and Harlan had first looked in on her yesterday—on her back, her head to one side, her eyes shut tight, her complexion pale. She looked just as exhausted, if not more so.

Jillian retreated from the room quickly and closed the door

softly. She stood there for a moment thinking, then decided to go to the baby's room. The shades had been drawn here as well, so she opened the door widely and went to the crib to look down at him more closely. He was dead to the world too.

Jillian thought he did have such a cute face. The features looked even more defined today. Did changes in infants occur this fast? she wondered. She couldn't recall. Anyway, he looked so sweet, so angelic in sleep; and she had to admit he was an amazing baby. She had hardly heard him cry and he seemed so content. Harlan and Dana were lucky to have come upon such a healthy child so quickly. Adoption could be such a gamble, she thought, and shook her head as she reviewed the tragic and strange events that had brought all this about.

She was about to turn away and go back downstairs when she noticed something. She leaned in closer to be sure. Yes, it was what she thought. The baby's carrot-colored hair—it was changing. Black roots were just visible above his scalp. She knew that babies' hair color could undergo changes early on, but for some reason the loss of the carrot tint was frightening to her.

It was as if the baby had had it carrot-colored just so it could endear itself to Harlan and Dana. And now that he was safely here . . . he could revert to his true color.

What a horrible, foolish thought, Jillian thought. *Babies are innocent, not evil. I've got to get hold of myself. God forbid I ever voice such an idea in front of Harlan or Dana.*

She looked at the baby once more. It didn't stir. It hardly breathed. In fact, she couldn't see any movement in its chest. Terrified at the prospect of crib death, she couldn't help but reach in and touch the child.

The moment her fingers reached his neck, where she hoped to feel a pulse, the child opened his eyes. She pulled her fingers back quickly, but it was too late. Nikos opened his mouth and wailed like she had never heard him wail before. She reached down to take him in her arms and soothe him, but everything she did seemed to intensify his anger more.

Moments later Dana was at the door. The vibrantly red nightgown she wore made her face and arms look ashen. She was so pale, she looked like a corpse. Her normally bright hazel eyes were dull, even sickly, covered with a gray film. Her lips were as bland as day-old dead worms and her hair was disheveled and stringy.

She became furious when she entered the room and confronted her. Her eyes widened, her lips writhed, and her shoulders lifted. Jillian actually lost her breath for a moment.

"What are you doing, Mother?"

"The baby . . ."

Nikos wailed harder at the sight of Dana. His little arms jerked spasmodically toward her and his face became blood-red. Dana practically lunged forward to seize the baby from Jillian. The moment he was securely in her arms, his crying stopped.

"What happened?" Dana asked.

"Nothing happened, Dana. I looked in on the child and became a little anxious when it appeared as though he wasn't breathing, so I reached down to touch him and—"

"You woke him!" Dana accused. "Why couldn't you just leave him be?"

"But, Dana, I told you, I was concerned about him, so I—"

"Just leave him. You don't have to be concerned. He's a perfectly healthy child. Perfectly healthy, do you understand?" She clenched her teeth. Jillian simply stared at her for a moment.

She watched Dana put the child back into his crib. The baby remained quiet, and both he and Dana turned toward Jillian. She looked back at them, never feeling more resented. Dana's reaction and present condition confirmed her fears—her daughter was on the verge of some kind of a nervous breakdown. She thought it would be best to calm down.

"All right, Dana. As long as everything's all right. Did you want anything? Can I bring you some coffee?"

"No. We've got to sleep."

"Okay, honey. I'll be right nearby if you need anything," Jillian said. She hesitated a moment to see what Dana would say, but Dana simply stared. She looked from her to the baby. Was it her imagination? The infant seemed to be wearing the exact same expression of disgust and annoyance. "Okay," she repeated, and rushed from the room.

Jillian went directly to her own room and closed the door. It was best she took a little nap now herself, she thought. All this was so unnerving and she was so tired. She sat on her bed a moment and listened. She couldn't make out any words, but Dana was talking to the child, talking to him as though he were old enough to understand her and even reply. Finally she heard Dana go back to her room.

All was quiet again. The house was filled with a funeral stillness, the kind of stillness that was unnerving.

She lay back. What's happening here? she wondered. My God, what's happening here?

She closed her eyes before she could think too much more about it, and in moments she was asleep.

The ringing of the phone woke Jillian. At first it seemed like the remnant of a dream because the sound was muffled. She opened her eyes and lay there looking up at the ceiling, trying to reorient herself. The ringing persisted and she sat up to listen more closely. She looked at her gold Piaget wristwatch and saw that it was nearly twelve-thirty. Then she scrubbed her face vigorously with the palms of her hands, got out of bed, and went to the guest-room door.

The phone continued to ring. She listened, looked around, and stepped into the hallway. First she went to Dana's bedroom, where the closest phone was. Looking in the doorway, she saw Dana in a deep sleep again. The phone on the dark oak night table beside her continued to ring. It amazed Jillian that her daughter could sleep through the sound.

She went downstairs as quickly as she could and picked up the receiver of the antique white replica of an early-twentieth-century dial phone and said hello. It was Colleen.

"What's going on there? I let it ring and ring. At first I thought I dialed the wrong number, so I dialed again," Colleen said breathlessly.

"I was asleep, and Dana . . . Dana's asleep. Maybe she got up to feed the baby while I was asleep and then went back to bed. I don't know. The phone finally woke me, but how it didn't wake her ringing right beside her is a mystery."

"Is she all right?"

"Not in my opinion. I can't wait for your brother to call. I hope he made that doctor's appointment."

"Should I come home?" Colleen asked.

"No, honey. There's nothing you could do here. I'll keep

busy around the house—make some lunch, take out the roast for supper . . ."

"All right. We're going to have that rally for the football team at the end of the school day, after all. I'll come home right after it ends."

"That's all right. Don't rush home to sit around and hold my hand. Just enjoy the rest of your day." She heard the doorbell ring. "Someone's at the door. See you later."

"See you," Colleen said, her voice small and sad.

Jillian cradled the receiver and went to the front door to greet Trish Lewis. The Lewises lived two houses down. Jillian had met Trish twice before. Trish had been one of Dana's earliest friends in Old Centerville Station, and Jillian knew she and her husband, Barry, occasionally socialized with Dana and Harlan. They had twins, a boy and a girl, in grade school.

"Jillian, hello. It's so good to see you," Trish said in her characteristically flamboyant manner. Usually Jillian enjoyed the thirty-three-year-old diminutive blond woman's histrionics. Both times she had met her before, Trish had behaved like a refugee from a community theater, impressed with her own body language and voice, out of breath, between this appointment and that, overwhelmed by a schedule that included carting her children from dentists to shopping centers to grocery stores and then rushing home to prepare Barry's supper, as though he were the only one in her house who ate an evening meal. Dana said she found her delightful and entertaining, and "always up, always energetic." Jillian thought she was nice enough, but she could be exhausting.

"Hello, Trish," Jillian said, and smiled weakly.

"Is Dana up and about? This is the first chance I've gotten to get over here. Naturally we were so sad about what happened, and then when we heard about the adoption, we were so happy for her and Harlan, but you know me—I waited until the last minute to get a baby gift, and then the twins had this art project to do. Don't ask," she said, her words flowing so fast, Jillian could only smile. "Why these teachers don't realize that the parents are going to end up doing the project, anyway, is beyond me. They expect so much from these kids. Just wait until Dana deals with elementary-school teachers. Where is she?" she asked, finally taking a breath and peering in behind Jillian.

It occurred to Jillian that Trish was speaking so quickly and being even more dramatic because of her own nervousness. She wasn't sure how to handle the situation, a situation that had begun as a tragedy and then quickly turned happy. It was only natural that she didn't know what to expect.

"Oh, come in, Trish. I'm sorry." Jillian stepped back to permit the five-foot four-inch bundle of energy to enter. A gust of air seemed to rush in behind her. "Dana was still asleep last time I looked in on her."

"Still asleep? Oh, you mean she went back to sleep. Naps—what a luxury. When did I do that last? I can't even remember." Trish smiled. "You must be so excited . . . a grandson."

"Yes," Jillian said. "Although Dana's been really exhausted caring for him."

"Breast feeding, I know." Trish tightened her face and pursed her lips. Then she leaned toward Jillian and lowered her voice to a whisper. "That was practically all she would talk about before she went in to have the baby. It got so I wished I was pregnant just so I could do it too. Imagine Barry's face when I said that," she said, straightening up and returning to a normal tone of voice. "Think I can peek in on him? Harlan told Barry the baby has carrot-colored hair."

Jillian swallowed, instinctively bringing her right hand to the base of her throat. She looked up the stairway and then back at Trish. She was actually terrified to give permission.

"I . . ."

"Oh, I know. You don't want to risk waking the baby. What, he just went back to sleep? I remember how I had to take advantage of those moments when the twins went back to sleep. They didn't always go back at the same time, so you can imagine what I went through," Trish said, raising her walnut-brown eyes toward the ceiling dramatically. "Anyway," she said, looking down at the baby gift she had brought, "give this to Dana and tell her I'll stop by later. After supper . . . well after supper." She smiled and squeezed Jillian's arm. "You look too young to be a grandmother."

"Oh, Trish, I don't know about that anymore."

"Really. And Dana's so proud of you. She never shuts up about you. Now, on the other hand, take my mother . . . still nags me to death and spoils the twins. Oh, Barry could just kill her, but that's what it means to be a grandmother, right? I'd better go," she added before Jillian could reply. "When did you get here?" she asked as she reached for the door. "You weren't here for the delivery, were you?" She bit down on her lower lip, as if she were trying to shut herself up. Her face grew pained-looking.

"No . . . no, I wasn't," Jillian said.

Trish nodded in understanding. Then she looked up the stairway. "She's been through a lot, poor thing. It's good you're here, Jillian. How is she, really?"

Jillian shook her head and Trish widened her eyes.

"She's not good. Very high-strung."

"Oh. Is there anything I can do to help?" Trish asked weakly.

"No. Harlan's getting her an appointment with the doctor and we'll see."

"She's not going to want to go on any medications. Not while she's nursing. I can tell you that," Trish said. She shook her head. "I see that you're very worried. Not sleeping, huh?"

"No, not much last night."

"Yes. We were up for a while in the middle of the night too," Trish said, remembering. She grimaced emphatically. "Buster wouldn't shut up."

"Buster?" Jillian smiled.

"Our five-year-old golden retriever. Barry finally had to go out and bring him into the house. Can you imagine? The Jensens' dog was howling too. Only they left him out to howl. Barry says sometimes a bobcat will come out of the woods or deer will wander onto our lawns. Regular jungle here compared to where you live, huh? Well, okay. I'll call later. Give her my love."

"Thank you, Trish."

"It'll be all right. Dana's such a strong-minded woman. Who else would even think of doing what she has done?" Trish added, revealing her own misgivings. She bit her lower lip again, glanced up at the stairway, and then left.

Jillian closed the door behind her and stood there feeling even more exhausted by Trish Lewis's lightning-quick visit. She wasn't really hungry, but she decided to make herself some lunch just to fill the time. The phone rang again just as she entered the kitchen. This time it was Harlan.

"Is Dana up?"

"No, Harlan. She might have been up earlier. I fell asleep."

"So, how are things?"

"Harlan . . ." She looked back to be sure Dana hadn't come down the stairway. "She's not right. I think she's on the verge of a nervous breakdown. You should have seen her before, when I went in to see the baby and the baby started to cry."

"What do you mean?"

"She was positively furious with me. I've never seen her like this, Harlan."

He was quiet for a long moment.

"Well, I made the doctor's appointment. When she gets up, you can tell her. It's ten-thirty tomorrow morning."

"Good. I want to go along," she said with determination.

"Fine. I have two-o'clock and four-o'clock classes today," he said. "And at eight tonight we have a faculty association meeting. Our salary negotiations have broken down again, but I'll see how things are before I decide to go," he added quickly.

"I'm going to put up the roast for supper," Jillian said. "I've been defrosting it," she added, looking over at the eye round on the counter.

"Great. Jillian, I'm sorry things are a little rough right now, but I'm damn glad you're here," he added. Tears filled her eyes. She nodded, her throat closing.

"Bye," she said softly, and hung the receiver in the wall cradle.

She took a deep breath and then went to the refrigerator and took out some cottage cheese and fruit, thinking she would eat lightly. Her stomach was too nervous for much else. As she sat there nibbling, she listened keenly for any sounds from upstairs. It was still so deadly silent in the house, a silence that continued to unnerve her. Finally she heard what she was positive were footsteps on the floor above. She left the kitchen and went upstairs. Dana wasn't in her room and the door to the baby's room was closed.

She went into her room to make the bed and wait. It took a while, but Dana finally emerged. She was coming down the hall toward the stairway when Jillian stepped out to greet her.

"How are you feeling, honey?" she asked. Dana looked up at her as though just realizing she was there.

"Okay," she said softly.

"Baby still asleep?"

"Yes," she said.

"Want me to get you some lunch?"

"It's all right. I'll go down and get something for myself," Dana said, and continued toward the stairway.

"Good. Trish Lewis was here. She brought a baby gift. I left it on the table in the entranceway."

Dana didn't reply. She just continued down the stairs.

"I'll change your sheets, okay? Freshen everything up while you're downstairs?"

"Thank you, Mom," Dana said. Jillian was encouraged by the enthusiasm in her reply, so she went to the linen closet and took out the sheets and pillowcases. She stripped down Dana and Harlan's bed and changed everything. The room was so gloomy because of the way the shades had been drawn down so tightly, keeping out all the daylight. She opened the curtains and lifted the shades. The room brightened and returned to life. She even opened the windows a bit to air out the stuffiness. She was nearly finished by the time Dana returned.

"Why did you open the windows, Mom?" Dana demanded.

"You need some fresh air in here, honey. You didn't realize how stuffy it was. Believe me."

"No, I want it darker. The light hurts my eyes," she said, putting a hand over her eyes to shade them. "And it's too cold for the windows to be open now."

"Dana, it's what they call Indian summer. Why, the air temperature must be at least—"

"It's too cold," Dana said, embracing herself.

"You're not feeling well, honey. I just hope you haven't picked up some virus or something." Jillian closed the windows and pulled down the shades again.

"That's better," Dana said, heading for the bed.

"It's not better." Jillian reached out to feel Dana's forehead but Dana pulled away.

"I'm all right," she snapped.

"No, you're not all right, Dana. You're sick, believe me. Anyway, Harlan called to say he's made an appointment for you with Dr. Friedman tomorrow at ten-thirty."

"What!?"

"An appointment. You're supposed to have one, anyway, and with the way you've been acting—"

"No! I'm not going to that doctor! I'm going to my own doctor, and not in the morning . . . tomorrow night."

"What do you mean?" Jillian was confused. "Your own doctor? I don't understand."

"It's my business, Mother."

"I didn't say it wasn't your business, Dana. But how come Harlan didn't mention this doctor and this appointment?"

"He didn't know about it," she said, and crawled into bed, pulling the blanket up to her neck.

"How could he not know about it?"

"This is a doctor one of the nurses recommended to me. I'd rather go to him, considering what happened. Now, please, Mother. I need to sleep."

"But—"

"I need to sleep," Dana repeated. "And for heaven's sake, don't do anything to wake the baby."

Jillian simply stared down at her. Dana had closed her eyes and looked like she could fall asleep in moments. She stood there for a few moments and then gathered up the bundle of dirty linen and left the room. She stuffed the linen into the laundry shaft. Before she went downstairs again, she hesitated in the hallway and listened by the baby's door. It was quiet. That pall of deathly silence had fallen over the house again.

Shaking her head in disbelief, she went back downstairs, wondering if she shouldn't try to reach Harlan at the college. It was quite uncharacteristic of Dana to go ahead and make a doctor's appointment with a new doctor without even discussing it with Harlan. Her daughter was so changed, she was hardly recognizable anymore, Jillian thought.

She saw that Dana hadn't touched the baby gift Trish Lewis had brought. It was where she had left it in the hallway. Why such disinterest? She paused in the hallway, thinking, and then went on to the kitchen to see if there was anything to clean up.

When she stepped into it, she stopped abruptly, gasping aloud. Again she brought her hand to her throat. She stood gaping at the kitchen counter, where she had left the eye round roast to defrost. It was nearly defrosted, but a sizable chunk of the softened part had been hacked off.

Dana had come down to eat something, and she had eaten a piece of raw meat.

❦ 5

The Centerville football team rally was treated like a school assembly and was to take place during the last period of the school day. It was held in the gymnasium. Black-and-gold banners predicting the impending victory over Pine Bush High had been quickly manufactured in the art classes and were draped from one side of the gym to the other. The team, its senior players wearing their school letter sweaters, had been assembled at the center of the floor, all standing with military posture, staring ahead, their faces so serious, it was as though they were about to face a firing squad instead of a wildly enthusiastic student body.

As the students were quickly herded in, the band played the school song. Controlled bedlam filled the air with an atmosphere of anticipation. Most of the teachers looked dazed; the students were animated, shouting, and waving at one another. After everyone was seated in the stands the principal introduced Coach Van Dermit, who, obviously uncomfortable with the dramatics of the pep rally, quickly presented all the members of the team. He made a short speech, promising to get the team to give its best effort.

Teddy was then introduced as the captain, and he made an equally short statement, thanking the student body for its support and seconding the coach's promise that they would give it their all. The cheerleaders did some cheers and the student body chanted along like a congregation of pagan worshipers. The school song was played again. The principal made a speech about sportsmanship, and the student body was dismissed moments after the bell announcing the end of the school day rang.

Throughout it all, even when Teddy spoke, Colleen found herself distracted. She couldn't help thinking about Jillian's description of Dana and the underlying tone of hysteria she heard in Jillian's voice during the phone conversation. Try as hard as she might, she was unable to overcome this sense of doom that was growing stronger and stronger within her. It was as though some giant shadow had been cast over her brother's house since Dana and the baby had come home, and no amount of sunlight—no matter how direct and how strong—could remove it.

"When do you want to study history?" Audra Carson asked her on the way out. Because of all the noise around them, they had to shout even though they were right next to each other. "This afternoon or later tonight?" She fingered her silver crucifix, as if her question were part of a catechism.

"What?" Somehow she had forgotten about the unit test and her and Audra's decision to study together. "Oh. Let me call you later and we'll see, okay?"

"Sure," Audra said. As usual, nothing disappointed or disturbed her, only now, for some reason Colleen didn't understand, Audra's pleasant disposition annoyed her. In the midst of Colleen's anxiety Audra smiled. But Audra could always smile. Encased in the protective bubble of her religious beliefs, she was immune to tragedy and sadness, apparently even unaffected by it when it occurred to others, close friends included. It wasn't that she was insensitive or uncompassionate; it was more that she dispensed sympathy and consolation with the professional expertise and aloofness characteristic of the way a good doctor or nurse could dispense medical treatment.

"Call you later," Colleen repeated, and hurried away from her. As planned, Teddy met her in the parking lot. She was out before him and waited impatiently. The sky had darkened, adding to her sense of gloom. She was anxious to get home now and see how things were. As usual, when he emerged, he sauntered out slowly, relishing the attention his teammates and other students were giving him. She got into her car and slipped behind the steering wheel before he arrived.

"Hey, what's the hurry? Aren't you going to the M and W?"

She had promised to join him at the root-beer and fast-food drive-in restaurant in Loch Sheldrake. The coach had decided to give the team the day off, and a number of them, along with their friends and girlfriends, were going to hang out awhile.

"No, I've got to get home," she said, punctuating her determination to do so by starting the engine.

"What's up?" Teddy grimaced and raised his arms.

"Problems," she said cryptically. He smirked, his eyebrows knitting emphatically. "Dana's not well," she added, sotto voce.

His expression didn't change. "She looked all right to me last night."

"Well, she's not all right. I told you what Jillian said when I called her at lunchtime," she said sharply.

His smirk evaporated. "So what are you going to do?"

"Help with something. I don't know. There'll be something. I just can't go off and forget about it, Teddy." She put the car into drive to signal there would be no changing her mind.

"All right, all right. I just thought with all the excitement, you'd wanna be part of it," he said, stepping back, his face cast in disappointment.

"I do want to be part of it, but I'm worried about everybody. I just wouldn't be good company right now," she added.

He nodded in reluctant understanding. "I'll call you later," he said, stepping back toward her.

"Okay." She leaned out the window and they kissed. Then he turned away quickly as she backed out of her parking spot and started away.

When she arrived home, she found Jillian alone, watching television in the living room. She was surprised that she was still wearing the blue housecoat she had been wearing at breakfast. She had done nothing with her hair or makeup, either, and her face looked even older than it had that morning. It was as though Colleen had been away for years instead of hours.

"Hi," she said, standing in the living-room doorway and embracing her books. She looked around quickly and realized Dana wasn't anywhere downstairs. "How are things now?"

"Oh, Colleen. Hi, honey." Jillian got up and turned off the television set. "I don't know what I'm doing watching soap operas. I never do. I watched three of them in a row and they all ran together for me." She released a thin, nervous laugh and ran her right hand through her hair, the expression on her face revealing that she had just realized how she was still dressed. "My goodness, I should change before Harlan gets home. He had a late-afternoon class today," she added, smiling.

Colleen didn't understand why, but her heart began beating quickly.

"How's Dana?"

"Dana? Still sleeping, I think. Last I looked, that is. She sleeps on and off all day," Jillian added, shaking her head. "And the baby—except for when I woke him—as far as I know, hasn't woke up either. Isn't that weird? I don't know. It seems weird to me," she added, quickly answering her own question.

"Did Harlan make the doctor's appointment?"

"Oh, yes he did. But it seems Dana made her own appointment with a different doctor. Harlan doesn't know yet."

"A different doctor?" Colleen turned and looked toward the stairway. "I'll go change. Can I help with supper?"

Jillian considered her a moment and then nodded.

"You can set the table. The way my hands are shaking, I'd probably drop something."

"Maybe Harlan ought to come home earlier," Colleen said, her worry increasing because of Jillian's unusually nervous demeanor.

"No, there's no point in driving him into a panic." She released another one of the thin, airy laughs and tugged on the collar of her housecoat. "I'll go change too. Come on," she said, and the two of them started up the stairs. When they reached the top, they stopped because Dana had come out of her room. She was wearing her blue velvet robe and she obviously had brushed her hair. She had tied it back in a dark brown bandanna.

"Dana," Jillian said, "you're finally awake. How are you feeling?"

"Good," she said, and smiled. "What time is it? It's so dark out."

"It looks like we might have some rain," Colleen said. "It's only a little after four."

"Oh." She looked very relieved. "I thought I missed a feeding. Mother, you mean to tell me you haven't gotten dressed yet today?" she asked, and laughed, sounding more like her old self. Colleen and Jillian looked at each other and smiled. Then they laughed too.

"Your air of relaxation is catching," Jillian offered in defense. Dana just shook her head.

"What's for supper tonight? I'm literally starving," she said. At the mention of food, Jillian's smile quickly dissipated.

"The roast beef," she said, recalling how she had found it hacked after Dana had been in the kitchen earlier.

"Great. Don't overcook it. I like it a bit on the rare side."

"Since when?" Jillian asked quickly.

"Since when? I don't know . . . since now," she said, smiling. "How's school, Colleen?"

"Good. We had a rally for the football team today."

"I'll bet that was fun."

"The coach and the team didn't look that happy about it. Coach thinks celebrating is premature."

"And Teddy?"

"Whatever the coach says is gospel. You know Teddy," Colleen said. "I'm going to change and set the table."

"I think I'd better take a shower and put on something decent," Jillian said, grateful for the relaxed, happy atmosphere that was more characteristic of the relationship between her and her daughter. She started for her room.

"I'll check on Nikos," Dana said. "Isn't it wonderful how long he sleeps?"

"Wonderful? You sure you're not drugging him?" Jillian quipped. Dana smiled and went to the baby's room. As soon as she entered it, Jillian turned to Colleen, who was standing in front of her bedroom door too.

"Am I going crazy or what?" Jillian asked, shaking her head. "One minute she acts one way and the next minute . . ."

"I told you . . . Harlan said it was all part of the postdelivery syndrome, whatever that means," Colleen said, and shrugged. "See you downstairs."

"Thanks, honey."

Dana's pleasant mood lifted the heavy gloom from Colleen's mind. As soon as she walked into her bedroom, she thought about Teddy up at the M and W, surrounded by all those girls, and regretted not having gone up there with him, at least for a little while. Then she remembered Audra and the manner in which she had treated her after the rally. She went to the phone and called her immediately.

"Come over right after you eat supper," she said, "and we'll study together, okay?"

"Fine," Audra said. "I wanted to see the new baby too."

"Good, see you about eight."

She changed into a pair of loose, older jeans and a gray sweatshirt and then started to let her hair down but reconsidered and left it in a ponytail. Just as she walked out of her bedroom to go downstairs, Dana appeared in the hallway with the baby. Nikos looked even more alert than before.

"Say hello to your aunt," Dana said, holding the baby in a sitting position, his head against her bosom.

"Hi, Nikos," Colleen said. She reached out and took his hand into her fingers. The baby looked up at her pleasantly and contentedly.

"Isn't he adorable?"

"Like a little doll," Colleen said, and she meant it. For the first time the baby appeared like a baby to her. He looked dainty and soft. Then she realized there was something distinctly different about him. She looked at him more discerningly. "I thought he had blue eyes," she said,

"What's that?" Dana turned the baby more toward her.

"Blue eyes. His eyes are darker, almost black, and look, his hair seems to be changing color too."

"Yes," Dana said, but not sadly or with any concern. "Babies go through so many changes during the first few months. It's as if they're born one person and become another," she added softly.

"Gosh, there's so much to know about bringing up a child," Colleen said with sincere amazement.

Dana laughed. "Don't worry, most of it is instinctive. Come on, Nikos," she said, "I'll feed you, and then I'll be able to go down and feed myself. Wave so long to your aunt," she added, and waved the baby's hand.

Colleen laughed and headed downstairs, bouncing lightly over the steps. It was better, she thought. Maybe things would be all right, after all.

Shortly after Colleen had the table set, Jillian appeared, this time dressed as smartly as usual. She wore an olive-green suede skirt, at mid-calf length with a rust-colored cotton pullover and matching cardigan. Around her neck she had draped a thick gold chain and she wore gold leaf earrings. She had swept her hair back and tied a dark brown ribbon just over the crown of her head to give the back of her hair a fuller look.

It all proved to effect an amazing metamorphosis, rejuvenating her once again and returning her to the young-looking middle-aged woman Colleen had gotten used to seeing.

"You look great."

"Thank you, honey. Let's see how the roast is doing. Can't overcook it or Dana will be disappointed. I've got creamed onions and string beans, as well as mashed potatoes. All-American meal. Got to build up your sister-in-law. She still looks so pale and tired."

"I know." Colleen followed Jillian into the kitchen and watched her put on the full-length blue print apron. "I'm not much of a cook yet," she said. "Whoever I marry is going to have to get test-pilot pay. My father hired Mrs. Wilson about a month after my mother died, and you couldn't touch her kitchen. She treated every meal as though it were a work of art. Actually, it was."

"Oh, you'll do all right. You can follow recipes as well as anyone else. Dana was always in the kitchen," she added, smiling at the memories. "She would follow me around, asking questions, even when she was only five or six. I think she cooked her first meal solo when she was only ten. She was never lazy and never balked about helping out.

"Why, my girlfriends used to remark about her all the time," Jillian went on, "comparing their own children, naturally, and complaining. Dana was special." She paused and thought for a moment. "You know, her father and I never had to get after her about doing her homework or cleaning up her room . . . anything.

"Oh, there were times we chastised her about coming home too late or hanging out with the wrong boy here or there, but when it came right down to it, she always made the right choices, the sensible choices. I was very lucky. I guess I got spoiled." Jillian laughed. "Imagine, my child spoiled *me*. Usually it's the other way around."

"She was very lucky, too, to have you as a mother," Colleen said.

"Thank you, honey. Well," she said, looking at the stove. "We're all set in here. Let's go into the living room and relax for a few minutes until Dana comes down and Harlan comes home, okay?"

"Fine," Colleen said. "Oh, what's that gift in the hallway?"

"Trish Lewis was by earlier and brought it for Nikos. Dana forgot to take it up. Why don't you run it up to her?"

"Okay," Colleen said, and went back into the hall to get it. She hurried up the stairs to Dana's room and knocked on the door. At first there was no response, so she tried the handle and discovered the door had been locked. She knocked again. "Dana?" After a long pause she responded.

"What is it?" Dana asked. Colleen thought her voice sounded quite raspy, almost like someone trying to imitate her rather than she, herself, responding.

"Jillian sent me up with the gift Trish Lewis brought for Nikos. You left it downstairs."

"Oh. Put it in his room, please."

"Okay." She shrugged at Dana's lack of interest, not even wanting to open it and see what Trish had bought.

Colleen had to put the light on in Nikos's room because the shades had been drawn down and the sky had become even darker. In fact, she heard the soft pitter-patter of the beginning of a rainstorm as the drops hit the side of the house, the window, and the roof. She looked around for a moment, deciding where to place the gift package, when a stain on the mattress in the baby's crib attracted her attention. She approached it slowly and looked down. Then, as if she were going to pet a potentially dangerous dog, she gradually lowered her fingers toward the spot and touched it.

Perhaps it was only her imagination, but she felt as if she had just brought the tips of her right forefinger and index finger to the surface of a stove. Her hand recoiled instantly, the stinging pain traveling with electric speed up her forearm and into her shoulder, the result of which sent an agonizing chill through her entire body. She shuddered and embraced herself, subduing a gasp. But she was unable to take her eyes off the spot.

Finally she looked at the tips of her fingers. There was no trace of the stain. She had half expected there would be, for although it looked dry, she was positive she was looking at a bloodstain. It had become a dark amber, but there was still a wet sheen to it, as though it had been freshly made.

Of course, she thought of that first time she had looked at the baby and seen what she thought was a drop of blood between its lips. She recalled how panicked Dana had become and how angry she was when no blood was found. Surely she couldn't miss seeing this. Maybe he had scratched himself. If it was serious, Dana would have shown more concern and they would have gone to the doctor. She didn't want to call her attention to it and get her angry again.

She looked once more at the stain, shook her head, and put the baby gift on the dresser. Then she started out.

She concluded that her imagination was in overdrive, for after she turned off the lights in the room she looked back and could swear that for a long second that bloodstain in the baby's crib glowed. She wanted to laugh at the illusion, but instead she fled from the room.

Dana came down and joined Colleen and Jillian in the kitchen. Colleen was sitting at the table, still listening to Jillian reminisce about her past, this time describing her own teenage years. She paused when Dana appeared in the doorway.

Dana had put on a dark blue skirt and a light blue blouse over which she wore a thick matching dark blue pullover scoop-necked sweater. She had removed the bandanna and had her hair brushed and pinned down neatly. The sallow look that had been in her face earlier was gone now, replaced by a sanguine tint that was so vivid, she looked absolutely feverish. Even her lips were more scarlet. The combined effect was to bring out the whiteness of her teeth. When she smiled, they flashed so brightly that they resembled the center of a hot flame.

In fact, it was this contrast between hot and cold that made her look so striking. She was dressed as though it were the middle of winter and the winds were blowing through the house, yet her complexion bespoke of an inner heat that looked absolutely all-consuming.

"My goodness," Jillian said, wiping her forehead with the back of her right hand, "I'm dying of the heat and you look like you're freezing."

"It is a chilly, dreary night, isn't it, Mother?" Dana asked. The rain had intensified, but it sounded more like a midsummer thunderstorm than a cold fall rain.

"Maybe it's because I've been working in this kitchen," Jillian said. "How are you feeling otherwise?"

"I'm fine, Mother. Why do you keep asking me that?" Dana said, and turned to Colleen.

Colleen had decided not to mention the stain in the baby's

crib just yet. If Dana hadn't brought it to anyone's attention, it was probably nothing, Colleen thought, and she didn't want to risk saying or doing anything that would change the mood of things right now.

"I like your hair in a ponytail," Dana said.

"Thanks. Teddy says it makes me look fourteen."

"So?" Jillian said. "Look fourteen. You'll look forty soon enough."

"I wish I could be locked into this age," Dana said, throwing her head back and running the palms of her hands over her hair. "I'd trade my soul for eternal youth."

"My goodness, listen to her," Jillian quipped. "Has a child and already thinks she's ready for the old-age home."

Colleen smiled tentatively, watching Dana's reaction.

At first Dana scowled but quickly changed into a smile and then a long, thin laugh that for some reason was bone-chilling. "My mother's right. I'm feeling sorry for myself." She looked at Colleen, her smile evaporating. "But it's not that easy having a beautiful teenage girl here to remind me of how quickly time does pass."

"What a thing to say," Jillian said. "I'd love to have someone as sweet and beautiful as Colleen around me all day long. Anytime you feel unwanted here, sweetheart, pack your bags and come live with me."

"I didn't mean to imply that she was unwanted," Dana said, finally coming in from the doorway and sitting down at the table. There was a moment's heavy pause. Despite Dana's denial, for the very first time since she had arrived at her brother's house, Colleen felt Dana was indeed jealous of her. Fortunately, before anyone could say anything else, Harlan came home, bursting into the house with a welcome energy and excitement.

He shook off the rain in the entranceway and quickly hung up his coat, calling out to them as he did so. Then he hurried down the hallway to the kitchen to join them. He kissed Dana, complimented her on her appearance, and announced that there was a good possibility that the faculty would be going out on strike.

"Really? A college teacher?" Jillian asked.

"We're up against the wall, Mom. Big meeting tonight, big

meeting." He slapped his hands together and looked at Dana again. "You look good, honey. Feeling stronger?"

"Of course, why shouldn't I? Breast feeding isn't incapacitating," she said curtly. He ignored her tone of voice.

"Right. So how's Nikos doing?"

"Growing fast, changing," she said.

"I did notice a change," Jillian said, turning from the stove. "His hair color."

"Really? I'd thought he'd be a chip off the old block," Harlan said. He smiled at the way Jillian looked at him, realizing she was surprised at how he fanned the fantasy of Nikos being his and Dana's actual child. Then he indicated Dana with his eyes, and Jillian nodded, although she still wasn't comfortable with the illusion. "What color is it becoming?"

"Black," Dana said. "And so are his eyes."

"Really? What do you know about that?" He rubbed his hands together vigorously and looked around. "Well, I'm starving . . . and everything smells so good in here."

"Go wash up. We're ready," Jillian said.

"On my way, on my way. The baby's asleep, huh?" he asked Dana.

"No, but he's not crying. Go look in on him."

"I will. Hey, Colleen, did you guys have that rally?"

"Yes," she said, smirking.

"It'll be all right. No jinx, you'll see. Love that ponytail," he said, and went out to wash up.

Harlan dominated the dinner conversation, jabbering on and on about the contract dispute between the college faculty and the college trustees. Everyone once in a while he paused and eyed Jillian and Colleen as they looked with awe at the way Dana ate. She had a voracious appetite and was gorging herself with large chunks of roast beef. Everyone stopped talking and looked as she took the meat dish and tipped it so that the blood from the meat would run onto her plate. Then she spooned it up like soup.

The sight of the roast-beef blood reminded Colleen of the stain in the baby's crib. She made a mental note to tell Jillian about it later on.

"Nursing certainly makes a mother hungry," he quipped.

Dana looked up, as though just realizing there were other people at the table. "Of course it does, Harlan. I'm eating for two of us now."

"And the way that baby eats, huh?" He smiled stupidly. "Going to be a football player, after all, Colleen. Sixteen years from now we'll all be going to the championship games. So," he said, putting his knife and fork down, "tomorrow I'll come right home after my nine-o'clock and take you and the baby over to Dr. Friedman's office."

Jillian shot a glance at Colleen, and both of them turned toward Dana, who at first acted as if she didn't hear him. Then she stopped eating and raised her head slowly.

"I'm not going to Dr. Friedman tomorrow morning, Harlan," she said nonchalantly.

"Huh?" He looked at Jillian, who tightened her lips and sat back. "Didn't Jillian tell you? I made the appointment."

"I made my own appointment, Harlan."

"With Dr. Friedman?"

"No. With Dr. Claret."

"Dr. Claret?" He looked at Jillian and then at Colleen, but neither spoke. "Who the hell's he?"

"He is a doctor I can trust," Dana said.

"But how . . . where did you find him?"

"One of the nurses at the hospital told me about him."

"I don't understand. How come you never said anything before?" She didn't reply; she went back to eating to finish the last pieces of meat. He waited until after she swallowed. "What am I supposed to say to Dr. Friedman?"

"I don't care what you say to him." She looked up, her eyes burning with intense anger. "He should have known; he should have prepared us."

"What? But the doctor explained it to both of us and you understood—"

"I understood nothing. And I won't place my baby's health and welfare in the hands of someone who missed something so fatal and significant. There's nothing more to say about it."

Harlan swallowed and sat back as though he'd been slapped. He looked at Jillian again. She got up and started to clear off the table. Colleen quickly jumped up to help.

"Well, what time is this new appointment with this new doctor?"

"Five o'clock."

"Five o'clock? But you know I have a five o'clock class tomorrow and—"

"You don't have to go. I can go myself," she said.

"And what am I, the hired maid?" Jillian said quickly. "I'll go with you. I want to meet this doctor too."

Dana turned to her sharply. "You don't have to do that, Mother."

"Why can't she go along? I'd feel better," Harlan said, practically pleading.

"I'll go, too, if you'd like," Colleen offered.

"I'm not an invalid!" Dana snapped. "Jesus!" Her outburst instantly dropped a curtain of silence. She looked from face to face and sat back. "All right, Mother. Maybe it's better if you drive me, anyway. That way I can concentrate on the baby," she said, but she still sounded sullen.

"Of course," Jillian said. "Please, Dana. Let me help you. That's why I'm here."

Dana looked up at her, her face softening.

"I know, Mom. Thanks." She looked at Harlan. "I'm sorry. I'm just still somewhat upset about what happened."

"Sure," Harlan said, quickly grasping the opportunity to calm things down. "It's understandable. I'll call Friedman's office and cancel your appointment."

"Thanks, Harlan." She patted his hand. "So. What's for dessert, Mom?"

Everyone laughed, as much from relief as from the humor of the moment.

"Homemade apple cake," Jillian said.

"With ice cream?" Dana asked, sounding like a little girl.

"Of course," Jillian replied.

After they had their dessert and coffee, Harlan went up to change for his meeting and Dana went up to get the baby. Colleen helped Jillian with the dishes and cleaning the kitchen. When they had finished, they went into the living room, where Dana was sitting with Nikos on her lap.

Once again Colleen thought the baby looked more like a baby should look now. He oohed and ahhed and smacked his lips. Dana kissed and embraced him and held him up to look at Jillian and Colleen.

"It's amazing," Jillian said, "how quickly his facial features are developing."

The baby's eyes appeared deeper, darker. His soft, pudgy cheeks looked longer, making his jawline more distinct, and his nose had thinned, although it looked perfectly straight. Jillian had to admit to herself that Nikos had the potential to be a very handsome young man.

"It's not amazing," Dana replied. "It just means he's healthy and well cared for."

"Sure it's all right for me to run off like this?" Harlan asked after he came down.

"Of course, Harlan. What you are doing is important," Dana said. "We'll be all right."

"It may be one of those long nights. We're going through the entire contract, sentence by sentence," he warned.

"Don't worry, Harlan," Jillian said. "Dana's not alone."

"Okay. I'm off to do battle with the forces of evil," he announced, and kissed Dana. He hesitated for a moment and then kissed the baby. "You're right, he's changing. Amazing, but I see his features developing right before my eyes."

"That's just what I finished saying," Jillian said, happy someone else saw things the way she did. So much of what was going on here seemed to sit on a borderline between imagination and reality. It felt good to have thoughts and impressions confirmed.

"He's going to be very handsome," Dana said. "Very handsome," she added, almost in a whisper.

"Right. See you later," Harlan said, and left.

For some reason, the moment he left, Colleen felt a sense of dread. The house suddenly was filled with a heavy emptiness. Dana held the baby against her body and looked at the silent television set as if it were on. Both Jillian and Colleen were amazed at how quiet the baby was.

"I don't think I've ever seen such a content child," Jillian said.

"It's the breast feeding," Dana replied. "I'm sure of it."

"I guess you're right. Well," Jillian said, "let's see some news, huh?" She turned on the set. Moments later the doorbell rang and Colleen remembered she was expecting Audra.

"That's Audra. We're going to study for tomorrow's unit test in social studies," she explained. Dana didn't seem to hear her.

She was playing with the baby's fingers and the baby was looking up at her silently, apparently as fascinated with her as she was with him. It was a warm scene.

"Hi," Audra said as soon as Colleen opened the door. "Am I too early?"

"No, right on time. Come in."

Audra wore a lime-green hooded cardigan sweater and a pair of jeans. She zipped down her sweater the moment she entered the house, revealing a black, long-sleeved cotton blouse, which made the silver cross between her breasts even more striking.

"I brought my maps too."

"Great. Come into the living room first and see the baby," Colleen said.

"Oh, good. My mother said she's going to knit something for him."

"Really? That's so nice of her. I'll have to tell Dana."

Colleen led Audra down the hallway to the living room. Jillian smiled as they entered, but Dana was sitting in the soft-cushioned beige swivel chair, facing the television set with the baby on her lap, her back to them.

"This is my friend, Audra," Colleen said. "Dana's mother, Jillian."

"Hi."

"Hi," Jillian said. Dana still did not turn around.

"Dana?"

Slowly Dana turned her head but kept her torso facing the television set, her upper body hiding Nikos from their sight.

"Hi, Audra," she said, and started to turn back.

"Audra wanted to see Nikos," Colleen said.

"Yes, congratulations, Dana."

"Thank you," Dana said, still not turning fully. Colleen smiled at Audra and stepped deeper into the living room. Audra followed.

"Audra says her mother's knitting something for Nikos."

"Oh, how nice," Jillian said. Dana said nothing. Colleen continued to lead Audra forward.

"He's so cute," Colleen explained. "Like a doll now," she added. Audra came forward and suddenly Dana turned around to reveal the baby.

"He is adorable," Audra said.

For a long moment Nikos remained complacent, his eyes barely open. Then he confronted Audra fully and his eyes widened.

Colleen would never forget how the baby's face became distorted. His mouth twisted in agony, the middle of his lower lip falling into his chin, the corners curling up as though invisible fingers had been inserted and were tugging vehemently, tearing the infant's face in half. His nostrils widened, his eyes enlarged, and his forehead wrinkled like an old man's. It was as if the very bones of his skull were being pressed outward, threatening to tear away the flesh and skin that hung over them.

And then he wailed. He screamed as if his very life were being threatened, the effort of that scream being so great, it brought blood to the surface of his face, drawing it up from his neck and torso so quickly, it left them deathly white. His little hands were clenched into fists and his arms began to jerk spasmodically as he kicked up his legs.

"What's wrong with him?" Jillian asked, standing. "He must be in some kind of pain, Dana."

Dana rose, glared at Colleen and Audra, and then hurried from the living room. Jillian followed behind her, but Dana was practically running away.

"Dana. What is it?" Jillian called after her.

"Nothing," she shouted back. "I'll take care of him." She was up the stairs before Jillian had taken the second step. A moment later the door of her bedroom was closed and then locked, the click definite and sharp.

Colleen and Audra came out of the living room slowly and joined Jillian at the foot of the stairway. For a long moment no one spoke.

"Cramps, maybe," Audra finally said. Both Jillian and Colleen turned to her so quickly, it was almost comical. "Well, that's very common with babies, isn't it?" she asked innocently, nervously fingering her cross. It drew both Colleen's and Jillian's attention, but neither responded. Instead they looked at each other and then gazed up the stairway.

"Let's just go study," Colleen finally said. Her throat was so dry, it hurt to speak.

Audra shrugged and smiled in her inimitable manner at Jillian as the two of them walked past her and up the stairs.

Jillian waited until they entered Colleen's room and all was quiet.

In fact, it was so quiet now that she could hear her own heart pounding. Its rhythm thumped up and down her body. She brought her hands to her ears, but that only intensified the reverberation.

A moan escaped and she placed her hands against her lips forcefully, but so forcefully, it was as if she were afraid of what she might hear herself say.

Still shaking from the baby's outburst, she made her way back to the living room and sat down, staring zombielike at the glow of the television set, not seeing, not hearing anything but her own images and thoughts—all of which swelled the ball of fear that had been born in the pit of her stomach.

She felt as if she, too, like her daughter had, might give birth to something already within the grip of death.

✥ 6

As he drove to his faculty association meeting, Harlan couldn't help thinking about the changes in Dana. To him they now seemed more than mere temporary personality adjustments. Dr. Friedman had made it sound as though they were like pimples or a heat rash. Soon they would disappear. Granted, not that much time had passed, and the doctor would have good reason to tell him to remain calm and patient. As he had said, "Give her a chance to digest all this emotional havoc." But Harlan was finding it difficult to ignore the sense of panic and doom that was intensifying within himself, and it was rare for him to be unable to put off or avoid unpleasant things.

Ever since the death of their baby and the adoption of Nikos, Dana had been developing into a complete stranger. He could see the concern in Jillian's face, and although he had done his best to minimize the changes in Dana, he knew that her mother instinctively would sense how serious things had become, especially now, when he, himself, was losing faith in the doctor's diagnosis. Surely she was gong to need psychiatric help if this continued much longer, and despite himself, he would have to do something about it.

Dana was obsessed with the child and had little or no patience for anyone or anything else. He couldn't think of anyone who usually was more sensitive to the feelings of others, who was more compassionate and more willing to sacrifice so that other people, especially people she loved, were happier than Dana. Look at the way she had taken Colleen into their home and made her feel wanted, he thought.

And whenever her mother visited them, Dana was continually concerned that her mother feel comfortable and appreciated. The relationship between them had always been something special. Perhaps because Dana was older than most women when they got married, or perhaps because she had developed more wisdom and patience; whatever the reason, she never resented her mother or saw her as an interfering person. From what well of negative personality traits had she drawn these new feelings and reactions? he wondered. He couldn't believe that they were always there, latent, waiting. She had never shown any evidence of them before.

There was no one at home or anyone with whom he was close enough to confide some of the troublesome, intimate details, but he had hoped to spend a few private minutes with Dr. Friedman to ask him about the way Dana was acting toward him. Whenever they were alone now and he attempted to kiss Dana, she would pull away. Of course, it would be a while before they made love again. He understood that, but why should she be repulsed by his kisses and why should she reject his embrace? Did she somehow blame him for the death of their baby? Did she believe it was because of a weakness in his genes that the baby was born with an aneurysm? True, both his parents had died of illnesses, but still . . .

The previous night, before he'd fallen asleep, he had started talking to her warmly about some of the changes they would make in the house, some of the things they would do for Nikos, and for a few moments she seemed like the old Dana—warm, soft, patient. He kissed her shoulder and stroked her hair, but he sensed her cringing as he did so. Be more gentle, he thought. Go slowly. He talked some more; he complimented her looks, and then, leaning over to kiss her on the cheek, he grazed her breast with his forearm and she exploded in a rage, evincing a violent, ugly part of herself, a part he never knew existed. He couldn't remember her ever being so angry.

But it wasn't the anger so much as the expression of it in her face that remained with him, even invading his dreams. It was as though something else, some horrible creature, lived just below the surface of her skin. It twisted her face. The whites of her eyes reddened and her normally soft hazel pupils darkened into a cold, vivid green that reminded him of mold. Her lips contorted and puffed out, as if her teeth were enlarging. Of course, by this time, he recognized that his imagination was running away with itself, but it also looked to him as if her shoulders thickened as they rose. For a second or so he actually felt physically threatened.

"Don't touch me there!" she commanded. "Don't you know how sensitive I am?"

"I'm . . . s-sorry," he said stuttering. "Is that normal? Are you all right?"

"Of course it's normal. Just don't touch me there." She glared at him a moment, and then her face calmed down because he nodded obediently. He lay back against the pillow and she went into a relaxed position too.

"Jeez, I hardly made contact," he said.

"It doesn't take much contact."

"How do you wear any clothing?"

"Don't worry about it. Let's go to sleep. I'm very tired," she added quickly.

"All right. As long as you're okay," he said. She didn't reply. He turned over and lay awake, thinking about her for a while, but then his own fatigue took control and he did fall asleep, driven deeply down into it by the vivid image of her face in rage.

Sleep was a form of retreat for him, just as immersing himself in this college contract dispute and the business of teaching had become an avenue down which he could flee from the trouble at home. He knew this and he felt somewhat guilty about it, especially about leaving it all in Jillian's hands. She was just as confused and upset as he was. He felt sorry for her, but at the moment he wasn't sure what course of action he should take.

Dana had gone ahead and made an appointment with a new doctor. She would see the physician without him, but perhaps even more importantly, whoever this doctor was, he didn't know her history. He didn't know what kind of a person she had been before. How could he judge the personality problems? How would he know how much of this was a result of postpartum blues and what, if anything, required treatment?

But he wasn't about to oppose her decision to see a new doctor. Perhaps he could see the physician afterwards by himself, and fill him in on some of this. He would get him to contact Dr. Friedman so he could get her medical history, he thought. Sure, that would help a great deal.

The simplicity of this solution made him feel better. Perhaps in time all the solutions would be this simple. Why shouldn't they be? He and Dana had always been so simpatico. Right from the beginning of their courtship they both had the sense that they were meant for each other, that if ever there was such a thing as two people being designed for each other, they were those two people.

He smiled at the memories. She had just come to work for Grant Kaplan's firm, the firm that handled his finances, when they met. Grant knew an uncle of hers who recommended her to him when Grant indicated he needed additional professional help. She had already given notice to the owner of the firm in which she was presently employed.

It was difficult for Harlan to believe that Dana never had been engaged or married before. She was so attractive, her warm, hazel eyes set in a cover-girl complexion. Whenever she moved around the offices, all eyes were on her. She had a grace and sleekness that radiated elegance. He loved the way she tossed her shoulder-length light brown hair behind her with the back of her hand and smiled at him. Was he on a movie set? Was he dreaming? This beautiful girl was within his reach, actually attracted to him.

He gathered from their early conversations that while she was getting her education and pursuing career objectives, she was determined to avoid any commitments that would compli-cate her life. She had such a firm grip on her emotions that she simply had them on hold until she was ready to come under their influence.

"At the time," she told him, "I thought I would rise faster and higher in the business world. You know what I mean. I saw myself as this sharp, efficient, corporate-executive type; but the first time a client asked me whether or not it would be efficient and intelligent to cut back on employees, I faltered. All I could think about was the misery being laid off would impose on the families of the employees. That was when I decided to relegate myself to the back room of the accounting office and fill out forms and pound adding machines. I would give the bottom line to someone else to do with what he or she may.

"It's a difference between a soldier on the front lines and an artillery man in the rear," she said, and he laughed.

"What kind of an analogy was that?" he asked.

"Don't you see . . . the soldier often sees the man he kills, but the artillery man, shoving shells into some cannon and then firing them into the air . . . it's like a game. It's impersonal and he can be aloof, unless he tours the area attacked."

"Oh."

Hey, he thought, this girl is far from shallow. She was well read, she appreciated his intellect, she wasn't pushy or demanding, and she didn't make him feel like a man with a limited future. She was as idealistic about his teaching as he was, seeing something creative about the stimulation of young minds. At last he had found a girl who wasn't self-centered, who wasn't Madonna's "Material Girl," who was no longer threatened by the prospect of someday being mainly a wife and mother.

At an age when he thought he was bordering on bachelorhood forever, he had met the girl of his dreams. He wasted no time proposing, and he would never forget the way she accepted.

"Why, Harlan," she said, "you proposed to me the first time you set eyes on me. It was written all over your face."

"Really?"

"Uh-huh. And although you couldn't see it then, I had already accepted. In fact, I was wondering why it was taking so long for a literature professor to put it into words."

He laughed at the recollection. The tears came into his eyes as he recalled the pride in his father's face when Harlan and Dana came to him and announced their engagement. Colleen was only eleven then, and it had been a while since there was another woman in her family. Dana sensed her anxiety immediately and immediately won her over. Right from the start the two of them were close.

Then came their attempts to have children and their years of failure until finally Dana became pregnant. He recalled the day they received the positive news, and their dinner of celebration. Maybe because it had been so difficult for her to get pregnant was why she'd become so obsessed with doing all the right things. And now this breast feeding . . . Whatever the reason, she was certainly determined that all would go well.

Now that he thought about it fully, the intensity surrounding her pregnancy, and then its tragic finale, it was no wonder her personality had undergone such a radical change. He would have to continue to understand, and he would have to get Jillian and Colleen to do the same.

We've got to give her time, he thought. *We've got to ease her back into herself.* He had been thinking he would talk to some of his closer friends on the faculty and see if any of them had undergone such psychological conflict after their wives had given birth, but now he decided against even that. He was sure none of them had gone through events in any way similar to the ones he and Dana had just gone through. They couldn't understand. There was no point in discussing this with any of them. They couldn't give him any advice.

For the time being, he would put it out of mind. He would immerse himself in the contract conflict and take advantage of that avenue of escape. Things will be all right, he told himself. He was always more comfortable with, and more willing to accept, blind optimism, anyway.

It might be a fault of mine, he thought, *but it's a good fault. It keeps me happy, and that keeps the people around and close to me happy. What's wrong with that?*

He could see his mother's face, the way she shook her head and pressed her lips together, and then he heard her answer.

"Mr. Ostrich. Just like your father," she said. "Go around with your head buried in the sand. But just remember," she added, nodding, "you can't keep it there forever."

He smiled at the memory and the wisdom, but he was unable to take heed.

"A good fault, a happy fault," he mumbled, and continued on toward the college, the night pressing behind and around him, a man oblivious to the fact that he was driving deeper and deeper into the darkness.

Jillian jumped at the sound of the doorbell; she was that much on edge. She rose out of the easy chair like a woman ten years her elder. These changes in Dana and the subsequent angst that had found a home within her had already had a significant effect on her physically. Rarely, if ever, did she feel her age. Her contemporaries usually depressed her with their talk of aches and pains. Their medicine cabinets were literally mini-drugstores. Most often she found herself associating with younger women. She had more in common with them. She certainly had as much energy and as much desire for activity.

Perhaps it was only a mental attitude, but it was effective. She thought young, and so she remained young. But something new and even a bit frightening was happening to her here. When she had first entered her daughter's home this time, it was as if she had crossed into another world, a world in which hours were like minutes, days like hours. She felt she had aged years. Suddenly there were aches in her shoulders and her hips. Suddenly wrinkles on her face were more pronounced. Most importantly, that rapport she had always had with Dana, a rapport that got its strength from her youthful viewpoint, was gone. It had slipped through her fingers almost before she had realized it was happening. She felt like someone who had tried to hold water in her fist.

She had had problems before. Life was hardly one smooth ride. She had even experienced a great tragedy, losing Brad in that freakish boating accident just when the two of them were beginning to enjoy their retirement. It had been as if they had begun new lives and were just rediscovering each other. Contrary to what most people might think, Brad at sixty-nine, and she at sixty-three, were quite romantic. They were in the midst of renewing their vows of love, and then suddenly, from out of nowhere, death slipped in between them and ended it.

It was cruel and it was hard to accept because at their age they were always preparing themselves for medical disasters—physical examinations that would result in dreadful news. People their age developed cancer or heart trouble. There was supposed to be trouble with cataracts, enlarged prostates, arthritis. Like the rest of America, they anticipated ending their lives with long hospital stays. They were readying themselves to be at each other's sides when and if their bodies succumbed to the ailments of time.

But instead, one afternoon, Brad was struck in the head by a swinging sail on a fishing boat and died instantly. She comforted herself by telling herself he would rather have died in such a way than to struggle with medications and procedures in some hospital. It was almost as if he died in battle, rather than withering away.

Somewhat stoic, hardened by the scars, she rose out of the tragedy and became stronger, more independent. She was determined that the unfortunate set of events wasn't going to end both their lives. That was something Brad would have hated to see happen. She told herself she had to go on for both of them now. Every bit of pleasure she garnered from Dana, she had to enjoy doubly. It became not only a duty to herself, but also to the memory of her dearly departed husband that she maintain her health and her vitality and go on for the both of them.

So up until now hardships, complications, and minor illnesses rarely had slowed her down. She fought back with a voracious appetite for life, proud of the way she had maintained her good looks and good health. But suddenly all that was changing. Time and age, both of which had been battering at her door, had found the door unlocked. Something here had done it—something overwhelming and powerful—and at present she was unable to fight back because she didn't know for sure who or what her adversary was. Confused and distraught, she struggled to maintain her sense of equilibrium and hoped that soon there would be some answers.

"Hi," Trish Lewis said when Jillian opened the door. "I said I'd be back after dinner. Dana up and around?"

"Oh, dear, I forgot about you, Trish." Jillian didn't step back to let her in.

"Something wrong?" she asked, leaning to the side to look past Jillian.

"Oh, something happened with the baby a little while ago and Dana went upstairs with him. I'm sorry. I told her that you were here earlier and—"

"Is that Trish?"

Jillian spun around. Dana was at the top of the stairway, the baby in her arms.

"Hi, Dana." Trish stepped up to the doorway and Dana started down the stairs.

"Come on in. It's all right, Mother. Everything's fine. Trish, I love the little outfit you bought Nikos. Thank you. Is Barry with you?"

"No. Poker night."

"Oh, right," Dana said, smiling. Jillian simply stared at her. Dana's face was full of color and vibrancy. Her eyes sparkled. She had brushed and pinned her hair down neatly and even put on a little lipstick. Now she wore her blue-and-white velvet robe. She looked relaxed, untroubled, healthy, and revived. She looked like her old self. Jillian shook her head in amazement.

"What was wrong with the baby?" she asked.

"Just a little gas, Mother. You can't get so excited every time he cries," she added.

"Me?" Jillian nearly laughed. Her smiled widened as she looked at Trish. "If you were here before—"

"It doesn't matter now," Dana said quickly. "Come into the living room, Trish, and fill me in on all that's been happening." She took Trish's hand.

"Let me see the baby first," Trish said. "Oh, he is adorable," she added when Dana turned Nikos so Trish could get a fuller view. Jillian noted that Nikos's hair had lost more of its bright orange tint. The black that had begun at the roots seemed to be climbing up the thin, short strands with remarkable speed, and the baby's eyes were considerably darker. "What a handsome little face for a baby this young," Trish said. She looked quickly at Jillian, and Jillian understood that Trish was wondering if the baby was indeed as young as it was supposed to be. Trish touched his cheek and Nikos closed his eyes.

"Maybe I should put him in his crib while I have the chance," Dana whispered. "I'll be right down again. Go on. Maybe you can give her a cup of coffee, Mom."

"Sure. Would you like a cup?"

"If you have some made," Trish said.

"What is there to making coffee? Go on into the living room," Jillian said, grateful for these pleasant moments. She was beginning to feel that Dana had become something of a schizophrenic, or maybe a manic-depressive. Such ups and downs, they were hard to understand.

"She looks great," Trish said as soon as Dana went back upstairs. "From the way you sounded before, I expected—"

"Believe me, she has bad moments," Jillian said.

"Never looked healthier to me," Trish insisted. Jillian nodded. "Maybe you're just being a neurotic mother, Jillian. Finally," Trish said, and smiled.

Jillian nodded again. "Who knows anymore?" she said in a tired voice. "Let me put up some coffee. I think I need it," she added, and Trish laughed.

Trish's visit with Dana went well. The two were just like they were before Dana had left to give birth and returned with Nikos. Jillian sat back and stared with pleased amazement as

Dana and Trish kidded about other people and Dana joked about Harlan as a father.

"You have to mark down every time he changes the baby's diaper," Trish advised. "Men have a way of exaggerating their contribution toward the care of babies."

"Right now he's understandably nervous about it," Dana said, "but he won't be able to use that excuse forever," she added, winking.

Jillian shook her head, her mouth wide open. Trish never would be able to tell from this conversation just how possessive Dana was with the baby. Was this dichotomy in her behavior deliberate or could it be that she really didn't see how she had been acting? It was a puzzle, all right, but for the present she didn't feel like rocking the boat. Things were going too well.

Audra and Colleen came down before Trish left. They visited a bit, too, and then Audra said she had to go home.

"I should too," Trish said. "Bonny Powell's baby-sitting for me, and I promised her mother it would be for just an hour or so."

"Everything all right with the baby, Mrs. Hamilton?" Audra asked before starting away.

"Oh, yes. Just a little gas," Dana said, smiling.

"Must have been high-test," Colleen quipped, and everyone laughed.

"For a moment there I thought he was reacting to me," Audra said. She shook her head, but held her smile.

"Oh, why would a baby not like you, honey?" Dana replied.

"Well, if you ever need someone to watch him for a while, I'd be glad to help," Audra said.

"Thank you, Audra. We might take you up on that, knowing how Colleen's social schedule is often so full these days."

"Uh-oh," Colleen said. "Time for me to make a quick retreat."

There was more laughter. She walked Audra to the door and said good night, after which she returned to the living room. Trish said good night and Dana went with her to the door, promising to work things out so she and Harlan could get together with Trish and Barry very soon.

"You can do it while I'm here," Jillian said. She had gotten up to help Colleen take the empty coffee cups into the kitchen and had just stepped into the hall. "That's what grandmothers are for—to be taken advantage of."

"That's right," Trish said. "Just ask Barry's mother. Maybe we can do something together this weekend, huh, Dana?"

"I'll see," Dana said. "The baby and I are going to the doctor for a checkup tomorrow."

"Well, I'm sure it all will be okay. Call you tomorrow night."

"Right," Dana said. She stood by the door after Trish left, holding it open for a second. Jillian watched her from the living-room doorway. Finally Dana closed the door. She started for the stairway.

"Why don't you come in and sit for a while, Dana? You and I have hardly had a moment's conversation."

"I was just going to look in on Nikos."

"But you only put him up there a short while ago. He's not crying."

"I'll check on him and be down," she said firmly. Jillian watched her go up and then followed Colleen into the kitchen.

"Every time I think she's coming out of it and calming down a little, she goes right back into it," Jillian said. "She's so intense about that child."

"Maybe the doctor will help tomorrow."

"I hope so, Colleen. I really do."

"Jillian," Colleen said after a moment, "do you really think it was only gas that made Nikos act that way before?"

"Why? What do you mean?"

"Well, when I brought Trish's gift up to Dana, she told me to put in the baby's room. She was nursing at the time. When I went into the room, I saw a bloodstain on the sheet in the baby's crib."

"Bloodstain! Bloodstain?" Colleen nodded. "Well, why didn't you say something before?"

"Well, the first time I looked at the baby," Collen said, "I thought I saw a drop of blood between its lips. Everyone got excited and there was no blood. Dana was actually angry at me, so I thought—"

"Bloodstain?" Jillian said again. "Maybe something is wrong and she's keeping it all to herself. That's why she's been acting so strange. Oh, poor thing. I'd better go up there and see about it." She started out of the kitchen.

"Jillian?"

"Yes?" Jillian said, pausing in the doorway.

Colleen just looked at her. She couldn't help it, she felt frightened; and nervous, as though she had just turned in a friend. She anticipated Dana's being angry that she had told Jillian about the stain. Colleen didn't know why she felt this way, she just did, only now she didn't know how to express it.

"Maybe she didn't want us to know, and if you say something—"

"Nonsense. How can she keep something like that to herself, anyway? Don't worry about it. You did the right thing in telling me," Jillian said, and continued on out of the kitchen.

Colleen sat down again to wait, still overcome with a sense of dread.

Jillian found Dana in the baby's room, standing by the crib. She thought it was the oddest scene. The baby wasn't asleep, yet it wasn't crying. He stared up at Dana, who stood with her palms pressed gently against her breasts, staring down at him.

A mother's infatuation with her infant wasn't remarkable; that wasn't what made the scene seem so strange to Jillian. Part of it was the intensity with which the baby looked up at Dana. His eyes were unmoving; he wasn't even blinking. He looked more like a doll, an inanimate replica. Nothing on his face moved—not his mouth, not his cheeks. His arms were at his sides, straight out, the fingers extended stiffly.

Dana was standing just as still. She didn't look amused and delighted with her baby; she looked mesmerized by him. From what Jillian could see, the expression on her face was so frozen, it looked painted on. Her eyelids didn't flutter, either, and neither baby nor mother looked as though they were breathing. It was as though if either moved, he or she would break the spell.

Jillian felt her heart begin to pound. Why this scene should be so frightening to her, she didn't know. All she knew was that something was wrong. Recalling the way Dana had reacted when she had come upon her in the baby's room earlier, Jillian stepped back and retreated a few steps into the hallway. She took a deep breath and then called. "Dana?"

Even though she knew Dana wasn't in her room, she pretended to go there first to look for her. From the doorway of her bedroom, she called again. "Dana?"

After a long moment Dana replied. "I'm with the baby, Mother."

"Oh." Jillian went back to Nikos's room. This time Dana was fixing the blanket around him in the crib, and the baby's eyes were closed.

"I was just coming down. What's wrong?" Dana said without turning to her.

"Well, that's what I wanted to find out," Jillian replied. She smiled softly and stepped farther into the room. "Is the baby all right?"

"Of course he's all right," Dana said, straightening up quickly. "I told you before. Nikos is a healthy baby, a wonderfully healthy baby." She pulled her shoulders back and pressed her lips together to signal her annoyance.

"Dana, please. Just listen to me for a moment. I know what you've gone through, and I'm sorry I wasn't here to be at your side when it all happened, but you've got to try to get a better hold on yourself."

"What are you saying? What's wrong?" Dana repeated. She looked at the baby quickly and then back at Jillian.

"I know you're nervous about the baby. It's understandable after what happened to yours, but if there's something wrong, you can't ignore it. Let me help. If we have to, we'll—"

"What are you talking about?" She stepped away from the crib so Jillian could get a full view of Nikos. "Look at him. Does he look like a sickly infant?" She held her arm out toward the crib and smirked.

Jillian hesitated for a moment, biting down gently on her lower lip. Then she took another step toward Dana.

"Is he bleeding somewhere . . . the circumcision, perhaps?"

"What? Bleeding? Of course not. Do you think I would simply sit around if my baby was bleeding?" she asked.

"Well, Colleen said that when she was in here earlier, she saw a bloodstain on the sheet in the crib, and I thought—"

"Bloodstain?" Dana brought her head back and then laughed, only the laugh was so shrill and so unexpected that it made Jillian take a step back and bring her hands to the bottom of her throat. She looked with amazement at the insane smile on Dana's face. "Bloodstain?" she repeated. "Obviously it's something she imagined. There's no bloodstain."

"Are you sure? Maybe you didn't see it yourself, honey."

"That's ridiculous," Dana said, this time with more anger in her face. Jillian simply stared at her for a moment. "Christ," Dana said, "I can't believe this!" She went to the crib and reached down to lift the baby.

"You don't have to—"

"Just look for yourself, Mother," Dana said sharply. The baby's eyes fluttered when she snatched him up. She did it rather roughly, Jillian thought, but he didn't cry or wake up. With her free hand Dana pulled back the blanket. "Look for yourself!" she commanded, and stepped away from the crib.

"I believe you, Dana. I only—"

"Just look, will you!"

Jillian saw the hysteria building in Dana's face. Nodding, she walked obediently to the crib and looked down at the clean white sheet. There was no stain.

"Satisfied?"

"Dana, we were only concerned about you and what you might be going through. There's no reason for you to be so resentful," Jillian said. Dana didn't reply. She put the baby back into his crib and fixed the blanket around him again.

"Do you really think I would ignore a bloodstain, Mother?" Dana asked, more softly this time. The change was so radical, it almost seemed contrived.

"I didn't think so, but it's no secret that I've been worrying about you. You're very nervous, very uptight."

"I know I am," Dana confessed. Her face started to crumble.

"Oh, baby, you know I only want to help you," Jillian said, moving to her quickly.

"I know."

They embraced. Tears came into their eyes. Jillian kissed Dana's cheek and they parted.

"I know I haven't been easy to live with," Dana said. "I know it's been hard on Harlan and Colleen and now you, but I'll get better. It just takes a little time."

"Of course. You want another cup of coffee?"

"No. I think I'll just go lay down now, Mother. Don't be angry."

"I'm not angry, Dana. Far from it. Of course, if you're

tired . . . We'll have a good talk in the morning, and I'll be with you when you go to see the doctor."

"Thank you. You're so sweet. I'm lucky to have you around, I know."

"You don't have to thank me, honey. Just let me help you."

Dana nodded. They embraced again and then started out of the baby's room. Dana looked back once before closing the door partway.

"Sure you don't want anything?" Jillian asked.

"No, nothing, thank you. I'll just try to read for a while and then get some rest."

"Okay. I'll be nearby if you need anything. Just shout."

"Thanks, Mom."

They kissed again and Jillian watched her go into her bedroom. She looked back at the baby's room and then went downstairs.

Colleen looked up immediately when she entered.

"She's going to read a little and then sleep," Jillian said.

"What about . . ."

"She was angry at first, upset that we would think she would hide such a thing, but she calmed down quickly."

"And the baby?"

"Nothing," Jillian said. "Thank God about that."

"What do you mean?"

"You must have imagined it, honey. I saw the sheet myself. No stains. Nothing."

"That's what I thought the first time, but this was different. I saw something between the baby's lips," Colleen said.

Jillian just stared at her. "I don't know. Sometimes, when you look at something bright and then look away, an image stays on your retina. Something like that . . . I read it somewhere," Jillian said after a moment.

"I didn't look at anything bright. I touched it too," Colleen added. "I know I did."

"Well, all I can tell you, Colleen, is that there was no stain, and I must admit that the baby did look fine to me. My God," Jillian said, shaking her head, "this has all given me quite a headache. I think I'm going to follow Dana's lead and go to bed. I'll take a couple of aspirins."

"I'm sorry," Colleen said. "I didn't think I imagined it."

"It's all right. Forget it for now. She is riding on quite an emotional roller coaster. One minute she's nasty and tight-lipped, and the next she's crying and kissing me. We'll see how it goes after the doctor visit." Jillian looked around a moment and then smiled. "Good night, honey."

" 'Night," Colleen said in a small voice. She watched Jillian go off, and then she got up and put out the kitchen light. She started for the stairway herself, then stopped abruptly in the hallway.

Why it should occur to her to do this, she did not know. She only knew that she had to see for herself. In the upstairs hallway, right next to the upstairs bathroom, there was a small cabinet door that opened on a metal shaft. They could drop dirty clothing and linen in it and the garments would fall directly into the laundry room, which was right off the kitchen pantry. It made things very convenient.

She went back through the kitchen without putting on the light, but she did put on the light in the laundry room and looked into the vat that caught the dirty clothing and linen. The bin was about one-quarter full, so it took her a few seconds to sift through it all.

She stopped when she found the crib sheet. The heat that rose up in her body nearly put her into a faint. She actually staggered.

Why would Dana lie, and how important was it to point this out to Jillian? Would Dana hate her for it?

The sheet actually felt hot in her hands. She folded it neatly, taking care not to touch the dried bloodstain, and then made a quick decision. She would say nothing for now, but she would hide this sheet so that later, if it became necessary, she could show Jillian she wasn't imagining things.

She decided to hide it at the bottom of her closet in her room. She put out the light in the laundry room, and then, with the sheet under her arm, she hurried like a thief through the kitchen and upstairs. Her heart was beating so fast, she found it hard to breathe. She had just reached the top of the stairway and turned toward her room when Dana appeared.

Miraculously she didn't turn toward Colleen. She walked like a somnambulist toward the baby's room, and Colleen, for once happy that Dana was moving in a daze, slipped quickly into her own room.

She closed the door behind her immediately and caught her

breath. Then, handling the small sheet as if it were something fragile, she knelt down at the foot of her closet and stuffed it under a carton filled with old shoes and sneakers.

She was so hot and sweaty, she had to take a shower before going to bed. Some time later, after she had put out the lights and slipped under her blankets, she turned toward the closet and, for reasons she did not understand, suddenly regretted bringing the sheet into her room. It was as if it could somehow do her harm.

Ridiculous idea, she thought, and turned over in bed so that her back was toward the closet. She fell asleep rather quickly but woke only minutes later because she thought she felt a wet, warm spot in her own bed. When she ran her fingers down the sheet, she thought she felt something, so she got up quickly and put on her lights.

There was nothing there. She shook her head and tried laughing at herself, but after that sleep did not come so easily because she had become afraid of her dreams. Locked in a battle with fatigue, she tossed and turned until the arms of Morpheus embraced her firmly and ended the struggle.

🔥 7

For almost the entire ride home the voices of Harlan's colleagues echoed in his ears. He had to laugh to himself, recalling the fervor and the dramatics with which some of them had spoken. And some of his fellow teachers had the nerve to call him histrionic. That was a laugh. How could he compete with Fred Leshner's don't-crucify-us-on-a-cross-of-legal-paper speech? And what about the way Ted Feldman quoted Martin Lurther King, Jr.'s "I have a dream" speech, and then the way Morton Weiss suddenly stood on his chair and shook his fist at the ceiling? No wonder it was difficult for most college teachers to think of themselves in the middle of a labor struggle. This was more like the final act of a Greek tragedy. Why, any moment he'd expected Zeus to appear to them on the end of a bolt of lightning.

Nevertheless, for Harlan the meeting had served its purpose. He'd been able to channel his frustrations and anxieties into the contract dispute and submerge himself in the sea of communal anger. They'd debated in the college cafeteria for well over three hours. A motion finally had to be made to limit the speakers' time. He couldn't believe how simple and to the point he was when he got his turn to speak, but the brevity was appreciated. He was sure some of the thunderous applause was simply in response to that, rather than to the content of his words.

In any case, he left the meeting mentally exhausted and was grateful for the feeling. As he drove along, he thought that surely now he would have little difficulty falling asleep.

Old Centerville Station certainly looked asleep by the time he reached it. The village, which really consisted of only one main street, appropriately named Main Street, had all of its stores closed. Some store owners had left lights on in windows for security reasons. That, plus the dull yellowish glow from the so-called improved streetlights, created a valley of illumination in which he could snake his way through the darkness. After that he had to go about a half a mile before coming to the turn leading into the residential area in which he lived, and the streetlights appeared again.

With the echo of some of the arguments voiced at the meeting dying away slowly, he turned onto his street, Highland Avenue, and then, almost as if he had crossed into another world, he felt his concerns over his job and the labor dispute slip away. Those thoughts fell back deeply into the caverns of his mind and were replaced with concern for Dana. He was like a man rising out of the confusion, an amnesiac returning to himself. The house, the familiar surroundings, the light over the front door—all of it pulled him out of the quicksand. He had returned.

He imagined that it was the mental turmoil into which he was now reentering that caused him to see the street and the neighboring houses in an ethereal, dreamlike way. The sky had cleared and the shadows cast by the full moon were deeper, longer. Lit windows looked like ghoulish eyes in the faces of houses that had become living, pulsating creatures; sentries guarding the entranceway to his private netherworld.

Everything was coming to life around him, inanimate and animate objects alike. The air was still, yet trees moved their long, twisted, knotty branches like octopi threatening him with their tentacles. The sidewalks undulated; the pavement became hot, the molten macadam gripping his tires and slowing him down. If he stopped, he would be drawn down into the boiling, black, oozing liquid. Before morning it would cool and harden, and no one would ever know that he was buried alive right below the street just outside his home. He had a maddening vision of himself entombed in his car, screaming right up until the moment of his death.

Right before he turned into his driveway, a bat flew so close to the windshield, he actually raised his arms defensively and veered to the right. He seized the steering wheel and hit the brakes, cursing as the car came to a halt. His heart was beating so quickly when he stopped before the garage door that he had to pause for a few moments to catch his breath before pressing the automatic garage-door opener. The door lifted and he drove in.

The house was filled with a disquieting stillness. With not

even the slightest breeze outside, there wasn't even the creak of a shutter. The heavy silence made him aware of the tiniest sounds he made: the squeak in his shoes, the passage of air in his nostrils. He felt like someone who lived deep inside his own body, surrounded by this monstrously noisy and awkward structure that was cluttered with vibrations. Bones ground against one another; liquids gurgled; gases churned. He could even hear his skin stretching and snapping.

He checked the rear and front doors to be sure they were locked securely, and then he put out the hall light and started up the stairs, pausing on the lower steps for a moment because he thought he heard something scratching on the window panels of the front door. It sounded like birds flapping their wings against it. He listened hard, but the noise was gone almost as quickly as it had come. Imagination, he thought again. He blamed it on the silence and the moonlight and continued up the stairs.

He paused on the landing. Both Colleen's and Jillian's bedroom doors were closed. There was no light slipping out from under either of them. The darkness made him even more conscious of his movements as he tiptoed toward his own bedroom. He considered looking in on the baby but decided against it, fearing that even the smallest sound might wake him and interrupt Dana's desperately needed rest. He entered their bedroom.

Dana had drawn the shades down so the moonlight couldn't come through the windows and illuminate the room. He knew she wasn't bothered by the moonlight as much as she would be bothered by the morning sunlight. He understood that if she could sleep, she wanted to. She had to catch it when it was available, considering the demands the baby was making on her. So he didn't complain about the way she blocked out the morning.

However, Dana had left the small, wall-outlet night-light on for him. It cast just enough of a glow for him to make out her dark image in the bed. She was on her back, her arms out over the blanket. Shadows over her face made it seem gaunt. The strands of her hair poured out from under her head. Somehow they looked darker, and for a moment it seemed as though she were reclining in a pool of inky liquid.

He decided to change in the bathroom and not risk waking

her. After he had done so, he slipped under the blanket
gracefully and lay listening to her heavy breathing. Actually he
was disappointed that she wasn't awake. He had hoped to
amuse her with his review of the meeting. But the rhythm of
her breathing, the fatigue that had settled in his muscles, and
the darkness that invaded his thoughts made his eyelids heavier
and heavier, until he couldn't resist closing them. In moments
his breathing rivaled Dana's in terms of its regularity. They
slept side by side like twins tranquilized by the night.

Dana's eyes snapped open. Even though Nikos hadn't cried,
she sensed that the baby was awake, yet for a long moment
Dana didn't move. She lay there staring up into the darkness,
listening keenly, anticipating something. She vaguely recalled
that she had had this feeling before, but now it was like an old
memory, hard to recall on demand.

Her mind had been that way lately. Thoughts and ideas were
hard to grasp and then hold on to for very long. Feelings,
images, and especially memories drifted in and out of her
consciousness. Everything was smoky, thin; even relationships, especially relationships. Sometimes when she looked at
Harlan now, he seemed like a complete stranger, and her
mother . . . her mother was more like an illusion, someone
not to be taken seriously.

But she could do nothing about it because even her realization that there was something about which she should be
concerned didn't last long. It came and went with lightning
speed, even now. A moment after she had these thoughts they
were gone, and she couldn't remember why she felt disturbed.

Suddenly she heard a faint scratching on the windowpane to
her right. Keeping her head stiff, she turned her eyes toward it.
The bright moonlight turned the shade into a transparent
screen. The silhouetted, winged creature that had pressed itself
against the glass grew right before her eyes, until its wings
spanned the entire window. It had happened before, and just
like before, she wasn't frightened by it; she was intrigued,
drawn.

Slowly, almost as if she were a shadow rising out of herself,
she sat up in the bed. The shadow of the silhouetted wings on
the window fell over her. She raised her hands to accept the
warm moonlight, washing her palms in the silvery glow. Then

she slipped off the bed, stepping on a shelf of air, as it were, for her feet never felt the floor. She glided to the doorway so silently, it all could have been in her imagination. Indeed, she had to look back at the bed to be sure she wasn't still lying there.

Harlan was on his side, his back to her, sleeping soundly. She turned from him and stepped into the hall. The night-light in the wall outlet lifted the darkness weakly. The thick shadows on the wall looked more like heavy, dark blue curtains raised tentatively from the floor of a stage. Her shadow was absorbed by them, as if she were a player making an exit from a performance; only, she sensed that her performance was about to begin.

She crossed the hallway to Nikos's bedroom door, hesitating before entering. Looking within, she saw he was awake in his crib. He turned toward her and his eyes lit with a catlike phosphorescence. Still he did not cry; he waited in expectation. She felt herself drawn to him by the now familiar tingle in her breasts.

When she lifted him from his crib, he released a soft hiss that reminded her of gas escaping from the burners on a stove. His body was as hot as something dangling over a flame, yet she didn't think of fevers or illness. The heat felt right. It was soothing, attractive. She clung to him, enjoying the feel of his cool lips against her own warm neck.

Her heart began to pound. She thought she could literally feel the blood circulating through her body, sense its movement and its rush toward every spot where Nikos's body touched hers. The tingle in her breasts spread electrically to other parts of her body. It was ecstasy. She closed her eyes and brought her head back, as if she were being caressed by some unseen lover.

After a few moments she turned and walked out of the room with the baby, carrying him high, holding the back of his head so that his face continued to press against her neck. It had come to her again—this need to leave the house. Something called to her, called to both of them. It was too strong to be resisted, and anyway, at this point she didn't have any urge to resist.

She went down the stairs carefully and stopped at the front door. After she unlocked it she tightened her grip on Nikos and then stepped outside, closing the door softly behind her.

Barefoot, and in only her sheer nightgown, she turned toward the street and the tall, dark shadowy figures that waited just beyond the reach of the first streetlight.

Jillian was surprised by the way she awoke. She heard nothing—not the baby crying, not Dana moving, no one speaking, nothing. It was as if some invisible person beside her in the bed had nudged her. For a moment, perhaps because of the confusion, she thought she was back home in her own bed with Brad beside her. It was years ago long before his death. She could reach over and touch his shoulder and be comforted by the knowledge that he was there—protective, strong, loving.

Maybe it was his spirit that had nudged her into consciousness. It was a great deal easier believing in that than in some of the other things going on around her these days. Besides, she had this ongoing faith that Brad did watch over her, even now, years after his death. She was his spiritual assignment.

He wanted her awake; he wanted her to realize something. What was it now? she wondered, and sat up slowly, listening. She spun around quickly when the shadow of something moved across her bedroom window. Whatever it was, it was gone. She had just started to recline again when she heard someone moving down the hallway.

Recalling what had happened the night before, she stepped out of bed, scooped up her light turquoise robe, slipped into her matching slippers, and went to her doorway. She opened the door and peered out just as Dana disappeared below the top steps.

"Oh, no," Jillian muttered to herself. "Not again."

She went into the hallway and to the stairway landing. Just like the night before, Dana hadn't put on any lights. What the hell was she doing? Jillian wondered. She looked back to see if Harlan had gotten up, but all was quiet and dark behind her. Determined now to get to the bottom of this, she started down the stairs. About midway down, she heard the front door open and saw Dana, carrying the baby, step out, closing the door softly behind her.

Terribly curious now, Jillian hurried down the remaining steps to the front door. By the time she opened it, Dana was below the driveway and on the sidewalk, heading up Highland

Avenue. The quiet residential street was otherwise empty: no other pedestrians; no cars driving by; most homes dark, except for their door lights, which had been left on to ward off potential burglars.

"Dana," she called, but Dana did not turn around. Barefoot and dressed only in her nightgown, she walked on. Was she sleepwalking? Jillian wondered. It could very well be a consequence of all this, she thought. She looked back, debating whether or not to rouse Harlan, and then decided there wasn't time. She hurried out of the house herself.

"Dana, wait. Where are you going?" she asked, but Dana continued on, as though she'd heard nothing. The baby wasn't crying, either. For all Jillian knew, he was asleep in her arms. It was difficult to move quickly in her slippers, but she broke into a fast pace. Dana seemed to be moving toward a pair of large maple trees in the lot just a few hundred yards from theirs.

"Dana," she called as she drew closer. She suddenly got the whiff of a most disgusting stench. The only thing she could think of was the putrid odor of rotting, dead animals. She had to stop for a moment and catch her breath. It was so oppressing, she thought she was getting the dry heaves. Dana, however, went on, undisturbed by it. Jillian reached out toward her, gasping, her mouth filling with saliva. "Dana, wait!"

Jillian swallowed hard and then rushed on after her daughter.

"For God's sake, Dana, where are you going this time of the night dressed like this? Don't you realize—"

She reached out to touch Dana's shoulder, but just before Jillian made contact with her fingers, Dana turned around. In the bright moonlight Jillian could clearly see both Dana's and the baby's faces. Once again they were only one face, but this time it took Jillian's breath away.

Harlan opened his eyes and started to stretch his arms out freely, a habit of his. More often than not, Dana was awake before him, but she'd lay there waiting for him to open his eyes. Then, when he stretched and groaned, she would turn over and he would kiss her.

He hadn't done that since she'd returned from the hospital, and his awareness of her being up at all hours of the night to feed and care for the baby made him more considerate in the morning. He stifled a groan, brought his arms down quickly, looked over, and saw that she was fast asleep.

She was turned toward him, her eyes shut tight, her lips puffed out just a bit. He took this opportunity to stare at her more closely. Jillian was right to be concerned, he thought. She did look pale. She had had more color in her cheeks in the hospital, he thought. Shouldn't she be getting stronger at home? Maybe she just didn't have the physical stamina for breast feeding. Hopefully the new doctor would see this and tell her if it was so. In any case, he wasn't going to be the one to suggest it. Might as well light a stick of dynamite under himself, he thought.

He studied her for a moment more and then slowly got out of bed. Of course, he couldn't help making some noise showering and dressing, but nothing seemed to wake Dana these days. She didn't even stir. If he didn't know better, he would think she'd died in that position on the bed, he thought, looking down at her. In fact, the thought seized him and he felt a cold panic. She looked as pale as a corpse and was hardly breathing. *Was she breathing?* He couldn't help it; he had to reach down to touch her.

She felt cool, but thankfully not cold. She moaned and her eyelids fluttered, but they didn't open. He quickly pulled his hand back from the side of her throat and waited. She wasn't going to wake up. How she could sleep so deeply? He shook his head and left the bedroom.

Before going downstairs, he decided to look in on the baby. The infant slept soundly, his face turned away from the door, but Harlan went farther into the room. He would take care not to wake him, but he wanted to see him. He hadn't had much opportunity to do so during the last few days and he felt guilty about it. He wished he had some of Dana's possessiveness when it came to the baby, but despite his original hope, he still had some difficulties adjusting to the idea that their own baby was dead and that Nikos was going to be their child.

Dana had an unfair advantage, he thought, by breast feeding. That gave her a strong physical tie to the child, whereas he had to develop a relationship. In time he expected he would, but he knew that meant he would have to take a more active role in caring for the child. *If she ever lets me,* he thought.

He looked down at the infant. The first thing that shocked him was the extent to which the baby's hair had changed color. It was nearly all black now, with only a vague remnant of the original carrot color in some of the strands. And the baby's face looked older, all of his features sharper. He even looked longer, more like a six-month-old baby, Harlan thought, not that he was that familiar with the size of babies. Nikos just looked enormous to him that morning.

Did they grow that fast or did their growth show itself more dramatically during the first month? he wondered. Why, the baby's fingernails even looked long.

"Amazing," he muttered, and shook his head. *At this rate we'll be tossing a ball back and forth before I know it,* he thought, and laughed to himself. He could just hear Dana's answer. It was the breast feeding, what else?

He left the room quietly, smiling, and moved quickly down the stairs. He had a nine-o'clock that morning and wanted to finish correcting the test papers from the previous day before the class started. He could have a good quiet hour in his office if he moved along.

He half expected his mother-in-law to be in the kitchen fixing coffee and breakfast again, but no one had come down yet. He put on the lights and went right to the cabinet to get the coffee. He decided he would just have some of Colleen's cereal and a quick cup of coffee.

His sister followed soon afterwards, rubbing her eyes as she entered the kitchen. Colleen had her hair down, a bandanna tying it just behind her head. She wore a light, white cotton blouse under her pale almond light wool pullover sweater, the color matching her eyes, and a matching mid-calf-length skirt with sneakers. He smiled at her neat appearance, thinking how much pleasure his parents would have gotten if they could see her now.

" 'Morning, Harlan," she said, and yawned.

"Still sleepy?" he asked.

"I had all sorts of terrible dreams," she replied. *"Terrible ones,"* she added for emphasis. He stood there nodding. She went for some orange juice and then sat down. "They were about the baby," she said. "Even though he was still a baby, he could walk and talk. Ridiculous dreams. Ugh." She shook her shoulders and drank her juice quickly.

"Well, at the rate he's growing, it won't be long before he does walk and talk."

"What do you mean?"

"He looks much bigger to me this morning. Probably because I haven't spent that much time with him, so his growth seems dramatic to me, but still . . . that kid's going to be a bull." He smiled and sat down to have some cereal. Colleen looked around.

"Surprised Jillian's not up yet," she said.

"Uh-huh. How were things last night?"

"Dana didn't tell you anything?"

"She was asleep when I got home, and she's still dead to the world. Why? Something else happen?" he asked, grimacing as though preparing for a blow.

"Audra Carson came over to study with me. I brought her into the living room to see the baby. Dana had him in her lap, and as soon as he set eyes on Audra, he went hysterical. Dana rushed him upstairs."

"And?"

Colleen shrugged.

"Turned out to be nothing. Gas, she said. Trish Lewis visited. Everything went well. We all had a good time. After Trish left, Dana went up to check on the baby."

"Uh-huh." He sat back, sensing there was more.

Colleen took a deep breath and then released it.

"Well, I didn't say anything to you because of that first time I saw the baby and thought I saw that drop of blood. But I saw a bloodstain on the baby's crib sheet yesterday."

"What?"

"I told Jillian, and she went up to ask Dana about it. Dana got angry again and said there was no stain. Jillian looked at the sheet and there wasn't."

"Thank God."

She hesitated. Colleen knew her brother; she knew how eager he was to avoid bad news.

"I saw it, Harlan. I didn't imagine it. I went to the laundry bin after Jillian went up to bed and I found the sheet with the bloodstain."

He lowered his spoonful of cereal.

"You're kidding."

"No. I took it upstairs and hid it in my closet. I'll show it to you."

"My God, why would she lie about something like that?"

"I don't know, Harlan. I didn't want to cause any more trouble, so I kept it to myself."

He stared at her a moment. Then he looked up. "I wonder why Jillian's sleeping so late. It's not like her."

"She's so uptight, Harlan. She's been trying, but Dana's ups and downs are getting to her."

He nodded.

"Dana's not going to like my finding the sheet and showing it to you, Harlan."

"Yeah, I know what you mean. Let me talk to Jillian first. Maybe I'd better see to it that I go along with them to this doctor today."

"You should, Harlan."

"What could be wrong with the baby? He looks so strong, so healthy."

"Might just be that he scratched himself. I think babies do that often, but why Dana would keep it a secret . . . I don't know."

"Just afraid of facing any problems," he said. She smiled, thinking that was her brother's problem. "You want me to make you some eggs or something?"

"No. I gotta get moving this morning" Colleen said. "I promised Teddy I'd meet him at the diner for some breakfast before school started. I broke a date with him yesterday and he's still upset."

"Sure," Harlan said, not really listening to her. She got up to leave.

"Talk to you later."

"Right," he said, staring ahead. She looked at him a moment and then went up to get her books.

Jillian's door was still closed. Colleen stopped by it and listened, but she didn't hear a sound. She hurried down the stairs and out to her car. She couldn't help feeling sorry for Harlan and all he was going through, but at this point she didn't know what else she could do. She backed out of the driveway quickly and turned to go up Highland Avenue, but she had just started to accelerate when she stopped, put the car into park, and got out.

She went up the sidewalk and picked up the slipper, studying it for a moment. Then she looked back at the house quickly. It made no sense, but she was positive this was Jillian's slipper. She got into her car and backed into the driveway, shutting off the engine and returning to the house. Harlan was still sitting at the table.

"Forgot something?"

"No. Harlan, I just pulled out and saw this on the sidewalk," she said, holding up the slipper. He shook his head, not understanding the significance. "It's Jillian's slipper. She wears them with that turquoise robe."

"Why was it outside?"

"I don't know. She didn't come down?"

"Not yet." He didn't move.

"Well, Harlan, we've got to ask her about it. What do you think?"

"I don't know," he repeated.

"I'll go knock on her door," she said, and hurried out and up the stairs. Harlan followed slowly. Colleen had just opened Jillian's bedroom door when he reached the stairway. He was nearly all the way up by the time she returned to the top of the stairway.

"What is it?" he said, seeing the confused look on her face.

"She's not in there and she's not in the bathroom. She's not anywhere up here."

"Where could she be? She's not downstairs."

"I don't know," Colleen said, looking down at the slipper as if the answer were written on the inside.

"Maybe she got up real early and went somewhere, huh?" Colleen shrugged.

"It's weird," she said. She looked toward her bedroom doorway. "Harlan, come look at the crib sheet. I want you to see it."

"What's the point, I—"

"Just come," she said. Reluctantly he followed her into her bedroom and watched her go to the foot of her closet. She lifted the carton off the folded sheet and pulled the sheet out, bringing it to her bed. He came farther into the room to watch as she unfolded it.

She did so and then turned it over quickly.

She turned it over again.

Then she looked up at him. He smiled in confusion.
She turned it over again.
"I don't understand," she said. She was nearly in tears. There was no bloodstain on the sheet.

🔥 8

"**M**aybe in your haste you grabbed the wrong crib sheet out of the pile of linen," Harlan said. Colleen looked at him, the possibility bringing hope into her eyes. He smiled and shrugged. While she went down to see, Harlan looked in on Dana and saw that she was still asleep. He went downstairs, and by the time he reached the kitchen, Colleen was emerging from the laundry room, the dazed expression on her face revealing that she hadn't found another sheet with a bloodstain on it.

"I don't understand," she said. "I saw it."

"Well, you might have wanted to see it so much that—"

"Harlan"—her face twisted in frustration—"I saw it. Why would I bring a clean sheet up into my room and hide it?"

"I don't know, Collie." She looked at him. Sometimes he called her Collie, a nickname her father had given her years ago, but Harlan was usually hesitant to use it, not wanting to bring up the memories. They stared at each other for a moment. "I'm not going to school," she said, sitting down petulantly. "I'd better not go anywhere until Jillian returns."

"Come on. I can't let you do that. I'll call in and cancel my nine-o'clock."

"It's all right. I won't be able to concentrate on much, anyway," she said. "Damn," she added, looking at the wall clock over the stove. "Teddy's waiting for me at the diner. He's going to be furious. I'd better call there and let him know I'm not coming."

"Are you sure you don't want to go to school?"

"Positive," she said with clear determination. He saw there was no sense in arguing, and since she was such a good student, anyway, he had no worries about her making up the work.

"Well . . . I can't imagine where Jillian would go off to this early in the morning."

"Maybe she went to get some Danish or some rolls for breakfast," Colleen suggested.

"Yeah. That's possible. All right," he said. "I'll call you in an hour or so. If there are any problems, I'll cancel my classes and come right home, okay?"

"Right," she said. She went to the cabinet near the refrigerator and dug the telephone book out of a drawer. After she found the number for the diner she called and asked to speak to Teddy Becker. Harlan left as she was waiting for Teddy to come to the phone. She didn't want to get into the business with the bloodstained crib sheet, and she didn't even mention Jillian's absence. She simply told Teddy she wasn't feeling well.

"I'll call you lunchtime," he said, his disappointment so heavy, she could feel it flowing through the line. "We've got our big practice today. Tomorrow's the league championship game," he added, as if he needed to remind her. She knew he was just trying to emphasize how much he felt neglected.

"I know," she said. "If I feel better, maybe I'll be able to see you tonight," she offered. He took it as the consolation it was, and they ended their conversation.

Now that she wasn't going to meet him at the diner, she thought she would make herself some breakfast, but when it came down to it, she couldn't eat more than a piece of toast. Sitting there, chewing slowly and reviewing the events around the bloodstained sheet, she didn't notice just how much time had passed. When she looked up at the clock, she finally realized that nearly an hour had gone by, and still Jillian had not returned.

She went to the front door and looked up the sidewalk. If one wanted to walk to the stores from Highland Avenue, one would have to go nearly three blocks east. It was at least a good twenty or twenty-five-minute walk, but she and Harlan had been up nearly an hour before realizing Jillian was gone. She would have had plenty of time to go and return. Where could she be?

Colleen retreated to Jillian's room to see if there were any clues. She found her light green leather jacket still hanging in the closet with the rest of her clothes. Of course, she could have packed another fall jacket, Colleen thought. She noted that Jillian's shoes were all neatly laid out at the bottom of the closet floor. It didn't look like any pairs were missing, yet Colleen wondered what had happened to Jillian's other slipper. What did finding her slipper out there mean, anyway?

Jillian was usually so meticulous about her things. In fact, that was what struck Colleen as most odd about the situation as she looked around the room. Jillian was not one to leave her room this messy. The bed was still unmade, and her blouse and bra were draped over a chair. It was all very puzzling. Colleen was about to leave the room when the sound of a dog barking below drew her to the window. She looked to her left and saw Trish Lewis's dog, Buster, hurrying down the street to join another dog that was on their property. Imagining how Dana would be if she were awakened by them, Colleen hurried downstairs and out to chase them off.

Both dogs had gone toward the rear of the house. She recognized the Irish setter as belonging to the Jensens, a family who lived toward the end of the block but who were the constant targets of complaints because of the lackadaisical way they handled their dog. Usually he was loose and on other people's property. Everyone threatened to turn him in to the dogcatcher, but no one actually made the call. Generally the Lewises had better control of their dog, though, Colleen thought. When she went around the back, however, she saw that Buster had torn his leash. Something had drawn him intensely from his doghouse.

Buster joined the Jensens' dog at the door to Harlan's toolshed. It was a small wooden building, four by eight, that Harlan had bought only a year or so ago. He wasn't much of a handyman when it came to work around the house, and Dana was always kidding him about being all thumbs. Either out of guilt or a secret ambition, he'd invested in more tools and equipment and then bought the small building to house them. Since then he had done a little painting, patched a hole in the foundation, and made grandiose plans to expand the rear deck.

The dogs were digging at the ground just under the shed door. Their barking became shrill and intense, and for the first time Colleen wondered if she could be in any danger approaching them this way. She looked around for something with which to drive them away and realized that now that they had this shed, everything had been stored neatly in it. Nevertheless, with some hesitation, she walked toward the animals until she got their attention.

Both dogs cowered when she shouted at them but didn't retreat from the property. They settled a dozen feet from the shed and continued to bark. She looked for a stone to heave at them and then wondered just what it was that made them so intent. She imagined that it was some small animal—a woodchuck or a gopher or whatever, which had made the shed its headquarters.

"Get out of here," she said to the dogs, and waved her hands at them. They moved farther away but still did not run off. She looked at the upstairs windows to see if Dana had been awakened. All the shades were still drawn, there was no sign of Dana, but if the dogs continued barking, it wouldn't be long before there was, she thought. "Damn," she said, and decided she would open the shed and get out a rake or a shovel and drive them off with that.

Harlan never locked the shed, even though there was a lock. They never had had any problems with vandalism or thievery on this quiet residential street. Most other people had developed urban paranoia and installed security systems and locked all their doors. She pressed down on the handle and opened the door. Because the rear of the shed faced east, there wasn't much light. She stepped forward hesitantly and peered in, looking from side to side for the appropriate weapon.

She was greeted by the terrible stench she had smelled the first night Dana had stayed awake with the baby. Her stomach churned as the juice, coffee, and toast she had just eaten began to return up her throat. So that's why the dogs were barking, she thought. Some animal had died in there. She gagged and started to close the shed door when something to her right caught her eye.

After Harlan had left for work and she had had time to sit alone in the kitchen and think, Colleen had come to the conclusion that her mind had been playing tricks on her. The apparently nonexistent drop of blood between the baby's lips, and then the bloodstain on the sheet, were, she decided, products of her imagination. Often people saw things that were not really there, she thought. Why she should have seen these things was a puzzle, but there was probably some logic to her imagining a bloodstain after she had imagined the drop of blood in the baby's mouth, followed by the incident in which the baby had made a small puncture in her finger.

So her first thought now was that things were not what they at first seemed to be. She nearly closed the door, laughing at herself. *I'm a fruitcake, all right,* she thought, and then opened the door farther and took a second look.

The blood drained from her face so quickly, she felt the cold numbness climb up her neck to replace it. Her head spun, and the food that had threatened to back up did so with a vengeance. A mixture of coffee, juice, and toast rushed into her mouth. She bent over immediately, clutching her stomach, and opened her mouth to permit the release.

Despite this reaction, she couldn't prevent herself from looking in and to the right once again. She had to confirm the horror; she had to guarantee herself that this was not a product of an overworked imagination. She nearly reached out to touch it, for it truly had become an *it* in her mind.

It was certainly not Jillian. How could this . . . thing, hanging on a hook, ever have resembled a human being, especially an attractive, vibrant one? It looked like some kind of stage prop, a costume, a replica of a person to be worn by another person who wanted to impersonate her.

Its hair hung down the sides of what looked like a shrunken face. The strands were now gray and as dry as thread. The skin of her face sagged like an empty stocking loosely attached to the base of her skull. The skin was bleached gray and filled with wrinkles. All the oil and moisture was gone from the surface of her face.

Below her closed eyes and to the sides were thin, yellowish stains over the creased and folded skin. Something had oozed out of her eyes and dried there. Because the face sagged so, the lower lip had dropped into a deep *U* and revealed the now pale white lower teeth, housed in gray gums. The upper lip draped over the upper teeth, nearly hiding them completely.

Her arms hung stiffly at her sides, the hands extended and the fingers locked straight. The turquoise robe that Colleen had always admired on Jillian now looked sizes too big. It had fallen from her shoulders and lay in a large fold around her back and below her flattened and depleted breasts.

Colleen gasped, fighting to regain her breath. She clutched her sides and took one more look at the thing on the wall. It was then that she saw the gash on the right side of Jillian's neck. It wasn't more than an inch or two, but the blood had dried in a rim around it, making it appear longer and wider.

"Jillian?" she uttered. Instantly the eyes flew open. They were as dry and as colorless as granite, and they looked as though they would fall out at any moment.

Colleen fell back. Her legs wouldn't obey, so she found herself sitting on the lawn. She screamed—or at least she thought she did, because she couldn't hear herself. It was as though her vocal cords had been cut. She turned over on the grass and fought her way back to a kneeling position.

The dogs, seeing her radical movement and behavior, began to bark more furiously. Yapping madly, they circled closer and closer, driving Colleen into greater panic. She crawled forward, tearing at the grass. Now she could hear herself. Her screams were so shrill, they drove a thin, almost electric vibration down the back of her spine and into the backs of her legs. She fell forward once before finally getting to her feet. Then she raced away from the shed, the dogs barking after her.

When she entered the house, she fell to the hallway floor. Unable to contain herself, she screamed on and on and on. She looked up to see Dana at the top of the stairway, her hair wild, her face in an ugly grimace. She was embracing herself. Colleen could see that she was speaking but couldn't hear her. Why couldn't she hear her?

She covered her ears, then uncovered them, and she screamed again. Dana started down the stairs. Outside, the dogs were in a frenzy, their barking so intense and continuous, they sounded more like a pack of dogs than just two.

Dana seized her by the shoulders and shook her. Colleen looked into her eyes, but what she saw there made her scream even harder. Dana's eyes were so cold and so colorless, they reminded her of Jillian's dead eyes locked in that stone stare.

Finally she felt herself shudder, and then it was as if someone dropped a black curtain between her and Dana. The last thing she remembered was the way she fell through Dana's fingers to the floor. It was as if she were made of wax and Dana's fingers were hot coils. She melted rapidly and landed in one shapeless pile at Dana's feet.

* * *

Colleen woke in her bed. Harlan was sitting at her side. He had put a cold, wet washcloth over her forehead. He smiled at her when she opened her eyes. For a moment she couldn't remember anything. She didn't know why she was there and why he was sitting staring at her. Her mind was a total blank. She couldn't even remember what day it was, let alone what time it was. She looked quickly around the room and at the doorway.

"Hi, there," he said. "How you doing?"

"What . . . happened?"

"That's what I'd like to know." He reached forward and took the washcloth from her forehead. "Dana called the school and I came right back. I found you on the floor downstairs. Dana couldn't lift you, of course, but she had a pillow under your head. I carried you up here . . . no small feat, I might add," he said, smiling, "and put the wet cloth on your head. We called an ambulance. They should be here any moment."

"Ambulance?"

"Sure, honey. You'll have to be checked out, no matter what. I'm glad you've regained consciousness, but what the hell did it? Dana said you were screaming incoherently. You woke her, and when she went to the top of the stairway, you were on the floor, clutching yourself as though you had stomach cramps. She went down to you, and you stood up, screaming even louder when she grabbed your shoulders. Then you fainted."

"Harlan," she said, remembering. The horrible images were coming back quickly. She closed her eyes.

"Easy. Just relax. I'm here with you now. Take it slow."

"Harlan," she repeated. "In the shed . . . go look. It's Jillian."

"In the shed?" He held his half smile.

She opened her eyes and nodded.

"It's horrible," she said. "She was murdered. Her body is hanging in there. Her eyes opened. It was ghastly."

"Christ." He stood up. "In the shed?"

"It's horrible," she repeated, closing her eyes.

"My God." He looked toward the doorway. "Dana," he muttered. "Oh, no. My God. I'll be right back," he said. "Don't try to move."

He rushed out and Colleen closed her eyes. The nausea was coming back because the vivid memory of Jillian's ugly corpse had returned. She turned over and buried her face in the pillow. She thought she might have passed out again, because she never realized Harlan had been gone. He was at her bedside again, only this time the ambulance attendants were right behind him. The two men rolled the stretcher in beside the bed so she could simply be rolled onto it.

"Harlan," she said.

"You have to go to the hospital, honey. You have to be checked out. I'll be right beside you the whole time."

She nodded and closed her eyes as she was gently placed onto the stretcher. She didn't look at the attendants; they were faceless, nameless nonentities, part of some necessary process. As they started to wheel her out the bedroom she reached up. Harlan took her hand.

"Where's Dana?" she asked.

"With the baby in our room. She's very upset. It's better she just stay there. I called Trish Lewis and she's coming over to be with her while we're at the hospital."

"Good."

They rolled her to the top of the stairway, and then she was lifted so they could carry her down the stairs. At the base of the stairway they lowered the wheels again. Harlan was right behind them. They paused at the doorway and lifted the stretcher so it could roll over the little rise in the floor. From then on it was easy. The attendants moved quickly to the rear of the ambulance and opened the back doors.

She reached out for Harlan again before they lifted her up and into it.

"Did you call the police?" she asked.

He looked at the two attendants before answering, so she looked at them too. Their faces were bland, expressionless. She thought they were more like robots, but she wasn't interested in them or in what was going to be done with her now. It wasn't the same as being taken to the hospital because of some illness. She knew what had caused all this. She would go through the examination, more to relieve Harlan's anxieties than her own.

"No, honey, not yet," he said.

"What? Why not?" She tried to sit up, but the straps held her fast. The attendants were lifting her now. "Harlan, why not? Harlan," she called back. "Why not?" she repeated more demandingly.

He leaned into the ambulance as she was set down inside it. She couldn't turn around, but he was just behind her head, his face close to hers.

"Because there's nothing in the shed, Colleen. Nothing. No dead body. Nothing," he repeated.

"*Harlan!*" she screamed, but he pulled back and the ambulance attendant closed the doors. "*Harlan, I saw her!*"

"Easy," the attendant who would ride with her to the hospital said. "You'll be all right. Just take it easy."

She felt the ambulance begin to move.

"*Harlan!*"

"He's right behind us, miss. Take it easy. You'll be all right," the attendant repeated. He started to put a blood-pressure cuff over her arm. She looked at him in amazement and then closed her eyes as the ambulance rolled on, its siren now clearing the way before it.

"They've given her something to quiet her down," Harlan said into the receiver. He was standing in the hallway of the hospital emergency room, just outside the examination room in which Colleen lay. "Some sedation."

"But, Harlan," Trish Lewis asked, "where *is* Jillian?"

"I don't know. I decided to call the police and report her missing. A detective will be at the house in an hour or so. I'll be here about a half hour more. If Jillian should return, call me here so I can call the police. How's Dana?"

"She's resting. Actually she's asleep. How she could sleep through all this commotion is beyond me. I'm sorry about Buster digging up some of your lawn," she added.

"That's my least worry. Thanks for helping out."

"Oh, there's nothing to thank me for. Just as long as Colleen's all right."

"Well, right now I'm not sure what the problem is. All her physical signs are good, thank God. It's something else. As soon as they have her set in a room, I'll be home."

"Okay," Trish said. "Oh . . . someone called here . . . a Dr. Claret. Dana spoke to him before she fell asleep."

"Dr. Claret? Right, right, her new doctor. All right, I'll hear about it when I get home. Thanks again," he said, and hung up the phone.

Colleen was unconscious by the time he returned to the examination room. The emergency-room doctor took him aside.

"She's had some sort of traumatic experience," he began.

"Well, I told you what she had said and what—"

"We're giving her a blood analysis, of course, but you might as well tell me if there is any history of drug use."

"Oh, no . . . not that I know of, that is. I don't think she's even puffed on a joint." He thought for a moment. "But who could swear for anyone these days . . . even your own sister?"

"Whether it was real or imaginary is not the point right now. She needs some intense rest, after which I suggest we have the hospital psychologist speak with her. Maybe he can calm her down or get to the bottom of her problem. If there is any evidence of drugs, we'll know shortly."

"I hate for her to wake up without me around," Harlan said.

"It'll be all right. The nurses will make her comfortable and you'll visit her later. You can't just wait around here, Mr. Hamilton."

"No, I've got an appointment with the police. The thing is, my mother-in-law isn't home and we don't know where she is."

"Which is something that might have triggered Colleen's imagination, especially if there is some drug involvement."

Harlan nodded.

"Okay. When should I call you?"

"Give us a couple of hours."

"Right," he said. "Thanks." He looked in on Colleen once more. Even in repose her face wore an expression of utter terror. His heart went out to her, for his was filled with a mixture of sympathy and guilt. Ever since his father died and Colleen had come to live with them, he had felt she was a major responsibility, not simply because she was his sister but also because his parents were no longer around to look after her. Dana sensed this in him right from the beginning, and right from the beginning she was very good about it, taking just as much interest in his teenage sister as he did.

Somehow he blamed this on himself. Something was going

on back at his house, and he had just let it go on. There was too much tension. The place was emotionally explosive. For all he knew, his mother-in-law had run off because she couldn't take it any longer herself. But why wouldn't she leave him a note, and why would she leave her clothing? Of course, she could have gone off for just a few hours or a day. It was just that something like this was not characteristic of Jillian.

Then again, look at how Dana was behaving. Everything she was doing was uncharacteristic of the Dana he had known these past years. He had a sick, empty feeling in the base of his stomach. Perhaps it had been wrong for them to adopt Nikos so quickly; perhaps they were being punished for spitting into the face of destiny. He shook his head. *Ridiculous idea,* he thought. *I'm going nuts too.*

The detective arrived at the Hamilton house just as Harlan pulled into the driveway. He pulled his car into the garage and came out to greet the man.

"Mr. Hamilton?" he said, stepping out of his vehicle.

"Yes."

"I'm Lieutenant Reis," the policeman said.

Harlan thought that either because he was anxious for the detective to look this way or because he really was, Lieutenant Reis fit his part. He was tall, at least six-foot-three, and broad-shouldered, a strong-looking man. His facial features were sharply chiseled with deep set, dark brown eyes. He had his hair cut very short, almost in a military crew cut. He did have an army officer's demeanor. There was an air of confidence and authority about the man that Harlan welcomed.

"Come on inside. Let's check first and be sure my mother-in-law hasn't called or returned."

"Right," Lieutenant Reis said. He followed Harlan into the house. Trish met them in the entryway.

"Dana's still sleeping," she said. She looked at the detective with interest.

"Trish, thanks so much. What about Jillian? Has she come home? Has she called?"

"Afraid not, Harlan," Trish said. "Except for that doctor, no one's called."

"Well, there it is," Harlan said, as if that explained the whole problem. Lieutenant Reis stared stoically.

"Well, let's go over the details here, Mr. Hamilton," he

said, "and think this out before we jump to any conclusions."

"Sure. You want any coffee?"

"I'll get it," Trish said. "Why don't you take him into the living room."

"Thanks, Trish. Right this way," he said, and Lieutenant Reis followed him in. Harlan indicated the couch, and Reis sat down. "Let me start from the beginning," Harlan said, "because I don't know myself what is important and what is not in a situation like this."

"Good idea," Reis said. For the first time his eyes widened with some interest.

Harlan began by describing the death of his and Dana's baby, as well as the subsequent adoption. He detailed Dana's emotional condition and explained the way in which his mother-in-law had reacted. He then told the detective about Colleen's illusions concerning the drop of blood, and then the bloodstain on the sheet. Reis's eyebrows rose but he didn't interrupt. Harlan was sure he was being illogical and incoherent after a while, rambling on about such things as Dana's appetite and his mother-in-law's description of Dana, up at night and wandering through a dark house. He was happy when Trish arrived with the coffee and he could pause.

Lieutenant Reis sipped his and stared silently for a moment. Trish sat on the soft-cushioned easy chair to listen.

"Now, what was this about a slipper?" Reis asked.

"Oh . . . that's why we got concerned about Jillian this morning. Colleen found her slipper on the sidewalk outside."

"I see."

"I told you about . . ." He looked at Trish. "About what she claimed she saw in the shed."

"Let's go back there so I can take a look," Reis said.

"Fine. Trish, can you just hang in a few more minutes?"

"Oh, no problem, Harlan," she said.

Harlan led the detective to the shed, and Reis went and looked around. "This mop and old jacket hanging on the wall could have caused the illusion," he said. He sniffed. "There's the odor of something dead in here," he added, and he and Harlan found a dead gopher. Its corpse looked a few days old. "Explains the dogs," Reis said.

"I have a neighbor who puts out poison for gophers. Looks like he got one," Harlan said.

Reis nodded. "Your mother-in-law . . . doesn't she know anybody around here she could have gone to see?" he asked.

"Not really. Oh, there are some people she's met through her daughter and myself, but I can't recall her ever becoming that friendly with any of them."

"You called her home?"

"She lives in Florida. She wouldn't go back there without saying anything and without taking her things."

Reis nodded. "Do you have any pictures of her? Relatively recent ones?"

"I don't know. . . ." He thought a moment. "I have something from last Christmas. She hasn't changed much. Actually she's quite a good-looking woman for her age."

"Well, why don't you give me that. I'll take down all the physical details you can add and we'll pass the information along so all our people can look out for her. At this point we have no evidence of any foul play. Just that slipper out here, but we can't make much of that. It could have been dropped from a bag or something. I wish I could do more for you, considering all you're going through right now with your wife and sister," he added.

"Thanks. I appreciate whatever you can do. I don't know what's wrong with my sister. Maybe she *did* see something; maybe she just had the location wrong."

"I don't know. Is there a basement in this house?"

"Yes."

"Well, I'll look through that, and I'll look around the neighborhood a bit, knock on some doors, and we'll see. In the meantime, if you think of anything else or anything else comes up . . ."

"Right. Okay, I'll show you the door to the basement and go get you that picture."

"Fine," Reis said.

They met fifteen minutes later in the entryway of the house. Lieutenant Reis said there was nothing unusual in the basement.

"Certainly no evidence of any foul play or any dead bodies."

"This is ghoulish, but I don't know what to think."

"We always think the worst," Reis said. "I see it all the time. Fortunately, what we think is not often the case."

Harlan nodded and handed him the picture taken last

Christmas. It had been taken in the living room. Dana and Jillian were standing by the tree.

"A fine-looking woman," Reis said.

"That she is," Trish said, looking over his shoulder. "I can't believe anything's happened to her . . . and on this street."

"Well, let's hold together, miss. The worst thing we could do is panic everyone on the block. Then we won't learn anything."

"He's right," Harlan said.

"I won't say anything," Trish said. "Except to Barry. My husband," she added.

"Good," Reis said. "All right. I'll call you if I learn anything, but in any case, I'll call you late this afternoon."

"Thank you," Harlan said. "Impressive guy," he added after the detective left. "I like the way he didn't just laugh everything off or tell us this was nothing to worry about. That's what they usually do in the movies."

"Right," Trish said. "God, Harlan, what you're going through! Go sit down. Rest for a while."

He looked at his watch.

"I will, but I'd better call the hospital and see how Colleen's doing. Thanks for everything, Trish."

"I'll call you later," she said. After she left, he headed for the kitchen.

The doctor told him that there were no traces of drugs in Colleen's body and that she was still under sedation. They agreed once again that it would be best for the hospital psychologist to have a session with her. Harlan thanked him and told the doctor he would be up at the hospital later in the day.

After he cradled the phone, he sank into the nearest chair and stared at the wall. What the hell was happening? he wondered. And why was it all happening so fast? His thoughts were interrupted by the sound of the doorbell. Hoping it had to do with Jillian, he shot up out of the chair and hurried down the hallway to the front door. He opened it and stepped back as though a gust of wind had driven him away from the opening.

A tall, stern-looking, but strangely attractive woman stood before him. She wore a dark red wool jacket over a nurse's uniform and carried a small suitcase in her right hand. Her coal-black hair was pinned up behind her head and her cap was pinned to her hair. She had jet-black eyes and fair skin, with just a tint of scarlet at the surface of her cheeks.

"Harlan Hamilton?" she said.

"Yes?" He looked past her and saw there was no car in the driveway. Someone had just dropped her off.

"Dr. Claret sent me."

"Pardon?"

"Your wife called Dr. Claret."

"My wife?"

"It's all right, Harlan," he heard, and turned around to see Dana at the top of the stairway. "She's come to help me. The doctor suggested it."

"Huh?" He turned and looked at the nurse.

"May I come in, please?" she said with an air of annoyance.

"What? Oh, sure." He stepped back.

"Dana?" the nurse said.

"Come right upstairs and I'll show you where you'll stay," Dana said.

"Stay?" Harlan asked. He looked from Dana to the nurse and then back to Dana.

"She's going to stay with us for a while, Harlan. I'll pay for it."

"I'm not worried about who's paying for it. I just didn't know, and . . ."

"Well, now you do, Mr. Hamilton," the nurse said. She extended her hand to him. "I'm Miss Patio, Rose Patio."

"How do you do," Harlan said. He took her hand. Her fingers tightened with surprising firmness around his. He brought his eyes up, and she met his gaze with a smile that began around her eyes and then rippled down her face to settle at the corners of her mouth. He felt his heartbeat quicken and a warmth travel across his chest, as though the blood there had been instantly pumped to the surface.

"I know you're having some problems," she said. "I'm an experienced maternity nurse," she added. "I hope I'll be of some help."

"Of course." He looked up at Dana.

"Thank you, Harlan," Dana said. "Right this way, Miss Patio."

"Rose. Call me Rose," she said, and started up the stairs. Harlan watched until she reached Dana, and the two looked at each other for a long moment before heading down the corridor. He stood there staring at the empty stairway until he realized what had surprised him.

It wasn't that Dana had agreed to take on a nurse for a while; many women did that when they first brought a baby home. And it wasn't that she had done this without discussing it first with him. With all that was going on that morning, it was actually good that Dana had taken control of something through a discussion with her doctor. He was happy about all of that.

What bothered him was a different realization.

The realization that she hadn't asked about his sister, nor had she asked about her mother.

And this realization left him cold and instinctively certain that Colleen had indeed seen something terrible. He felt it was only a matter of time before he would too.

✿ 9

Just before returning to the hospital to see how Colleen was doing, Harlan went upstairs. He had been waiting for Dana to ask him to bring up the foldaway bed from the basement and place it in the baby's room for the nurse. But after Rose Patio went upstairs, Dana never called down to him. In fact, the house became rather quiet, and he saw neither of them.

He found Dana asleep in their bedroom and the door to Jillian's room closed. The nurse was not in the baby's room. He was disturbed because Dana obviously had placed the nurse in Jillian's room without finding out what had happened to her. Dana's indifference was inexcusable. Just so much could be attributed to her condition, he thought. Now, driven by an uncharacteristic overt anger, he woke her.

"I want to know what's going on here," he demanded, standing by the side of the bed. Dana looked up at him, blinking rapidly, as if she were trying to remember who he was. Her look of confusion annoyed him. "Dana, do you hear me?"

Without replying, she moved farther away and turned her back to him, intending to go back to sleep, but he wouldn't be rejected. He went to the other side of the bed and shook her shoulder again. This time she moaned but with such force and in such a deep, unrecognizable voice that he actually stepped back.

"Dana!"

She opened her eyes more forcefully and confronted him.

"What do you want? I'm trying to get some rest. Nurse Patio says it's very important. She says I'm emotionally exhausted."

"Where is this nurse? Why is she in Jillian's room? I thought you would ask me to bring up the foldaway and we would put her in the baby's room," he said rapidly.

"Foldaway? You expect her to sleep on a foldaway? Don't

you know how important she is now? Don't you understand anything? If I'm not well, the baby will suffer. Don't you care?" she asked, her face twisting with disgust.

"Me? Care? How about you? What about your mother? You haven't even asked about her, not to mention Colleen. How can you give some stranger your mother's bed when we don't even know what's happened to her?"

"She left," Dana said, and closed her eyes. Then she opened them again abruptly, as if remembering something. "We had an argument."

"What?" Harlan asked. She didn't respond. He stepped closer to the bed. "What did you say?"

"I said," Dana responded, speaking with what obviously took great effort, "we had a fight."

"You and Jillian? Why, I never once saw—"

"I'm telling you what happened, Harlan. We had a fight and she ran out of here, threatening to leave. So she left. It's probably better, anyway. She wasn't able to handle my breast-feeding Nikos. It bothered her. And you really don't know my mother, Harlan. She has a low toleration level. She's spoiled. My father spoiled her, and she remained so, even after his death. She lives like some kind of princess in that lavish Florida home, and if anything is in any way distasteful to her, she can't take it. Understand? So she used our argument as an excuse to leave."

"But she didn't take her things. They're still in the room," he protested.

"She left in a highly emotional state. She doesn't need those things. She has dozens of replacements. I'm really upset about it, Harlan. I'm just trying to ignore it so that it doesn't bother me."

"And you're not helping her one bit," the nurse said. He spun around. She had entered the room behind him as silently as a shadow. Now she stood between him and the doorway, the flush in her cheeks and her neck so vivid, she looked as if she were suffering from some kind of rash. Her dark eyes were larger, her gaze more intimidating. When he had first seen her in the doorway, he had thought her a tall woman, but right now she seemed to swell right before his eyes. Her shoulders lifted and her bosom rose, so that the bodice of her uniform looked as though it were under some strain.

Yet she wasn't ugly or grotesque, even though her sexuality seemed in some way threatening to him. He felt that the clinging white uniform gave her figure a deceptively antiseptic and safe appearance. It didn't neutralize her and make her asexual the way some uniforms made women. Instead he felt that this uniform was worn as a disguise. Beneath it throbbed a hot, passionate body, one that was eager to consume. He was drawn to her with the same fascination a young boy has for the center of a small candle flame. He would tease himself by bringing his finger dangerously close. Perhaps he would pass it through the flame rapidly and escape being burned. It was a thrilling call to pain and danger.

There was something in the nurse's eyes that told him she knew and understood his feelings. She had seen it in men before. He felt exposed, embarrassed, and had to turn away.

"Why didn't you tell me about this before, Dana?" he asked. He heard the way his voice trembled. He felt the nurse's indignant stare on the back of his neck. Her presence was too strong to be ignored.

"I was hoping she would return and not act like a child," Dana said, and looked past him at Nurse Patio, who had come up on his right. Out of the corner of his eye Harlan thought he saw her nod.

"This is incredible."

"Mr. Hamilton," Rose Patio said, moving closer. "Dr. Claret has sent me here because your wife has undergone a considerable amount of emotional strain. It is essential that we keep her isolated from any further excitement. Do you understand?" she asked. She was inches from him now. He thought he could feel the heat radiating from her body, but he chalked that up to his imagination.

"How could he make any diagnosis without seeing her?" Harlan asked.

"He will see her today. In the meantime it doesn't take a medical genius to prescribe rest, does it? Considering what she had gone through, that is."

"Please, Harlan," Dana said. She closed her eyes. He stared down at her for a moment.

"All right," he said, feeling very insecure. Maybe he was complicating things. Maybe he was causing more problems.

"I'm going to see how Colleen is doing. You know she's in the hospital, and—"

"Mr. Hamilton . . ." Rose Patio said. She touched his arm. He was sure he felt great warmth at the tips of her fingers. They seemed capable of burning through his shirt sleeve and singeing him. He actually stepped away from her. She gestured toward the door. He looked at Dana once again, saw that she was already going back to sleep, and headed out of the room. The nurse followed. She closed the bedroom door behind her softly and stepped into the hall with him.

"What is going on here?" he demanded.

"Look, Mr. Hamilton, I wouldn't tell your wife any more about your sister just yet. She's on the edge of a nervous breakdown as it is. You can imagine how it was for her, being the one who was here when your sister was hysterical. Under the circumstances Dana handled things quite well. But all of this has taken its toll," she added, pronouncing each word slowly, carefully, as if she were talking to a complete idiot. "I've seen the symptoms hundreds of times, Mr. Hamilton. She's in a very fragile state. With the loss of her baby, the problem with her mother, her own sensitivity . . . she has enough to contend with. Let's wait until she's a little stronger before we lay any more on her, okay?" she said, finally reaching a reasonable tone of voice.

He looked back at the closed bedroom door. Somehow Miss Patio had made him feel as if he were harming Dana simply by talking to her. He was the one who was looking unreasonable now. There was no question, however, that he—and even Jillian—had felt Dana was on the verge of a nervous breakdown. Perhaps this nurse was not altogether wrong. After all, she had come at a doctor's behest.

"Yes, I understand," he said. "It's just that everything seems to be happening so fast."

"It's more often than not that we can't control events that affect our lives, Mr. Hamilton. Our only recourse is to move in rhythm. If you resist, bend a branch too far, you break it," she said, her voice dropping into a most seductive and sensual tone. He felt a warmth climb up the inside of his thighs, as though he had just lowered himself into a tepid bath. Rarely had a woman's voice stimulated him so.

He noticed that the top two buttons of her uniform had come

undone. The rose tint in her neck spread down to the peaks of her breasts, now revealed as they ballooned out of the top of her firmly fastened bra. He tried to swallow but couldn't. It was as if he had lost control of all his bodily movements. His heart began to pound, driving the blood to the surface of his face. He felt the heat. Finally he nodded obediently. She smiled and he seemed capable of relaxation again. He took a deep breath. "I've got to get to the hospital," he said, his voice so low that it was nearly a whisper.

"It will be all right here, Mr. Hamilton," she said. "I'll watch her closely."

He nodded again.

"I hope," she added, "that everything will be right with your sister as well."

"Thank you," he said, and hurried down the stairs, anxious both to see Colleen and to flee from the intimidating nurse. Just before he backed completely out of the driveway, he looked at the house and saw that the nurse was drawing down the shades and closing the curtains in all the windows. He didn't understand how it had happened, but now, when he looked at his home, a house he had restored with color and brightness, it appeared old, haggard, dark, and deserted. It gave credence to superstition. He was willing to consider seriously the ordinarily otherwise fantastic idea that evil, or the devil, or something similar had come down this quiet residential street and pointed its finger at his home.

The shadows fell like rain and soaked the house in gloom. He feared it would take the brightness of a thousand mornings to lift the bleak curtains away and was afraid of what it would cost them all in the end.

Despite what Dana had told him, Harlan couldn't accept that Jillian would leave the house in a huff and not take her things. Even if they had had an argument, his mother-in-law would have spoken to him before leaving. He felt certain about this, as he drove away from the house toward the hospital. He couldn't question Dana further about the supposed incident, especially with that nurse hovering around. But now, away from both of them, he thought more clearly and decided that Dana's explanation of recent events was inadequate. Even so, he would call Jillian's home in Florida later, just to be sure.

By the time he reached the hospital, Colleen had come out from under sedation, although she was still somewhat dazed. He learned that so far none of the medical tests performed on her revealed anything abnormal. She had been moved to a semiprivate room. Right now there was no one in the other bed, so she had complete privacy. He drew a chair to the side of the bed and held her hand.

"What happened to me?" she asked.

"You had a bad experience, and what I guess they'll eventually call an emotional breakdown, but thank God, nothing else seems to be wrong. You need some rest, that's all. There will be a different doctor coming to see you in the morning."

"Different doctor?"

"Psychologist. Give him a chance to help," Harlan pleaded.

"Help?" she asked. She struggled to sit up. "Everybody thinks I'm crazy, is that it? Is it, Harlan?" she repeated when he didn't respond immediately.

"You've got to try to relax, Colleen. Only then will you get any better," he added, smiling. Everything was getting to be overwhelming. Why were the two most important women in his life both in the throes of hysteria? How would this end? He had to work; he had to go on with his life. How often could he cancel his classes before the department head would be on his back? Right now he couldn't imagine teaching either Shakespeare or basic composition.

"Harlan, I did see Jillian in the shed," Colleen insisted. She clenched her fists on her lap and pressed her lips together. "I'm not going crazy. I swear."

Go easy, he thought. "I know. Now let me tell you what has happened so you can get things into perspective, okay?" he said. Colleen nodded. He thought that if he spoke to her in a calm, reasonable tone and didn't sound as though he were patronizing her, she would remain calm and listen. "I looked in the shed myself, of course, and found nothing . . . no one. Then I called the police and they sent a detective, a good one, and he and I searched the shed. He found a dead gopher, which explained the smell, and then he pointed out a mop and an old jacket hanging on the wall. We think you saw that and imagined something terrible."

"Mop? Jacket? There wasn't any mop and jacket."

"Of course not . . . to you, that is. You saw something else, Collie. It happens to people. Jeez, it's happened to me on occasion. You know, you're thinking about something so intently, and then you glance at something and your mind takes over. It's understandable—no big thing."

She shook her head.

"Now, Colleen, what's the sense of you insisting on something that isn't there? I told you, I had a police detective on the scene."

"Then where's Jillian? Did she come home? Did she call?"

"No. Dana claims that they had a fight and Jillian left the house."

"A fight? I can't believe it."

"Right now that's all we have to go by. The detective has taken a picture of her, and he's looking into it. Hopefully it will be resolved soon."

"How's Dana?"

"She's not so great. The doctor sent over a nurse to stay with us for a while. Her name is Patio, Rose Patio."

"A nurse?"

He nodded. "I suppose, under the circumstances, with Jillian gone, you here, me having to go to work . . . it's a good idea," he said, but not convincingly. Colleen, even in her somewhat dazed state, picked up the negative vibrations.

"You don't like her?"

"Not particularly, no. But that's not important as long as she can do her job," he said.

"Why don't you like her?"

"She strikes me as a bit too . . . cold," he said. "Impersonal. But," he added, "maybe that's the way people in her profession have to be . . . efficient, stern." He shrugged. "It's the first time I've ever had a nurse living in the house." He smiled. "It'll be all right after you come home. We'll handle her," he said, and winked. "Besides, I don't imagine her having to be there more than a few days or a week."

"Where's she sleeping? The baby's room?"

He shook his head. "The guest room," he said.

"But what about—"

The phone rang, and for a moment they both looked at it.

"Maybe some of the kids found out about me already," she said. "It doesn't take long for news to spread around here."

She lifted the receiver. "Hello? Yes, just a moment," she said, sounding disappointed. "It's for you." She handed the receiver to him.

Harlan took it slowly, afraid something else had happened at home. "Yes? . . . Oh, Lieutenant Reis. . . . No, it's all right. What do you have?" Harlan asked, then listened. "I see. Yes, that is really unusual, but I was going to call you afterward and tell you something that makes more sense now. My wife just told me that she and her mother had an argument and that was why her mother left. . . . I understand. Well, thank you. I had a feeling you'd be of great help. . . . Yes. Thanks again," he said, and hung up the phone. Colleen, looking more alert and anxious, waited patiently. He turned to her slowly, shaking his head.

"What is it?"

"The detective knocked on some doors in the neighborhood, and then, on his own initiative, went to interview some taxi drivers, and then to the bus station. A clerk at the bus station recognized Jillian from the picture and said she had purchased a one-way ticket to New York City late last night. He's absolutely positive it was Jillian."

"I don't understand." Colleen sat back against her pillow. "What did I see this morning?"

"Huh? Oh, the mop, the jacket."

"I don't understand," she repeated, shaking her head. She turned to Harlan. "How come we didn't hear them arguing? When did this happen?"

"During the night, I guess. Shortly after you and I fell asleep, I imagine."

"And Jillian just left? I'm so surprised. Where did she go to stay?"

"I don't know. She has friends in New York. I know that. Oh, well," he said, standing. "At least one part of this mystery is solved."

"I want to go home, Harlan. Please," she pleaded.

He nodded. "You will. Soon. I promise. But don't you see, honey? Now it's more important than ever that you have a session with this doctor tomorrow."

She nodded reluctantly.

"I guess." She looked down and then looked up again quickly. "But what about the big game? And Teddy?"

He thought for a moment. "I'll be here right after the doctor sees you, and if it's all right, I'll get you out and you can make the game."

"Promise?"

"Of course."

"Thank you, Harlan. I'm sorry I turned out to be so much trouble. Especially on top of everything else."

"Nonsense. That's what a teenage sister is supposed to be, trouble. You'll be all right. We'll all be all right," he said. He leaned over and kissed her on the cheek. "Besides," he added, "as I told you, I'm going to need help dealing with this nurse."

"I'll help you."

They both laughed.

"Talk to you later," he said, and started out.

"Okay. Tell Dana I'm sorry," she added. He shook his head. What a great kid she was. He only wished he and Dana had a daughter who would grow up to be like her.

On the way out of the hospital, he realized he could still make his late-afternoon class. He didn't want to do so, however, without checking home, so he phoned. Nurse Patio answered. At first her voice surprised him because it was weird to hear a stranger answer the phone at his house.

"How's Dana?"

"Resting comfortably. All is well," she said. "How is your sister?"

"Better."

"That's good."

"Maybe it will be all right for me to go to my late-afternoon class," he said.

"Of course it will. I'm here, and after Dana wakes up, we're going to see Dr. Claret."

"Oh." He thought for a moment. "Well, maybe I shouldn't go to my class then."

"Mr. Hamilton, the purpose in having me is to take the pressure off you and your wife. I assure you I am capable of taking her and the baby to see her doctor," she said sternly.

"I understand. All right," he said. "When Dana wakes up, tell her that her mother was seen buying a bus ticket to New York late last night. Apparently it all happened as she said it had."

"I'll tell her. Even though she and her mother did not have

a pleasant parting, this news will be of some relief to her. Don't think your wife was insensitive about it all, Mr. Hamilton. Once she told me some of it, I had her put it out of her mind to protect her own well-being."

"I see," he said, but he was amazed that the nurse had such influence on Dana so quickly. Even though he thought it demonstrated how effective and professional she was, he couldn't help but feel anxious about her.

"You go and enjoy your class, Mr. Hamilton. I'll have dinner ready when you return."

"Really? Thank you," he said. "Bye."

He stood by the pay phone for a moment. She cooks too? He shook his head. He was really impressed. Maybe this nurse was a very good idea at this time, he thought. Maybe he should just try to take it easy now, he concluded, and left the hospital feeling relaxed and lighthearted for the first time all day.

Harlan's class proved to be just the relief he needed. Most of his students had done the required reading, *Macbeth,* and liked what they had read. Because they were prepared, he was at the top of his form. The discussion was stimulating. Some of his brighter students made interesting points. It wasn't until nearly the end of the period, when he had to discuss the psychological significance of Lady Macbeth's famous line—"Out, out, damn spot"—that he was reminded of his situation at home. Lady Macbeth saw spots of blood on her hands, the blood of the king she and her husband had killed, even though that blood was not really there. Of course, what she imagined was a result of her overwhelming sense of guilt.

All this led him to theorize about Colleen. Did she imagine the blood between the baby's lips and on the sheet because she resented the baby? Did she somehow see the baby as a threat to her relationship with him and Dana?

Ever since his father had died and Colleen had to come to live with him and Dana, he had concentrated on how all of it was affecting Dana. In his mind she was always the one to be protected. She was the one who had to make sacrifices. But what about Colleen? Because she was such a good student and such a reliable young lady, he never thought of her as having any mental weakness or emotional problem.

He hadn't been fair to her, he decided, but what was even more important, he hadn't been sensitive to her pain and her feelings. Now that he analyzed it the way he should have from the beginning, he realized that in her mind Colleen had substituted him and Dana for her parents. Sure, that made sense. She had lost one set of parents, and now she was on the verge of losing another, losing them to a new child, the baby. Nikos.

Sibling rivalry, he thought. Classic. Most of this was her subconscious at work. She was unaware of it herself; that's why she was so confused. This whole fantastic thing with Jillian—seeing a corpse in the shed—all of it was simply a way of gaining attention, the attention Colleen feared she was losing to the infant.

"Out, out, damn spot." Thank you, Willy Shakespeare. He slapped his hands together. Hopefully the psychologist would arrive at some of these conclusions himself tomorrow, he thought, but just in case he didn't, Harlan decided to have a short talk with him afterward and point some of it out.

He was feeling rather self-confident and cocky when he left the college and headed for home. In a few days it would all blow over. Colleen would be home tomorrow. Hopefully Jillian would call, and he or Dana would calm her down. The new doctor and this nurse would help Dana regain her strength, and they would be a family again. Once again his usually dominant optimism took control.

The neighborhood no longer looked gloomy to him. Shadows were thinner and weaker and not threatening. They hid no unseen horror. The houses looked quaint or attractive or warm. The neighbors he saw working on the lawns or standing around waved as he drove past. There was a friendly, safe atmosphere, a climate of contentment. All would be well.

He pulled into his driveway, parked the car, and entered the house. Already something new and pleasant had been added: he heard music. The stereo in the living room had been turned on, and one of his tapes was playing. Interestingly enough, it was one of his classical pieces, the Carmina Burana. Dana wasn't especially fond of it; she usually complained that it frightened her because it sounded like something used as a sound track for a horror movie, but he loved it, loved the chanting chorus and the heavy, melodic rhythms. It was great music to read by.

There was no one in the living room, however, so he put down his briefcase and rushed upstairs, taking two steps at a time. His bedroom door was closed, but he turned the knob softly and opened the door. He didn't enter. He stood there staring in. Dana was lying back against a couple of pillows, her eyes closed. She was bare-breasted, her hair down, her face as pale as he had ever seen it. But her bosom was tinted pink, the color sweeping up from under the fullness of her breasts and turning into her cleavage in a wide, ribbonlike streak. Her nipples were very dark, the circles the color of dried blood.

He felt drawn to her, stimulated and eager to press his lips to that bosom himself. Rarely before had her neck looked as smooth and as soft. He fantasized his naked body against hers, both of them brought to such heights of sensuality that they were like two matches rubbing against each other, about to ignite, their tiny flames crossing and merging until they consumed each other with their hot passion.

Yet in seconds this sexual imagery gave way to something more frightening. He sensed a threat; he felt himself quiver. There was another presence here, a power that had already claimed Dana's sexuality, a force coming between him and her. These conflicting feelings confused him, and for a moment he couldn't move forward into the room or back out of it.

Suddenly he saw the blanket over her lap and abdomen quiver. Dana didn't open her eyes, but seconds later the baby's head emerged. He watched with fascination as the infant struggled upward, toward her breasts, emerging as if in second birth. It wiggled with snakelike movements, inching closer and closer, until it brought its head up and its lips down around the nipple of her right breast. Dana's eyelids fluttered. Her right hand came up and over the blanket to rest on the baby's back as it fed.

"Mr. Hamilton," the nurse whispered, and Harlan turned around to see her coming out of the baby's room, folding a blanket as she did so. "I didn't hear you come in."

"I just did," he said. He looked back at Dana.

"She's nursing. We just returned from the doctor's office."

"What did he say?"

She smiled. "All's well. Why don't you wash up, shower, change, do whatever you do when you come home from work, and then come downstairs. I'll give you all the details after we have dinner," she added. "I made a roast beef."

"A roast beef? We just had—"

"Pardon?"

"Nothing. It's not important. Sure. Thank you. Fine," he added. "I'll be down right after I shower and change." He looked in at Dana and the baby again. This time she had the child cupped on her arms and her eyes were wide open. "Hi," he said.

"Hi. How's Colleen?"

"Resting comfortably." He walked into their bedroom and began to loosen his tie, watching the baby feed. He could see the muscles in the back of its neck vividly. Once again the baby looked bigger to him. Its head, its shoulders, its back— all looked twice the size. Could he be imagining such a thing?

"Gaining weight fast, huh?" he said, indicating the baby.

"Yes. Dr. Claret says his growth is wonderful. He gave him a perfect bill of health."

"Really? What's he like?" Harlan asked, taking off his shirt and undershirt.

"Very kind and gentle. A fatherly type," she said. "I'd say he's in his early sixties. Patient man, willing to take the time to explain everything. Made me feel very comfortable, very secure."

"Dr. Friedman always did that," Harlan said, slipping out of his pants.

"Yes, but this is different," she said emphatically.

"Oh?"

"I like him, Harlan. He's very thorough."

"Fine. That's what counts the most when you visit a doctor, a sense of confidence in him. What did he say about you?"

"I'm doing all right. A little undernourished, considering," she said, indicating the baby. Nikos didn't seem to let up on nursing for a moment.

"I can understand that. The nurse told you about your mother buying a bus ticket?"

"Yes," she said, grimacing. "I don't want to talk about her right now. It's too upsetting."

"So unlike her," he said, and shook his head. "All right. I'll shower and get dressed for dinner. Seems we have a cook as well as a nurse."

"She's wonderful, Harlan. So professional. You understand why I need her, don't you?"

"Of course."

"She bathes the baby, changes him, cares for me . . . just for a little while."

"No problem," he said. He bent over to kiss her on the forehead, but the moment his lips touched her skin, the baby pulled back from her nipple and wailed. Harlan stepped back instantly. "What is it? What?"

"It's okay," she said, embracing the child. "It's okay. He lost his hold." When she returned him to her breast, the baby stopped crying immediately.

"Wow. Talk about your heavy eaters. I'm not coming between him and his meal," he quipped. He shook his head and then went into the bathroom to shower. By the time he came out, the baby had been returned to his room and Dana was putting on a robe.

"Now I'm starving," she said. "I'll meet you downstairs."

"Fine."

He dressed quickly and joined her and the nurse in the dining room. Their fine china and best wineglasses had been set out. Two long red candles had been placed in silver candlesticks at the center of the table and lit. The lights had been turned down. Dana sat smiling, the glow of the small flames softening her face and casting a yellowish-white veil over her. There was a sparkle in her eyes. Her lips looked soft and wet, their fullness drawing him to them. He liked the way the light danced over the silver serving trays and dishes and reflected off that part of her smooth, white neck that was exposed. It turned her skin into alabaster. Indeed she looked like a statue come to life, the mythical Galatea brought to life by Pygmalion. At this moment she embodied all his fantasies.

Harlan couldn't remember when he'd last felt this romantic. She sensed it and held her hand out to him. He took it and kissed it, and she giggled. He leaned over and kissed her lips, pulling back just as the nurse brought in a platter of sliced beef floating in a pool of blood.

"When you said you were making dinner, I had no idea you had this in mind. This is fantastic," he said.

"Thank you, Mr. Hamilton."

"Please . . . call me Harlan."

"Harlan." She served Dana, placing piece after piece of beef on her plate. Then she poured the bright red gravy over it. It looked uncooked, as if it had been drained from the meat before it had gone into the oven. Dana didn't seem concerned. Rather she looked more pleased. She was at the food quickly, almost as though she were the only one at the table. He smiled and shook his head at Nurse Patio. She looked at Dana approvingly and then smiled at him in what he thought was a rather warm way.

Harlan took his seat and looked over the table. There were baked potatoes and string beans, bread, cranberry sauce, and a bowl of salad. He reached over to look at the bottle of wine. He had never heard of the brand and was surprised at the vintage.

"Where did we get this?"

"Dana and I picked it up on the way home from Dr. Claret's," Nurse Patio said. She took the seat directly across from him. Dana was on his left, as usual.

"Looks . . . interesting." He poured a little into his goblet and inhaled its scent. The nurse watched him intently. "Very interesting," he said. She nodded.

"I'm glad you like it. It's one of my favorites."

"What a dinner," he said. "Fantastic." He started to pour some wine into Dana's glass. "Oh, is it all right for her to have this? I seem to remember some prohibition against alcoholic beverages when a woman is breast-feeding. Dana?"

Dana looked up, impatient with the interruption.

"What?"

"It's perfectly all right, Harlan," Nurse Patio said. "As long as she doesn't drink the whole bottle."

"Great." He poured Dana half a glass. Nurse Patio passed her glass to him and he filled it. Then he filled his own. "To everyone's health," he said. Dana stopped eating her meat and raised her glass, tapping his.

"Thank you, Harlan," she said. "Thank you for being a great and wonderful husband. I'm sure you'll be just as great and wonderful as a father."

"Of course he will," the nurse said. It sounded more like a

threat. I'm sure he will," she added, and lifted her glass toward him.

"Hope so," he said with a smile, and he drank his wine, quite aware that the nurse was watching him just as intently as she watched Dana.

🔥 10

Colleen's friends began calling her shortly after the school day had ended. Of course, Teddy was the first, promising to visit as soon as practice ended. Hearing his voice ask "So what happened to you?" brought tears to her eyes. She told him it wasn't something she wanted to discuss over the phone. And he couldn't talk long, anyway.

Audra was one of the first of her friends to visit. She had called her mother the moment she found out about Colleen, and her mother picked her up at school and drove her directly to the hospital. The two of them arrived like angels of mercy, never really asking for details about her malady but promising to pray for her. Audra's mother had the same gentle, brown eyes as Audra, set a little too closely in her round, soft face. It was easy to see that Audra eventually would have her mother's chubby figure. They were so physically alike. Audra was one of those children who looked to be the offspring of a single parent. It was as though her father had never really existed.

During Audra's visit, her mother toured the hospital ward, visiting people she knew or people who were related to people she knew.

"It's nice of your mother to bring you up here so quickly," Colleen said.

"My mother and I often come up here," Audra told her. "We visit patients, try to cheer them up, pray for them. Especially during the holidays."

"Really? You never said—"

"I don't like to talk about all the things we do. It's prideful, and pride can be a very bad sin. Anyway," Audra said, reaching behind her neck to unfasten her chain, "you're a special person to us. I want you to have this." She brought the chain around her neck and handed Colleen the large silver cross.

"Oh, no, I couldn't . . . it's yours. It's special to you."

"I told you: You're special to us. Besides, there would be nothing that would give me more pleasure than seeing you wear it. Hopefully it will bring you the Lord's attention, and He will watch over you as he has watched over me."

Colleen held the cross in her hand for a moment. Although she had gone to Sunday school when she was in grade school, her parents had not been especially religious people and had never bought her any religious jewelry. She never had been one to believe in the miraculous power of icons. In fact, when she first set eyes on Audra, she was a little put off by the ostentatious cross. It was one of the biggest crosses she had seen on anyone other than a priest or minister. Actually, she hadn't realized until now that it was solid silver.

"This is a very expensive piece," she said, looking down at it. It stretched from the tip of her index finger to the top of her wrist. "I can't—"

"There's no good in having things if you can't give them to and share them with people you love," Audra said. She smiled softly and closed Colleen's hand over the cross. "At least wear it for a while. Unless," Audra said, as though she just realized the possibility, "it makes you uncomfortable to do so."

"Oh, no," Colleen said. "It doesn't make me uncomfortable." She looked down at it again. Oddly enough, even though the cross grew heavier the longer she held it in her palm, the weight didn't annoy her; it gave her comfort, a sense of security. It was something substantial. Also, she liked the way the luminescent surface caught the light in the room and then seemed to hold it. Perhaps it was a quirk of sorts, an unusual characteristic of solid silver, but after a moment it appeared more like the light was originating from the cross rather than being reflected by it. It warmed her palm and she nodded, smiling.

"Here, let me help you with it," Audra said, and fastened the chain around Colleen's neck. The cross fell between her breasts, about midway down. That same comforting warmth that she had felt in her palm now settled in her chest. She ran her right forefinger down the cross and then sat back. "It looks good on you."

"Thank you," Colleen said. When Audra's mother returned to her room, she saw the cross on Colleen and smiled as if she had known Audra would give it to her.

"We'd better be on our way, Audra," she said. "We have some other errands yet."

"Okay. Think you'll be going home soon?" Audra asked.

"Oh, tomorrow. My brother promised to check me out so I could go to the game, as long as everything's all right."

"That's wonderful, Colleen," Audra's mother said.

"Maybe you'll come over tomorrow night," Colleen suggested, "and help me catch up on anything I missed today and tomorrow."

"Sure," Audra said. "After dinner."

"Have a good night," Audra's mother said, and they left.

Some of Colleen's other girlfriends arrived. They proved to be quite a contrast to Audra and her mother. These girls rushed in, already out of breath. The hospital scene obviously made them nervous. They all talked loud and fast and giggled a great deal. When they found out Colleen was in the hospital because of emotional problems, they all grew quiet instantly. She didn't want to get into the causes, not with any of them.

"But I'm over it," Colleen said quickly, and they broke into their chatter and laughter again. By the time they left, Colleen was grateful for the peaceful moments. Only minutes after she was served her dinner, Teddy arrived. As promised, he had come directly after practice.

They kissed, and he immediately asked about the cross.

"Audra was here," she said.

"Oh, that explains it."

"I couldn't turn her down, especially since her mother and she came right over after school. And," she said, holding it out and looking at it, "I'm not so sure it won't bring me good luck now."

"So what's wrong with you? You look great," he said.

She pushed the tray of food aside. The thin slices of turkey looked unappetizing, and the potatoes pasty. She had only nibbled on the vegetables.

She proceeded to tell Teddy everything, beginning with the first time she had seen the baby and had thought she had seen the drop of blood between his lips. He listened attentively, his eyes growing larger and his mouth opening more and more as she went on. When she described what she thought she had seen in the shed, he was positively aghast. Then she told him about Harlan and the detective and what they had learned, and the horrified expression left his face.

"So you imagined it all?"

"Something like that. I'm seeing a psychologist in the morning, and then hopefully Harlan will pick me up and take me to the game."

"I'm glad of that. Without you in the stands I wouldn't be worth a damn."

"Sure," she said, even though she saw by the warm longing in his deep black eyes that he was sincere. For some reason such a demonstration of affection made her nervous. Perhaps it was part of her condition, she thought. Her emotions were fragile. Everything frightened her. Despite her wish to ignore it all, she had to admit to herself that something wasn't right. The vivid recollection of whatever she imagined she'd seen in the shed had shattered her well-being.

"I mean it," Teddy said, determined not to let her make a small thing of his expression of love. "It means a lot to me to know you're up there. When I see you . . . it gives me support. Really," he said, smiling.

"I know," she confessed. Tears came quickly to her eyes and she dabbed them with her napkin before they ran too far down her cheeks.

"What is it?"

"Nothing," she said. "I can't help it. Part of what has happened to me, maybe. I feel like crying all the time now." She forced a smile. "I'll be all right," she said quickly. She pushed her tray farther away and they kissed again, just as a nurse entered the room.

"Hey, hey," she teased. She waved her right forefinger at him. "No riling up the patients."

Teddy blanched.

"You're supposed to eat that stuff," the nurse said, pointing to the tray full of food.

"It's . . . ugh," Colleen said, and shook her head.

"Nothing wrong with her," the nurse said. Teddy waited for the nurse to leave.

"Want me to run down and get you a Big Mac or something?"

"No. I'm not really that hungry, anyway." Teddy leaned over and tasted the turkey.

"Not that bad." He continued to eat.

"You jocks eat anything, as long as it doesn't move." He laughed but ate some more. Her warm smile returned, and he felt reassured that she would be all right.

"I told you the other night you were imagining things. But some of this is wild. What do you think made you imagine all that stuff?" he asked.

"I don't know. Maybe . . . maybe I can't deal with the baby and with the way things have changed at the house."

He nodded as though he understood, but since she didn't understand, herself, she knew he was just being polite.

"You probably won't be able to go out after the game, though, huh?" he said, anticipating the disappointing reply.

"I don't imagine so. Hopefully I won't be on any medication, but you've got to expect that they'll tell me to take it easy."

"Yeah. Well, everybody's up for it. I think we're ready," he said, and ate the last piece of turkey. "I hope I won't be depressed afterward."

"You won't." He shrugged and started to pace. She laughed at him. "You? Acting nervous? What happened to the famous Iceman?"

"He melted." She laughed again, and he came back to the scat beside her bed. He suddenly had a very satisfied smirk on his face. "Does taking it easy mean I can't come over to see you tomorrow night, either to celebrate privately or cry in your arms?"

"No, silly. Of course you can come over. Oh, I told Audra to come over and bring me the work I missed. But she won't stay long," she added.

"Okay," he said. They talked a while longer and then he left. The hospital aide brought her some coffee, and then Colleen called home to speak to either Harlan or Dana. She was surprised to hear a strange voice say, "Hamilton residence."

"This is Colleen," she said. She heard laughter in the background. "Is my brother there?"

"One moment, please."

"Who was that?" she asked when Harlan got on.

"Oh, that's the nurse, Nurse Patio," he said, and laughed.

She heard him cover the mouthpiece with his hand and say something. There was more laughter.

"Harlan?"

"Hi, honey. So how are you doing? Did you eat?"

"A little. What's going on there?"

"We're having dinner. The nurse made it. Actually, it's a wonderful dinner."

"Have you heard from Jillian?"

"Who? Oh. No, nothing."

"How's Dana."

"A lot better. A whole lot better," Harlan added in suggestive overtones that Colleen found embarrassing. He sounded strange, almost drunk.

"Have you been drinking?" she asked.

"Huh? Oh, just a little wine. So you're doing okay? Good. Everything's going to be all right."

"You're going to come up here in the late morning, right?" she asked.

"Right after my ten-o'clock linguistics class," he said, pronouncing it "linwistics." He laughed at his pronunciation. "Have a good night's rest," he said.

"Harlan . . ." she began, but he had already hung up.

She looked down at the receiver as though she could see through it and witness what was happening at the other end. Then she cradled the phone and sat back in the bed, wondering. After a few moments she realized she was clutching the large silver cross, as though she had already become dependent upon its holy powers.

As soon as Harlan ended his phone conversation with his sister, he returned to the dinner table. Actually, he thought, Colleen wasn't far off the mark when she asked him if he had been drinking. He felt pleasantly high from the wine and imagined that his behavior, the sound of his voice and his laughter, had revealed it.

But it was good wine, very good wine. He had already drunk three glasses. After all the tension and the excitement of the past few days it felt good to let himself go. Overdoing it a little with the wine was just a small extravagance, anyway, he thought. The nurse produced a second bottle, so he didn't feel guilty about pouring himself a fourth glass. Dana had only the one, but Rose Patio had as many as he did, only she didn't look in the least affected by it. She sat as straight, held her head as high, and continued to look at him with clear, coldly analytical eyes.

"You know," he said, "I'm not really a connoisseur of wine. Actually, it's very rare that I drink any . . . practically only when we go out to dinner, huh, Dana?" He laughed but he didn't think she had even heard him. She had taken a second helping of meat and was concentrating on that. So he directed himself entirely to the nurse. "But this wine is absolutely delicious. The thing is, it has a flavor all its own, very distinctive, sort of a cross between cherry and . . . I don't know . . . something a bit salty. It has a lot of body, a fullness," he said.

He turned the glass in his fingers and watched how the candlelight filtered through the dark red liquid, making it seem more like a glass of clear, red rubies. He laughed and sipped some more, holding the wine in his mouth, bathing his tongue in the flavor and texture, and then swallowing it quickly, closing his eyes as he did so.

"You drink it as though you're making love to it," Nurse Patio said.

"Huh?"

He stared at her across the table. Her white uniform seemed to take on a scarlet tint. It was so tight on her, it was easy to imagine her naked body beneath it. He envisioned her skin to be as crimson as the blush on a ripe peach, although her breasts were milk white and peaked with strawberry nipples. It was strange how he thought of her body in terms of things to eat, especially after so satisfying a meal, but she stirred his appetite in a deeper, even frightening, way. He felt an unusual craving for food, unusual because this hunger wasn't simply the normal desire for edible things with which to nourish his body; it was sexual as well, almost as if the very act of consuming food could bring on an orgasm.

The more he looked at the nurse, the more desirable she became. He rubbed his eyes and looked at Dana. She sat back, chewing. Her loosened robe fell open. For a moment he thought about her bloated bosom. The vivid memory of the baby pressing its lips around her red, erect nipple returned. However, during this quick recollection, when the baby pulled back, wine spurted from Dana's breast instead of milk. The vision added more heat to his already warm body.

"The way you hold that glass . . ." Nurse Patio continued. "So affectionately. You caress the rim with your lips and then you drink," she said. Dana laughed, but it was such a sharp, hard laugh, his eyes widened and he sat up straighter.

"I'm just—"

"Fucking the wine," Dana said, and laughed again.

"What?" He looked from her to Nurse Patio, but her expression was unchanged. He started to smile. "What did you say? I can't believe she said that. Did you hear that?"

"I heard it," Nurse Patio said dryly, as if to say "So what?" Dana laughed again and then pushed her plate away.

"God, am I full."

"No wonder. You ate five pounds of beef," Harlan said.

"Oh, I did not." She grimaced, the creases in her forehead appearing like deep, bloodless incisions in her head. "So what? I'm eating for two," she said. She turned to the nurse. "Right?"

"Positively. For two. But maybe you ought to rest now," Nurse Patio said softly. Harlan looked at Nurse Patio quickly. She spoke to Dana almost as though they had been lovers.

"Oh, no, let me help with the dishes," Dana protested.

"That won't be necessary. Go on upstairs. Make yourself comfortable. Later I'll bring you some warm milk."

"Warm milk?" Harlan said. He started to laugh.

"What's wrong with that, Harlan?" Dana demanded.

"Nothing wrong with it. It's just that you never had warm milk after a meal before. Usually you have coffee. Warm milk sounds like something you give an elderly person."

"Well, tonight I'm having warm milk. It's what Nurse Patio thinks will be best," Dana said, not hiding her annoyance. She pressed her teeth together and pulled her lips back into a snarl.

"Fine," Harlan said, somewhat oblivious to the intensity of her response. "Whatever Nurse Patio says is fine with me," he added, smiling. He lifted his glass to toast the nurse.

"You're acting very silly, Harlan. Very silly," Dana said, and got up. "If anyone needs coffee, you do."

"I have some coffee for him," Nurse Patio said. She eyed him as a marksman would eye a target, closing one eye and tilting her head to the side. "Don't worry about him."

"Good," Dana said, and started for the stairs. She paused. "Thank you for everything, Rose," she said.

"It's quite all right. A pleasure," the nurse said. Harlan turned to watch Dana continue toward the stairs. Then he turned back to Nurse Patio. She stood up and approached him slowly. He couldn't take his eyes off her. When she came this close to him, he picked up a pungent, attractive scent. Inhaling it made his mind reel. It was more intoxicating than the wine. She reached down to take his hand. "Why don't you go into the living room, Harlan? Take your wine with you. I'll bring you some coffee in a while, okay?" Her voice was already soft, far-off, a voice from a dream, something forbidden that had escaped the confines of fantasy and entered his reality.

"Sure. Thanks," he said, and stood up. "Oh, shouldn't I help you with this?"

"No. It's no problem. Go on. Relax."

He nodded and obediently went to the living room. He felt a little unsteady and giggled at himself when he reached up for the wall to guide his way. He took great care not to spill any of the wine from his glass. He stood in the living-room doorway for a moment, thinking about where he wanted to sit, and then made a lunge for the couch, laughing even louder at his own unsteadiness.

Slowly, sipping the remainder of his wine, he suddenly felt himself sinking into the soft couch. He closed his eyes and sat back. He didn't know how long he was there before she came to him; it felt as though he had been asleep for some time. When he opened his eyes again, she was standing before him, only this time the illusion of being able to look through her uniform was so strong, he really thought she was naked. He blinked rapidly and wiped his eyes. His imagination was running away with him, and he was both a little frightened and embarrassed by his budding erection.

"Are you all right, Harlan?" she asked.

"What?" He looked around, not aware of how much time had passed. He had even forgotten coming into the living room. "Oh, yes, yes." He saw that his wineglass was empty. Now his mouth was filled with a strange stinging sensation, not unlike the one that followed the eating of a hot pepper. "I feel a little funny," he said.

"Oh?"

She sat beside him. Once again he smelled that strong, alluring scent. It was so sharp and so provocative, he closed his eyes. A rainbow of colors flashed under his lids and he sighed, his body feeling so soft, so pliable, it was almost as though it had been turned into a sponge. When he opened his eyes again, she was leaning toward him. Her face was so close, he could see the thin film of wetness on her lips.

"You've been through a great deal, too, Harlan. Doctors never think about the pressures on the spouse. Sure, Dana is going through some turmoil, but so are you," she said. Her voice was softer, friendlier. Gone was the correct, hard tones of the professional, aloof nurse. She touched his shoulder. The warmth from her fingers traveled with lightning speed down his back and across his chest. The sexual excitement that had come over him so quickly, and so surprisingly, continued to build.

"Oh, I'm all right," he said. He thought about getting up quickly and going upstairs, but he couldn't take his eyes off her. Another button on her uniform had come undone. The material retreated from her cleavage, and the pinkish white skin of her breasts slipped farther out of the grip of her bra.

"You need sympathy and comfort too," she whispered, her lips molding around the words, holding the vowels like bubbles between them. "I'm here to help you as well, Harlan."

Her right hand moved up the inside of his thigh so rapidly that when her fingers touched his building erection, he didn't pull back. Nor did he pull back when her lips met his. She pressed her tongue into his mouth quickly, finding his and triggering a surge of sexual electricity down into his chest. He felt as if his whole body lit up. His heart thumped madly, the beat so hard and fast that it frightened him, but she was so aggressive and so firm, he didn't resist.

Later he would try to tell himself that he didn't realize what was happening. He had been so stimulated at dinner. Dana looking so voluptuous, her lips moist, her eyes bright, that robe slipping away from her bosom, had aroused him, and then the desire had retreated, leaving him hanging on the edge of passion. The hunger he had sensed at the table came over him more forcefully now. He told himself his feelings were only natural. It had been so long since he'd made satisfying love. And then there was the wine. Much could be blamed on that.

She peeled his clothes off so gracefully and quickly, he hardly realized it was being done. All the while he felt numb, as if her tongue had stung his own and transferred some anesthetic into his body. In moments he was naked. She spread him out on the couch, laying him out as if he were a handicapped patient in a hospital bed, stroking his chest, running her hands down his arms right to the tips of his fingers and then pressing her palms against his sides and over his lower stomach, circling his erect penis as though it were not to be touched. She came so close, however, that he practically felt her hand slip over him. She continued down the inside of his legs, separating them softly as she did so.

Finally she stood up and slipped out of her uniform and undergarments, while he watched dumbly, unable to move, unable to speak, fascinated with the way her breasts inflated as the tight bra was pulled away.

Lying beside her, he thought his own pale white body—with its tiny, dark hairs curled over his chest and legs—looked like the more fragile and feminine one. Although she had a woman's figure, there was something hard and sharp about the way her waist curved and her buttocks lifted.

When she brought her lips close to his again and he was able to look into her eyes, he found himself looking into an infinite pair of eyes, two tunnels with mirrored walls that reflected the dark pupils endlessly, deeply. He sensed himself falling into those tunnels, slipping, sliding along the icy surfaces. He reached out in vain, his fingers unable to grasp anything to prevent his continued descent. Yet he didn't scream; he fell mutely, like one unable to understand the true significance of what was happening.

The dizziness that came from the illusion of falling down the mirrored tunnels and the pungent scent of her body, hot against his, caused him to close his eyes and act like a patient under treatment. He was vaguely aware of her hands gripping him around his ribs. He thought she was actually lifting his body and turning it to fit him comfortably between her legs.

Though he vaguely understood that he was being seduced, was being unfaithful to Dana, he couldn't prevent himself from becoming sexually stimulated. Her breasts softened against his chest, and her nipples were pressed against his own.

Yet this lovemaking was different and in many ways unreal.

He had no sense of her as an individual. A parade of women passed through his mind: women he had fantasized making love to and women he *had* made love to—they all merged into a common female, eventually faceless. When his orgasm came, it seemed to come within him instead of within her, as if all of this had been a fantasy.

He came out of it like a man rising from the bottom of a dark, cool pool of blood, gasping and swinging his arms around, pulling himself up from unconsciousness and frantically throwing off the blanket of sleep. He shouted once and opened his eyes.

"Easy," she said. She slipped off him, rising as though she were made of an airy substance. "Relax," she said. "You're all right now. All's well. You'll feel better now. I was happy to help you," she said, and began to dress herself.

He looked around in confusion. Had he really made love to her? She was smiling down at him as though he had. He looked over his naked body and then sat up quickly.

"You should get dressed," she whispered, then smiled. "You don't want Dana to find you like this."

"What?" He looked at the open doorway and then hurried to get his clothing on. She left as he did so. A few moments later she returned, carrying a tray with a cup of coffee on it.

"Better drink this," she said.

"What happened? What did we do?"

"Nothing terrible," she said. "Sometimes," she said, "sex is a kind of therapy—a treatment, if you will. And I'm here to help. Don't think of it as anything more, if you like." She was smiling licentiously now. Her face looked so different. The sternness was gone, as well as the coldness in her dark eyes.

"I've never been unfaithful to my wife before," he said. "Never."

"Poor Harlan." She reached out and ran her right hand over his cheek. "Don't think of it as being unfaithful. If you want, I'll explain it all to Dana."

"No! What are you, mad?" He looked toward the door again. "Look, I'm sorry. It must have been the wine. I don't know what I was doing. I shouldn't have led you to believe I wanted any . . . any . . ."

"Sex?" She laughed. "It certainly didn't seem that way. Drink your coffee," she ordered, her voice returning to its more commanding tone. He took the coffee and sipped it, his eyes never leaving her as she stood over him like a nurse administering medication to a patient. Satisfied, she turned to leave. "Wait," he called.

"Yes, Harlan?"

"I . . ." He looked at the couch again. "What should I do now?"

"Why, go to sleep, Harlan. You're tired. You need your rest. It's been an exhausting day," she said, and left him. He stared at the empty doorway for a moment and then drank the coffee eagerly, as if convinced it was the correct prescription. After he finished it he got up and went upstairs to see how Dana was doing. He was still in a bit of daze, finding it hard to believe he had just made love to a woman who was practically a stranger. And in his own house! Him! Harlan Hamilton, a man who shied away from the young, attractive coeds in his classes as if they all carried the AIDS virus. A man normally so shy, the students called him Mr. Blush because of how quickly his carrot-tinted complexion turned crimson.

Dana was sitting up in bed reading, just the way she often did before the baby had been brought home. She looked brighter, stronger, far less pale and tired than before.

"Wonderful meal, wasn't it?" she said when he entered the bedroom.

"Yes." He couldn't help feeling guilty. Now he wondered if that guilt was evident in his face. Would Dana know what he had done? Would she see it, sense it? How could he explain?

"Isn't she an amazing woman? I feel so much more secure now that she's in the house, don't you?" For a moment he couldn't respond. "Don't you, Harlan?" she demanded, putting her book down and leaning forward.

"Well . . . yes, I'm glad she's here. It was a good idea." He was afraid to give her any other answer now, afraid of rousing any suspicion.

Dana smiled and nodded with satisfaction, as though he had recited an answer she had taught him a long time ago. "I'm going to read a little more," she said. "I don't feel as tired tonight. The extra vitamins, the good food, being relieved of some of the work with the baby . . . it's all revitalizing me," she said.

"I'm glad. You do look better." He approached her and

kissed her on the forehead. Her skin felt cool, healthy, not hot and steamy like before. For a moment he had the urge to tell her about the incident with Nurse Patio; he wanted to confess, but he was afraid of what would happen, what damage it might do to her apparent recovery. "I'm a bit sleepy, though," he said, standing back. "Drank too much of that wine. The coffee helped, but I think I'll turn in."

"The light won't bother you?"

"Not tonight. Nothing will bother me tonight," he said, and went into the bathroom to brush his teeth. He sensed that he really would sleep like a baby.

That made him laugh: sleep like a baby. Nikos was certainly the king when it came to that. That baby could sleep, but he supposed all babies slept long hours. It was during those hours of sleep, Dana had once told him, that they would do most of their growing, and growing was certainly something Nikos was doing. Maybe because he slept so much, he thought. He laughed at the idea. Little Rip van Winkle.

It had been a long, difficult day. It was good to be bringing it to an end. Morning, with its bright sunlight and new start, would initiate his stream of optimism again. He would bring Colleen home. Dana would continue to get stronger, they wouldn't need the nurse anymore, and their difficult start would come to an end. There truly would be a new beginning.

He looked at himself in the mirror. Had he really just made love to that woman? It had happened so quickly, and he had made no effort to resist. Not really. He shook his head. Maybe it had been only a dream. Maybe it hadn't happened. Maybe it'd been an illusion caused by the wine. Could he convince himself of that? If only he could . . . he could live with that.

He started to brush his teeth, but he was so tired, he could barely move the bristles back and forth over the enamel. He'd rinsed out his mouth, put the brush back in the cabinet, and started to turn away when he saw it: a red spot on his neck that reminded him of the hickey Marlene Cross had given him when he was only in the ninth grade. He'd worn it like a medal of honor, proud of the evidence that he had been passionate with a girl like Marlene. All his buddies had been jealous.

But this was different . . . this proved something else. Dana hadn't noticed, or if she had, she hadn't thought anything about it. He took some talcum powder and spread it over the reddened area. Satisfied that it was hidden enough, he went out to the bedroom. Dana looked up from her book again.

"I'm getting tired," she said. "It won't be much longer, anyway."

"It's okay." He had his hand over the spots on his neck.

"Anything wrong?"

"No," he said quickly. "All's well," he added, and then realized that was the way Nurse Patio had put it.

All's well for whom? he wondered. But he didn't wonder long. Moments after his head hit the pillow he was in a deep sleep. So deep, in fact, that he never heard Nurse Patio come into the bedroom, nor did he hear Dana get up to follow her out with the baby.

He heard nothing but the echo of his own unanswered questions.

❦ 11

Anticipating Harlan's arrival at the hospital, Colleen got dressed. She felt a great deal more confident and secure about herself this morning, especially after her session with Dr. Lisa. The forty-five-year-old psychologist had a calmness about him that put her immediately at ease. His light blue eyes were the color of the morning sky. He had long, feminine eyelashes and a small, thin mouth; yet his diminutive nose and high, sharp cheekbones didn't make him pretty-faced as much as they gave him a gentle, firm look. She could see that at one time he had had hair only a few shades lighter than Harlan's, but he had begun to gray early, which made his short cut look more like a cross between blond and red.

He introduced himself and then sat in the chair beside her bed. Even though he smiled warmly and joked with the nurses, Colleen sensed he was all business. He measured his words carefully, focusing intently on her answers. After the initial tension she felt about him seeing her, she was convinced of his sincerity and realized that between them they might arrive at a solution to her problem. She liked the way he forced her to analyze herself and then kept her from being too hard on herself.

"Sure, the manifestations of what you're going through are bizarre," he said after they had talked for nearly an hour. "They took a rather dramatic turn: drops of blood, bloodstains, a grotesque corpse in a shed. I'm not surprised, though, given the kinds of graphic and vivid images of horror young people are exposed to today. *Nightmare on Elm Street*? *Friday the Thirteenth*? *Halloween Part Twelve* . . ." He shook his head. "Have you seen any of those?"

"All of them. Some more than once," she confessed.

He dropped her chart on the foot of her bed and sat back, folding his hands behind his head. She relaxed too.

"I know I felt insecure about the baby's arrival, and maybe I exaggerated Dana's personality changes, but I can't believe I would want to see the baby hurt," she protested.

"That part of yourself that felt threatened by the baby reacted." He shrugged. "Unaware of your own subconscious and its capabilities for violent and evil thoughts, you accepted everything at face value. You had no reason to think otherwise. But," he said, leaning forward and slapping his knees, "you've obviously thought all this out very well yourself, Colleen. I'm almost extraneous here. Thanks a lot for making my job a lot easier." He smiled at her and she nodded.

"But what's it going to be like for me now?" she asked.

"Oh, I'm not going to say that all will be hunky-dory. You have some adjustments to make. There is some tension in the house, naturally. But I think when you have reactions or thoughts now, you'll be able to take a second, more objective, look at things and in effect calm yourself down.

"What I mean to say is, I believe you have the wherewithal to handle your problems on your own. Of course, if you come to something that is overwhelming and you feel threatened, you can remain calm by reminding yourself you have people who can and will help you. I'm going to leave my card with you. Call me anytime. I mean that. No matter what time of the night it might be."

"Thank you," she said. "Do I need any medication?"

"Definitely not."

"Can I go home today?" she asked quickly.

"Of course. There's nothing more that can be done for you here. Just take it easy for a day or two. You did have a rather intense shock to your nervous system, even though the cause was in your own mind. The net result wouldn't have been any different had there really been bloodstains and corpses hanging in sheds. Understand?" She nodded. "I have the number where your brother can be reached," he said. "I'll call him and tell him it's all right to come pick you up."

"Thank you," she said.

"By the way," he said, "I'm the youngest of four children, all boys. My three older brothers would have drowned me in a potato sack if they could have. Now we all couldn't be any closer."

"Why does it have to be this way?" she wondered aloud. "Why are our feelings and emotions so complicated?"

"Why? I don't want to get into that. It just is, and part of life, part of being mature, is dealing with what is or what has to be. I think you're going to be just fine," he added, and then left.

Now, as she stood by the window in her hospital room waiting for Harlan's arrival, she wondered if Dr. Lisa really had that confidence in her or simply said the things he had said as a means of building her up. Did he say such things to all his patients? Anyway, what difference did it really make, as long as it worked? she thought.

"Great, you're all ready," Harlan said as he came through the doorway. She spun around to greet him and immediately was struck by his appearance. His hair was unbrushed, looking as it would when he had first gotten up. He looked pale and tired, his eyes slightly bloodshot. The knot in his tie was sloppy, the tie itself uneven. She was surprised because Harlan was usually meticulous when it came to his clothes, especially the clothes he wore to school.

"Hi. You spoke to Dr. Lisa?"

"Yep." He looked around nervously. She sensed a tenseness in his demeanor. Gone was the usual subdued manner, the laid-back posture, and the calm expression that sometimes annoyed Dana. Her sister-in-law often said something could blow up in the house or catch on fire and Harlan would simply get up slowly, almost reluctantly, and quietly dial the fire department while she jumped around and screamed hysterically. Right now he looked more like a drug addict frantic about his next fix.

"Everything else all right?" she asked.

"What? Yeah. Wonderful. Everything's much better. Come on, I'll get you home so you can shower and change and go to the game."

She didn't ask him anything else about things at home until she had checked out of the hospital and was in the car. The way he had fidgeted around in the hospital corridors and the administration office made her think he was pressured for time.

"Your next class isn't until two-thirty, right?"

"Huh? Oh, yeah," he said.

He was very distracted, almost oblivious to what he said or was doing. She saw that he drove a lot faster than usual, making his turns sharply, accelerating and passing cars. Was this her conservative, calm brother?

"How are things between you and Nurse Patio?" she asked.

"What? Good. Why?"

"Why? Yesterday you said—"

"She's good," he said quickly. "She's professional. It's good we have her." He turned to her sharply, his eyes wide. "Don't say anything critical about her to Dana. Don't do that."

"Who said I would, Harlan?" She shook her head, a half smile on her face. "I'm the one who was in the hospital, but you're the one acting kind of strange."

"Me?" He produced a short, nervous laugh. "Actually, I didn't have too good a night."

"The baby was up?" she asked innocently.

"No. I don't know. Maybe. Yeah. I think so, but that wasn't what kept me from having a good night's rest."

"What was it?"

"Too much wine at dinner," he said, smiling. "You can hallucinate from drinking too much alcohol, you know."

She misunderstood him. "That's not what happened to me, Harlan. I didn't drink any wine first."

"Oh, I know. I had a good talk with this psychologist. Right on the money. Yeah. I know. So you'll go to the game." He turned to her again, his face twisted in what looked to be a painful grimace. "Just ignore Nurse Patio if she bothers you. Stay to yourself. Do your own thing. She won't be with us that long."

"I'm not worried about it, Harlan," she said, surprised at his outburst. She shook her head and looked out the window for the rest of the ride home.

The first thing that struck her about the house was how dark it was. All the curtains and shades were drawn. There were no lights on in any of the rooms. She paused in the doorway as though they had entered the wrong house and looked at Harlan for an explanation, but he seemed oblivious.

"Why is it so dark in here?" she asked.

"Oh. Nurse Patio says we have to keep it that way. Something to do with the way the light affects Dana and the baby. Put the lights on as you need to, but don't leave them on when you're finished."

"What does light do to them?"

"I don't know. Sensitivity. Something like that. I'm not the professional, she is," he snapped. The sharpness of his reply was so unexpected, she actually stepped back, as if he had slapped her. She saw he didn't regret his tone of voice, either. Surprised, she looked around and then rushed up the stairs to her room.

The door to Jillian's room was partly open. She peered in as she passed and saw all of Jillian's things piled up in the far corner. The nurse's suitcase was open on a chair against the wall. She shook her head, still finding it hard to believe that Jillian would just walk out of the house and go to New York, fight or no fight.

In her usual way she turned on her stereo and put a tape into the deck as soon as she entered her room. The action was practically automatic. Harlan kidded her about it often, saying he was going to hook the stereo up to the door so it would go on and off as it opened and closed.

While Cat Stevens sang "Hard Headed Woman," she sat on her bed thinking. Harlan was acting weird, all right, but *Keep calm*, she told herself. *Just keep calm*. She turned her attention to her wardrobe and thought about what she would wear to the big game. Just as she started to sift through her garments, there was a loud, hard knock on her door

"Hello," Nurse Patio said. Colleen gazed at her in the doorway. Colleen was surprised because she had assumed she would be much older. She thought she was attractive, with her silky black hair and jet-black eyes. Her facial features looked sculpted, proportional, but coldly statuesque. She did have a hard, stern look, and her posture was so perfect, it seemed as if she had a steel backbone.

But Colleen thought the uniform clung to her body almost obscenely. The milk-white cotton material, tucked in under and around her breasts, looked like a bra. It was possible to make out her collarbone and ribs. After having seen nurses in uniform at the hospital, this one looked more like a caricature. Colleen couldn't help stepping back. Nurse Patio ignored the look of surprise on Colleen's face.

"Hello," Colleen said.

"I'm Nurse Patio, Rose Patio. I'm sure your brother told you why I am here."

"Yes."

"You'll have to make that music lower," she demanded.

"Oh. I didn't realize . . ."

"For a while we all have to start thinking more about Dana and the baby."

"Of course. I'm sorry." Colleen turned and quickly went to the stereo to lower the volume, but when she looked back at the doorway to see if Nurse Patio approved, she was already gone. "Jesus," she said, and shook her head. She closed her door and turned her attention back to choosing her clothing for the game.

She dressed in her black-and-gold sweatshirt, black pants, black Reeboks, and gold socks. Looking at herself in the mirror, she recalled the last time she'd worn this outfit to a game. Bobby Stuart had asked her if she wore black or gold panties too. She laughed at the memory. Now, of course, she had added one additional thing to her outfit: the silver cross. She pulled it up from under the sweatshirt and draped it between her breasts.

Satisfied that she looked healthy and vibrant and that all traces of her short, but dramatic, hospital stay were gone, she left her room, intending to have something to eat and then go off to the game.

She found Harlan in his den/office, going over some paperwork. He had put on only the desk lamp and was hovering over his papers in the small amount of light. When she asked him if he wanted her to make him some lunch, he didn't reply. Thinking he was too deeply involved in his work to hear her, she shrugged and went to the kitchen to make herself a sandwich. Just as she sat down at the table, the phone rang. Before she got to it, it stopped. Nevertheless she picked up the receiver, hearing voices. Nurse Patio had answered the phone upstairs. She was speaking to Trish Lewis.

"Yes, I am the nurse Harlan hired," Colleen heard her say to Trish.

Trish simply said "Oh."

"I'm afraid Dana can't be disturbed for a while."

"Is she all right?"

"She'll be just fine, as long as we give her what she needs and help her along. For the present she must be sheltered from any excitement."

"Of course. If there's anything I can do . . ."

"Thank you, but there's nothing."

"I see. Is Harlan at home? I wanted to ask him about Colleen," Trish said.

"Hi," Colleen interjected. "I have it," she added for Nurse Patio's benefit, but she didn't hear her hang up. "I have it," she repeated. There was a click. "Hi, Trish, I'm home."

"Oh, how are you, honey?"

"I'm better."

"Who is that woman?" Trish asked. Colleen laughed.

"Someone from the KGB, I think."

"How are you?" Trish repeated.

"Okay. Really," Colleen emphasized.

"I heard they traced Jillian," Trish said, tiptoeing over the words. "Found out she bought a bus ticket to New York."

"Yes. I know. I think I realize what happened to me now, although I still can't understand Jillian going off like that."

"You haven't heard from her?"

"Not yet."

"How is Dana?"

"I haven't seen her yet. I think I'll have to make an appointment through her nurse," Colleen said, and laughed.

"Yeah. It sounds like it. All right. You call if you or Harlan need anything, okay, honey?"

"Sure thing. And thanks," Colleen said. "Talk to you soon," she added, then hung up. Before she got back to the table to eat her sandwich, Nurse Patio was in the doorway. Colleen turned because she actually felt the woman's presence before hearing or seeing her. Hearing her was practically out of the question, anyway. The woman must walk on air, she thought, even though those soft white shoes looked like they would squeak.

What had happened cast a chill over her. It was as though the woman's cold, dark shadow knifed through her back and stabbed her in the heart with a blade of ice. Colleen shuddered, and that was when she turned to the doorway.

Nurse Patio looked taller, wider, her breasts more swollen. She had her hands on her hips, the elbows extended so that she blocked the entire doorway. "That wasn't very polite," she said.

"Pardon?" Colleen said.

"When you heard I was on the phone, you should have gotten off, not listened to the conversation and then interrupted me, making me feel as though I were the rude one listening in on you."

"That's ridiculous," Colleen said. "First off, that was Trish Lewis, Dana's close friend, and she wanted to speak to either me or Harlan. Why do you answer the phone, anyway?"

"What is it?" Harlan asked, coming up behind Colleen. She turned to him, disgusted. "She's angry because I picked up the phone after she did and overheard her conversation with Trish Lewis."

Harlan looked at Nurse Patio. She lifted her hands from her hips and pressed them over the top of her chest. Her eyes now glowed like hot coals, the black having an orange tint.

"She listened in and interrupted," Nurse Patio said.

"Did you, Colleen?" he asked softly.

"It was Trish Lewis, Harlan. For God's sake!"

"That's not the point. It's all right, Nurse Patio. It won't happen again," he said. She nodded, smiling with satisfaction.

"Harlan!" Colleen's eyes filled with tears. "I didn't do anything wrong. If anything, she should have called you to the phone to speak to Trish."

"I'm sure she was only trying to do the right thing. We've got to keep Dana quiet for a few days. She's been through some terrible times."

"But, Harlan—"

"Let's forget about it," he snapped. "Please, let's try to get along and not make big things out of small things. Not now. I need some peace around here!" he said. His face exploded. His cheeks reddened, his eyes widened, and his mouth twisted in at the corners. Then he clenched his fists and raised his arms for emphasis. She couldn't believe she was looking at her brother.

She looked back at the front entrance to the kitchen, but Nurse Patio was gone. The woman moves around like a ghost, she thought. She sat down, avoiding Harlan's gaze. After a moment he returned to the den. She tried to eat, but her appetite had diminished. She could only pick at the sandwich. Disgusted, she went back upstairs to her room, intending to finish with her hair and makeup, but she paused when she saw Nurse Patio standing in Dana's bedroom doorway. The nurse turned expectantly as she approached.

"Can I speak to her?"

"Just for a moment. The baby's about to feed," she said firmly.

She entered the bedroom. All the lights were off and the room was lit only by the thin rays that leaked in around the shades and curtains. Dana was sitting up in the bed and had the baby cradled in her arms. She was staring down at the infant and didn't look up when Colleen walked into the room. Colleen glanced back. Nurse Patio was right behind her.

"Hi, Dana," she said, and stepped up to the bed. Dana turned her head slowly, as though she were in a daze. At first she said nothing. Colleen looked down at the baby. His eyes were still closed. For a moment she didn't think it was the same child. He looked so much bigger, months older. All the baby fat was gone from his face. His cheeks were lean, the jawbone emphatic. His facial features were as formed as a mature man's. In fact, the well-developed nose, the strong, full mouth, and the deep-set eyes made him look freakish. It was almost as if a twenty-year-old man's head had been transplanted onto a baby's body.

The thing that shocked her the most, however, was the complete change in hair color. There was absolutely no trace of the carrot tint, neither in his head of hair nor in his eyebrows, which were now coal black. His skin was darker too. It was as if he had been sunbathing. She thought the child looked too old and too big to breast-feed.

"Colleen . . ." Dana finally said. There was something in the way Dana pronounced her name that tore at Colleen's heart. It was as though she were pleading for something, calling out, appealing for help.

"Dana, what's wrong?"

"Nothing's wrong," Nurse Patio whispered loudly from behind. "Don't even suggest that anything is wrong," she ordered.

"What is it, Dana?" Colleen asked, ignoring her. She thought Nurse Patio grunted or made some kind of a strange, guttural sound just as Dana opened her mouth to speak. Instantly the baby's eyes snapped open, but instead of looking up at Dana, he looked at Colleen.

His face twisted as his eyes widened. He lifted his little fists in the air and screeched. The high pitch and intensity of the wail was so sharp, it made Colleen close her eyes and step back. Dana clutched the child frantically to her body, but his screaming continued, growing even louder and more intense. Nurse Patio came forward to stand between Colleen and the baby. As soon as her body blocked Colleen, the baby's cries were subdued. Soon he was only sniveling.

"What is it?" Colleen asked. Nurse Patio turned on her abruptly. In the darkened room, with the subdued light behind her, Nurse Patio seemed more ominous. Her dark eyes, draped in shadows, were like empty sockets. Colleen felt she was looking into the face of a corpse. Indeed her cheek and jawbones seemed to rise up against the skin, pressing out emphatically when she spoke.

"It's that cross," she said, nodding at Colleen's chest. "The baby is frightened by it."

"What?" Colleen reached up and put her right hand over the silver cross. It felt positively hot. "I don't understand."

"It catches the light, and the gleam is frightening to the baby," the nurse said.

"Where did you get that?" Dana asked. Nurse Patio didn't move out of the way, however, so Colleen had to talk around her.

"Audra gave it to me when she visited me in the hospital yesterday," she said, and heard her voice crack.

"Don't wear it in here," Dana said. "Don't wear it near the baby," she added, as if the words had been memorized.

"I won't . . . I'm sorry, Dana," she said. "I only wanted to see how you were. I'm sorry." She turned and ran out of the room, quickly retreating behind her own door. Once safely in her own bedroom, she caught her breath and then sat on her bed. She touched the cross and turned to her vanity mirror. There was no question that it stood out, but why should a baby be frightened by such a thing?

She remembered now how Nikos had first reacted to Audra. Audra had been wearing the cross then too. Maybe Nurse Patio was right. But how could she know such a thing so quickly? Was it because she was an expert with babies? That's what Harlan would say, she thought. She was positive of that.

It seemed like she couldn't do anything right. Here she was home only a few hours, and already she had had a bad confrontation with Nurse Patio and had disturbed Dana and the baby. Tears streamed down her face. It wasn't all her fault, was it? she wondered. It all made her so tired, she wasn't sure she should go to the game.

Then she thought of Teddy. It would be better if she got out of the house for a while, anyway, she concluded. She dropped the cross inside her sweatshirt and left her room. The hallway was empty and quiet. Dana's bedroom door was closed. She went downstairs quickly and looked for Harlan. She found him on the couch in his den, just sitting there staring down at the floor.

"Are you okay?" she asked when he looked up at her.

"Yeah." He forced a smile. "I'm all right. Off to the game?"

"Uh-huh. What about dinner? Did you want me to get something or make something?"

"It's all right. Nurse Patio's cooking liver."

"She's doing the cooking again?"

He nodded. "You'd better take it easy, Collie. Come right back, okay? You'll have a good dinner tonight. No junk food. I promised Dr. Lisa you would eat right and rest for a day or two."

"I will," she said. "Harlan, I . . ."

"What?"

"I'm sorry about what happened before, but she does seem too bossy."

"That's the way some professional nurses are. They have to be like that because they have a great deal of responsibility," he said, but she didn't think he sounded convincing.

"Dana looks awfully tired, Harlan. Are you sure that woman's helping her?"

"Tired?" He thought for a moment. "She goes up and down. It'll be like that for a while. At least that's what Nurse Patio said the doctor said."

"The baby seems so big. Maybe Dana shouldn't be breast-feeding him, Harlan."

"Don't worry about it, Colleen. I told you, we have professional help now," he said sharply.

"But—"

"Please!"

She saw the frustration and the anger building in his face, so she looked away.

"All right," she said, turning back to him. "I won't make

any trouble, but I don't like that nurse," she blurted, and left the den and the house before he could respond.

Harlan rose slowly from the couch and walked through the wake of Colleen's dramatic exit. Her words lingered in the air like the stale odor of decaying flesh, for despite what he had told her, he still felt something was indeed degenerating here: his marriage; his relationships with the people he loved; his very life. And the thing that was so painful, that made it so hard to accept, was his failure to understand how it all had occurred and why it had occurred so quickly.

Sure, he could blame his sexual encounter with Nurse Patio the previous night on many things, not the least being his own weakness; but the fact was that it had happened—he had made love to another woman right under his wife's nose—and it had left him feeling drained and compromised. That complicated everything, especially having Nurse Patio here to assist Dana. The truth was, he didn't feel he could place his full trust in her.

For one thing, he didn't know the doctor who had sent her, and he didn't know anything about her background. All he knew was that Dana liked the new doctor and Nurse Patio. He wanted to speak up about this and might have before, but now, after what he'd done, it wasn't going to be easy. He rationalized his failure by telling himself it was for Dana's sake, after all, that they had Nurse Patio at all. He realized his desire to get rid of her was purely selfish. He wanted to get rid of her so he wouldn't be reminded of what he had done last night. Now, because of that realization, he was overcompensating and defending her to Colleen when Colleen was right. Nurse Patio had no right answering their phone and turning away their friends without consulting him first.

Poor Colleen, he thought, he would have to find a way to make it up to her, especially after what she had just been through. Oh, well, he thought, Nurse Patio won't be here that long. The trick now was to get through the period during which she would.

He went upstairs to see Dana and found her asleep in bed, so he tiptoed out and went in to see the baby. Nurse Patio was in her own room with the door closed. Nikos must have just been put into his crib, Harlan thought, because he was still moving around, even though his eyes were closed.

Harlan studied him. Colleen wasn't exaggerating—the baby

had grown considerably in a short period. In fact, to Harlan, the child looked at least a foot or so longer. He thought he must have gained ten pounds or more as well. He was disappointed in how quickly his hair color had changed. He didn't have the same reaction to the baby's face he had had when he first set eyes on him in the hospital and immediately afterward. Then the baby had been pudgy and cute, his face full of possibilities. His features had become sharp and more definite, and, as stupid as it was to feel bad or complain about it, the baby looked like someone else's child.

But it had always been someone else's child; Harlan had been wrong to fan the illusion that it was theirs. Now, because the baby was taking on its true identity, he felt bad about it. This was his own fault, he decided. And, anyway, if Dana wasn't having this kind of reaction, why should he?

Of course, Dana had a stronger tie to the child. Because of the breast-feeding, the infant was dependent upon her and obviously had developed a strong physical attachment to her. As he continued to look down at the baby, he wondered how he would go about developing a relationship with Nikos. Shouldn't he start caring for the infant soon too? Right now the child barely knew him, if he knew him at all.

This was another reason to resent Nurse Patio. As long as she was here, she would stand between him and his adopted son. Whenever Dana wasn't caring for it, Nurse Patio was. He was totally blocked out of the experience. Such a thing probably wouldn't have been as important to him if the child was really his child, he thought. It was part of the irony, but there would have been inbred things, genetic things on which to depend for a strong relationship. But here, in this case, he felt a need to work at developing a relationship. It wouldn't come naturally.

The baby grimaced, and Harlan figured it was gas. That was something he knew about babies—they had a lot of gas. They had to be burped properly. Surely Nurse Patio had done that.

Harlan was tempted to reach down and pick up the infant. The truth was that he hadn't even held him since they had brought him home. He wasn't really asleep yet, anyway, he thought. He leaned over the crib, but as soon as his fingers touched Nikos, Nikos opened his eyes. Harlan laughed at the look of surprise on the baby's face.

"Don't you know who I am? I'm going to be your old man, buddy. Yes. I'm your father."

He affectionately touched the baby on the chest with his right forefinger. Nikos didn't cry, but his eyes followed every one of Harlan's movements closely. Harlan felt that the baby's body was tense. The infant didn't trust him.

"Hey," he said, "it's all right. I'm not going to hurt you. You're getting to be a big boy fast." He felt the baby's shoulders. There was a surprising firmness to them. "In fact, you're a little football player. I know, don't tell me, it's the good food."

The baby stared up at him with such intensity, Harlan had to laugh again. He ran his right forefinger up the side of the baby's face and over the top of his head, exploring the child with the same kind of curiosity that a baby would have for the things in its immediate world.

"In a way we're both developing, Nikos. This is just as new for me as it is for you. Believe me, little buddy," he said. The infant's eyes moved all the way to the side, watching where Harlan's fingers went. "I can sense it. You're going to be a tough one, maybe a Dennis the Menace, huh? Nobody's going to push you around. Nobody's going to threaten and intimidate Nikos Hamilton. Yeah."

The baby turned its head toward Harlan's right hand as Harlan brought his fingers around to the baby's chin. Nikos opened his lips gently.

"Uh-uh. No. This is not another feeding, you little hog."

He started to take his fingers away from the baby's face, and the infant lifted his head from the sheet and literally seized Harlan's right forefinger between his lips. Shocked by the quickness and the firmness of the move, Harlan didn't withdraw his hand until he felt a stinging sensation at the end of his finger. Then he pulled his hand back quickly and looked at the tiny pinhole in his skin, from which a small bubble of blood was beginning to emerge.

"What the hell . . ."

He looked at the baby.

"You little devil. How could you . . ." He reached in with a determined curiosity this time and brought his thumbs to the sides of the baby's mouth, pulling the lips up and away to expose the gums. He saw two distinct spots of white enamel in the top gum and ran his thumb over them, feeling their sharpness. "Cutting teeth? Already? God, they feel sharp. How does Dana—"

"Mr. Hamilton!"

He released his hold on the baby and turned around to face Nurse Patio.

"What are you doing?" she demanded, her hands on her hips. At this moment she looked more like a Marine drill sergeant than a nurse.

"Visiting with my son, or is that against some rule?"

"It is if you prevent him from taking his needed nap and get him riled up. Dana just fell asleep and—"

"All right, all right," he said. He looked down at the baby again. It continued to stare up at him with the same intensity. It didn't move, didn't utter a sound. "He's cutting teeth already. And they're sharp."

"So?"

"Well . . . how will Dana . . . I mean . . . can't the baby hurt her?"

She smiled at him condescendingly and then uttered a short, thin laugh, shaking her head.

"Of course not. The baby instinctively knows where its source of food comes from and won't do anything to harm that source. There's a relationship between the infant and its mother that's positively spiritual," she said, changing her expression quickly to one of deep reverence.

He was impressed. "No kidding?" He looked down at the baby again. "Quite a kid, quite a kid."

"Yes, he is."

"You've taken care of babies before—a number of them, I assume."

"So?"

"Is there anything unusual about him? I mean, he seems to be growing so fast and—"

"No. There's nothing unusual. He's just an exceedingly healthy and content child right now, and it's all working well for him. Don't do anything to disturb it," she warned.

"Why should I do that?"

She straightened up, the material tightening around her bosom as though that were answer enough. He blanched.

"I gotta get to work," he said. "Got a late-afternoon class."

"I know. I have your schedule pinned up in my room."

"You do?"

"Of course. I have to know when you are available, Mr. Hamilton," she said, but he thought she said it in a very seductive tone.

"I see. Okay. Dana's asleep, so I'll just leave. Tell her I'll—"

"I know what to tell her," she said. "Don't worry about Dana."

He stared at her a moment and then nodded. She wasn't going to step out of his way gracefully. He could see that.

"Excuse me, then," he said. She leaned back, but as he passed between her and the doorjamb, she leaned into him again, her breasts caressing his arm and shoulder. He didn't stop, however. If anything, the touch had driven him down the hall a lot faster. He thought he heard her laugh as he descended the stairs.

When he stepped outside, he felt as if he had just stepped out of a steam room. His heart was beating madly and he was very flushed. He vigorously scrubbed his face with his palm and looked around. Except for the rhythmic barking of the Jensens' dog, the street was deadly quiet. It looked more like an empty movie set. There was no movement, no sign of life in the houses. He felt like yelling "*Action!*" and bringing the world back to life.

He started for his car, parked in the driveway, and stopped when he looked back at the shed. Strange, he thought, how something so innocuous had become the object of such fear for his kid sister. He saw where he and the detective had left the door open, so he went back to it. Just before he closed the door, he looked in at that mop and jacket, trying to imagine how they could have formed such a horrible illusion for Colleen.

How had they gotten in here, anyway? he thought. He hadn't put them there. Must have been something Dana had done. He couldn't ask her about it, though. Not right now. He didn't want to bring up something so ugly.

He closed the door and turned away, looking up at his house as he did so. Something caught his attention in the window of his and Dana's bedroom. The curtain moved. Suddenly Nurse Patio appeared, standing in the window, looking down at him. She wore what he thought to be a smug smile.

And in her arms she held Nikos, who looked like he was smiling in the same way. In fact, it wasn't until that moment that he realized what it was that bothered him so much about the baby's newly formed facial features.

He looked a lot like Nurse Patio, especially around the eyes and mouth. His face was taking on a similar sculpted look.

It was almost as if he were her child and she had come surreptitiously to take care of him.

He looked back only once before getting into his car, and saw that they were both gone from the window. Perhaps it had only been an illusion, he thought. Perhaps he had caught Colleen's problem.

Shaking it from his mind as best he could, he drove off to work.

✹ 12

Dana felt herself shrinking in the bed. She wasn't really asleep but was midway between consciousness and unconsciousness; in some dazed, drunken state. She was vaguely aware of her surroundings, but at the same time falling back into a dreamworld. She fought against it, even though she was so tired that she longed for respite. There was something horrible waiting for her the moment she fell into unconsciousness, some terrible, lifelike nightmare. She knew that the shriveling of her body was only the beginning of it, so she tossed and turned and struggled against losing her grip on reality.

But she couldn't stop the deflating of her body. It was as though she had been pumped with air and then sprouted a leak. Where was the leak? She ran her hands down her hips and over her legs, searching for it, hoping to feel the air escaping. She brought her palms up over her pelvis and lower abdomen, sliding her hands back and forth, but she felt nothing. Gradually she brought her fingers to her breasts, and only then did she feel the leak. The air was escaping from her nipples. If she listened hard enough, she could hear the silvery *sssing* that sounded like breath gently blown through closed lips.

She pressed her hands against her breasts to stop it from happening, but the pressure continued to build, making it harder and harder to hold her palms there. Her nipples became stiff and sharp. They were starting to become painful, as though they were nails being pressed into her hands. She moaned and held on as long as she could, but finally she had to pull her hands away.

Now, instead of air, blood spurted from her breasts. She screamed and sat up.

For a moment she did nothing. Then she rubbed her eyes and waited for them to focus. Nurse Patio was standing there at the foot of the bed with Nikos in her arms. She was smiling, but the baby was simply staring, its face harder, colder, its dark eyes unmoving, now more like two shiny black onyxes set in tiny pools of pearl. He smacked his lips. He began to squirm, reaching out for her.

"What happened?" Dana asked.

"You must have had a bad dream. It's nothing. Put it from your mind."

"It was so real." She looked down at her bosom and screamed. "My God, what happened?"

"It's nothing. Relax," Nurse Patio said quietly, even though there were large, bright red bloodstains on the bodice of Dana's nightgown.

Dana touched them gently and looked at her fingers. The blood was there, fresh; it had just happened. She looked up at Nurse Patio and held her hands toward her.

"Look!"

Nurse Patio continued to smile. She put the baby down on the foot of the bed and went into the bathroom, returning with a damp washcloth. She took each of Dana's hands and washed the blood off the tips of her fingers.

"Just take off the nightgown," she said. "I'll see to it."

"But what happened?"

"You broke a capillary. No big deal," Nurse Patio said. "Come on. Lift your arms."

Obediently Dana did so. Nurse Patio helped lift the nightgown from her body, crumpling it into a ball and dropping it to the floor. Then she guided Dana back to the pillow. Dana watched her as she brought the washcloth to her breasts and carefully cleaned away any traces of blood.

"Nothing to worry about," she said. Dana glanced down at the baby. Nikos squirmed and grunted, clawing at the blanket in an attempt to pull himself toward her.

"But the baby . . ."

"There's no problem. I told you, it's all right," Nurse Patio said. She put the bloodied washcloth with the crumpled nightgown and lifted the baby from the bed, bringing him up to Dana. "He's hungry again," she said. "You can see that."

"But it seems like I just fed him, and besides, shouldn't I wait awhile to see what more will happen?"

"Nothing more will happen."

"But suppose another capillary breaks while I'm nursing? Maybe we should call Dr. Claret."

"It's nothing," Nurse Patio said, widening her smile. "You'll see. Here. Take him to you."

"But—"

"Take him," she said more firmly. Dana stared at her and then looked at the baby. He grimaced and started to cry. "See? I told you he's very hungry."

"Oh, dear," Dana said. Reluctantly she reached up and brought the baby to her bosom. Nikos was at her nipple instantly. Nurse Patio stood over them, watching, a wide smile on her face.

"He's growing so well, so fast. It's wonderful," she said.

"I'm so tired right now. I feel like I could fall asleep with him at my breast."

"It wouldn't matter. It's all right. Close your eyes."

"Really? You won't leave, though, will you?"

"I'll stay right here, right next to the bed, until he's satisfied again," she said. She reached down and wiped some strands of hair from Dana's forehead. Dana was grateful for her soft, loving touch. She closed her eyes and then opened them quickly. "I'm here," Nurse Patio said. "Relax." Dana closed her eyes again.

The baby was drawing the liquid steadily and firmly, but that sense of shriveling came over Dana again. Her legs felt as though they were shortening, being drawn higher and higher into her hips, her hips becoming more and more narrow. Her ribs closed in on her lungs. It was getting harder and harder to breathe. She started to open her eyes and felt Nurse Patio's fingertips on her lids.

"Sleep," she said. "Sleep."

Dana eased her hold on the baby, but he didn't move; he didn't shift position. After a moment her arms fell to her sides. They felt as though they were telescoping in toward her shoulders. Her hands became as small as the baby's. Everything was shrinking except her breasts. They were rapidly filling up with all the blood in her body.

She continued to battle against unconsciousness, but the fatigue that came over her rose up her body like a heavy, warm blanket. Its ascent couldn't be prevented. Soon it was at her chin, and then it was nearly overhead, shutting her into the darkness. She sank deeper and deeper into the bed as the mattress came over the sides of her body to engulf her. The baby was getting heavier and heavier, and pressing her down as it suckled.

Before she lost consciousness, she had the distinct impression that her own bed had become her coffin. She tried to scream, to show that she wasn't really dead, but the lid was being closed over her, anyway.

The last face she saw was the face of Nurse Patio, who had pulled the blanket back. She looked down at her and smiled. Her lips moved. "It's all right," she said. "There's nothing to worry about. It's all right."

Then she brought the blanket all the way over Dana, and all went dark.

Colleen was exhausted. She could barely talk. Her throat was raw from screaming and cheering. As soon as the gun ending the game was sounded, she raised her arms and jumped with the crowd from her seat, actually feeling as though she were being lifted by the roar and the thundering of their feet on the stands. The game had been close up to the beginning of the second half, the lead seesawing back and forth; and then Teddy led one successful drive after another, maintaining a two-touchdown lead right to the final moments. They were the league champs.

Moments after she started away from the stands, Colleen sensed that she was indeed very tired. She had misjudged the effect the emotional drama had had on her over the past thirty-six hours. That, plus the excitement of the championship game, worrying every time Teddy got the ball, feeling every blow to his body, riding the emotional roller coaster of a successful pass, and then an unsuccessful one, was overwhelming. Her legs felt shaky.

She got to her car as quickly as she could, avoiding as many of her friends as possible. She knew everyone would try to talk her into celebrating with them, but she had promised Harlan she would go right home, and now she believed she truly had better. By the time she reached the driveway, she had settled down a bit, yet she still thought that right after dinner she would go up to her room to rest.

She found Harlan in the living room watching the news. He

hadn't even heard her arrive. She thought he looked tired and small in his easy chair. He was staring at the set as if he had been watching television for hours and hours and had become mesmerized by the glow. He still had that uncharacteristic disheveled appearance: His hair was unbrushed and his tie was loosened and lopsided.

"Hi, Harlan. We won. Much bigger than anyone expected."

"Oh. Really? Great." He sat forward and looked around as though he had just woke up. "Fantastic," he mumbled. "How are you?"

"A little tired. My throat feels like I swallowed sandpaper," she said, pressing her fingers gently over the front of her neck.

"Sure. It's only natural. So," he said, "we won. Teddy's a hero again."

"He was great. He's supposed to drop over later."

"Uh-huh."

"Should I help with dinner?"

"Oh. No. Nurse Patio is in the kitchen. Everything's been done."

"And how's Dana?"

"She's . . . been sleeping," he said, as though just realizing it. "Ever since I came home. The baby too," he added. Colleen looked at him, debating whether or not to say anything else about it, but recalling how he had reacted before, she just nodded.

"I'll go up and change."

"Yeah, good. I told Nurse Patio that as soon as you arrived, we would eat."

"Be down in a jiffy," she said.

"We'll be in the dining room," he said, getting up. She saw that he rose out of the chair as though he were years older.

"You all right?"

"Yeah, sure. Just a tough day. Still a lot of strike talk. A lot of tension. Everywhere," he added sadly. She nodded in understanding and left to change.

She wasn't going to look in on Dana, but when she came out of her room to go back downstairs, she thought she heard a distinct moan. Since the door to Dana's bedroom was open, she walked over to peer in.

Dana was in bed, but her eyes were open and she was staring up at the ceiling.

"Hi," she called, but Dana didn't respond, nor did she look her way. She simply continued to stare at the ceiling. "Dana?" Still nothing. Colleen walked farther into the room, moving tentatively, her arms folded under her breasts. "Dana?" She stepped up to the bed. Dana turned to her slowly. Colleen thought she was exceedingly pale. There was barely any color in her lips and her eyes looked so glassy. "Hi. How are you doing?"

Dana blinked rapidly but didn't respond. She stared at Colleen as though she didn't know who she was.

"Are you all right? You act like you're in a daze or something."

Still she didn't respond. Instead she closed her eyes and turned away. Colleen stood there staring down at her, debating whether or not to try to wake her. She decided she would call Harlan upstairs and turned to go out of the room when Nurse Patio suddenly appeared in the doorway.

"We're waiting on you," she said. "Dinner's getting cold."

"What?"

"Your brother sent me up to fetch you, but you weren't in your room."

"Dana's not feeling well," she said. "She looks terrible."

"She's simply tired. She's been up all day with the baby today. He was a little more difficult than usual and it has fatigued her. Just let her rest."

"She doesn't look well," Colleen insisted. "She's terribly pale."

"She had no fever and her blood pressure is good. I told you, she's simply tired. After a good night's rest that paleness will be gone."

"I don't believe you," Colleen insisted. "I think she's sick."

"Don't you dare talk to me like that. Don't you think I know what I'm doing?" Nurse Patio snapped. Her shoulders rose and her head seemed to sink between them. Colleen thought she looked like some kind of bird. Even her hands, the fingers curled inward, looked more like claws.

"No," Colleen said defiantly, "I don't."

She rushed past her and down the hall to the stairs. She found Harlan sitting at the dining-room table, looking as distracted as he had when she had first come home. He was chewing lazily on a piece of bread.

"Harlan, you've got to go upstairs," Colleen said.

"What is it?" he asked, not much animation in his face.

"Dana doesn't look well to me. I think she's very sick."

"Well, what does the nurse say?"

"She says she's all right, just tired. But I don't believe her, Harlan. She's wrong. She's not a good nurse. She may be a good cook, but she's not a good nurse," Colleen insisted.

"Now, Colleen, I told you—"

"Something's not right, Harlan," she said with determination. "You don't have to be a nurse to know when someone looks terrible. Go see for yourself. She's as pale as a ghost and she can't even keep her eyes open. I don't think she knew who I was!" she added, her arms out for emphasis.

He stared at her a moment and then took a deep breath. "All right," he said, standing up. "You sit down and start to eat, and I'll look into it. What we don't need now is any more hysteria."

"Okay, I'll stay here and be calm if you'll just go up and look at Dana," she said, taking her seat. He shook his head and left. A little more than five minutes later he returned and took his seat again. She waited while he poured himself some wine. "Well?"

"I went in. She was sitting up in bed talking to Nurse Patio, going over the menu for the week. The nurse is a nutritionist, you know, so she's planning foods that will help build Dana up."

"But how did she look? How did she act?"

"She's a little tired. As the nurse explained, the baby was difficult today, so it's not unusual. Yes, she's pale, but not any more than she has been. The nurse says that will go away soon. She's building up her blood, giving her vitamins, but as far as her not being able to recognize anyone . . ."

"She didn't respond when I said hi. And then when she looked at me—"

"Yeah. She says she's sorry, but she was just waking up from a long nap. Let's start on this stuff before it gets too cold," he said, lifting the cover off the silver serving dish. "Smells delicious."

Colleen watched him serve himself the food.

"What about Dana? When does she eat?"

"She ate already. The nurse brought it up to her."

"She can't even get out of her bed," Colleen said. "Don't you see—"

"All right, already," he said. He slammed the lid of the tray down. "I told you, she's getting better. We have a nurse here. You don't have to like her. It's not important whether or not you like her, as long as she does her job. I'm tired of all this," he said.

The tears came to her eyes quickly. She shook her head. Then she got up from the table and ran out of the room.

"Colleen!"

She didn't respond. She bounded up the stairs to her bedroom and slammed the door. For a moment she just stood there. Then she flopped on her bed and began to cry, pausing when she heard the nurse's footsteps go by her door and down the stairs. She wiped her face and lay back against her pillow. The fatigue and tension had made her eyelids heavy. She kept them closed, and in seconds she was asleep.

A gentle knocking on her door woke her. She looked at her Garfield clock and realized she had been sleeping for nearly two hours.

"Who is it?" she called.

"Audra. Are you all right?"

"Oh. Come on in, Audra," Colleen said, and swung her legs out over the bed. "Hi."

"Aren't you feeling well?" Audra asked. She stood just inside the doorway, her arms full of books and notebooks.

"I'm okay. Just tired. Come in and close the door." Audra did so quickly. "Sit down," Colleen said, indicating the desk chair.

"Your brother said you weren't feeling well before, but he said it would be all right to come up to see you."

"I'm all right. He's the one who's not all right. How did he look to you?" she asked with interest. Audra shrugged.

"The same, I guess. What's supposed to be wrong with him?"

"He's been hypnotized by that . . . that nurse," Colleen said. "Did you see her?" she asked quickly, her eyes wide.

"You mean Rose Patio? She greeted me at the door."

"What's so funny?" Colleen asked, seeing the big smile form on Audra's face.

"I must have looked terribly shocked. I didn't know there was a nurse here, and my first thought was that something had happened to you. The nurse was amused by my expression, I guess. Anyway, she introduced herself, explained why she was here, and took me to see Harlan. I thought she was very nice."

"God, she's horrible. How can you not see that?" Audra shrugged again. "You're so oblivious to everything," Colleen said sharply. "You're too damn trusting and too nice to people who are stabbing you behind your back."

"Maybe," Audra said, unperturbed by Colleen's outburst, "but these people are the ones to be pitied, not me. They're the ones who are suffering."

"Huh?"

"They're in some mental anguish, otherwise they wouldn't be so belligerent and hurtful."

"I can't stand it," Colleen said, looking away. At this moment Audra's sweet smile and gentle, hopeful eyes were annoying. Colleen needed an ally, someone to commiserate with and share her outrage. Instead she had all-forgiving, all-loving Audra. "My sister-in-law is very sick, but my brother thinks Nurse Patio is doing everything right. Whatever she says, goes."

"Oh. Well, a nurse should know a lot more than we do about it," Audra said. "I can understand why your brother feels that way. What does Dana think?"

"She doesn't think. She's exhausted, sick," Colleen said. "Jesus," she added.

"You should pray for her," Audra said. "I'll pray for her."

Colleen looked at her innocent friend and laughed. She shook her head and went to the window. She had forgotten that the window looked down on the shed. Instantly the vivid recollection of Jillian's ugly corpse flashed across her eyes. She moaned and covered her face with her hands.

"Colleen?"

"It's all right, it's all right. Look, I'm a lot more tired than I thought. Maybe we'll go over this tomorrow. I think I'll take one more day off from school."

"Of course. I'll come over after school tomorrow if you like, and bring the additional work. I have everything written out for you on this notepad," she added, and tore the sheet out of the small pad. "I'll leave it for you, and if you feel better during the day tomorrow, you can start to catch up."

"Thanks." She took a deep breath. "I'm sorry, Audra."

"Oh, there's nothing for you to be sorry about." She stared at Colleen for a long moment, until Colleen realized why.

"I'm still wearing your cross. It's under my blouse. The last time I wore it outside, it bothered the baby."

"Oh?"

"Yeah," Colleen said, anxious to drive home a point that Audra might appreciate, something that would show her the negative side of the nurse. "The baby cried just as he did when he first saw you, and the nurse said it was because of the cross, because the light reflected off it and frightened him. How do you like that? She even has Dana believing it."

"Gee, I never thought of that. I'm sorry if it's true."

"It's not true, dammit. It's stupid. Don't you see?" she said, the frustration turning her face red. She extended her arms toward the floor. "Maybe the nurse doesn't like it, so she said that. Maybe she hates God," Colleen added, her eyes looking angry.

"But the baby did cry," Audra responded softly. "I suppose it doesn't hurt not to wear it out in front of him for a while," she said.

Colleen kept her arms extended and her neck stiff for a moment and then relaxed her body. She shook her head and then nodded, as if she were getting advice from an unseen source.

"What's the use?" Colleen said. "I'll talk to you tomorrow, Audra. Thanks for the work," she said, turning from her.

"You're more than welcome. I'm sorry you're not feeling well yet." She started for the door. "Oh," she said. "Isn't it wonderful about the game? I heard Teddy was fantastic."

"Yes, he was," Colleen said, her voice softer. Her heart felt lighter when she thought about Teddy. And he was supposed to come over very soon now. At least she would have him to confide in, and he would understand why she was so upset. Now that she thought about it, it was ridiculous for her to get angry at Audra. Audra was a child, kept in a world characterized by an Adam and Eve innocence. She didn't suffer because she never knew she was in pain. It would only be cruel to make her realize it, Colleen concluded.

"I wish I could have been there," Audra said, "but I do the shopping for Mrs. Finklestein today. She's eighty-one, and it's hard for her to get around anymore since she developed eye trouble."

"I know. It was a nice thing for you to do." Colleen smiled. "I'm sorry I was a bit short with you, Audra. Thanks again."

"I'll see you after school tomorrow," Audra repeated. " 'Night."

" 'Night."

Colleen watched her leave and then went to the desk to look over the work she had brought. She wanted to keep herself occupied until Teddy arrived.

Audra paused at the foot of the stairs. She never liked to leave Colleen's house without saying good night or good-bye to her brother and sister-in-law. She thought it was rude just to walk out of someone's home. It was so quiet downstairs, though, that she hesitated. Nevertheless, she turned into the corridor and walked toward the kitchen, looking for Harlan. She peeked into the living room but saw no one, so she continued on, heading for the dining room.

"Can I help you?" Nurse Patio asked.

Audra turned abruptly. Nurse Patio was behind her, but she hadn't heard her approach and Audra wondered from where she had come.

"I was looking for Mr. Hamilton. I wanted to say good night."

"Oh? Leaving so soon?" the nurse asked with a pained expression.

"Yes. Colleen's not feeling well enough yet. I'll return tomorrow."

"I see. That's too bad. You're the girl who gave her that beautiful cross to wear, aren't you?" Nurse Patio asked, stepping closer to her.

"Yes," Audra said. Instinctively her hands went to the small valley between her breasts where the cross had always lain. "I'm sorry if it caused any problems for the baby."

"Problems? Oh." Nurse Patio smiled. "You mean when Colleen leaned over the crib and the cross swung out? Yes, Dana got very nervous about that."

"That was the reason? I thought—"

"It's no problem as long as she remembers to keep it inside when she's near the baby. Babies grab on to things, too, and put everything in their mouths, especially babies that are breast-feeding," she said. Audra nodded. "I'm sure you understand. But I think it was a wonderful thing to give your friend. It's something personal and yet something that can be meaningful to others."

"Yes," Audra said. "That's exactly how I feel about it." She smiled. This nurse was quite nice. Why did Colleen feel so negative about her? she wondered. Was it part of her problem? Poor Colleen, unable to see the good in people, as well as the bad, she thought.

"Well, how's the schoolwork going?" Harlan asked, stepping out of the den.

"Not too well tonight, Mr. Hamilton. Colleen's not feeling that great yet, so I'll come back tomorrow. I just wanted to say good night to you," Audra said. She wondered for a moment whether or not she should tell him and the nurse more about Colleen. She was afraid Colleen would be angry with her for doing so, but she was not happy leaving her in such a bitter state up in her room. She looked at Nurse Patio, who was smiling warmly. "She's very unhappy, Mr. Hamilton."

"Yes, I know," Harlan said quickly. "We'll do what we can to make things better for her. She'll be all right," he added.

"I hope so," Audra said.

"Colleen might have overdone it today," Nurse Patio said, looking at Harlan, "considering what she's gone through. She probably shouldn't have gone to the game." She turned back to Audra, and Audra nodded. "She'll be fine in a day or so. It's nice of you to be so concerned for your friend. Colleen's lucky to have you."

"Oh, I'm lucky to have her."

"Don't worry, we'll look after her," Nurse Patio said, smiling. She patted Audra gently on the shoulder. "I'll walk you to the door," she added.

"'Night, Audra," Harlan called.

The nurse opened the door for her.

"You walked all the way?" she asked.

"Yes, I don't mind it. It's really only about a mile or so, so it's not too bad—until it starts to snow and it gets terribly cold, that is."

"Yes, I know what you mean. Well, good night Audra. I'm sure I'll see you again," she said.

"God willing," Audra said.

"Yes, God willing," Nurse Patio replied, and followed it with a short laugh. It was the only off-key note in her friendly melody, but Audra didn't think about it. She smiled back and stepped outside. Nurse Patio closed the door behind her and all was still.

Audra looked up at Colleen's bedroom window before she started down the quiet, residential street. Colleen wasn't standing there, but she thought about her troubled friend and felt sorry for her. She wished she could have done more. Tonight, before going to sleep, she would say a special prayer for her, and after she described Colleen to her mother, explaining how troubled she was, she was sure her mother would pray for her as well.

Audra turned her attention back to the street. There was a heavy silence about it, and the hush that hung over the sleepy houses and dark trees was so thick, it amplified every sound, no matter how slight it seemed. As she started down the driveway her own footsteps echoed with an unusually loud reverberation, even though she wasn't walking quickly.

Perhaps the gloomy atmosphere came from the low ceiling of clouds that blocked out the stars and moon, she thought. Even the streetlights seemed depressed by it, making their normally bright glow look thin and pale yellow. The narrow corridor of illumination barely extended past the sidewalk. She had the impression that night was still closing in, the shadows oozing over the lit areas and gradually extinguishing them. But there was no one but her to complain.

It wasn't unusual for there to be no traffic and no people. At this time in the evening on fall nights, inhabitants of Old Centerville Station, just as the inhabitants of most of the small villages and hamlets in the Catskills and similar semirural communities, retreated to the warmth of their homes and gathered around their television sets the way ancient man gathered around campfires. Audra imagined them staring at the flames, hypnotized in almost the same fashion, glad to ignore whatever nocturnal dangers lingered outside their small, protected areas.

Darkness had a way of driving people into themselves,

Audra thought. All the stores and businesses in town, except for the all-night convenience store and the self-service gas station, were closed. Even stray dogs and cats found their nooks and crannies and retired early.

Audra never minded the silence, nor did she really mind being alone. Solitude gave her the chance to meditate and pray, offering her the best opportunity to be close to God. She knew that her classmates and others her age, even Colleen, couldn't appreciate what she felt and how deeply fulfilled she was whenever she sensed she had God's attention. These were golden moments, moments when she believed she was most alive and most meaningful.

Being afraid of the dark or of being alone never occurred to her. Her faith was her shield; not only did she feel protected, but also she had a sense of her destiny. Nothing bad could happen to her until or unless God willed it so, and if He did, it wouldn't matter how bright it was outside or how many people she was with, anyway. She truly felt sorry for people who lived in fear, for it meant they had little faith.

She was about half a block from the corner of Highland and Turtle, just between Colleen's home and the Jensens', when the Jensens' dog started to bark madly. She thought that because of the clapping sound of her footsteps she was the cause of it, so she started to walk faster, hoping she would be far enough away from the dog before his barking disturbed people.

But the dog's barking intensified and became shrill. She had to pause to listen, because the animal sounded more like an animal in pain than an animal warning away intruders. As suddenly as the barking had started, it stopped. She continued to listen, but there was nothing more coming from the Jensens'. She imagined Mr. or Mrs. Jensen had come out to quiet the animal and might even have brought it inside.

Just as she started to walk again, she heard someone behind her call out her name distinctly. She turned. Whoever it was who had called her had done so in a loud whisper. At first she thought she might have imagined it, for she saw no one. Then the woman stepped to the border of the shadows so that there was just enough light to wash the mask of darkness from her face.

It took only a few moments for Audra to remember the face, realize who it was. She smiled pleasantly and walked toward her, never once wondering why the woman didn't come farther forward into the light.

In fact, as Audra drew closer, she stepped back into the shadows and drew Audra back into the darkness with her. In moments the silence closed in around them, smothering Audra's screams almost before they began.

✹ 13

The ringing of her telephone jarred Colleen from her deep thoughts. She literally jumped in her seat. She had been working on her school assignments, and for a while that had kept her from thinking about anything unpleasant. When she gazed at her clock, she realized that Teddy should have been there by now. It was getting to the point where she knew he wouldn't come; it would be too late. That had to be him on the phone then, she thought, calling to offer some excuse. She wasn't in a forgiving mood, and although she regretted her belligerent feelings, she answered the phone abruptly, not attempting to disguise her unhappiness. However, the tiny voice on the other end changed her attitude instantly.

"Hello, Colleen? This is Lucy Carson. Is Audra there, please?"

"Audra?" For a moment Colleen wondered if Audra had been with her tonight or last night. That was how confused the question left her. "Audra? Why, no, Mrs. Carson. Audra left." She looked at her clock and tried to remember exactly when. It didn't seem possible. "Nearly two hours ago."

"Oh, dear. Did she say she was going someplace else before coming home?" Audra's mother asked. Colleen could hear the barely subdued note of hysteria.

"No, not that I remember. She's not home?"

"No," Lucy said, her voice so small that she sounded like a little girl. "I'm a little worried now," she explained. "Audra would call before going anywhere else, anyway."

"She didn't mention anyone else," Colleen repeated. "I've been in my room since she left," she added.

"Oh, dear," her mother said again. "I wonder what I should do."

Colleen recalled the time Bernie Hodes had run away from home and his parents called the police. They didn't really begin to look for him until nearly twenty-four hours later. Their experiences with missing teenagers told them that nine out of ten times the teenagers were safe. They had been either neglectful or uncaring when it came to informing their parents. The police tended to categorize all teenagers as one type, so they would react the same way to Audra's mother's call. She knew they would be polite and take down all the information Lucy Carson gave them, but she didn't expect they would search for Audra this soon. Of course, she didn't want to tell Lucy Carson this.

"Maybe she met one of our friends and they asked her to help with something, some schoolwork. Knowing Audra, she would just go and do it," Colleen offered. It was the best she could come up with, but she did want to alleviate Mrs. Carson's fears, as well as her own.

"Yes. Maybe she did," Lucy Carson said skeptically. "It's just that she would call. If you should hear anything . . ."

"I'll call right away, Mrs. Carson."

"I wonder when I should call the police," she thought aloud. "I don't want to cause a lot of trouble for anyone, but I'm getting very worried."

"Tell you what, Mrs. Carson. I'll take a ride along Audra's route home," Colleen said suddenly. "Maybe I'll catch her walking home from someplace."

"Oh, I hate to bother you so late."

"No, it's all right. It won't take me long. If I don't see her, I'll let you know."

"Thank you, Colleen. Bye."

Where could she be? Colleen wondered. It wasn't like Audra not to call her mother. She put on her black-and-gold sweatsuit jacket and hurried downstairs. Harlan came out from the living room to see where she was going.

"It's late. What's up now?" he asked with some annoyance. She still couldn't get used to Harlan being so impatient and intolerant.

"Audra never got home. Her mother's quite worried."

"Really? Well, maybe she stopped by to see someone else."

"I told her that," Colleen said. "But Audra wouldn't do that without calling her mother. It's been nearly two hours since she left here," she added. "I'm going to ride along her route home and see if I can find her."

"Maybe she should just call the police," Harlan said, shaking his head.

"I'll be right back," Colleen said quickly, and left before he could add anything. She got into her car and backed out of the driveway before she put on her headlights. The rays knifed through the darkness. She hadn't noticed when she had looked out of her window earlier, but it had begun to rain. The light drizzle and fog diminished visibility considerably. All sorts of possibilities went through her mind. Audra may have taken a ride with someone, a stranger, when it had begun to rain. She was so trusting a person. Perhaps that was why she never reached home.

"Oh, Audra," she muttered to herself, and suddenly felt very guilty about it all. If she hadn't been short with her, if she had only controlled her emotions, she and Audra would have done their schoolwork, and then, when she saw it was raining outside, she would have driven her directly home.

She drove very slowly, looking from side to side. When she reached the corner of Turtle and Highland, she saw a familiar vehicle just ahead. It made a turn onto Main Street and picked up speed, but before it pulled away, she recognized that it was Teddy's car. What was he doing here? Why hadn't he come to her house?

She had to make a turn and go in the opposite direction to head for Audra's house, so she couldn't pursue him. Once again she drove very slowly, searching the sides of the street, looking for a sign of her innocent friend walking home. She saw nothing. By the time she reached Audra's house, she had a very sick feeling. Instead of going back home and then calling her mother, she pulled into their driveway and went to the front door. Lucy Carson was at it instantly.

"Oh, Colleen," she said. She had her hands pressed against the base of her throat, her short, stubby fingers interwoven. It wasn't until this moment that Colleen realized how childlike and fragile Audra's mother really was. She was able to deal well with other people's problems and tragedies, but when it came to her own, she looked lost, confused. "When I heard the doorbell ring, my heart nearly stopped beating."

"Audra didn't get home since you called me?" Colleen asked, already knowing the answer.

"No."

"She wasn't walking along the way. It's raining now too," Colleen added.

"Oh, come in, come in," Lucy Carson said, stepping back quickly. "I wonder what I should do."

"I think you'll have to call the police now," Colleen said. "Come. I'll talk to them too," she added.

"Thank you, dear," Mrs. Carson said, and they went to the phone.

The dispatcher took down all the information as nonchalantly as Colleen had expected he would. She tried stressing the seriousness of the situation by repeating and emphasizing Audra's habits and strong sense of responsibility. The dispatcher must have been impressed because he told her a patrol car would be sent out immediately to do basically what Colleen had done. He promised that the patrolman would stop at the Carson residence and pick up a recent picture of Audra too.

"Well, they're going to do something about it," Colleen said. "There's nothing to do but wait and keep the phone free so Audra can call if she has to."

"Oh, right. Thank you so much, Colleen. You've been a great help."

"It'll all prove to be nothing, and we'll laugh about it later on, I'm sure."

"Hopefully. In the meantime I'll pray."

"Yes. So will I," Colleen said, and realized she meant it. "I won't call you, but please, call me, no matter what time of the night, as soon as you find out something."

"Of course, dear. Thank you," Lucy Carson repeated.

Colleen pressed her fingers against the cross under her sweatshirt and recited her prayer as she drove; as she recited it she pictured Audra standing in her doorway, promising to return the next day with the schoolwork. It brought tears to her eyes. She tried to get hold of herself before she pulled into her own driveway. If there was one thing she didn't want right now, it was to have another emotional breakdown. Harlan would go absolutely mad. He might even send her away, claiming she was becoming a real threat to Dana's well-being. Maybe she was.

It wasn't until she opened the door that she remembered Teddy's car. Where had he been going? Where had he been? It was a night filled with confusion and mystery.

Harlan had just turned off the television set and come out of the living room to go upstairs when she entered the house.

"So?"

"No sign of her, Harlan. Her mother and I called the police, and they're sending out a patrol car to search. It's so unlike her to do something like this."

"Well, what do you think happened?"

"I don't know. I'm just afraid she accepted a ride from someone and . . . you know."

"Oh, boy." He shook his head. "With all that young girls are being told about going with strangers . . ."

"Audra's . . . trusting," Colleen said.

He nodded. "I'm tired," he said. "Going up to bed. I think you had better do the same thing. And whatever you do, whatever you find out, don't tell Dana about this. Not right now," he added, widening his eyes to emphasize just how intense things were.

"I won't. You left a light on in the kitchen," she said.

"Nurse Patio is in there preparing a late snack for Dana."

"Oh?" She shook her head and went up the stairs. He followed slowly.

After she closed her door she thought about Teddy again. She couldn't stand not knowing why he had been near her house, but hadn't come over, especially after indicating he wanted so much to be with her to celebrate the great victory. She decided to call him, half expecting that he wouldn't answer. Perhaps he was still out celebrating with his teammates. But he picked up the phone instantly.

"Hi. Where were you?" she asked quickly.

"What do you mean?"

She explained what had happened with Audra and when she had seen him.

"You're kidding," he said. "I came to your house."

"What?"

"That nurse greeted me at the door and told me you weren't feeling well at all. She told me Audra had just been there but had to leave immediately. You were supposed to be going right to sleep."

"She what? She had no right to do that. Why did you listen to her?"

"Why? I don't know. Your brother wasn't around, and here

was this nurse in uniform . . . I just felt . . . I don't know. How was I to know she had no right to do that?" he asked with annoyance. He didn't like the way she was blaming it all on him. "You were up in your room and you had been in the hospital . . ."

"I'm sorry," she said. "I didn't mean to yell at you. It's just that it makes me so mad. Damn her. I'm going to tell my brother about this."

"Maybe she felt she was only doing the right thing," he said.

"It's not that, Teddy. You don't know what's going on here," she said, lowering her voice to a loud whisper. "She's taking over everything. She answers the phone, she turns away Dana's friends, my sister-in-law is getting weaker and weaker but she has Harlan convinced she's not—"

"You sound like you're getting back to the way you were," Teddy said. For a moment she couldn't speak. Her throat closed and her eyes teared. She couldn't swallow, but she took a deep breath.

"Teddy, don't you believe me?"

"Yeah, yeah, it's not that."

"Yes, it is," she said. "Never mind, I'll handle this myself. I'm going to sleep. Good night," she added, and hung up before he could say another word. She sat there for a few moments, the fury building up in her. What was she going to do? What *could* she do?

She got up and went to Harlan and Dana's room, hoping she could call him out and tell him what had occurred, but the door was closed and she was afraid of waking Dana. She saw from the light in the hall and entryway that Nurse Patio was still downstairs. Her rage still strong, she went downstairs and found her in the kitchen, cutting raw roast beef into thin slices. For a moment she was able to watch her unnoticed.

Although she had to admit that there was something very attractive and obviously very sexy about Nurse Patio, there were times when she looked more masculine. Right now, when Colleen viewed her from behind, her back looked wider, her shoulders fuller. Her neck looked thicker and more muscular as well. She cut through the meat with ease, the muscles in her arms and back rippling against the tight uniform.

Even before Nurse Patio turned to confront her, Colleen had a great sense of dread. Fear weakened her rage. She felt herself begin to tremble. The air had become so still. Her feet were suddenly glued to the floor and she had the familiar, horrible feeling that she was melting. She had had this grotesque image in her mind when she had returned to the house, hysterical after seeing what she thought was Jillian's deformed corpse in the shed. Once again she felt as though her body had turned to wax. Now she was dripping down into a small puddle between her quivering legs. Nurse Patio would scoop up the hardened material and mold her into candles to be burned at these culinary feasts she prepared for Harlan. He wouldn't even know that the tiny flames before him were consuming the flesh and blood of his sister.

She closed her eyes and then opened them as a way of erasing the bizarre imagining. She heard a thin, scraping sound against the window above the sink. It was almost as though someone had run her fingernails over the pane.

Nurse Patio looked first at the window and then turned sharply toward her, holding her body at an angle to block Colleen's view of the meat. Colleen gasped. The woman's face looked distorted; all her features were larger. Her beautiful, catlike eyes lost their slimness and were more like the bulging eyes of an enraged bull. Her widened nostrils complimented that image. Her lips turned rubbery and stretched into a mad smile.

Then, as suddenly as this distortion had occurred, it began to disappear. Her face softened and reformed, returning to the face of the dark, Indian-like beauty Colleen had first confronted. Even so, there was an ugly sneer at the corners of her mouth and around her eyes.

"Sneaking around the house?" she asked.

"I'm not sneaking," Colleen said. "I came down here to see you specifically."

"Oh? How can I help you?"

"You . . . you had no right to stop Teddy from coming in to see me. You had no right to tell him those lies."

"What lies?" She turned her body completely to her now, holding the bloodstained meat knife out. There was even some blood on her knuckles.

"You said I was too sick to see anyone," Colleen said, eyeing the blade.

"Well, weren't you? Your little religious friend had to leave because you were so upset," Nurse Patio said, still smiling. "I was only trying to do what was best for you."

"You had no right. You're not my nurse. You're Dana's. Don't you ever do anything like that again. Don't answer my phone or greet my friends," she added, building courage with every word. "I'm going to tell my brother what you did," she added.

Nurse Patio smiled. "Why, dear, he already knows," she said. "And he thought I did the right thing."

"You're lying."

"Ask him yourself, and after you do, you can apologize."

"I'll never apologize to you. I think you're doing terrible things here!"

"Now don't get yourself all excited again, Colleen. If there's one thing your brother and his wife don't need, it's an hysterical teenager on their hands these days." Her smile evaporated and she took a few steps forward, still holding the knife straight out. "If you do have another emotional break-down, I'm going to have to recommend to Harlan that he send you someplace else for a while . . . at least until Dana gets strong enough to deal with someone like you. Do you understand?"

Nurse Patio's face began to revert to the state it had been in when Colleen had first entered the kitchen. Colleen stepped back. It seemed to take all her effort and strength to move her feet. For a moment she thought they really had been glued to the floor. She was tempted to look down to see if there was any evidence she had stepped in some sticky substance. Her heart was beating so fast, she thought she might pass out. Her head was getting very light.

"I don't know who you are, but you're evil. You're evil," she repeated, and turned to run off. Nurse Patio's laughter followed her to the stairway. She paused at the base of it to catch her breath and then went up to her room.

For the first time since she had moved in with her brother and her sister-in-law, Colleen Hamilton locked her bedroom door.

The first thing Colleen realized when she opened her eyes in the morning was that Audra's mother hadn't called. She didn't think the woman would forget to, and she was certain that if

Audra had returned and learned about all that had occurred, she would have called herself to apologize for worrying everyone. Something was seriously wrong.

She sat up, debating what to do. She knew that Audra's mother was probably hovering over the telephone, and that its ringing would jab pins and needles into her heart, but she couldn't contain her own concern and curiosity. Besides, maybe there was something else she could do for Lucy Carson, she thought, and with that as a rationalization she dialed. As she expected, Audra's mother lifted the receiver after the first ring.

"It's Colleen," she said after the woman's tiny hello. "What's happening, Mrs. Carson?"

"Oh, Colleen. I've heard nothing. I've been up all night. I keep calling the police but they haven't been able to find her. Something's happened to her, something terrible," she said, and started to cry. For a moment Colleen couldn't speak. Then the right words came.

"Hold yourself together, Mrs. Carson. Audra's going to need you when we find out what's happening. You've got to be strong."

"Yes, yes."

"Do you want me to come over?"

"Oh, dear. No," she said after a moment. "You go to school. I'll be fine."

"Are you sure? Is there anything you need?"

"No, dear, thank you so much."

"I'll come over as soon as I can, Mrs. Carson."

"That's very nice of you, Colleen. You're a good friend, a true friend. Audra's only friend," she added, and Colleen was unable to speak. She nodded and squeezed out a good-bye before hanging up. For a while she just sat there. Then she decided to get up and get dressed. She would go to school. Sulking and moping about the house would do no good. She had to get herself together again; she had to become active and strong, for she sensed she was involved in some kind of a battle, even though she was uncertain as to who the actual antagonists were.

Nurse Patio was one; that was for sure, she thought. She was surprised to see her bedroom door still closed. She had imagined the woman would be downstairs preparing Harlan's breakfast, continuing to develop her influence over him. She was shocked to find Harlan asleep on the couch in the living room. He was still in his pajamas. Confused, she went to the kitchen and put up some coffee. When she returned to the living room, Harlan was stirring.

"What happened, Harlan? Why are you sleeping down here?"

"Oh. What time is it?" he said, rubbing his face.

"A little after seven."

He nodded and sat up, shaking his head to loosen the hold fatigue had on him. His eyes were bloodshot. He looked up at Colleen, who stood staring at him.

"Bad night," he said. "Terrible night."

"What happened?"

"Dana tossed and turned and moaned something terrible. I thought she was in some kind of pain. I called in Nurse Patio, and she gave Dana some warm milk and asked that I sleep downstairs so Dana could be more comfortable. I wasn't getting any sleep, anyway, so I did what she said. It must have been about four in the morning before I finally came down here."

"What's wrong with her?"

"Nurse Patio thinks she might have to stop breast-feeding and take some sedatives. She's bringing her to see the doctor today, and he'll decide. All of it . . . the death of the baby, the pressure of taking care of Nikos, the situation with Jillian, and . . ." He hesitated.

"And me," Colleen said.

"Whatever. All of it has been too much. She's a nervous wreck. I don't know," he said, shaking his head. "I don't know."

Her brother looked very small and weak to her. She realized why he had always avoided personal conflict and controversy. He simply didn't have the strength to stand up to them. Right now he looked overwhelmed, beaten down. She felt sorry for him, but she was also disappointed. If at any time in her life she needed someone with strength, she thought, it was now.

"Audra wasn't found last night," she said. "I called her mother. There's no trace of her."

"My God. That poor kid." He shook his head. It seemed to be the only action he could take.

"I decided to go to school," Colleen said with determination. "I've got to get back into the swing of things."

"Good idea," he said.

"I put up coffee."

"Great. I'll take a quick shower and get dressed. This all has to happen the night before my biggest day of the week, the day I have most classes."

She nodded, but she was losing her sympathy for him. He shouldn't be feeling so sorry for himself, she thought. Not with all the problems other people around him were having. And by now he should have realized how terrible Nurse Patio was instead of placing even more faith in her and becoming more dependent upon her.

By the time he came down, she had finished her breakfast and gotten her things together.

"Everyone's dead to the world up there," he said, and poured himself some coffee.

"Did you know," Colleen said before leaving the kitchen, "that she turned Teddy away last night? Told him I wasn't well enough to see him?"

"You weren't feeling well. Audra had to leave," he said.

"She had no right to do that, Harlan. And you had no right to let her. You and Dana have become more like her prisoners in this place, and now she's trying to do it to me."

"Colleen," he said with a sigh, "really . . ."

"Forget it," she said, and rushed away from him. She went out the front door, got into her car, and backed out of the driveway, but about a block down the avenue she stopped because she saw a patrol car parked in front of the Jensens' house. Thinking about Audra, she got out to see what she could learn. She found both Mr. and Mrs. Jensen standing by the side of their house, talking to a patrolman. Everyone turned to her as she approached.

"What's wrong?" she asked.

"My Lollypop," Mrs. Jensen said.

"What?" Colleen asked. She looked at Mr. Jensen, who smirked. Colleen had never been very fond of the man. He was always quite surly, even reluctant to wave hello or acknowledge Harlan and Dana.

"Our dog," he said. "One of our friendly neighbors," he added, and smirked.

"I don't understand," she said, looking to the policeman.

"Their dog's dead. Its neck's been broken."

"Oh, my God. I'm sorry."

"It happened last night," Mrs. Jensen said. "But I didn't realize it until I went out to feed her. And we had just tied her up, too, after what had happened at your brother's house," she said. Her eyes grew small, as though she had just concluded that Harlan had taken revenge for the dogs digging up some of his lawn.

"I can't imagine anyone on this street doing this," Colleen said, but she was impatient with the problem of a dead dog when there were bigger problems. "Do you know anything about my friend?" she asked the patrolman. "Audra Carson?"

"The missing girl? No, nothing yet. You have any information that might help?"

"No. She had been visiting me," Colleen said with disappointment.

"Missing girl?" Mrs. Jensen said. "Oh, dear. What a night. My poor Lollypop," she repeated. Colleen turned away and hurried back to her car so she could continue on to school.

Ever since she had begun a romance with Teddy, he met her at her locker in the morning, just before homeroom. That morning he wasn't there. She saw him down by the auditorium, surrounded by other students—mostly girls—who were reviewing the championship game. When he started away from the auditorium, they moved along and behind him as if they were attached. She saw that he had seen her, but she slammed her locker shut and walked off to homeroom.

He didn't catch up to her until the bell rang for the first period, and even then he was followed by what was rapidly becoming his entourage of adoring fans.

"Calm down some?" he asked her.

"For your information," she said, spinning around abruptly, "Audra is still missing. The police have been unable to find any trace of her."

"No kidding." He turned around to see if any of the other students had heard what she'd said.

"A dog was killed on my street," she added. Even though she didn't see how it related to the situation with Audra, she wanted to impress him with the events. "The Jensens' dog. Someone broke its neck."

"Jesus."

"But I suppose all this is my imagination," she said, and started for her first-period class.

"Hey, wait a minute." He reached out to seize her by the elbow, but she didn't stop walking. "Why are you so angry at me?"

She stopped and looked at him. The students who had been with him caught up.

"When we can have a word in private, without your fan club, I'll tell you," she said, and continued on. She heard the comments and whistles. "What's got into her? Her time of the month, Ted? She wants you all to herself, Ted." There was some laughter, so she walked even faster.

They didn't meet again until lunch period. This time he came up behind her, scooped her arm into his firmly, and directed her toward the east exit.

"We've got to talk," he said. "In private."

"Sure you have the time?" She let him lead her into the parking lot. They got into his car.

"Now, what's going on?" he asked.

"I'm just tired of everyone thinking I'm the bad one, the crazy one."

"I don't think that," he protested. "You're just so intense about everything lately. I don't know what's happened with you anymore. It's not all my fault. You've got to admit that I'm not exaggerating. You ended up in the hospital, didn't you?"

"Thanks, Ted."

"Well? Didn't you?" he persisted. She looked down at her hands in her lap.

"Things are bad at my house. Even this horrible nurse has finally come to the conclusion that Dana might have to stop breast-feeding. She's very ill, mentally and physically. My brother's beside himself. I don't even recognize him anymore. Now this terrible thing with Audra." She turned away from him and pressed the side of her face against the window as she gazed out at the parking lot. "Just when I need someone to be strong and be with me, you're wrapped up in your glory days. You're just like everyone else in my life right now, self-centered," she said.

"Now hold on," he began.

She held back the tears, opened the door, and got out of the car. Before she was halfway back, he stopped her.

"Listen to me. Listen, will you?" he said, turning her toward him roughly. "All right. You're right. I've been distracted by all this," he said, waving his hands, "but for God's sake, Colleen, we won the championship yesterday and I led the team to that victory. It's only normal . . ." He looked away. "I admit I've been impatient with you and I'm sorry."

She looked at him and then nodded.

"You're right. It's not all your fault. I'm uptight. I know it. I just don't know what to do. I know something's happening to my brother and my sister-in-law. There is something peculiar about the baby. And I know something happened to Jillian. No matter what they say," she added quickly. "Now, with Audra missing . . . don't you see . . . it's not all my imagination."

"Well, what do you think it is?" he asked, impressed with what she was saying.

"I don't know, but I'm going to find out."

"What are you going to do?"

She thought for a moment. "I'm going to try to find out more about the baby, about the family that gave it to Harlan and Dana."

"What good is that going to do?"

"I don't know right now," she said, "but I've got to do something, learn something that will make Harlan come to his senses before it's too late for everyone."

"All right," he said. "I'll help you." He put his arm around her. "I care too much about you to see you so damn upset all the time."

"Thanks, Ted."

He kissed her, and then they heard her name called. When they looked toward the exit, they saw Mr. Stevens, the principal, beckoning.

"There's a detective in my office," he said when they approached, "who wants to talk to you about Audra Carson."

"Oh, no," Colleen said. "Has something happened to her?"

"Just come along," Mr. Stevens said. He looked at Ted. "Alone," he added.

Lieutenant Reis stood up as soon as Colleen entered the office. Mr. Stevens, obviously following some prearranged plan, nodded at the detective and then stepped back out of his own office, closing the door so Colleen would be alone with the policeman.

"Colleen, hi," he said, and introduced himself. "Please sit down." He indicated the chair across from his. "I didn't meet you, but I met your brother the other day."

"Oh," she said. "You're the one who found the mop and jacket?" He nodded. "So you think I'm unstable."

"No, I don't. Fortunately, what you thought you saw, you didn't. But I'll tell you," he said, shaking his head and smiling, "for a normally quiet, residential street, your street has become a little wild. There was a dog brutally killed there last night."

"I know. I stopped at the Jensens' on the way to school."

"And now Audra Carson left your house last night and never made it home. What can you tell me about that?" he asked, sitting back.

She shrugged. "Nothing more than I told her mother. She didn't stay at my house long. My brother and . . . and Nurse Patio, can tell you that," she said, smirking.

"Nurse?"

"Helping with my sister-in-law."

"Oh. And Audra didn't say anything about going anywhere but home, is that it?"

"Uh-huh."

"If you know where she might be and you keep it from us, it would be a crime at this point," he said, tilting his chin toward his chest.

"I can't believe you said that," she said. She shook her head. "Don't you know how bad I feel about this, especially for her mother? Jesus." She looked away.

"That's okay. I'm glad you're angry. That proves to me that you're sincere. But other teenagers have been known to cover for one another, Colleen. Did Audra have a fight with her mother? Did something happen between them that would cause her to run away?"

"Absolutely not. No mother and daughter could be closer."

"What about a boyfriend? Is Audra in some kind of trouble?"

"You mean, is she pregnant?" Reis started to nod. Colleen smiled and shook her head. "Nothing could be further from the truth. She and her mother are very religious people."

"Religious girls get in trouble, too, Colleen."

"Not Audra, not like that."

He stared at her a moment and then nodded.

"Okay. Is there anything you can tell me that might help?"

She looked at him a moment. Should she start? she wondered. Should she tell him how Harlan had changed, how Dana was getting sicker and sicker, how the baby was strange? Should she tell him about the bloodstain that had disappeared from the sheet? Where would she begin? What would he believe, especially after the shed incident? How did any of it relate to Audra, anyway?

She shook her head.

"Any ideas, theories?"

"I'm just afraid she took a ride with someone."

"Someone she knew?"

"It wouldn't matter. Not to Audra. She'd trust the creatures from *Aliens*."

"Who?"

"Anybody. She's that way," Colleen said. "That's what I'm trying to tell you. She has faith in everything and everyone. She cares too much for her mother to do anything like this to her. Something's happened. Something terrible has happened!" she said emphatically but immediately realized that Lieutenant Reis was afraid she would get too emotional and suffer another breakdown. He nodded and stood up, anxious to end the interview.

"Okay. If something should come up . . ."

"I wouldn't wait a second to call you."

"Good." He handed her his card. "Anytime," he said.

Ted was waiting for her. She told him what had happened and then they went to their afternoon classes. They decided he would come to her house about an hour after school so he could see the way things were. First she was going to pay a visit to Audra's mother and try to comfort her.

She got home just minutes before Ted arrived. She found it dark and quiet, but she didn't open a curtain or raise a shade. When Ted entered, it was the first thing she pointed out to him.

"It's the way she keeps the house now . . . like a morgue," she said. He looked around and nodded.

"Where is everyone?"

"Asleep, I guess. All the bedroom doors are closed."

"What are you going to do now?"

"I've been thinking about it. Let's go to my brother's den," she said. "He won't be home until much later today."

"What for?"

"I want you to stand guard at the door while I look for something," she said. He followed her through the house and watched as she rifled through the drawers and files in Harlan's den.

"What are you looking for?" he whispered.

"Papers," she said. "Adoption papers." About ten minutes later she found something. "It's from the lawyer," she said. "At least it's a start. The family name is left off," she said, reading down the document, "but I recall Harlan telling me the name. I'm going to call the lawyer's office and see if I can get him or his secretary to give me their address."

"Will they do that?"

"Maybe. They don't have to know why I'm looking for them. I'll tell them . . ." She paused and looked at him. "What will I tell them? Any ideas?"

"You have something that belongs to them . . . an inheritance."

"Why not?" she said. "Thanks. Knew you were good for something more than passing a pigskin."

"Thanks a lot," he said.

He watched her dial the number. She listened, and then after a moment she hung up the phone. "So?"

"The phone's no longer in service. And there's no alternate number."

"A lawyer? Never heard of them going out of business," Teddy said.

She looked at the paper. "It's in Kerhonkson. Let's go there. It's only twenty-five miles."

"Really?"

Colleen didn't reply. She was already charging through the house. "I guess really," Teddy mumbled, shook his head, and hurried to catch up with her.

✤ 14

Colleen and Teddy sat in his car and stared at the charred, boarded-up building before them. It was obvious that it had been the scene of a serious fire some time ago, a fire that had gutted it badly. The entire right side of the building had fallen in, and part of the roof had collapsed.

"You're sure this is the address?" Teddy asked. Colleen looked at the paper and then leaned over to show it to him. He read it and shook his head. They were on a side street just outside the village of Kerhonkson proper. They were definitely at the address printed on the stationery. "Makes no sense," he said, returning the document to her.

"Drive back into the village," she said. When they got there, she told him to pull up to the drugstore. "I'll be right out." After a little more than five minutes she emerged from the store, looking dazed or in deep thought.

"What did you find out?" Teddy asked after she got in.

"The building burned last year. There's been no lawyer's office in it, not even before it burned. It housed a hardware store and two apartments above."

"So maybe the address is just printed incorrectly on the stationery," Teddy said. Colleen shook her head. "Why not?"

"The druggist, Sam Cohen, owns this store and has lived here all his life. He never heard of this lawyer. Then he did something we should have done back home. He took out the phone book, turned to the Yellow Pages, and we looked down the list of attorneys. He's not there," she said.

"What the hell . . ."

"Let's go home. Quickly," she said.

When they finally pulled back into her driveway, they saw they were right behind Harlan, who had obviously just this minute returned from work. Colleen considered it the first piece of good luck she had had in a long time, for she would be able to speak to him without the possibility of Nurse Patio or Dana overhearing.

"See how wild he looks?" Colleen said to Teddy as Harlan approached. It was as if he had ridden with his head out the window. The red blotches on his forehead and cheeks made his face seem chapped. Strands of hair fell randomly around his forehead and temples.

"Hey, champ," Harlan said, extending his hand. "Congratulations again. Heard all about the game."

"Thanks, Harlan."

"Harlan," Colleen said, "we've got to talk to you before you go into the house."

"Oh?" He looked at the house. "Something happen to Dana?"

"No, no," Colleen said. "But, Harlan, something's not right about all of this. I always felt it, and you know how I feel about Nurse Patio—"

"Now, Colleen, don't start with that again," Harlan said, eyeing Teddy.

"Just wait. Listen." She got out of the car and came around to him. Teddy remained seated behind the steering wheel.

"What is all this?" Harlan demanded. He took a step back, as though afraid to come into any contact with her.

"I did something that might upset you, Harlan, but I did it because I was convinced something wasn't right, and now . . ." She looked at Teddy. "Now I'm sure something's not right."

"What is it this time, Colleen?" Harlan asked. He leaned over, as though his briefcase had suddenly gained enormous weight.

"I went into your den and found the lawyer's papers."

"What lawyer's papers?"

"Concerning the adoption," she said.

"You did what?" He straightened up. "What?"

"Just listen for a moment."

"But why? Why did you do that?"

"I wanted to learn what I could about Nikos's family."

"For what reason? I don't understand," he said, turning from her to Teddy. He looked quickly at the house and stepped farther back, as if to be sure to keep out of hearing range of anyone inside.

"I . . ." She hesitated. She didn't want to get into her feelings about the baby with Harlan—not just yet. "I think something strange is going on, and I just wanted to find out more about them. Anyway, we tried to call the lawyer, only that number is not in service. So we drove out to Kerhonkson to his office."

"You did what?" He looked at Teddy. "You too?" Ted looked down.

"But there wasn't any office, Harlan. The lawyer's address doesn't exist. Never did. It's a burned-out building that had been a hardware store. And what's more," she said quickly, "the druggist, a man who has been there all his life, never heard of a lawyer named Garson Lawrence. He's not even listed in the Yellow Pages under attorneys!"

For a long moment Harlan said nothing. The muscles in his face twitched. He sucked in his lips and looked toward the house, an expression of utter terror forming on his face, which reddened even more, his cheeks swelling as he took in a deep breath.

"My God! Don't you realize what you could have done! Don't you understand anything? So the lawyer used a false name and false address . . . that was to protect the people . . . to keep the adoption secret . . . to protect their identity and the identity of everyone involved. You've endangered the adoption. If Dana should find this out . . ." He turned to Teddy. "How could you go along with this?"

"I'm sorry, Harlan. I mean . . ." He looked to Colleen.

"Harlan, I don't understand. This isn't right. Why would a lawyer—"

"You have no right to poke your nose into this. You have no right! Where is that paper?"

She held it out and he snatched it from her hands.

"Don't ever do anything like this again . . . ever," he said. He looked at Teddy. "I'm disappointed in both of you," he added, and rushed toward the house, folding the paper quickly and stuffing it in his briefcase as he hurried along.

Colleen said nothing. The tears streamed down her face.

"Jesus," Teddy said. He started his car. "I'd better get the hell home."

"Teddy, he's irrational," she said. "You can see that. You

don't believe that whole thing about hiding names and identities, do you?"

"I've heard that families who give up babies do want to keep it secret, Colleen. That isn't unusual. Better let things calm down," he said. "I'll call you later, huh?"

She didn't reply. He backed out of the driveway, leaving her standing there staring at the house. After a moment she lowered her head and started for the front entrance. Before she reached it, Harlan came out, closing the door softly behind him. She looked into his face. It appeared as though he had gone completely insane. He worked his mouth in and out and pulled his eyelids up with such intensity, she thought his eyes might pop out.

"Harlan—"

He raised his right hand like a traffic cop.

"Don't say . . . anything else about this. Not in there," he added. She saw there was no point in arguing, so she nodded quickly, hoping to calm him. He did relax his shoulders. "Nurse Patio just told me Jillian called," he said. "She's sorry about the way she left the house, and she's coming back tomorrow night. I'm to set up the foldaway bed for Nurse Patio in the baby's room," he added.

She looked up quickly. Her heart began to pound, and she pulled back the corners of her mouth in a grimace of terror, her eyes wide and looking as wild as his. They truly looked like brother and sister, siblings reared in a house of horror.

"What?"

"So, you see," he said, "this confirms it. Everything is just your imagination. For a while there you even had me imagining things," he added. "Now put it to a stop," he said, waving his right forefinger at her. "You hear me? Just stop!" He turned and went back into the house, softly closing the door behind him.

When she reached out to open the door, she found her hand shaking so badly, she couldn't close her fingers around the knob. It took both her hands to turn it. Then she caught her breath and entered the house.

She paused in the entryway. Nothing she could think of at that moment was more terrifying to her than looking into Jillian's face after what she had thought she had seen in the shed.

* * *

Dinner was to be served later that evening because Nurse Patio was taking Dana to see Dr. Claret. Colleen was surprised to learn that Harlan wasn't going along. He said Dana had asked him not to, claiming he made her too nervous. He laughed about it, but it was a strange laugh, the laugh of someone on the verge of a breakdown himself. Colleen didn't question anything. She set the table and then went up to her room to wait.

She heard Nurse Patio and Dana get the baby, and she listened at her door as she talked to Dana about the visit to Dr. Claret, stressing how much he wanted to see her and how important it was that they go quickly. Although Colleen didn't hear Dana's replies, she had the sense that Nurse Patio was convincing Dana, that Dana had offered some resistance. It was confusing, especially in light of the way Dana had reacted to this physician before.

"Maybe Harlan should come too," she heard Dana say as they walked by Colleen's door.

"Oh, no," Nurse Patio replied.

"I'm afraid," Dana said, and they started down the stairs.

Why was she so afraid suddenly? Colleen wondered. She thought about it a moment and then made a quick decision: She would follow them. The phone rang just as she started out her bedroom door.

"How are things now?" Teddy asked.

"I can't talk. I'm going to follow Dana and Nurse Patio to the doctor's office."

"What? Why?"

"I can't explain. I'll call you later."

"Colleen, no—"

Before he could say anything else, she hung up and hurried out of her room and down the stairs. Harlan was in the kitchen seeing to some of the cooking duties Nurse Patio had assigned him. She opened the front door softly and slipped out just as Nurse Patio and Dana pulled away from the house. Then she hurried to her own car. She got in but didn't start it or turn on her headlights until Dana and Nurse Patio had turned off Highland Avenue. Watching suspense stories on television had taught her that much, she thought.

She turned on the headlights when she reached the main

street and then followed Dana and Nurse Patio as they headed
for the outskirts of Old Centerville Station. She had no idea
where they were heading, but she thought it was odd that they
turned down Church Road. The secondary road went on for
miles before it reached a major highway and took travelers
either to the city of Middletown or the bigger villages of
Monticello and Liberty. There were so many shorter, easier
routes to these places. And why would a doctor have an office
out here? she wondered.

Her question was answered nearly ten minutes later when
they turned up a hard-packed dirt driveway and headed toward
a farmhouse a good thousand yards off the road. Before she
turned in to follow them, she switched off her lights again and,
using only the illumination of the moonlight, drove her car
very slowly over the driveway, her tires crunching over the
stones and sand. She saw the back lights of Dana's car go off
as it pulled up to the house, so she stopped and waited until she
heard the car doors close. Then she went a little farther, until
she found what looked to be a safe clearing off the driveway.
She parked her car there and went the rest of the way on foot.

The Indian summer days that they had been enjoying meant
unusually warm afternoons and crisp, clear evenings. Tonight
the moon looked enormous to Colleen, and she was grateful for
the bright illumination. Out at a place like this, so far from
town, an overcast or even a partly cloudy evening would make
it impossible to move around without a flashlight. The gravel
driveway was narrow and full of dips and holes. At some
places along the way the vegetation had been permitted to grow
unchecked along the sides of the drive. Long, thin, spidery
branches from bushes and small trees reached over the road.

In fact, the closer Colleen drew to the farmhouse, the more
she was impressed with the lack of maintenance. The fields
were overgrown, the fences broken. Even the grass right in
front of the farmhouse hadn't been mowed for some time.
There were pieces of disabled and rusting farm machinery
visible here and there. They looked like the corpses of
nocturnal creatures left to rot in the dark. Disuse left a tractor
forever precariously tipped. A long, flat wagon, its wheels
removed or broken, lay on its side.

Walking alone in the darkness made her more cognizant of

the stillness. Before this, she had been oblivious to the way the end of one season and the beginning of another had drawn down the curtain on many sounds in the night. The evening was no longer filled with thousands of insects going through their ritual symphonies. Peepers had metamorphosed. Birds were either asleep or on their way south. This far from the village, even the occasional car horn was muffled.

The silence made her even more aware of her own footsteps and heavy breathing. Every sound she made was amplified. She was sure she was being so loud, she would signal her arrival to the inhabitants of the old farmhouse, so she crouched down and practically tiptoed the remaining distance.

It had been difficult, if not impossible, to see just how run-down the building was. This was one of those early twentieth-century structures characteristic of this part of the Catskills. Like so many others, obviously it had begun as a small home and then been expanded as the family took in boarders to complement their meager farm income. Now the expanded, long front porch dipped. Some floorboards had popped up, and the railings were cracked and broken in spots. A second-story window shutter on the west side of the building dangled dangerously. Even in the darkness Colleen could see where the siding had peeled, where boards hung loose.

The house had a fieldstone foundation and there were two windows on each side, both now boarded up. She had been in the basements of old houses like this one before, so she knew it probably had a hard dirt floor. Although the house most assuredly had indoor plumbing, she saw an outhouse behind the building, adding more evidence to support the theory that the home's beginnings dated some time back.

But who would live in a place like this now? How could a doctor live there and have an office there? she wondered. It made no sense, but more importantly, it added to her anxiety. Perhaps she should turn right around and see if she could get Harlan to come up here, she thought. Then she realized he would simply rant and rave about her interfering again and poking her nose about where it didn't belong. Whatever she had to do, she had to do herself.

She started toward the lit windows at the west side of the house, moving through the tall grass quickly but carefully.

She didn't want to trip over anything and signal her arrival to the inhabitants.

There were no shades or curtains over the windows. In fact, she saw where two windows in the dark portion at the rear of the house were broken. Avoiding the pool of pale yellow light that spilled from the lit windows, she wove her way through the pockets of darkness around the house until she was against the side of the building. Then she inched toward the window until she was able to see in.

At first, because of the angle at which she was able to look in, she saw no one. She realized she was looking into a living room. There was a brick fireplace directly across from the window, but it looked as though it hadn't been used for years. The screen had fallen into it and looked rusted and torn. The floor of the room was covered with a thin, very faded brown carpet, and the walls were papered with a scarred, beige-and-blue flower pattern. There was a bookcase against the far wall, but there were no books in it, nor were there any artifacts or knickknacks. She saw one high-backed, deep brown, cushioned chair in the corner.

She squatted, moved under the window to the other side, and peered in again. Nothing she had imagined, nothing she had sensed, not even the horror she thought she had seen in the shed prepared her for this. She felt as though she had just fallen into a pool of ice water. The blood hardened in her veins. Every joint froze. A scream originated in the very essence of her being and grew louder and louder as it struggled toward her lips. Even her thoughts seemed trapped. It was as if her brain protectively folded into itself in her skull, denying and refusing to accept what her eyes reported.

Naked from the waist up, Dana sat on the long, heavy-looking, old gray couch. Her arms, extended, lay atop the couch. Her head was back, her eyes wide open as she stared up at the ceiling. She was the center of some grotesque ritual.

Nurse Patio squatted in front of Dana and held the baby by its waist as it suckled at Dana's right breast. The baby seemed to be growing as it did so. It was twice as long, twice as wide and twice as heavy as Colleen remembered him to be.

As strange and terrifying as this scene was, it was not half as horrible as what went on around it. Standing behind the couch and to her right was a dark-skinned black-haired man who held

Dana's right wrist down against the couch with both his hands, the fingers of which were long and thin, with nails that extended for inches. They looked more like claws. His eyes were a luminescent red. As he stared down at the baby nursing, his mouth writhed into a smile that looked more like a snarl.

And from out of his mouth loomed two long, narrow teeth that came to a sharp point.

Across from him, on the other end of the couch and behind Dana, was a woman, as dark and as tall as he was. Her long black hair fell loosely about her shoulders. She, too, had red luminescent eyes. Out of her mouth emerged the same threateningly sharp fangs as she pulled her lips back into a similar smile. She held Dana's left wrist down against the couch.

Sitting just to the right, calmly observing, a more gentle smile on his face, was a distinguished-looking elderly man who fit the description of Dr. Claret. He was dressed in a suit and tie and sat back in the dark gray easy chair.

Colleen finally found strength enough to pull herself back from the window. The numbing cold that had come over her body was quickly replaced by a terrific heat. It was as though her blood had defrosted instantly, but as it began to flow through her veins freely again, it caused a painful burning sensation. She embraced herself and moaned. Instantly she covered her mouth. She felt like two people, one controlling the other. If there was one thing she didn't want to do, it was to alert those creatures within to her presence.

The realization of what she had seen was so overwhelming that she had to question the truth of it herself. She had to look in one more time and confirm that this was just not another one of her illusions, the product of a distorted imagination. This was indeed reality.

When she looked in again, she saw that Nurse Patio had pulled the baby back from Dana's breast. A thin trickle of blood ran from the nipple. The baby began to wail. Everyone laughed, the laughter of the man and the woman so deep and reverberating, it made Colleen tremble. Nurse Patio brought the baby back to Dana's breast.

Colleen turned away and took a few steps back this time. It was all coming to her now, all of it making some sense. She really had seen a drop of blood on Nikos's lips that day. There definitely had been a bloodstain on the sheet, and when she had put her finger in the baby's mouth, it had drawn her blood because it wasn't human, at least not entirely so.

It was probably their baby, she thought, or maybe . . . maybe the offspring of the vampire man and Nurse Patio. That was why Nurse Patio had come to their house—to supervise the growing and feeding of her own horrible child, a blood child.

And this was why Dana was getting weaker and sicker every day. Gradually they were making her into one of them. Actually the baby was doing it. That's why it was taking longer. That was why she was so possessed by the child. It wouldn't be long before she would be dead, or, to be more accurate, one of the *undead.*

Instinctively Colleen reached down and pulled up the cross that Audra had given her, the one Nurse Patio made her keep under her clothing. If ever she needed the power of prayer, she thought, it was now. She held it in her hand and whispered.

"Oh, God," she said. "Please, God. Help me. Help me." As she spoke, she backed farther and farther away from the house. How was she going to convince Harlan of this? Would he come up here with her? Could she get him now? How much longer would they be there, anyway? How could she expect him to believe any of this if he didn't believe the simpler things?

She had to go somewhere else for help, maybe to Dr. Lisa, her psychologist, or maybe to Lieutenant Reis. Would either of them believe her? Teddy . . . Teddy would listen, she thought. She had to get to Teddy and get him to come back up here with her. Maybe together . . . sure, if she could get someone else to corroborate what was going on, everyone, including Harlan, would listen. Maybe there was still time to do something to stop all this. There had to be time; there had to be.

She turned to run back to her car but hesitated because she heard the definite sound of someone coming around the house. Her heart was beating so fast, she couldn't get her legs to move fast enough. She started to walk away, afraid to look back, but she sensed that whoever it was, was coming fast, almost flying.

She broke out into a trot and then into a sprint. Even in the bright moonlight it was hard to see exactly where she was going. She tripped over some discarded piece of equipment and went flying into the grass. The ground here was softer, wetter

She had difficulty getting back to her feet. The damp earth smelled sour. The wetness on her hands felt more like blood than water.

She was talking to herself now, chanting words of encouragement and comfort between prayers, promising herself it would be all right, fingering the cross as she did so. "Just get back to the car, lock the doors, and start it up. It's easy," she said. "Oh, God, please be with me. Please. Easy. Then you'll get help. Don't stop; don't look back. Get your breath. It'll be easy."

Whoever it was who had come after her went off to her right and passed her in the darkness. She didn't see anything, but she sensed it, sensed him or her moving by quickly, flying. She hoped that meant she hadn't been discovered.

Cheered by the possibility, she got into a smooth rhythm again and sprinted over the grass to the gravel road. Once there, she caught her breath and headed quickly for her car.

But just as she approached it, she saw that someone was waiting for her. The moonlight seemed to intensify, as if the moon itself moved to direct more of its illumination onto the creature. The darkness was peeled away, and Colleen stopped only a few feet from the car.

It was Jillian, dressed in the nightgown and robe she had been wearing the night of her disappearance. Of course, the moonlight changed the color and texture of her complexion, but she looked as young and alive as ever.

"Jillian?" Colleen said. "Oh, Jillian. Thank God. Did you find out about Dana too? Have you brought anyone with you? Harlan? The police?"

Jillian stepped forward and smiled, and when she did so, she pulled her lips back as far as those people in the old farmhouse had. And the same long, sharp teeth emerged.

Colleen screamed and grasped the silver cross around her neck as Jillian continued toward her. Jillian seized Colleen's hair to pull her forward. When Colleen raised both her hands to push her away, the silver cross glittered in the moonlight, and Jillian's grip softened. She put her right hand over her eyes and reached forward with her left to grab at the chain around Colleen's neck. Her prehensilelike fingers and long nails caught it and pulled at it. Instantly the heavy cross fell from Colleen's neck to the gravel road below.

Jillian reached forward once again to seize Colleen's hair, pulling her head and neck toward her. Colleen twisted away, but when she turned to run, Jillian caught some of her hair in her fist and pulled her back so hard, Colleen fell backward, hitting the gravel road hard. Jillian started tugging her to her feet.

Colleen saw the cross on the gravel. It seemed to capture the moonlight and call to her with its reflection. Eagerly she reached out for it, taking it in her hand. When Jillian knelt down to take a firmer hold on her, Colleen swung her fist around, the neck of the cross extended like a knife, and caught Jillian in the cheek.

Colleen was amazed at how the cross pierced Jillian's skin, which seemed as if it were paper. She felt it stop when it hit her jawbone. Then, as if it had control of itself, the cross continued to tear a long gash down through her cheek until it emerged.

Jillian screamed and fell back, covering her face with her hands. Colleen sat back on the gravel road and watched in amazement as Jillian's body began to shake. In moments it began to crumble. Because she was bathed in the moonlight, every aspect of Jillian's demise was visible to Colleen. She would wish later that it hadn't been.

Her skin, which looked as thin and as translucent as a thin lamp shade, fell into her body as if it were being consumed by a fire burning within. Her eyeballs rolled out, leaving two deep, dark caverns from which poured a greenish slime, running down and into her mouth. The skinless skeleton collapsed into itself as she silently fell into a heap of dust, now covered by the turquoise robe. In moments it was over, and once again all was deadly quiet.

Sobbing, embracing herself tightly, Colleen stood up and inched her way around the pile of bones and dust under the robe. She was afraid it might all take form again and become one of those horrid creatures. Had it really been Jillian, or had it assumed her form and image? That was definitely the robe she had worn, the robe she had seen dangling on the dried corpse in the shed.

She stuffed her hand into her mouth to keep herself from crying out and backed up to her car, afraid to take her eyes off the pile. When she felt her body against the car, she reached behind herself to take hold of the door handle. Once she grasped it, she turned quickly and got into the car, locking the doors immediately. She put the cross into her pocketbook.

For a moment she sat there, unable to take the correct action, unable to make her fingers turn the key in the ignition. Ahead of her, the farmhouse loomed as before, its few lit windows still lit. It remained just as desolate-looking. She neither saw nor heard anyone or anything moving around. Finally she turned the key and the car started. No longer caring about whom she would alert, she put on her headlights.

As soon as the light hit the turquoise robe covering the pile of dust and bones on the gravel road before her, she screamed. It seemed to her that it was indeed moving. She fumbled with the gearshift to get the car into reverse. Then she accelerated, but a little too hard and fast. The car jerked backward, the tires spitting up the gravel, and she flew across the driveway into a ditch on the other side. The rear tires dangled. No matter how hard she accelerated, they did not make contact with the ground. The car would not move.

"Oh, God, no," she cried. Her body shook uncontrollably. She had been sobbing ever since Jillian's decomposition, but she hadn't been aware of it. Positive now that she had made enough noise to make everyone aware of her presence, she stopped trying to get the car moving, turned off the ignition and lights, grabbed her pocketbook, and slipped out quickly. Without hesitation she started running down the gravel road toward the highway. She didn't look back once.

She tripped twice on the gravel driveway, each time catching herself before her face hit the ground, but the gravel tore into the palms of her hands and the resulting pain was excruciating. Gasping for breath, she stopped when she reached the main highway. It felt like little pins and needles were being pressed into her ribs. When she looked back up the driveway, she saw only darkness and heard nothing. The headlights of an oncoming automobile cheered her. She stepped farther into the road and waved, but the driver, either afraid of stopping for someone on such a deserted road or not seeing her altogether, drove right on by.

She moaned, looked back up the driveway once more, and then started to trot down the road in the direction of Old Centerville Station. Another car came by, and the driver did the same thing, even speeding up when she waved at the vehicle. Although the moonlight lit her way, she felt the darkness closing in around her, swallowing her up, digesting her into the horror of what had just happened.

She tried to run harder, faster, now driven by an overwhelming fear. She sensed that if she stopped, if she tried to rest, she might not start again. Every shadow in the road, every dark shape ahead, looked ominous. As she ran, she avoided looking back, terrified that if she did, she might see one of the creatures running right beside her, smiling, its teeth gleaming in the moonlight.

A closed service station appeared ahead. She vaguely recalled it and slowed down as she approached. Perhaps someone lived behind it or perhaps was still there. She ran right up to the office window and pressed her face against it, but all was dark within. She shook the door handle and called out. "Anyone here? Please! Anyone?"

There was no response. She looked back up Church Road toward the driveway that led to the horrid old house. As far as she could see, there seemed to be no one coming, but the shadows still looked very threatening. Frantic now, she prayed for another oncoming vehicle. She vowed she would throw herself in front of it to make it stop.

But none came.

After a moment she looked toward the other side of the service station and saw a pay phone. She charged forward like someone who had been lost on a desert and had just discovered water. When she reached the phone, she rifled through her pocketbook quickly, locating some change, but when she found it and lifted the receiver, she hesitated.

"Who should I call first?" she wondered aloud. "Harlan? Maybe they have control over him already. Maybe . . ."

She thought again and searched through her pocketbook, holding some paper and cards up so she could read them in the moonlight. She found the one she wanted and dialed the number. A deep female voice answered.

"Police."

"I have to speak to Lieutenant Reis immediately," she said.

"Who's calling?"

"Colleen Hamilton. He'll know. Please, hurry. It's an emergency."

"One moment."

There was what seemed to be an interminable delay until Reis finally announced himself.

"It's Colleen," she said.

"Oh, Colleen. Sure. What have you got?"

"Do you know Church Road outside of Old Centerville Station?"

"Sure."

"I'm at a service station. It's closed."

"Shell?"

"Uh-huh."

"I know where it is. That's Carnesi's place. What about it?"

"Hurry here and you'll see," she said. "You'll see it all," she added. "But hurry."

"Exactly what—"

"Hurry," she said, and hung up before he could ask anything else. Then she leaned back and closed her eyes. Something startled her, and she opened them again, screaming as if she were being attacked. After a moment she stopped and looked around. There was nothing. The road was quiet and the garage just as still and deserted.

She found some more change and quickly dialed Teddy's number. When he answered, she just started to cry, mumbling his name between sobs.

"Where are you? What's happened now?"

She got hold of herself and told him where she was.

"My car is stuck in the driveway," she said.

"What driveway?"

"Come quickly. You'll see."

"Be right there," he told her. "Take it easy. I'm coming."

She hung up and just leaned against the wall of the phone booth and let herself slide down into a sitting position. Then she embraced her knees, pulling her legs against herself protectively, and leaned her face against her thighs. She closed her eyes, sobbed silently for a few moments, and then grew quiet.

She was unaware of any movement around her, so she didn't see or hear the bat slide through the night air. It landed on the garage rooftop and closed its wings around itself protectively.

Silhouetted against the fire-red and orange moon, it looked enormous. Moments later it was joined by a second, and then by a third. The nocturnal trinity hovered beside one another like pigeons preparing to swoop.

Colleen raised her head slowly. Sensing the danger, she fumbled through her pocketbook until she located Audra's cross. She held it up toward the moonlight, and it glittered brightly, holding back the darkness like a single candle. She gathered up all the faith within her and willed it down her arm and into the cross. It fed the gleam as she waited and waited and waited. . . .

✤ 15

Since he lived closer, Teddy was the first to arrive. He found her squatting by the phone, frozen in position, her arm extended as she held up the cross. She didn't appear even to have heard his car. As soon as he saw her, he got out and approached, calling to her; but she didn't turn to him. He had to squat down beside her and touch her shoulder to make her aware of his presence.

She screamed. Then, realizing it was Teddy, she embraced him, holding him as tightly to her as she could.

"Teddy, oh, Teddy. Teddy."

"Hey," he said, pulling back from her. "Easy, easy. What's going on? Where's your car?" he asked, looking around.

"It's back there. On the driveway. I got stuck."

"Driveway." He squinted at the darkness. "What driveway?"

"The one leading to the old farmhouse."

"Farmhouse?" He shrugged. "Well, where is it? Let's go see if I can get it out."

"No!" She pulled away from him and stood up.

"What? Why not?"

"Wait. Let's wait. Lieutenant Reis is coming. I called him before I called you. He should be here any moment."

"You called the police for a stuck car?"

"No. God, no. No." She put the cross back into her pocketbook.

"So?" he said, holding out his arms. "What's this all about?"

"Jillian is dead," she said. "I didn't imagine it. She was one of them. She tried to . . . tried to kill me too."

"Jillian? Dana's mother? She's dead but she tried to kill you? I don't understand. She's one of what?"

Before she replied, they both turned to see Lieutenant Reis

pull up beside Teddy's car. He got out slowly and flipped a cigarette across the road.

"What's going on? This have something to do with the missing girl?" he asked as he approached.

"I don't know," Colleen said.

"Huh?"

"It's my sister-in-law and her mother. Her mother's dead," she said. "I killed her with this." She pulled the cross out of her pocketbook. Lieutenant Reis looked at Teddy, but he shook his head.

"You killed her? What is this, your imagination running wild again?"

Colleen took a deep breath and started to explain. She began with what she overheard Dana say in the hallway as Nurse Patio was taking her to see Dr. Claret. When she finished describing Jillian's demise, Reis put his hands on his hips. He looked at Teddy and saw that even he wore an expression of amazement.

"Is this some kind of prank? A joke? Because if it is . . . if you two brought me out here to make a fool of me——"

"No, honest. Please, you've got to believe me. I'll take you back to the car and the . . . what remains of Jillian. Then we have to go up to the farmhouse and get my sister-in-law out of there before they . . ." She shook her head. "Maybe she's one of them already," she said.

"Vampires?" Lieutenant Reis said. "And a baby who sucks blood as well as mother's milk?"

"I saw it myself," she said. "I saw it. Please. Just go up there."

"What about you?" he asked Teddy. "You see this too?"

"No, sir. She followed them without me. I just got here."

"Uh-huh. Where's your brother? Does he know you're out here chasing vampires?"

"No. He doesn't understand any of this. I think they have him hypnotized or something."

"Hypnotized," Reis said dryly. He shook his head.

"If you'll just go up there with me, you'll see I'm telling the truth. There'll be no question about it this time. Please," Colleen pleaded. He studied her for a moment. "At least look at the body," she said.

"All right. Both of you get into my car," he said. He

watched them get in, looked around, shook his head, and then got in himself. They drove up to the gravel drive and pulled in, Colleen repeating her description of how carefully she had followed Dana and Nurse Patio. They quickly came upon her car in the ditch.

"See?" she said, as if that proved everything she had told them. Reis angled his vehicle so that the headlights swept back and exposed the back end of her car.

"Might need a tow truck for this," he said.

They all got out. Teddy went directly to her car. He stepped into the ditch and looked at the rear wheels.

"Maybe if we put our weight on the rear bumper, she'll make contact with the ground and pull forward," he said.

"Forget the car for a moment," Lieutenant Reis said. "I want to see this corpse." He turned around. Colleen lingered by his car. "Well?"

"It's right ahead, there on the road," she said, pointing. "Under the bathrobe."

"I see." He went to his car trunk and took out a large flashlight. The beam cut a narrow tunnel of light through the darkness as he started forward. Teddy joined him, and Colleen followed a good four or five feet behind. They walked on up the driveway and then stopped.

"So?" Reis said. Colleen came up beside him. "Farther up the road, I suppose?"

"It's got to be," she said.

"Uh-huh." He walked on. Teddy took her arm and they followed. After another dozen yards Reis stopped again. "You said it wasn't far from your car."

"I don't understand." She looked ahead at the farmhouse. It was completely dark. "They heard us coming," she whispered.

"Huh?"

Teddy squeezed her arm tighter, as if to get her to shut up, but she pulled away from him and went to Lieutenant Reis's side.

"They heard us coming, so they gathered up her body and took it someplace. Then they put out all the lights. Don't you see?"

Reis stared at her a moment, then directed the beam of light toward the old farmhouse. What he saw made him shake his head.

"Who the hell could live in there? That place looks like it's been deserted for years. Let's get out of here," he said, and started to turn away. She grabbed his arm.

"I'm telling you the truth! They have Dana in there. Please," she pleaded again. "Keep looking."

"Look, miss, I appreciate—"

"Wait," Teddy said suddenly. "Let me borrow that flashlight a minute."

Reis gave it to him, and he and Colleen watched Teddy go up the driveway another dozen yards or so. Then he beckoned to them.

"What?" Reis said, approaching.

"Look at this," Teddy said. "A definite set of tire tracks."

"So? She drove up here."

"But she said she pulled over into that clearing. Her tracks are there. These go on toward the house."

"Maybe she drove up there too. She's not rational. She doesn't know what she's saying anymore."

"You can check the tire size from this impression," Teddy said. "It doesn't look like her tires. They're wider than the ones on a Mustang."

"So even if someone else did drive up here, what does that prove? She might have followed a couple of passionate teenage lovers. Great place to park," Reis said. He leaned toward Teddy and lowered his voice. "She probably saw the boy kissing his girlfriend passionately on the neck, and the rest is a product of her wild imagination."

"I know, but shouldn't we search a little more?" Teddy asked.

"Look, do you see any cars up there?"

Teddy stared ahead and then shook his head.

"So?"

"Maybe they pulled it behind the house."

"Jesus," Reis said. He looked back at Colleen, who stood waiting and watching intently. "Do you believe that fantastic story?" Reis asked.

"I don't know what to believe," Teddy said. "I'm going to run up and take a quick look behind the house, okay?"

"I've got a better idea. Let's drive up there," Reis said. "Then we'll come back and see if we can give her car some traction and end this horror show."

"Okay," Teddy said.

After they all got back into his car, Teddy put his arm around Colleen. She leaned her head against his shoulder and they drove up to the old farmhouse. Teddy got out quickly and, taking the flashlight with him, went around to the rear of the house while Reis examined the front porch and door. Teddy returned a few moments later.

"Nothing," he said. "But there was a car parked here. See?" He directed the flashlight beam at the tire tracks.

"Lovers," Reis repeated. "No one has been living in this run-down place. That's for sure. Much less a doctor." He came off the porch.

"You're not going inside?" Colleen asked him.

"What's the point, Colleen? There's no one here. What we've got to do is get your car going, if we can, and get you home to get some rest."

"You think I made it up?" she said sadly.

"All I know is that there is no decomposed body on the road, there is no car, there are no people with long teeth . . . that's all I know," he said. "Get in," he commanded. They did. Then he drove back to Colleen's car. He and Ted got out and stood on the bumper, shaking the car up and down.

"Get in, Colleen," Teddy told her. "Start it up and put it in drive."

She did so, and when they jumped up and down, the tires got enough of a bite so she could drive the car back onto the road.

"Thanks a lot," Teddy told him.

"Listen," Lieutenant Reis said, seizing Teddy by the upper arm, "take my advice. Get your girlfriend home and keep her there, will you? She's got some serious problems. She should go back to see that psychologist up at the hospital."

"Okay," Teddy said softly.

"I'm going to have to call her brother and let him know about this," Reis said. Teddy nodded and then got into Colleen's car and rode with her back to the closed gas station. Reis pulled ahead of them and then went on down Church Road.

"Now everyone will be convinced I'm crazy," Colleen said. "And no one will help Dana."

"He's going to call Harlan and tell him about this."

"Oh, God." She thought for a moment. "Teddy, I'm not going home tonight."

"What do you mean?"

"I can't go back there, not tonight. I know what I saw, and I know what happened. I'm going to come back up here in the morning, when it'll be possible to see things clearly. I'll find some evidence. I will," she said with renewed determination.

"Jesus, Colleen." He shook his head. "I don't know if I can let you do that."

"What do you mean, let me? You have nothing to say about this, Teddy Becker. I don't care if you believe me or not."

"I didn't say I didn't believe you. You saw something there," he added.

"I saw exactly what I said I saw," she replied firmly.

"All right. Let's take it a step at a time. Where are you going to go tonight, if you don't go home?" he asked calmly. She thought a moment.

"I'll go to Audra's house and stay with her mother. Harlan will accept that. I want to, anyway. I should have stayed with her last night."

"I see. And then, in the morning, what will you do if you come up here and do find . . . something."

"I don't know. Teddy," she said, "if they are what I think they are, if they are vampires, then they won't be awake during the day. Yes," she said suddenly, full of realization. "That's why Dana and the baby slept so much during the day. Don't you see? That's why the baby was always up and alert at night."

"You know you're scaring me," Teddy said.

"But it makes sense." She got out of the car.

"Where are you going now?"

"To call Harlan from the pay phone before Lieutenant Reis calls him," she said. He got out and followed her, standing by her as she dialed and spoke.

"I'm eating with Mrs. Carson," she told him when he said Nurse Patio was serving supper shortly. "How long have Dana and Nurse Patio been back? . . . I see. How is Dana?" She listened for a few moments. "Maybe she should be in a hospital, Harlan. . . . I know. I know. Okay. I'll call you from school. . . . No, I have everything I need. Good night, Harlan." She slowly cradled the receiver.

"What is it?"

"They returned home, all right. Probably while I was down here waiting for you and Lieutenant Reis. Harlan says Dana is very tired and anemic, according to this Dr. Claret. She has to take high doses of iron and vitamins. He says she'll no longer be breast-feeding the baby."

"Really? How does that fit in with everything? I mean, if Nurse Patio and this doctor don't want her to breast-feed anymore, then—"

"It doesn't mean anything," she said quickly. "Harlan will never know when she does breast-feed. He believes everything Nurse Patio tells him."

"After Reis calls him, he'll call Mrs. Carson to speak to you and demand you go home."

"I know, but I won't go home. I don't want to be in the same house with Nurse Patio," she said, and shook herself to rid her body of the chill.

"You're determined to come up here again, huh?" Teddy said.

"Yes, Teddy. I have to. Don't you see? If I don't prove that I saw what I said I saw, it will all go on until Dana's dead and one of them."

"All right. I'll meet you here at the gas station at seven-thirty in the morning. My parents will think I'm going to school. I'll go through the place with you. But after that," he added quickly, "you've got to promise you'll stay away, that you'll go to school and then back home to be with your brother."

"I promise," Colleen said.

"Wait for me," he said. "I'll follow you to Audra's house just to be sure you're safe."

"Thank you, Teddy. I knew in the end you'd be with me."

"Yeah, we'll both share a cell in the loony bin." He kissed her quickly and went for his car.

As they pulled away the bats that had been resting atop the gas station's roof surged into the air, swooped down toward the road, and then flew off toward the old farmhouse. When they flicked their wings, it sounded like wooden matches being struck. In moments they were swallowed up by the cool shadows that embraced them.

And the silence they left in their wake was as cold and as empty as the silence between the stars.

Lucy Carson was grateful for Colleen's company, even though to her, Colleen appeared high-strung and tense. She assumed it was because of her concern about Audra. She wanted to give her something to eat, but Colleen refused. They sat in the living room and talked for over an hour.

"I haven't moved from this house," Lucy said. "I'm afraid to miss a phone call, either from the police or someone who knows something."

"I can understand," Colleen said. "Mrs. Carson, I'd like to stay with you tonight."

"Oh, you don't have to do that, Colleen. I'm sure your brother would rather you were home."

"No. No," she repeated more softly. "I want to be with you. At least one night. I want to do it for Audra. Please. I won't be any trouble."

"I know that, dear." Lucy Carson's eyes took on that childlike innocence again when she smiled. "It is very kind of you to think of someone else. Of course you can stay here. If you want, you can sleep in Audra's room."

"I'd like that," Colleen said.

"I already changed the bedding. I've been working around the house all day, sometimes doing the same things twice. Just to keep my mind off things," she explained. "Whenever that phone rings, it's like a small explosion. My heart jumps and I lose my breath. Most people who know us aren't calling. They realize I'm waiting anxiously.

"So," she added, taking a deep breath and pressing her palms together as if to follow what she had said with a prayer, "it gets dreadfully quiet in here."

"I don't mind it," Colleen said. She sat back on the couch and closed her eyes.

"You look very tired yourself, dear. Are you sure you're all right?"

"I'll be okay." Colleen stared at her for a moment. "Mrs. Carson," she said, "do you believe in the existence of evil creatures . . . things people think are imaginary or science fiction . . . horror creatures?"

"I believe in the existence of the devil," Lucy Carson said.

"And I believe he takes many different forms in his efforts to destroy our souls."

"Why does God let it happen?"

"He doesn't. We do," Lucy said softly.

Colleen sat up and leaned toward her. "What do you mean, 'we do'?"

"If we have faith in our hearts, true faith, then it can't happen. But," she added, shaking her head, "unfortunately, even if we have deep faith, we are vulnerable to evil if we don't remain vigilant. Audra is such a trusting soul. In a way that's my fault. I built such a tolerance into her. She believes anyone or anything has some good in it."

"But if we believe and we are vigilant, we can defeat these evil creatures, we can defeat the devil?"

"Most definitely," Lucy said, and smiled. Colleen nodded and then closed her eyes. She was very tired now. Her body felt as though it weighed twice as much. "I think I'll get ready for bed," she said.

"Of course. It's nice of you to have sat here this long and talked to me. I'll go up and turn down Audra's bed for you."

"Thank you," Colleen said. Just as she started to rise, the phone on the dark walnut table beside Lucy Carson rang and they looked at each other in anticipation. "It might be my brother," she said quickly.

Lucy Carson lifted the receiver, swallowed, said hello in her tiny, frightened voice, and then smiled.

"Yes, she's here, Mr. Hamilton. One moment." She handed Colleen the receiver. "I'll go up to turn down the bed," she repeated, and left Colleen alone in the room.

"Hello," Colleen said.

"What have you done, Colleen?" Harlan asked immediately. His voice sounded tired and thin. "What has come over you? I just finished talking to the police. I thought you were going to put all this to a stop. I thought you understood—"

"I know. I'll explain everything tomorrow."

"I want you home right now. Do you understand?"

"No, Harlan. There still hasn't been any trace of or information about Audra. I'm not going to leave Mrs. Carson. She needs someone here with her. I'll be all right. I won't go anywhere or talk to anyone tonight. As a matter of fact, I'm going to sleep in a few minutes."

"You followed them? That's what you told the police?" he asked incredulously.

She hesitated. There was no point in going over the story again, especially with him in this state of mind, she thought. She sensed that it would only enrage him further, and cause more problems. He might even come over to the Carson house and make a scene in front of Lucy.

"I don't want to talk about it now, Harlan. I'll talk about it tomorrow."

"You're damn right you will. And to that psychologist at the hospital. I'll make an appointment right after my first class in the morning."

"Make it for after school," she said, thinking ahead. "I've got to go to school. I can't miss any more work."

"What? You're going to school?"

"I'll come directly home, and you and I can see anyone you want," she added to appease him. He was silent a moment. "Okay?"

"Don't you dare go anywhere else but school, Colleen. And don't you dare tell anyone else these stories."

"Okay. And, Harlan . . . please, don't tell Nurse Patio where I am tonight if she should ask. Do that one thing."

"You're a sick girl, Colleen. I'm sorry to say it."

"Please don't," she repeated.

"You should come home," he said after a moment.

"I'm going to sleep right now," she said quickly. "Good night, Harlan." She hung up before he could reply.

"Everything's ready for you, dear," Lucy Carson said as she returned to the living room.

"Thank you."

"I'm going to sit up a while longer. I'll only lie awake in bed, anyway."

"Maybe I should stay with you," Colleen said. "I don't have to go to sleep."

"No, no. I'm just going to be a little while longer. Go on. We'll have a good breakfast. It's comforting just to know you're in the house, and especially in Audra's room. Thank you so much for being so thoughtful."

Colleen got up, and Lucy Carson kissed her on the cheek.

"Have a good night," she said. "God bless you."

"Good night," Colleen said, and went upstairs to Audra's room.

The Carson house was much smaller than her brother's. It was a Cape Cod style structure with a Queen Anne sloping roof and small eyebrow windows in the front, even though there was no attic, just a crawl space. Audra's room was at the front of the house, a room only half the size of Colleen's, but it was a clean, warm, comfortable room with light blue wallpaper, a light maplewood trundle bed, and matching dressers with a rectangular mirror over the smaller one. There was a portable stereo tape deck set in the left corner on the aqua-blue nylon carpet. Colleen recalled that Audra mainly had only religious tapes, what some called religious rock and roll.

As soon as she walked into Audra's room, she stopped and looked around sadly. There were so many reminders of her friend, of course, but the one that hurt the most was the picture she and Audra had taken with Teddy a month ago. Audra had it in a frame over her large dresser. The three of them were standing by Teddy's car. Audra looked so small and vulnerable in the picture. It was almost as if Colleen could have predicted then that something terrible would happen to her.

There was a large cross over Audra's bed, a Bible on the small night table, and some religious magazines in a rack beside the dresser. On the post at the head of the bed Audra had draped a half dozen different-sized crosses. Some were on silver chains, some on beaded ones. Colleen sighed and embraced herself. She could feel safe in a room like this, she thought.

She went to the bathroom, washed up, and returned to the room quickly. She saw that Lucy Carson was still downstairs. She felt sorry for her, but she was exhausted. She took off her clothing and slipped under the dark-blue comforter. She felt snug and secure, even though the horrible things she had seen kept returning. She fought back the persistent images, but what seemed to keep them firmly at bay was her taking the large silver cross out of her pocketbook and placing it beside her on the pillow.

She quickly fell asleep after that and didn't open her eyes until a loud scratching sound on the window woke her. She stirred and looked toward it. At first she thought it was a large bat, its wingspan the width of the glass pane, but then it changed before her eyes and she thought she saw Audra peering in at her.

She sat up and rubbed her eyes to rid herself of the illusion, but the face was still in the window. She heard Audra calling to her, begging her to open the window and let her in. Was she in a dream, or had she indeed awakened? she wondered. She couldn't think very well. She felt drawn to the window, drawn to open it.

Colleen turned and placed her feet on the floor and started to get out of the bed. The face changed back into the large bat's and then to Audra's. The mouth moved slowly, the words coming forth in a distorted, low tone but it was distinctly Audra's voice.

"Colleen . . . Colleen . . . let me in. Colleen . . . Colleen."

She stood up.

"Audra?"

"Colleen . . . let me in. I want to be home. I want to be with you. Please . . . open the window."

She started for the window but stopped. Something stronger drew her around. She looked down at the pillow and quickly reached for the cross. With it in her hand she turned back to the window; only now the face was gone, and so was the sound of Audra's voice.

Cross in hand, she went to the window and peered out at the night. The breeze nudged the branches of the trees. Their dry, orange-and-yellow leaves fell like tears into the shadows. Some floated farther and landed in the pools of white light created by the streetlights. She listened but heard nothing more.

Still feeling as though she were in a dream, she glided back to the bed and crawled under the comforter. She placed the cross beside her, and once more sleep came in gentle, welcome strokes. When the morning light woke her, she could barely remember getting up to approach the window during the night. What she did remember seemed too much like a dream to be taken seriously, anyway.

She didn't focus on it. She went to the bathroom and dressed quickly to have breakfast with Lucy Carson and meet Teddy at the gas station. Before she left Audra's room, she thought about the things Lucy had told her about battling the devil in all his forms.

Convinced now about the power of the cross, she put it back into her pocketbook and added a handful of the crosses Audra had draped over the bedpost. Then she hurried downstairs to begin what was going to be the most dangerous and important day of her life.

🔥 16

"**A**udra's been gone too long now," Mrs. Carson said the next morning after thanking Colleen for staying the night and keeping her company. "I'm prepared for the worst."

"Oh, we mustn't give up hope," Colleen had replied weakly. "Something happened, but maybe she's still all right."

Mrs. Carson had smiled, as if she were the one who had to humor Colleen.

"I'm praying for her soul," she'd said simply, then had closed the door softly. For a moment Colleen had been unable to walk away, so bathed in sorrow and pain was she. Her chest had ached so. She had wanted to go back into the house and embrace the woman, but she had to go on. It was time. Maybe somehow, some way, she would do something that would change the dismal prophecy both she and Lucy Carson had in their hearts.

As she drove to the gas station on Church Road to meet Teddy, she gradually replaced sorrow and pity with anger. If Lucy Carson was right, then the forces of good could win over the forces of evil. She had to have faith in goodness, of course, but she had to have faith in herself as well. All that had happened to make her doubt herself would be pushed aside. She had to prevail, and she was determined now to do so. In a strange way she had been hardened, scarred by the terror. She felt anointed, prepared for battle.

"Get in," Colleen said quickly when she arrived at the gas station to meet Teddy. He had been standing by his car, waiting. He looked hesitant, confused.

"Just leave your car where it is," Teddy said, "and we'll go in mine. I'd better do the driving this time," he added. She nodded. Teddy was impressed with her look of determination. Her eyes were clear, her gaze intent.

"I asked Steve Carnesi about that farmhouse," Teddy said as he walked with her to his car.

"And?"

"The family that had owned it lost it in a tax auction about six months ago. Someone else bought it."

"Who?" she asked.

"Well, he's never seen them but their name is Niccolo."

"Niccolo!" She stopped walking. "You said Niccolo?"

"Uh-huh."

"Don't you know who that is?" she asked, her face becoming animated. He looked puzzled. "No, you couldn't. I never told you. That's the name of the family from whom Harlan and Dana adopted the baby."

"Are you sure?"

"Of course I'm sure. In fact, I remember asking Harlan if that was why Dana wanted to name the baby Nikos . . . sounds like Niccolo."

He stared at her a moment.

"Maybe we ought to call Lieutenant Reis again."

"For what? Do you seriously think he would come down here this morning? Come on," she said, and got into his car. He hesitated.

The previous night, after he had followed her to the Carson house and seen her go in safely, Teddy had done more thinking about all this. Despite his strong feelings for Colleen, he had to agree with the detective and Harlan. Her stories and supposed sightings were getting more and more incredible. Of course, he had no background and no experience with mentally disturbed people, but she was looking more and more like one. Why this suddenly should have happened to a bright, outgoing girl like Colleen, he couldn't say; but it had. Mental illness was a mystery to him, anyway; he didn't expect any less of its causes.

Was she telling the truth now? Had the baby's family been named Niccolo, or had her bizarre mind turned everything into this wild conspiracy filled with creatures and decomposing bodies? Maybe he was doing something terribly wrong by taking her up there that morning. Maybe it would lead to even more trouble, and this time he'd be blamed for it, he thought.

"I don't know," he said. He opened his car door and got in. She looked over at him curiously.

"Don't know about what?"

"About whether or not we're doing the right thing going up there by ourselves. I mean . . . it *is* trespassing, and if we go into the house, that's like breaking and entering, isn't it? What if this family comes up while we're there? What are you going to tell them, that you saw vampires in there last night and returned to check it out?"

She looked at him a moment, opened the car door without speaking, and got out.

"Colleen!"

She didn't turn back. She went directly to her car and got in. He started toward her, but she turned on her ignition and shifted into gear quickly. He practically had to jump out of the way as she pulled out of the gas station and onto Church Road.

"Colleen! Wait!" he screamed, running after her, but she didn't slow down. Moments later she was turning up the driveway to the farmhouse. She drove very slowly and very carefully, watching the sides of the gravel road and looking keenly for any signs of Jillian's turquoise robe. In moments the old farmhouse loomed ahead.

That morning, in the bright sunshine, it appeared far more dilapidated than it had during the night. She could understand why the detective thought it ridiculous that anyone lived there. The porch railings dangled, the gray siding had rotted and fallen off in places, the upstairs windows were broken, and the lawn was so overgrown that it covered the small sidewalk that led up to the porch steps.

In the daylight the farm machinery didn't look ominous, just old, discarded, rusted, and broken . . . pieces of equipment simply falling into disuse. Could the house itself be something supernatural? she wondered. Could it actually undergo a metamorphosis at night, come alive just like the undead? Why not? Perhaps they had imbued it with some of their power, some of their evil spirit.

Colleen pulled up beside it just where Nurse Patio and Dana had parked and got out of her car slowly. It was a cool morning. The sun had actually just begun to burn the frost off the brown grass and yellow weeds. Cumulus clouds were gathering on the western horizon. Their dark, nearly horizontal bases looked ominous. It was as though they threatened to bring back night and revive the undead. She slung her pocketbook over her shoulder, took a deep breath, and started for the house.

Other than her own footsteps over the gravel and then the flagstone walkway, there were no other sounds until she reached the steps of the porch and went up to the rickety landing. At that point she could have sworn the house moaned. The structure seemed to sway before her. She was surprised to find the door unlocked. Actually it was partly open. The jamb had cracked at the left top corner and the door itself couldn't be completely closed. She pushed it farther open and entered.

There was a short entryway, its hardwood floor buckled and warped in spots. She paused. Why shouldn't she expect one or more of the creatures she had seen the night before to be waiting for her behind one of the doorways ahead? Perhaps they didn't sleep during the day. Few people believed such evil creatures really existed, so how much was actually known about them?

She fumbled with her pocketbook and drew out the large silver cross Audra had given her. Holding it before her like a torch in the dark, she proceeded to go all the way down the entryway to the first doorway on the right, the one that opened onto the room she had peered into the previous night.

The furniture looked far more dilapidated and worn. She could see that the bottom of the couch on which Dana had been held down with the baby at her breast had fallen out. Some of the springs were visible. The chair in which the elderly-looking man had sat supervising the ritual had a long tear down the center of its back. The rug had a wide, oval-shaped hole worn near the middle, revealing the pale brown wooden floor beneath. She stood there studying the room. Had this indeed been the site of that horrifying scene?

She stepped farther into it and looked for some sign of inhabitancy, but there was nothing to indicate anyone had been there recently. She listened keenly. The breeze had picked up, and now a loosened shutter tapped gently against a window frame.

Suddenly the house was filled with many different sounds. Boards creaked, walls groaned, pipes vibrated. Something made of cloth flapped and snapped. To her it was as if the house were trying to warn her, to urge her to flee. She turned around quickly because she thought she heard footsteps, but there was no one there.

Undeterred, she left the living room and went on through the house. She looked in at what had probably been a sitting room and at a room that was most certainly the dining room. Then she went on to the kitchen, where she found the floor literally ripped up, the appliances rusted and broken. It looked to her like vandals had been through the place. Young boys often roamed through deserted houses and bungalows, scavenging, wrecking, having a good old time of it. They must have been here, she thought.

How could this have been the same house she'd looked in last night? she asked herself again. Surely there was something magical; there had to be. She peered in at what was once the pantry and saw that there was a door at the rear. When she opened it, she realized it was the entrance to the cellar, often used to store canned and jarred fruits and vegetables in houses like this.

Of course, it was much darker downstairs because the basement windows had been boarded up, and obviously there was no electricity. *But how had they lit the living room last night?* she asked herself quickly. *Were there lanterns? God, I couldn't have imagined it all. I couldn't have.* However, the contrast between what she had seen and what actually existed was so great, she was beginning to doubt herself.

She searched the kitchen, opening cabinets and looking into drawers. Finally, under the rusted-out sink, she found a kerosene lantern. There were matches there too. Encouraged by her discovery, she lit the lantern and went back to the entrance to the cellar. The light pushed the darkness back, revealing a very sturdy-looking stairway. With the lantern in one hand and her silver cross in the other, she began her descent. Behind her, all the sounds in the house seemed to become amplified. It seemed as if the wind had broken through every window and door and was now rushing about madly from room to room. She even imagined it was calling her name.

But it was too late to turn back; she had come this far, and she would see what had to be seen and do what had to be done.

Teddy had stopped running after her and had stood watching

her car go on toward the long driveway that led to the old, deserted farmhouse. He caught his breath and considered his options. Of course, he would have to go after her. He didn't intend for her to rush off like that and go by herself, but now he believed that this would never end. He had to do something to stop it.

He returned to the gas station and went directly to the pay phone. For a moment he thought about calling Lieutenant Reis, just as he had suggested to Colleen, but he opted instead for a call to Harlan. At first he thought he had dialed the wrong number. The male who answered didn't sound at all like Colleen's brother. His voice was deeper and his speech slow, like someone under hypnosis.

"Harlan?"

"Yes. Who is this?"

"It's Teddy Becker."

There was a long pause, and then Harlan, in a voice that sounded more like his, responded, "What's up, Teddy?"

"I'm sorry to have to call you to tell you this," he began, "but Colleen's still on this thing."

"What thing? What are you talking about?" Harlan asked quickly.

"She thinks she saw something horrible last night up at this old farmhouse off Church Road. The driveway is the first on the right, just past Carnesi's garage. She thinks the nurse took Dana there and—"

"I know all about that," he said quickly. "Lieutenant Reis called me last night."

"Yeah, well, she still believes that's what happened."

"Is she going there now?" he asked quickly. "Instead of going to school?"

"Yes. I'm calling from the pay phone at the garage. I was supposed to go with her this morning. I thought it would convince her that nothing had happened, and that it all would come to an end, but I can see that it hasn't. Something's not right with her, Harlan. I'm only afraid that—"

"I'll be right up there," he said quickly. "Wait for me at the garage."

"Well, she's already gone without me. It's deserted now but was recently bought in a tax auction by a family named Niccolo."

"What was that name?"

"Niccolo. Colleen says—"

"Did she tell you the name?"

"No, Steve Carnesi did. Anyway, Colleen says—"

"Just wait there. I'm on my way," Harlan said, and hung up before Teddy could say any more. He held the receiver in his hand a moment, shrugged, and then cradled it.

He looked up the highway toward the old farmhouse. Maybe he should have just gone up there with her as they had planned, he thought. He didn't like just standing there waiting for Harlan.

No, he decided, he had done the right thing. What if she went bananas on him up there? He wouldn't know how to handle it. It was better that her brother would be coming too. He got into his car, leaned back in the seat, and closed his eyes. He would wait.

Colleen stopped at the foot of the basement stairway. Just as she had thought, the basement floor was hard-packed dirt. The fieldstone foundation walls were uncovered. Pipes running under the upstairs floor were exposed, as was some of the electric wiring. So much had been done after the house had been built. It was one of those old places that would always have an unfinished look.

To her left and just ahead was a wall of shelves. There were still some empty jars and some old, rusted utensils on it. To her right was the water heater and the water pump. When she turned all the way to her right, however, she confronted the main area of the basement, a large underground room that ran the length of the house. She lifted the lantern and directed the light in that direction.

Almost immediately she saw them: three narrow crates shaped like coffins. She hesitated, the lantern shaking in her hand. The illumination trembled over the floor and walls of the dark, dismal basement, making the shadows shudder. That now familiar, horrible scent of decaying animals reached her and she gasped. She fought back the urge to dry-heave, even though her stomach churned painfully, and then she went on. As she did so, the moving light changed the shape of the shadows. They looked like ghosts sliding along the walls, following her progress.

The floor of the basement was wet and soft here. Some underground spring had broken out in the far right corner. There was a great deal of clay in the ground, and that gave the earth a bloody tint. The dampened dirt floor clung to the bottom of her feet like wads of discarded chewing gum. Once again she had the sense that the house was warning her off.

She paused at the first coffin and lifted the lamp so the light would wash the darkness off the lid. Then, holding her cross and the lantern in her right hand, she slid the lid off and looked in.

Laid out in a dark black suit, his ebony hair dull and even somewhat gray was the tall man she had seen holding down Dana's right arm the night before. His face was bone-white, but there was an amber ring around his eyes. His lips, although mostly turned in, were as black as charred wood. That odor of rotting flesh was so strong, she had to hold her breath.

At least she had found him, she thought. Now all she had to do was bring Lieutenant Reis back here. She was about to leave and do just that when the tall man's eyes snapped open. For a moment she could not move. His gaze was mesmerizing. Then he smiled and revealed his long teeth.

She screamed, but before she could move, he reached up and seized her left wrist. Instead of sitting up, however, he began to pull her down into the coffin with him. She struggled, but his grip was so powerful, she felt her skin begin to tear and slide away from her flesh. It was as though he had fingers of fire.

She started to bring her right hand down, intending to drop the lantern and struggle to free herself. He looked up at the light just as she lost her grip on the cross. It struck him in the chest, and then he screamed the most shrill and chilling scream she had ever heard.

He released his grip on her wrist and waved his hands at the cross, as though he were trying to put out a small fire that had started on his chest. Indeed, smoke rose from the area on which the cross lay. She stepped back quickly and turned to flee. His continual screams reverberated throughout the basement. She had to cover her ears. After another moment, however, they ended.

She turned and looked back at the coffin. Puffs of dust rose up out of it. For a long moment she just stared in anticipation, but nothing happened. She raised the lantern and looked around the basement, but nothing moved. Content that she was safe, she went back to the coffin and peered within.

The gray-black dust continued to rise up from around the decaying skeleton, and out of the sockets of the skull oozed a green slime. The skeleton still seemed to be sizzling. She saw that the cross had burned through the tall man's rib cage and now lay on the bottom of the coffin. She covered her mouth and backed away.

But she didn't rush up the stairs and out of the house. Now it was clear to her what had to be done. She reached into her pocketbook and took out the additional crosses she had instinctively taken from Audra's bedpost that morning. Then she went to the second coffin, slid off the lid, raised the lantern, found the female who had held down Dana's left wrist during the ritual the previous night, and dropped the cross between her breasts just as her eyes opened.

The female's scream was no less shrill than the tall man's had been. However, she was able to sit up in the coffin and gaze out at Colleen, even though the cross had already burned a hole through her chest. She reached out as if to plead for help, and then crumpled into dust and bones right before Colleen's eyes. The skeleton collapsed back into the coffin. She looked in at it and saw the same gray-black dust rise around the decaying bones and the same green slime emerge from the eye sockets.

Then she went to the third coffin, found the elderly man who was supposed to have been Dr. Claret, and followed the same procedure. His scream seemed deeper. She had the sense that he was much older than the other two. He didn't pull himself up, but he extended his arms and clasped his hands together, as if there were an invisible rope dangling from the ceiling and he was trying to grasp it and pull himself up and away from his destruction. His arms crumpled and his hands fell downward. When she looked into his coffin, she found the same results she had in the other two.

She stepped back from the three coffins. At least that was over. The horrid creatures were no more. In the quiet moments that followed, the full impact and realization of what she had just done came upon her and she began to sob. Crossing her left arm over her breasts and holding the lantern out, she started for the stairs. She was nearly there when she heard her name being called and turned to look out at the darkened basement again.

At first she saw no one. Then a dark shadow coming from the far left corner took shape. It was Audra.

"Audra," Colleen said as she approached her friend. Audra backed away from the light, holding her hand up in front of her face. "The light bothers you?" Colleen placed it on the dirt floor and took another step toward her.

"Yes," Audra said.

"What happened to you? What did they do? Have they kept you prisoner here? Your mother is so worried."

"Yes, I am their prisoner," Audra said.

"I've destroyed them," Colleen said proudly. "I used your crosses. They can't hurt you anymore. Come on. Let's get out of here quickly."

Audra smiled.

And Colleen saw the lengthened, sharpened teeth.

"Oh, God, no!" Colleen stepped back.

"Yes," Audra said, but Colleen thought her smile softened. "Take my hand, Colleen," she said, offering her hand. "Be with me."

"No!" Colleen retreated another step.

"Just for a little while. You must have faith. If you have faith, you can help me. I need your faith. Please. Help me," she pleaded. There was something so appealing in her voice, Colleen couldn't help herself. Audra's hand drew closer.

"I'm afraid," Colleen said.

"Don't be. Believe in the power of goodness. Colleen, help me," Audra pleaded again. Colleen couldn't keep her hand from going out to her friend. She looked at her arm as if it were not connected to her, as if it had a mind of its own. She saw her hand close in on Audra's, and then she felt her fingers touch her.

Audra's fingers were cold, hard. Their grasp was quick, powerful. She jerked her arm to pull it back, but it was too late. Audra's hand was frozen to hers. She sensed that she would have to tear away from her own skin to pull her arm back now.

"Be with me," Audra said. "Your faith will be enough for both of us. Please, help me."

Colleen felt herself soften. She took one step, and then

another, until she was right beside Audra. This close to her, she was able to see the thin capillaries in her eyes, which had become gray and dull. Her skin looked chalky and her hair was stiff, the color fading.

"Don't pay any attention to my body," Audra said. "It's not my body any longer. It's my prison. Come, be with me," she said again, and led Colleen deeper into the darkness. Colleen gasped. The odor of death and decay was so strong, she nearly swooned, but she felt a desperate need to maintain her consciousness.

In the deeper darkness, Audra's eyes were luminescent, her breathing heavy. She sounded like someone with asthma. Colleen stopped, hoping to retreat, but Audra pulled her forward.

"Have faith," she repeated. "Be with me."

"Audra, no—"

"I need your faith," Audra said. "The goodness in you was strong enough before, it will be strong enough now."

"But I'm afraid," Colleen repeated.

Suddenly Audra pushed open the door to the outside. The daylight rushed into the basement and Audra screamed. Yet her grip of Colleen's hand remained firm, secure. She started to bend over and stepped away as if the sunlight were water flooding in, pushing her back; but she resisted, and, with Colleen's hand in hers, forced herself forward into the light.

They both stepped out into the yard, the basement door closing behind them. Audra suddenly straightened up.

"Walk with me," she said in a raspy voice. "My friend," she added and took a few steps forward. Her grip loosened on Colleen's hand, but Colleen did not pull away. She and her friend moved away from the house. She felt Audra weakening until finally, she went to her knees.

"Audra," she said. "How can I help you?"

"You already have," Audra said and turned to her, smiling. This time, her smile did not reveal the sharpened teeth. "God bless you," she said and fell back on the tall grass.

Colleen knelt over her, still holding her hand.

Harlan stopped his car beside Teddy's and got out. Teddy opened his eyes and sat up abruptly as Harlan opened the car door and got in.

"Where the hell is she?" Harlan demanded.

"Just a little way up the road. I'll take you there," he said, moving quickly to start his car and put it into gear.

"We're taking her right to the hospital," Harlan said. "Right to the hospital. I can't have her in the same house with Dana. Not until she's definitely cured of all this."

"I understand," Teddy said.

Harlan turned to him. "You did the right thing in calling me."

"I hope so. I know she's going to hate me for it, but I thought it was better you were here." He turned off the road into the driveway and downshifted.

"What the hell . . ." Harlan said when he saw the house ahead. "She thought Nurse Patio brought Dana here to see a doctor? No one's lived here for years. Any fool can see that."

"I know," Teddy said. "That's why I called. I couldn't imagine—"

"Jesus, she *is* sick."

"There's her car."

"What the hell is she doing in that shack?"

They pulled up beside her car and got out.

Harlan contemplated the house. *"Colleen!"* he shouted. They both waited. *"Colleen, get out here, dammit!"* After a moment he started for the front door, Teddy right beside him. Harlan looked down at the porch's cracked floorboards. "Watch yourself," he said. "It's dangerous just entering this rattrap." He walked through the doorway and looked around. *"Colleen!"*

"Why doesn't she answer?" Teddy asked.

"Maybe she's hiding somewhere, embarrassed. I don't know." Harlan went farther in, looked into the living room and continued on through the house.

Teddy went ahead of him and into the kitchen. "She's not in here," he said when Harlan arrived. "Where is she?"

"Dammit! *Colleen!"*

"Colleen!" Teddy shouted as well. They both waited but heard nothing. "What do we do now?" Teddy asked.

Harlan shook his head, his face tightening with frustration and anger. "I hate to go upstairs in this place. We'll probably fall through the floor." He started to turn and then stopped. "What's that door?" he asked, nodding toward the pantry.

Teddy peered into it. "Looks like a pantry or storage area. Wait, there's an open door in here." Harlan joined him and they both looked down the stairway. "It's the basement," Teddy said.

"Colleen, are you down there?" Harlan called. They waited a moment, but there was no response. "Jesus. All right, let's look," he said, and started down the stairs. Teddy followed right behind him. They both paused at the foot of it. When they turned to their right, they stared in confusion.

The kerosene lantern, still lit, was resting on the dirt floor just to the left of the coffins. It cast enough illumination for them to see most of the basement.

"What the hell is this?" Harlan said. "They look like . . ."

Teddy started for the coffins first. "God, how it stinks in here," he said. He paused and looked into the first one. "Holy shit," he said. Harlan was at his side.

"What is this?" Harlan asked, looking around. "Some old burying place? Someone turned this basement into a tomb."

Teddy looked into the other coffins, covering his nose and his mouth with his hands as he did so. "Corpses in both," he said. He looked back toward the stairway. "So where the hell is Colleen?"

Harlan went to the kerosene lamp and lifted it, directing the light toward the darkest areas of the basement. There was no sign of her. He caught sight of the outside doorway. "Maybe she went out this way," he said. "Come on."

Teddy joined him quickly, and they moved across the basement to the door.

It was Colleen, tears streaming down her face.

"My God," Harlan said, looking down at Audra's corpse. "What happened to her?"

"The same thing that happened to Jillian," Colleen said. "They made her one of them. But it was different for Audra. She was too pure, she was too good," Colleen said, looking down at her dead friend.

"Those corpses in the coffins . . ."

"I did that," she said. "I put the crosses on them. They were vampires. Such things exist. As Audra's mother said, the devil can take many forms. He simply seeks out our own darkest fears and crystallizes them."

Harlan nodded, thinking about Nurse Patio. There was a

dark part of him that she had appealed to; there were fears in him that she had crystallized.

He looked back at the house and then at Colleen, the full realization of what went on and what was still going on coming to him. "She did bring Dana here last night," he said, "didn't she?"

Colleen nodded. "It's the baby," she said. "He's one of them."

"Oh, God. Oh, no. Is it too late for Dana?"

"I don't know," she said.

He backed away from the scene, shaking his head. "I've got to get home. I've got to get back." He turned and ran around the house to Colleen's car.

"We'll be right there," Teddy shouted after him. He reached down to help Colleen stand. She started to rise and then stopped, opened her pocketbook, and took out one of Audra's crosses. She placed the chain carefully in Audra's fingers, taking care not to touch her body with the cross.

"She was special," she said softly. "Too special, even for them." Teddy nodded and helped her stand. They both looked down at Audra's body. "We can't do any more for her," she said. "Let's hurry. Maybe there's still something we can do for Dana."

They started away, walking quickly to his car. Harlan was already down the driveway and on his way home.

The moment he entered, he sensed a different sort of stillness in his house. Something heavy and dark was gone. Shadows that had been oppressing, that had loomed like spies ready to report even his thoughts to his enemies, were no longer there in the same form. His home had been unfriendly to him. He had felt betrayed by every creak in the floor, reporting his whereabouts whenever he moved from room to room. Every time he had approached the stairs that led up to what had become Nurse Patio's domain, he felt threatened. He usually lumbered up, his legs feeling heavy, his eyes directed down, not even looking side to side, moving like a man wearing blinders, afraid to look, afraid to see and to realize what was going on around him.

But these changes he now sensed did not encourage him. He was not sure that the emptiness he felt did not portend disaster.

He had come too late. Dana's very soul had been stolen from her, right beneath his eyes.

This time he rushed up the stairs, screaming Dana's name. Despite the vacuous feeling he had sensed when he had first entered the house, he still expected to confront Nurse Patio at the top of the stairs. He imagined her standing there, her body more formidable and threatening than ever, and he feared that he did not have the strength and the power to get past her in time. When he reached the landing, he clenched his fists and looked around madly. Seeing no one, he charged forward into his bedroom and found Dana, lying in bed, her right arm over the side, her head back, her mouth open.

"Dana!"

He rushed to her side and took her hand into his.

"Dana, Dana." He reached down and embraced her, lifting her body to him and rocking back and forth with her on the bed. Her body was cold, but he felt a subtle movement. Her eyelids fluttered against his cheek. "Oh, God!"

He scooped her body into his arms, and with a strength he never realized he had, he carried her out of the bedroom and down the stairs. Teddy and Colleen arrived just as he reached the door.

"Quickly. She's still alive!" he said.

They helped him get her into his car. They put her in the backseat, and Colleen got in beside her.

The initial examination at the hospital emergency room revealed her blood pressure was so low, it was amazing her heart was still beating. They began blood transfusions immediately.

"She must have a leak somewhere," the emergency-room doctor told Harlan, and he and Colleen nearly laughed.

"There's no leak," Harlan said with a confidence that astounded the young physician. "Just keep building up her blood. I'm the same type, so let me donate immediately," he added.

Colleen stopped him just before the doctor led him off. "What about—"

"I heard no one there. Don't do anything until I'm ready to go back with you. I'll call Lieutenant Reis myself and tell him what's up at the deserted house and then have him accompany us home," he said.

She nodded, and she and Teddy waited in the emergency room until Harlan was finished and the doctor reported that Dana was rallying.

Lieutenant Reis and two patrolmen met them in the hospital parking lot. The look on his face told them he had already visited the old farmhouse and discovered everything Harlan had described to him, especially poor Audra.

"All right," he said, "let's start from the beginning."

"I'll ride with you back to our house," Colleen said, "and tell you all that I know."

Reis looked at Harlan.

"And this time you had better listen to her," Harlan said.

Lieutenant Reis nodded. She got into his car with him, and then she began her story.

EPILOGUE

Neither Harlan nor Colleen expected that Nurse Patio or the baby would be at the house when they arrived from the hospital. On the way Lieutenant Reis listened attentively to Colleen's story. However, despite Dana's condition, what he had found in the basement of the deserted farmhouse, what had happened to poor Audra, and what allegedly had happened to Jillian, he struggled to find other explanations.

"It's not that I don't believe you," he told Colleen. "I do. My guess is this was all part of one of these off-the-wall cults. You know what I mean?"

"Believe what you want," she said. She was tired of trying to convince people, and anyway, it didn't matter anymore. Audra and Jillian were dead, the baby and Nurse Patio were gone, and Dana was on her way to recovery. There wasn't anything she could change.

At the house, Lieutenant Reis took descriptions of Nurse Patio and the baby. Harlan turned over the papers from the lawyer, Garson Lawrence, and Colleen and Teddy told him of their futile search for such a man. He said he would check on the owners of the old farmhouse. Sometime later he would phone to tell them there was literally no trace of the Niccolos. Harlan thanked him for calling and told him it was nothing they hadn't expected. He told Colleen he thought Lieutenant Reis was a little annoyed by his attitude.

"He was hoping to locate them and fit all this into a safe, acceptable explanation," Harlan said. Colleen nodded. She understood the detective's need to do so. The nightmares, the visions, and the images still lingered. Sometimes at night she would awake, thinking she had heard Audra's raspy voice. The wind at her window, a shadow cast by a street light, the barking of a dog—all of it, any of it, would send her reeling back through a tunnel of horrible memories. She didn't need the psychologist to tell her it would take time.

Dana's mental recovery occurred simultaneously with her physical recovery. She quickly returned to her old self. When Colleen visited her in the hospital with Harlan, she was as friendly and as warm as she had ever been.

"I feel like someone who just came out of a coma," Dana said. "Everything is so vague in my memory. It's almost as if . . . as if I'm still in the maternity ward and I dreamed it all."

"I wish you had," Colleen said.

"I know. Poor Mom. Still no trace of her?"

"Nothing." Harlan said. He had asked that Colleen not tell Dana they had found Jillian's robe in the basement of the old house. There was nothing with it—no bones, no dust, nothing.

"Somehow I feel responsible," Dana said.

"Knowing what we know now," Harlan replied, "there's no reason for you to feel that way. You had no control of your actions or thoughts. I think your mother understood that, and that was why she was so upset and wanted so much to do something about it. But," he added, looking away quickly, "even I couldn't help her. Even I was under their control to a certain extent."

He had thought about telling her of his sexual incident with Nurse Patio, but he resisted, partly out of his own feelings of guilt and partly out of his desire to spare her any more pain.

"All we wanted," Dana said in a small voice, "was a child."

He embraced her. Colleen turned away. She would be the one to embrace Lucy Carson. She would be the one to stand beside her at Audra's funeral. Afterward, alone with Lucy Carson in her home, Colleen would tell her about Audra's power over the forces of evil.

"She was special," Colleen said.

"Thank you, dear. Thank you for giving me the comfort and for caring so much about Audra," she said.

Weeks went by. Dana got stronger and once more became her vibrant, beautiful self. She talked about returning to work at the accountant's office. The labor dispute at the college was settled, and Harlan dived back into his teaching with vigor. Colleen studied hard and made some more friends. They didn't have their first snowfall until nearly Christmas, but Teddy and she both had joined the ski team. The terror they had all lived through began to thin out, even though it never really left them.

Harlan took the crib apart and they closed the door to the baby's room. Everything that had to do with the infant was removed from the house. Lieutenant Reis called again to report that they had made absolutely no progress with the case.

"Nurse Patio and the baby seemed to have disappeared off the face of the earth," he said.

"Hopefully," Harlan replied. He knew that the detective still couldn't understand his lack of interest in the baby, but he didn't care about it anymore. Reis never called again. He figured if they had any questions, they would call him.

One day late in January, Colleen and Teddy returned from a ski meet. It had been snowing softly all day, one of those snowfalls that makes people think of sleigh bells and Christmas lights. Both of them were energized from their vigorous afternoon of exercise. Colleen's face in particular was red, her eyes sparkling with life. She and Teddy were beginning to regain their momentum. Shadows were merely shadows again.

They burst through the front door, exploding with laughter and energy. Harlan was already home from work and the house was filled with the delicious aroma of a roast turkey dinner. Teddy had been invited the day before. As they took off their winter coats and removed their boots in the alcove, Harlan and Dana came out of the living room and stood before them, holding hands and smiling.

"Men lost, women won," Teddy said.

"Figures," Harlan said. "That's the way it's going to be for the rest of your life, buddy. Get used to it."

Teddy laughed but Colleen held her smile. She looked from Dana to Harlan, sensing something. "What is it?" she said. Instinctively she felt for Teddy's hand.

"We have a surprise. An announcement," Dana said. "I was going to go back to work, as you know, but Harlan told me to hold off making that decision. Well, I'm glad now that I did."

Colleen squeezed Teddy's hand so hard, he looked at her, puzzled.

"Why not?" Colleen asked.

"Because I worked a miracle," Harlan said, smiling.

"Harlan Hamilton . . ." Dana said.

"I mean, *we* worked a miracle."

"I'm pregnant again," Dana said. "I didn't think it could happen, because it took so long the first time, but it did."

"Well?" Harlan said when Colleen didn't respond.

Colleen's lips trembled, her smile widening.

"Congratulations," she said. She went forward and embraced Dana, and Teddy shook Harlan's hand.

"Extra celebration tonight," Harlan said. "Wine at dinner." He slapped his hands together. "And, boy, am I hungry!"

"I'll second that," Teddy said.

"Come, tell me about the ski meet," Harlan said, and he and Teddy headed for the living room.

Dana stood smiling at Colleen. "If it's a girl," she said, "I'm going to call her Jillian."

"Oh, I hope it's a girl," Colleen said.

"Me too. Don't tell Harlan. Come, help me with the dinner," she said, and Colleen followed her into the kitchen.

Later that night, just before she went to bed, Colleen looked out of her bedroom window. She stared down at the shed and thought about Jillian.

And she thought about Dana's pregnancy.

And she hoped—no, she prayed—that it was what Harlan and Dana thought . . . a miracle.